When three sexy bachelors ~~in~~ ~~er,~~
they have no idea their soon-to-be dream pad is already
occupied . . . by a foxy she-devil out for revenge!

Praise for Lexi Davis and her debut novel

PRETTY EVIL

"Lexi Davis combin[es] romance, spirituality, and suspense.
. . . Her hip portrayal of the characters and heartwarming
message of friendship, love, and faith are inspiring."
—Cydney Rax, author of *My Daughter's Boyfriend*

"A terrific story that contains humor, spicy sex, and a great
spin on the paranormal genre. . . . The witch is crafty, and
the book's humor contagious."
—*Romantic Times* (4 ½ stars)

"A complex, hysterical, and progressive plot. . . . Original in
its contents and very well written. . . . A notable first novel."
— *Book Review*

with sharp
. The prem-
is's writing

ace Review

iction.com

of the sea-
is born."
Covington

The After Wife

Also by Lexi Davis

Pretty Evil

The After Wife

Lexi Davis

POCKET BOOKS

New York   London   Toronto   Sydney

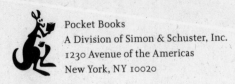

Pocket Books
A Division of Simon & Schuster, Inc.
1230 Avenue of the Americas
New York, NY 10020

Copyright © 2009 by Lois Roberson Kimp

First Pocket Books trade paperback edition March 2009

POCKET and colophon are registered trademarks of Simon & Schuster, Inc.

For information about special discounts for bulk purchases,
please contact Simon & Schuster Special Sales at 1-800-456-6798 or
business@simonandschuster.com.

The Simon & Schuster Speakers Bureau can bring authors to your live event.
For more information or to book an event contact the Simon & Schuster Speakers
Bureau at 866-248-3049 or visit our website at www.simonspeakers.com

Designed by Aline C. Pace

Manufactured in the United States of America

10 9 8 7 6 5 4 3 2 1

Library of Congress Cataloging-in-Publication Data
Davis, Lexi.
    The after wife / by Lexi Davis.
       p. cm.
    1. Witches—Fiction. 1. Title.
    PS3604.A9724A69 2009
    813'.6—dc22   2008032835
      ISBN-13: 978-1-4165-0526-6 (trade pbk.)
      ISBN-10:   1-4165-0526-1 (trade pbk.)

To my family,
and everyone who believes in God,
hard work,
and dreams

Acknowledgments

To those who helped make this book a reality, thanks you; my agent, Sara Camilli, my editor, Brigitte Smith, and everyone who gave me creative feedback. To all of you who purchased and enjoyed reading *Pretty Evil,* and to my ever-growing readership, I am deeply grateful. Most of all, I thank God for His inspiration.

❧ CHAPTER 1 ❧

*N*ia Youngblood crept down the hallway of a Las Vegas hotel behind her boyfriend, Malcolm Smalls, who was dressed like a spy in a black shirt, black shoes, black cap, and dark shades. When he paused, she paused. She shifted her duffel bag and tugged the back of his shirt. "Who are we looking for?"

"The enemy."

"But, Mal, it's one o'clock in the morning and—"

"Shh!" Malcolm placed a finger across her lips.

She pushed it away. "This is not how I planned on losing my virginity. You act like it's *Mission: Impossible.*"

"No, it's harder."

Malcolm was right. At twenty-four, Nia's love life was like a suspense thriller with every potential sex scene so far being a near miss.

Nia sighed. "I was hoping for a romantic candlelit dinner, maybe soft music . . ."

"Shh!" Malcolm yanked her around another corner and hurried her down the long wine-colored carpet on the twenty-sixth floor of Treasure Island hotel. Malcolm had been her on-again-off-again boyfriend for six years since high school, but his appeal was beginning to wear thin. Twenty-nine and finally out of law school, he was already grabbing for fame and fortune, and right now a chance to get busy with Nia. After his court case had recessed for the day in Los Angeles, he'd convinced her to hop a short flight to Las Vegas. He'd told her he had a foolproof sexual rendezvous planned where they could escape whoever was making it impossible for him to make love to her.

Malcolm plunged his keycard into the door's slot and rushed Nia inside the room. Although her hopes of a romantic first experience had been dashed, Nia remained excited and optimistic. Not a virgin by choice, but by circumstance—always *unusual* circumstances—she was more than anxious to explore the fiery side of her sexuality.

She dropped her duffel bag on the bed and sat next to it, fidgeting and hoping that the intimate soul connection she'd yearned for since puberty was about to happen. Malcolm put out the DO NOT DISTURB sign and quickly locked the door.

"Mal, relax. You're making me nervous."

"Shush!" Malcolm tilted his head toward the door, listening. Nia listened, too, but only heard silence, though she knew silence didn't necessarily mean no one was there. Someone was always watching her. Someone possessive, jealous, and not necessarily human.

Nervous, she tugged at her thick sepia hair, twisting a wavy lock around her finger. Malcolm yanked the curtains closed, but a slither of light from the Vegas Strip remained. After checking the bathroom, he came out and complained, "Every time we try to do it, something crazy weird happens."

Nia tried to downplay it. "It's probably just coincidence."

"Twenty-nine times?"

"You counted?"

"Every cold shower." Mal turned off his cell phone and tossed it on the nightstand. "Nothing's going to stop us this time, not even the hounds of hell."

"Wow, Mal. Great romantic imagery." Nia rolled her eyes. "Got any goblins to go along with those hounds?"

She wasn't worried about hellhounds. She knew hell had creatures far more dangerous and seductive than ornery mutts, and one of them kept a constant eye on her.

Mal snatched off his black cap and hurried out of his black clothes. He clicked off the lamp and rushed at Nia, popping buttons off her blouse. A melting hot surge rushed through her warm body, reminding her of all the nights she'd fantasized about being with a real man. Aroused, her womanly places quivered, moistening with anticipation, but Mal was in such a hurry she had to struggle to catch her breath.

"Mal, slow down." She grabbed his hand. "This is my first time. I want it to be special."

"If I get some, it *will* be special," he said, but he saw the glare in her eye through the sliver of light. "What? What else do you want?"

"I want you to talk to me."

"Talk?"

"Yes," Nia said. "Tell me what every woman wants to hear at a moment like this."

He was clueless; his brows wrinkled like a fault line.

She sat up, still waiting. "I'm talking about the *L* word."

"You're a lesbian?" Malcolm's face caved in.

"Love!" Exasperated, Nia huffed, "I want you to say you *love* me."

Mal looked at her in amazement. "Why would you bring

up something like that at a time like this? Are you *trying* to kill the mood?"

"Mal, it's my first time. I'm nervous. I need reassurance." She watched him carefully, knowing how he avoided the truth whenever possible. "And don't lie to me," she added.

Mal moved back, balancing himself on one elbow. He saw the seriousness in her eyes and came up with something. "You're lucky, Nia. You've got the lust factor."

"The *what* factor?"

"You're a lust magnet." He leaned in, talking more to her body than to her. "You've got these joyously juicy breasts, wild tigress hair, and big sexy eyes that speak to men."

"Oh, yeah?" Nia widened her eyes. "What do they say?"

"They say, 'Behind these big innocent eyes there's a freak waiting to be unleashed.'"

"Really?" Nia exhaled, baffled.

"And that's my mission—to unleash the freak in you." He nudged her down on the bed. "So relax and let me bring her out."

Nia leaned back awkwardly and took a deep breath. Mal wasn't her dream man, but he did have one crucial thing going for him—he stuck around. Despite the weird events that always surrounded her, Mal didn't ask questions. When she'd break up with him—which she did frequently due to his lying, cheating ways—she'd try to date other guys, but they'd soon get scared away, and she'd end up back with Malcolm. After six years of putting up with him, at least she knew what to expect. Plus, Mal's appetite for sex was as huge as hers. Nia's blood ran hot and her urges were intense but yet to be satisfied, and Mal made no secret of his horny intentions.

Suave in a self-absorbed way, Mal flashed his "practiced" smile, the one designed to win over jurors, and ditched his underwear. He crawled on top of her, smothering her mouth with kisses designed to keep it shut. Nia sighed and tried to relax.

She closed her eyes, thinking of her many sexual fantasies while she explored his male anatomy, touching fleshly objects she'd only dreamed about.

Malcolm's cell phone rang.

He ignored it and continued kissing, grappling, and grinding, but the phone kept ringing.

Distracted, Nia squirmed. "Mal, your phone is ringing."

"Impossible. I turned it off," he said dismissively, and parted her legs with his knee. The cell phone's speaker clicked on by itself and a woman started leaving a message:

"Hello, Malcolm, you naughty sex machine. It's Vicky. I'm still reeling from that wild animal sex we had last night . . ."

Malcolm jumped off the bed and reached for the phone, fumbling with it, trying to turn it off, but the speaker's volume increased. *"I got the video you e-mailed from your camera phone, you sly devil. I'm watching it now and getting hot all over again."*

As the woman moaned, Nia stiffened.

Mal chuckled nervously. "Obviously, it's a wrong number."

Nia gritted her teeth. "She said your name, Mal."

"There are lots of Malcolms in the world, so don't go jumping to conclusions."

"Just don't let our naughty video get out or both our careers will be in the toilet. I look forward to many more stiff sentences from you. See you in court tomorrow, you wild animal. Grrr!" Vicky gave a lusty growl, then hung up.

Malcolm slammed the phone into the nightstand but it bounced off, ricocheted into Nia's hands, and played the video of him and Vicky. Speechless, Nia watched the amateur porn of her boyfriend sexing a woman with gigantic breasts. Her palms shook with anger.

"It wasn't me." Malcolm threw up his hands. "I swear."

Nia zeroed in on Malcolm's face. Hot tears filled her eyes.

He mumbled some lame excuse about a possible twin

brother before finally caving in. "C'mon, Nia, give me a break. Trying to have sex with you is harder than paying off a student loan. Every time I try, something crazy happens, like this!" He pointed at the phone. "There's something weird going on with you, Nia."

"Mal! None of this is my fault." Insulted, she picked up a pillow and hit him with it. "Besides, you're the one who cheated!"

"Until there's conclusive proof, I deny everything."

Nia reached for her blouse and put it on, then quickly scooted into her pants. Mal paced the floor, scratching his head and muttering, "*Who* took that video?"

Nia knew who'd taken the video, but she wasn't saying. "Doesn't matter who took it. They did me a favor." She grabbed her duffel bag, slung it over her shoulder, and headed for the door. "Forget it. It's over!"

He followed her. "Hey, I paid for this room. There are no refunds."

"Refund the six years I wasted with you." She flung open the door. "Good-bye, Mal."

At two A.M., Nia caught a cab to the Las Vegas airport and boarded the next plane heading back to Los Angeles. In late November, the desert city known for its sin and heat was chilly, but Nia wore no sweater. She didn't even own a coat, because she didn't need one. Among other weird things about her, Nia's body always ran hotter than normal.

As Nia boarded the plane, she wiped smudged mascara from her eye. She hated wearing makeup, but Malcolm liked it. Once again, she'd tried her hand at romance but things had only gotten worse. Nia searched for her seat while wracking her brain trying to remember where she'd seen *Vicky* before. Disheartened, she slumped into her seat and noticed a flight attendant staring at her.

The woman in the blue uniform approached. "Excuse me, miss, but where did your companion go?"

"My companion?" Baffled, Nia sniffed back a tear. "I'm traveling alone."

The attendant pointed to the seat next to Nia, the only empty seat in first class. "The gentleman asked me to make sure no one took his seat. He seemed very protective of you."

Suddenly alert, Nia shifted uneasily. "What did he look like?"

After all these years, she'd never actually seen his face. The attendant described him as best she could. "A tall, well-dressed gentleman in a dark magenta suit. I couldn't really see his face because the cabin lights malfunctioned, but he seemed the quiet type, with a very powerful presence. Almost overwhelming, you know?"

Yes, Nia knew.

The attendant continued, "He had an exotic look, perhaps a foreign citizen, but I couldn't place his nationality. I wouldn't be surprised if he was royalty of some kind since he had such a commanding presence and a definite edge."

"An edge?"

"Yes, like someone you wouldn't want to cross."

Nia remained purposely expressionless, though her insides turned to mush.

"We're ready for takeoff, but he's nowhere in sight." The attendant backed up slightly, disappointed. "We may have to take off without him."

Antsy, Nia sat back in her seat. She fastened her seat belt and tightened the strap. "He'll show up again. He always does."

As the attendant left, Nia looked again at the empty seat. Out of nowhere, a rose appeared. A single long-stemmed rose with thick, velvety petals in the lavish color of royalty—purple. Attracted by its mystique, Nia picked up the purple rose. She slowly ran her fingers along its long, smooth black stem; its razor-sharp thorns gently pricked her skin, sending a piercing tingly sensation through her body. A densely sweet, familiar smell emanated from the rose, like burning molasses. Nia's body temperature increased the way it always did whenever *he* was near, and minuscule beads of perspiration replaced the dried-up tears on her cheeks.

During takeoff, she brought the petals close to her cheek, brushing their velvety thickness gently across her lips. "Please," she whispered into the rose, knowing he could hear her, "just let me go."

❧ CHAPTER 2 ☙

*N*ia had been up all night, and her mind was buzzing like a broken radio. Her flight landed at LAX, but her emotions continued to soar. She took a shuttle to the self-parking area, jumped into her gold Mustang Shelby, and left the airport. The sun wasn't up yet. Neither was the traffic on the 405 freeway. Nia headed north and drove well over the speed limit to her house in Northridge.

She'd figured out who Vicky was, but after all these years, she still hadn't figured out how to deal with her mysterious dark pursuer. Solving one out of two mysteries would have to do, for now. After inhaling the purple rose's sweet, alluring scent one last time, Nia tossed it into the trash compactor, where she'd tossed so many others. She cuddled up on her red sofa, took a quick nap, then arose and ate a hearty breakfast of eggs Benedict and homemade hash browns. Nia showered, changed clothes, and headed to the downtown L.A. courthouse.

When she arrived, court was already in session. Malcolm had caught an early flight back to Los Angeles and was present in all his pompous glory, prosecuting a gang of teenagers who had protested against a land developer building a mall that would destroy half their neighborhood. Nia had begged Mal not to take the case, but he'd said the money was too good to turn down.

The trial had been carried over from last week due to his clever legal maneuvering. She'd attended and made a last-ditch effort to get Mal to change his mind, but when he'd refused, she'd left a few minutes after the judge had taken the bench.

Nia glared at Mal as she searched for a seat. She settled into a seat directly behind the opposing counsel's table. She hadn't noticed the other lawyer before, but she certainly did now. Thirtyish, about six foot four, with a great physique; he was built like an NBA guard. His hair was short and looked as soft as his eyes—a deep, rich shade of brown, like full-bodied Brazilian coffee. He looked scrumptious in his suit, which was tailored just enough without being showy. He wore his clothes well, along with an attractive, self-confident demeanor. When he bent over the defendant's desk to retrieve papers, Nia noticed something else.

"Mumm, great tush," she mumbled, then asked the man sitting closest to her, "What's his name?"

"That's David Wrightwood, the defense attorney," the man said, then added, "If on judgment day I find myself dangling over a hot pit of burning coals, I'll want him representing me."

"He's that good, huh?"

"Justice crowns the head of the righteous." He nodded admiringly toward David.

Nia wasn't sure what all that meant, but now she realized why Malcolm had bad-mouthed this guy—he was jealous. David

Wrightwood clearly had it going on. But Malcolm was known to pull out all the stops to win a case, and it looked like he was doing just that. Polished and slick, he flashed the jurors his winning smile and accused the teenagers of obscure, impossible-to-understand violations to purposely confuse the jurors.

She peeked again at David Wrightwood. Not only was he cute, but he remained cool, composed, and focused despite the fact that Malcolm clearly had the judge's favor, based on her facial expression and body language.

"Ahem!" Nia faked a cough, trying to get David Wrightwood's attention. He turned and looked at her, but so did the judge and bailiff. David smiled. The judge and bailiff didn't. He turned his attention back to the trial.

"Ahem!" Nia grunted louder, disrupting the court again.

The judge pounded her gavel. "Are you acting in contempt of court?"

"No, but I have some important evidence regarding this trial."

David Wrightwood looked puzzled. He asked the judge, "Your Honor, may I request a brief sidebar council?"

Though clearly perturbed, the judge allowed it. David leaned over the rail toward Nia, smelling as good as he looked, like a fresh fantasy.

Nia whispered, "I've got something that will get you a mistrial. From the looks of things, you could use it. You're losing this case."

"I disagree. But what've you got?" David's dark eyes looked even softer up close. She could practically smell the coffee beans brewing, and it made her thirsty. She pulled Malcolm's phone from her pocket.

Mal, who'd been watching Nia closely from across the room, saw the phone and panicked. "I object!"

"You object to what?" the judge asked.

"To—to whatever's about to happen."

The judge overruled Mal's objection but peered at Nia and David Wrightwood impatiently. David looked at the phone. "A cell phone? That's what you've got?"

Nia turned it on and played the video. David frowned. "Porn?"

"Look closer. Recognize that guy?"

He squinted and focused. "That's Malcolm Smalls, the prosecutor."

"It gets better." Nia pointed out the woman's face. "Get a load of *Vicky.*"

David's eyes widened. "The Honorable Judge Victoria Bowden?"

Nia nodded. "Without her bifocals, her gavel, or her *panties.*"

David turned toward the judge, who had no idea what they were looking at. He smoothed his hand down his handsome face, thinking quickly, then handed the phone back to Nia. "Hold on to this and follow my lead."

"Okay." Nia leaned back in her seat, nervous, hands fidgeting with the phone.

David quickly turned his attention back to the trial. "Thank you, Judge Bowden. I'm ready to proceed now."

The judge called the court back to order. "Do you have new admissible evidence to present to the court?"

Nia clutched the phone and prepared to stand. She was sure this whole fiasco would wind up on Jerry Springer.

David Wrightwood said, "No, Your Honor."

Nia's mouth fell open. "But what about—?"

He threw her a *trust me* look and told the court, "I've presented all the truthful and pertinent facts, and now I rest my case. I trust the jury will do the right thing."

"Do the right thing?" Nia exclaimed skeptically, letting out

a loud gasp. David gave her a *just relax* sign, but she ignored it and stood, holding up the phone. "But I've got—"

"I object!" Mal yelled again.

Nia yelled across the room back at Mal. "Of course you object. You cheater!"

The judge banged her gavel again. "Order!"

Nia turned to the judge. "You're good at banging things, aren't you? Especially other people's boyfriends."

"Arrest her for contempt!" Judge Vicky ordered the bailiff. The bailiff proceeded toward Nia, but David Wrightwood stepped in front of Nia protectively. "Your Honor, please. I ask for clemency—"

"Clemency?" Nia interrupted David. "Why should I ask for clemency? He's the one who got caught with his pants down," she exclaimed, then pointed at the judge and added, "and her with her robe *up*."

Realization finally struck Judge Vicky. She dropped her gavel and stared at the cell phone. "Wait," she told the bailiff quietly. "On second thought, just take her out of here."

As the bailiff escorted Nia out, she glared at Malcolm and then at David Wrightwood. David backed up to the rail and whispered to her, "Have faith. Trust me. I've got this."

As Nia walked out, the judge dismissed the jurors to deliberate, but the jury's foreman stood up and said, "We don't need to deliberate, Your Honor. We've already reached a verdict."

Nia slowed, despite the bailiff's nudging.

The foreman continued, "We, the jury, find in favor of the defendants."

The courtroom buzzed loudly. Nia stepped out and waited in the lobby. The teenagers and their families poured out of the courtroom, rejoicing and showering David Wrightwood with thanks and admiration.

The first chance he got, he broke away and came over to Nia.

She asked him, "Why didn't you show the video?"

"Because I wanted to save you."

"Save me from what?"

"Embarrassment. More heartache." He looked at the phone. "I'm assuming that Malcolm Smalls is your boyfriend."

"My *ex*-boyfriend."

"If I'd exposed him, it would have caused you more pain."

"But he deserved to be busted."

He didn't dispute that point. "But you didn't."

"Why should you care about my feelings?"

"Because the less time it takes you to get over him, the sooner you can go out with me." He smiled broadly, winking.

Nia backed up. "Excuse me?"

"I'm sorry, did I say that out loud? I meant to only think it." David's cute smile was contagious. Nia couldn't keep from blushing.

Malcolm exited the courtroom, his face lined with worry. David looked at him with contempt. "Why were you with a guy like that anyway?"

"It's a long story."

"I've got time, over dinner tonight."

She was warming up to this charming guy. "You're very persistent. I like that, but I don't even know you. Why should I have dinner with you?"

"Because it's my birthday."

"You're lying."

David took out his driver's license and showed her the date. Sure enough, it was his birthday.

"Get outta here! You weren't lying."

"Trust is a beautiful thing." As he put his license away, this gorgeous, *truthful* guy was starting to make her forget how mad she was at Malcolm.

She informed him, "I don't believe anything until I see it, and even then, I don't always believe what I see."

Puzzled by her statement, he asked, "Where does faith come in?"

"It doesn't. Not in my crazy life."

People continued walking past them and the lobby started to empty. "So, do I get the opportunity to persuade you otherwise?"

"Can you accomplish so great a feat over dinner?"

"I can try, if you let me."

Nia fidgeted with the cell phone. "I don't know. That's asking a lot. I've pretty much given up trusting all men right now."

David shook his head, confident. "If that were true, you wouldn't be standing here right now, looking up at me with that small spark of hope inside those beautiful brown eyes."

❧ CHAPTER 3 ❧

*D*avid Wrightwood had never seen eyes as bright and lovely as those of the woman standing in front of him. He'd just won a big case, a case many thought was impossible to win. Usually after a victory, he'd go out and celebrate. But right now all he could think about was not letting this beautiful girl slip through his fingers before he even knew her name.

"I'm David Wrightwood." He extended his hand, and she took it.

"Nice to meet you, David. I almost got arrested in there. Thanks for saving my butt."

"A butt as lovely as yours deserves saving. I thoroughly enjoyed it. How about your other parts, do they need rescuing too?" he asked pretentiously, admiring the way she burst into laughter. "Finally . . . just like Christmas."

"What's like Christmas?"

"Your smile. It took so long to get here, but now that it's here, I wish it'd never leave."

She scrunched up her nose. "Umm, that was kind of corny, don't you think?"

"Yeah, but it made you smile." The lobby had emptied of all but a few people. "Are you going to tell me your name, or do I have to stand here and suffer?"

"Nia." She smiled with slightly dimpled cheeks. "Nia Youngblood."

He considered this for a moment. "In Welsh, *Nia* means *radiance*."

"How did you know that?"

"I'm amazingly smart." He held her gaze, then admitted, "Okay, one of my college buddies just had a baby girl and named her Nia, so he told me. But I'd still like for you to think that I'm amazingly smart."

She laughed at the coincidence. "And you've been waiting to meet a girl named Nia and use that line on her?"

"No, I think I've been waiting to meet *you*." He grinned, then added, "But did the line work? Did I win your company for dinner?" She glanced toward the water fountain as if someone was there. But he didn't see anyone.

Pushing aside her playfulness, she got a little more serious. "Are you married?" she asked, looking him in the eye.

"No."

"Engaged?"

"No."

"Living with someone or currently involved?"

"No."

"Got a hundred baby mamas?"

"None, that I'm aware of."

"Any perverted or maniacal tendencies?"

"Zero."

She placed her finger on her chin and considered his answers, while he waited. Her lively brown eyes seemed to emit the warmth of a thousand sunrises, he thought, feeling warmed all over.

"I'll supply my Social Security number and a background check, if that'll help," he said.

With no makeup and only a dab of lip gloss, this girl sparkled with raw beauty.

Having made up her mind, she grinned slowly. "So . . . what time is dinner?"

Relieved, he tried to shake off the butterflies he felt in his stomach. "Give me your number and I'll tell you."

Nia pulled an unpaid parking ticket from her pocket and started jotting down her number. "I'm innocent, by the way," she said, referring to the ticket. "They painted the curb red *after* I parked there."

"I believe you." David chuckled.

After the courtroom lobby emptied, one guy remained. Stocky, midthirties, with thinning, rust-colored hair, he stood behind Nia like a warning sign. Johnny Spivek, David's best friend, had overheard their conversation. David mouthed at Spivek, *Leave us alone,* and went back to laughing with Nia. Nia handed him the ticket with her number on it.

"If you take this, you'll also have to pay for the ticket."

David took it. "Not a problem."

Nia heard Spivek's not-so-subtle cough and turned around. David introduced them. "Nia Youngblood, meet Johnny Spivek."

Spivek interjected, "*Detective* Johnny Spivek, LAPD." He eyed Nia's parking ticket. "When do you intend to pay that?"

David interrupted. "Don't mind him. He gets a bit overzealous about his job sometimes." He pulled Spivek off to the side. "Hey, do you mind? I'm trying to ask her out."

"I couldn't help but notice the gaga expression plastered

all over your face," Spivek said as he continued to inspect Nia. "She's cute," he admitted, but he also noticed the way she kept looking over her shoulder, as if she thought she was being followed. "But she could be trouble."

"You've said that about every girl I've met since the small incident with Cher-Ling."

" 'Small incident'?" Spivek raised an eyebrow. "Three protective restraining orders on her before I finally had to arrest her for going bonkers on your automobile is no small incident."

"That has nothing to do with Nia." David smiled at Nia and hoped she couldn't overhear them. Nia smiled back, shifted to her other foot, and looked over her shoulder again.

Spivek cast a concerned look at David. "I'm just trying to look out for you, Wood."

"Thanks, pal, but I can handle this." David nudged him aside and returned to Nia, whistling nonchalantly.

Nia smiled. "So, you have an ex-girlfriend who went bonkers on your car and had to be arrested?"

Embarrassed, David explained. "Cher-Ling had a small psychiatric problem. *Bipolar,* I believe, is the correct term. I wasn't aware of it until about a year into our relationship when she stopped taking her meds." He quickly changed the subject. "How about I pick you up at seven?"

Nia thought about it, then smiled. "See you at seven."

As she walked away, David stared unabashedly at the sexy sway in her curvy hips. Spivek saw his expression and nudged him, trying to break the trance. "That's the same way Samson looked at Delilah. Watch yourself, Wood."

"With a smile like that and hips like those, I'll take my chances." David chuckled, admiring the view. "Besides, it's just dinner. It's not like I asked her to marry me."

Spivek glowered at David. "If it's company you wanted

on your birthday, you should've said something. I would have taken you out for a pizza and bowling."

David finally tore his eyes off Nia and looked at Spivek's bearded face and squat body. He shook his head. "Somehow, it's just not the same."

✌ CHAPTER 4 ✌

*W*hen Nia got back to her house in Northridge, a two-story English Tudor home in Running Springs Estates, she hurried through the double doors, kicked off her shoes, and ran up the winding rose-colored tile staircase. David was intelligent, funny, and sexy—everything she wanted. Sure, there'd be some things about Malcolm she'd miss, but at the moment, she couldn't think of what they would be.

She ran into her bedroom and ransacked her closet. She wanted to look good for her date with David. She wasn't that into clothes, preferring T-shirts and jeans over anything else. If her ponytail holder matched the color of her tennis shoes, she considered that fashion. Malcolm, on the other hand, had been a self-absorbed, fashion-obsessed show pony and always complained about her casualness.

Nia stripped out of the tan suit she'd worn to court. Wearing nothing but a baby-blue lace bra and matching thong, she tossed clothes from one messy pile to another before she finally decided on a simple dress to wear. She hung the dress on a hook and threw the other clothes back into the closet. For the time being, she put on her workout clothes. The kids would be coming soon.

After getting no sleep the night before, Nia was an emotional whirlwind. David had sparked something inside her that she didn't even know was there. Nia ran downstairs to her gourmet kitchen, thinking about David. His short black hair was perfect for running her fingers through. At six foot four with an athletically fit physique he was the perfect match to her five foot five curvy body. She pulled five packages of wieners from her fridge and poured them into an industrial-size pot filled with water, then turned the flame up high.

She watched the wieners start to boil. Heat bubbles arose from the bottom of the pot as the meat plumped and rotated in the roiling water. As the temperature gradually increased, she couldn't help thinking about *him*—her secret dark lover. Not *lover* in the technical sense, since she was still an official card-carrying member of the V Club—*V* as in *virgin*—but he'd filled so many of her nights with dark, steamy erotic thoughts and fantasies that she felt sexually experienced, even if she hadn't actually done anything. He'd certainly whetted her appetite and built up her craving for the real deal.

David Wrightwood could be the real deal.

What is David like in bed? she wondered, and turned the flame up higher. For a virgin, Nia knew a lot about sexual heat, mostly from lucid dreams. She knew how it felt to seethe with desire. The low whirring sound of the gas blowing through the burner reminded her of *him* again, and the many nights he'd hovered over her sleeping body around midnight, whispering naughty things in her ear. His deep voice would resonate, rubbing and warming her like the blue flames coming out of the burner. His words would enter her subconscious and manifest themselves in her body, creating passionate physical responses.

In her reverie, she leaned in too close to the burner, and its flame licked the tip of her sleeve and caused a small flare. Nia quickly snuffed out the flame with her hand, knowing her body soaked up heat like an asbestos doll. Another one of the weird things about her—Nia didn't burn.

She heard a flurry of knocks on the side entrance door and checked the clock: three P.M. She hurried to open the door. A porch full of rowdy, rambunctious teenagers dressed in oversized Sean John shirts, hoodies, and expensive sneakers poured inside her house, roughhousing and playfully bickering.

They greeted her with head nods, peace signs, and hugs as they dropped their backpacks and extra articles of clothing in her game room and made themselves at home.

The boys immediately spilled out the back door, heading for the basketball court and her huge backyard. Most of the girls went into Nia's kitchen to finish gathering the hot dogs, chips, and sodas.

Nia met with the three tutors she'd hired to help her with after-school mentoring, who had also arrived. After checking their lists, Nia tapped the shoulders of the teens who needed to catch up on their homework or get tutoring and pointed to the desks lined up along the side of the game room.

Jay Wells was one of the teens who needed tutoring. Tall and lanky, with a baby face, he lived next door and held a special place in her heart. He was one of the first teens she'd recruited six years ago when her dad bought her the house and set up her trust fund. She'd watched Jay grow from a hyperactive ten-year-old boy into a sensitive young man.

Jay dropped down into a desk and frowned up at her. "You okay, Miss Nia?"

"Yeah, Jay. I'm fine. Why?"

"You look all dreamy, like you're sick or in love or something weird like that."

"I'm not sick or anything weird like that." That left love. Nia blushed and couldn't help thinking about David again.

"Good, 'cause I graduate in two more years, and I know you gonna hook me up with a real nice graduation present." Jay put up his hands like he was driving a car.

"You want a car?"

"It doesn't have to be new. I'll settle for that old used Mustang Shelby you drive, if you want to go the cheap route." Jay grinned, all teeth and kissing up.

"That's an expensive muscle car." Nia pushed his head. "First pass chemistry and driver's education, then maybe we can talk about it."

Jay gave a thumbs-up and Nia walked away laughing.

Over the next few hours, more teens trickled in, transforming Nia's house into an after-school hangout for the neighborhood's latchkey kids and other at-risk youths. Nia didn't see "future parolees," as Malcolm called them. She saw a bunch of bored kids with lots of energy and no place to go.

Nia helped tutor the kids, coached them, counseled them, and broke up fights, but mostly she played with the teens, working up a good sweat and releasing pent-up energy of her own. Ping-Pong, billiards, basketball, and touch football. Laughing, cracking jokes, stuffing themselves with hot dogs and junk food—this was Nia's idea of the perfect job, and she spent every weekday from three P.M. until bedtime doing it.

"Let's get this game started!" she yelled after the tutoring and homework was done. "Everybody who's not a wuss, get your butts out on the field! Now!"

Nia nominated herself as team captain and got a game of touch football going. She could relate to these kids. Her father had made a small fortune in real estate, but after she was born, he took up keeping company with Jack Daniel's and preferred pouring his problems into a shot glass to spending time getting to know his only child. He never married her mother, who'd been MIA most of Nia's life. Nia later learned that her mother's absence was probably a good thing, given her piss-poor mothering skills.

Nia's father set her up with a trust fund that would embarrass Paris Hilton and paid cash to move her into this grand house in Northridge when she was only seventeen. Other than an occasional phone call, he kept a safe distance from Nia's life and affairs, having decided that he couldn't do anything non-financial to help her. She would have gladly given up her trust fund for a normal life.

"Stop trying to cheat, Jay. Your foot was out of bounds." Nia teased her favorite teen.

"No, it wasn't!" Jay fussed.

Nia loved playing and arguing with the teens. Pouring her time, energy, money, and affection into them helped ease her own disquietude.

"Heads up, Miss Nia! Catch this!" Jay yelled, and threw the football.

Nia ran and jumped for it. She dove, caught the ball, and rolled on the grass. "Yeeeah!"

At twenty-four, she had as much energy as the teenagers, maybe more, and enough heart to go the distance. "What time is it?" she yelled at Bear, a slow-moving, burly kid who stood on the sidelines keeping score.

Bear checked his cell phone. "Almost seven o'clock."

"Oh no!" Nia sprang to her feet. "I've got to get ready for my date!"

Disappointed, Jay picked up the football. "I hope you ain't going out with that asshole Mr. Malcolm."

"Jay, watch your mouth. Malcolm is not an asshole. He's just an ass." She grinned. "And no, I broke up with him last night."

"Good! I couldn't stand that dude."

"Me either," Shayla agreed, trying to catch Jay's attention. At nineteen, Shayla was older than the other kids, but she liked hanging out. Shayla and Nia were close. They talked about everything, but Nia kept telling her that Jay was just a kid and to stop looking at him in that way. But Shayla was hot to trot.

Shayla said, "Malcolm looked okay, but his eyes were too close together. You can't trust people whose eyes are too close together."

Jay continued ignoring Shayla. "Miss Nia, you broke up with Malcolm, but you always take him back."

"Not this time. Besides, I met somebody else."

"Who?" Shayla asked. "Is he cute? Does he have lots of cheddar?"

"It's not about money, Shayla." Nia headed for the back door.

Shayla caught up with her. "That's easy for you to say. You've got it made." Shayla huffed. "Girls like me need to marry rich to get what you've already got."

Nia turned around. "Despite what you think, my life is not exactly ideal." Without elaborating, she continued, "As for David, I have no idea how much money he has, but one thing is for sure—he is *definitely* cute!" Nia gave Shayla a high five. "Now come on. I need you to do my hair."

Nia hurried inside the house and Shayla followed.

৫ CHAPTER 5 ৯

*D*avid purposely arrived at Nia's house a few minutes early to see if she was the prissy type who took too long to get ready for a date. After dating Cher-Ling, a professional model, he was tired of waiting an extra hour to eat.

When Nia swung open the door on the first buzz, he was pleasantly surprised. She was ready, albeit out of breath. "Happy birthday!"

"Yes, it certainly is, and what a gorgeous birthday present." He ran his eyes down her dress. Nia looked stunning, dressed in a simple but sexy tangerine-colored dress that hugged her shapely curves and reminded him of tasty exotic fruit. "You do for that dress what James Brown did for R&B music."

"What?"

"You put the *soul* in it! Whew!" David pretended to wipe sweat from his forehead.

"That's exactly the reaction I was hoping for." She took his hand and pulled him inside.

Nia was all grin. Nothing was self-conscious or fake about her. She wore little if any makeup with a generous dab of luscious-looking lip gloss. He'd never seen a woman so comfortable in her own skin.

As he followed her into the living room, he couldn't help but notice her house was expensive, with square footage to spare, but she'd decorated it more like a rich kid's dorm room than a pricey adult home. Bright, boldly painted walls, a red sofa, wicker chairs, sports memorabilia, two Spider-Man lamps, and an antique popcorn machine on wheels parked next to a home theater system with a jumbo plasma screen. A sad-faced clown portrait hung above the red sofa, and a small black-framed photo of a lion stalking in an African desert was propped on the theater system. The close-up shot captured the savagery in the lion's yellow eyes.

David worked with people who aspired to this level of living, people who felt a big house was a measure of success. David struggled for something far less material but equally ambitious. He just wanted to be happy. The problem was, he couldn't clearly define happiness yet, but he hoped he wouldn't have to wait much longer to find it.

Nia did a sweeping motion with her hands. "You like?"

"Yes, I like a lot," he said, keeping his eyes on her.

"I meant my house."

"Yeah, that too." He marveled. "How'd you get all your hair up into that neat bun?"

"My friend, Shayla, attended cosmetology school before she flunked out. She does my hair for me."

"You look like a princess."

"Thanks." Nia surprised him with a kiss on his cheek. Most of the stunningly beautiful women he knew collected

compliments like party favors, but Nia seemed genuinely ap-
preciative.

"You're very welcome."

"Come meet my kids." Nia headed toward a back door.

He turned too, surprised. He didn't know she had kids
and only hoped their daddy wasn't lurking somewhere near
with a baseball bat. She swung open the patio door.

"Hey, kids! Say hi to David!"

David stepped outside and nearly fainted when he saw a
backyard full of teenagers.

"Hey, whassup!"

"How's it hanging, homie?"

"Yo! What's poppin', G?"

They greeted him with sagging pants and do-rags, gum-
chewing, lip-smacking, sweaty, wisecracking, basketball-dribbling
teenagers, some as tall as him. And none of them looked like
Nia.

An older girl with too much mascara who looked like a
walking Maybelline commercial cooed at him, "How you doin'?
Nia was right, you *are* cute."

"Back up, Shayla," Nia warned.

A tall, baby-faced teenage boy palmed a football. "Hey, do
you ball, man?"

"Uh, yeah, I play a little." David turned back to Nia. "You
tricked me. These aren't your kids."

"Yes, they are. Every one."

"Hey, watch out!" somebody yelled, but before David could
turn back around, he heard the familiar whooshing sound of a
ball flying through the air. The tall boy had let loose the football and thrown it at David. David instinctively put his hands
up, but not before the football hit him square in the chest with
a loud *thwack!* Staining his gray suit with grass.

Everybody gasped, especially Nia. "Jay!"

Jay frowned, defensive. "I thought the dude could catch! Not my fault."

"David, I'm sorry," Nia said, her voice hushed.

He looked down at the football lying at his feet, then at Jay. He burst out laughing.

When the kids saw him laughing, they started laughing too. Nia was still in shock. "What? You're not mad?"

"Oh, yeah. I'm mad. One of your kids said I can't catch." David quickly loosened his tie and picked up the football. He cocked back his arm and threw the ball straight at Jay like a pro. Jay saw the rocket coming, ducked, and let it hit Bear square in the chest. Laughter broke out across the whole yard.

David cocked his finger at Jay. "*That's* how you throw a football." He glanced back at Nia. "Why didn't you tell me there was a game going on?" Before she could answer, David pulled off his jacket and shoes and ran toward Bear. He grabbed the ball up again and turned toward Jay. "Let's see what you got."

David squatted, prepared to run. Jay immediately squatted too and tried to block David, but David plowed past him with the speed of a pro athlete. Jay chased him but David was faster. He yelled to Nia on the sidelines, "Where's my backup?"

Nia didn't hesitate. She kicked off her shoes and ran to help David.

When he looked back and saw Nia trying to keep up in her tangerine dress, hair falling down in her face, he couldn't help laughing so hard that Jay caught him. He threw all his weight into David and tackled him. They both hit the grass, and David slid to within inches of the goal line.

Panting and feeling all of his thirty-one years of age, David lay flat on his back. He teased Jay, "You didn't catch me. I tripped."

Jay jumped up. "No way! I caught you"

Nia flopped down next to David, breathing hard, too. "I'm so glad you're not angry."

"Why should I be mad? That was fun."

She looked at the wet grass stains that smudged his pants. "I'll pay for your suit."

"No. Seeing you here next to me, all sexy and breathing hard, is worth more than the price of a suit."

Nia blushed. "That was a good run."

"Not good enough. I wanted to score a touchdown for you." He helped her back up to her feet and handed her the football.

"You did. Trust me, you did."

❧ Chapter 6 ❧

Fifteen minutes later, Nia had showered, washed her hair again, and drenched it with moisturizer. She'd just started blow-drying it when she heard a knock on her bathroom door. She cracked the door. David was standing there wearing nothing but a white terry cloth towel wrapped tightly around gorgeous damp skin and slender abs beneath a broad come-hither chest. A tiny scar ran horizontally near his left nipple, but even that looked sexy on him. Freshly showered, he'd left the guest bathroom and come into her master bedroom.

Nia's mouth fell open, her hand went limp, and she blasted him in the face with hot air.

"Oops. Sorry." She turned off the hair dryer.

David blinked several times to recover from the blast, then snuck a peek at the pink towel she was wearing. "Since the first time didn't work, how about we don't get dressed this time?"

"Excuse me?" The heat she felt now wasn't from the blow-dryer.

"I mean, let's not get dressed up for our date. Let's just do it casual."

"Hmm, that sounds kinda sexy. If you're okay with wearing that towel for the next few hours, I'm game."

David tried to hide his blush. "What I meant was, let's dress casually."

"You mean like T-shirts and jeans?"

"Yeah, but on one condition." He leaned against the door frame. "Your jeans have got to be tight."

She cocked her head teasingly. "You want to see me in tight jeans?"

He bit his lip, sneaked another peek at her pink towel, and nodded. "*Skin*-tight."

Nia shifted her weight to her right hip. "I think I can swing that."

"I bet you can." He winked. "And if you need help getting into them, just holler." He leaned off the door's edge and started walking away.

She stopped him. "Hey. What do I get out of this deal?"

He turned back around. "Huh?"

As Nia's eyes roved down his towel, her mind filled with naughty thoughts. Judging by the huge bulge in the front of David's towel, he was packing serious heat. He must have taken a very warm shower or must have been thinking about her. Either way, she was quite impressed. "Do you really think you can walk into my bedroom half naked and fully gorgeous, then just walk out without giving up a thing?"

He responded with his own naughty smile. "What would you like me to give up?"

"Let's make a deal." She lowered the dryer to the floor by

its cord and slowly walked toward him, with mischief sparkling in her big brown eyes.

"Name your game."

"I wear a pair of my tightest jeans for you, and in return, I get your towel."

"But . . ." David paused. "I have on nothing underneath."

"Yeah, I know." Nia giggled low and sexy as she walked past him to a full-length mirror. With her back toward him, she fiddled with her towel and threw him a teasing look. "Unless you don't want to see me in skintight jeans."

"Okay. I'll call your bluff"—David walked up behind her, his reflection filling the rest of the mirror—"and raise you a towel."

"What do you mean?" she asked over her shoulder.

"I mean, ladies first." He gave a sensual chuckle and he eyed her towel.

Aroused by his sexy proposal, Nia grinned. "You dare me?"

His dark eyes glinted with gamey anticipation as he brought his chin close to her wavy brown hair, gaining a clear view of her body in the mirror. "Yes."

Slowly, in sexy daredevilry, Nia dropped her towel.

David lowered his eyes and saw the strapless blue lace bra with matching panties that she had on beneath her towel. He shook his head, smiling. "You tricked me."

She ran her hand along the lace, smirking. "A towel for a towel, that was our deal, unless you're chickening—"

Before she could finish her sentence, David dropped his towel.

He'd moved closer, strategically positioning himself be-hind her, letting her body block his in the mirror. All she could see was the edge of his naked body. As he stood inches behind the lace of her blue panties, her eyes drifted down his defined abs and stopped at the seductive V-shaped line that cut inward heading toward his masculine wonderland.

Nia swallowed as his tantalizing image sent a feverish jolt through her womanly regions, where the climate quickly grew hot and moist. His deep, rich Brazilian-coffee eyes added to the heat. Swooning slightly, she accidently leaned back and the tip of his hardened flesh brushed the small of her back. The storm that had been brewing in her nether regions quickly escalated to a category-three hurricane.

"Oh . . . my . . ." Nia exhaled so hard her hot breath fogged the mirror. By the time she turned around, he'd securely fastened the towel just below his sexy navel.

Flushed and disappointed, she squealed, "You cheated."

He chuckled. "Guess you're not the only one with a few tricks." He pointed to her closet. "Now find those tight jeans."

David left her bedroom but she remained giddy, excited, and unabashedly horny as she quickly squeezed into her tightest pair of jeans.

Several minutes later, Nia came downstairs. She stopped at the doorway and watched as David called all the teenage boys into the game room. Still wearing the towel, he picked up his wallet, took out two crisp hundred-dollar bills, and held the money up, gaining the boys' full attention.

"These two bills go to the first young man who runs home and returns with a fresh clean shirt, a decent pair of size-thirteen sneakers, and a nice pair of denim pants in my size, thirty-four, long, that don't hang a foot below my butt."

Without hesitation, the boys jetted out the door, knocking over chairs as they went.

Nia stood in the doorway staring at him. "Gosh. I'm going to miss that towel."

Surprised, he turned around. When he saw the super-tight

jeans hugging her curvy hips, he leaned back, obviously pleased. Slowly, she walked to an overturned chair, making sure David was watching, and bent *waaay* over, poking out her butt in sexy slow motion.

David's eyes were glued on every inch of her seductive ploy. "Wow."

"Translate that for me."

"It means, *wow.*" He tightened his towel. "How did you get into those jeans? I told you to call me if you needed help."

"I didn't need any help getting into them, but I may need help getting out."

David bit his knuckles and warned her, "You'd better stop flirting with me, or else."

"Or else what?"

"Or else the next time this towel drops, things could get out of hand."

"Hmm, is that a threat?" She closed the small gap between them. "Or are you just bragging?"

His nose grazed her freshly washed hair. "I'm just telling the truth."

She lifted her chin, staring at his juicy lips. "Can I be the judge of that?"

As he brought his lips close to hers, they heard a noise. Nia turned and saw her friend spying on them. "Shayla, what are you doing?"

Shayla nodded toward David's towel. "Hoping it drops."

"Shayla," Nia huffed, but she couldn't blame her for trying to sneak a peek.

Jay ran back inside with the clothes, beating the others. "Here!" Breathing hard, he slammed the clothes on the table and immediately held his hand out for the money.

David looked at the clothes. "Where are the shoes?"

Jay lifted his oversized shirt and pulled two sneakers from

the pockets of his sagging pants. "Size thirteen." He held out his hand again.

David laughed. "Guess you're faster than I thought."

"Uh, Jay lives next door," Nia tattled. "All he had to do was hop my backyard fence."

Jay grabbed for the money, but David held on to it while inspecting the clothes. "These clothes look a little too conservative for you, Jay."

Nia tattled again, "That's because they belong to his father."

"I can't wear your dad's clothes," David said, scoffing. He played like he was putting the money back in his wallet.

"No, wait!" Jay stopped him. "My father's cool with it. When I told him you were paying two Benjamins, he said to give him half and bring them back dry-cleaned."

Tickled by Jay's reply, David gave him the money. The other boys ran through the door carrying clothes just in time to see Jay scoop up the money and do a victory dance.

While the other boys grumbled and roughhoused, David took the clothing into the guest bathroom to get dressed. Nia had asked one of the tutors to stay late, thinking she'd be on her date by now, but since she wasn't and it was getting late, she helped the teens pack up their stuff to go home. Everyone left, except for Jay, who slipped into the kitchen to wolf down the last hot dogs.

Shayla stayed behind, too. Most nights, she'd stay later and they'd pop popcorn, watch movies, and lie on Nia's living room floor, talking girl talk. Nia never told Shayla she was still a virgin because she didn't want to lose credibility, especially since Shayla proudly boasted of her many sexual exploits.

"Thanks for doing my hair, Shayla."

Shayla pouted a bit. "Why thank me? You just messed it up again."

"Sorry." Nia felt bad. She knew that styling hair was one of the few things Shayla took seriously. Since graduating from high school, Shayla had fumbled through different jobs with no real direction or plan for her life. She lived with her aunt in a tiny apartment, and they constantly bickered about money. Nia slipped Shayla a few twenties for her effort. "You did a good job. I should have been more careful."

"You? Careful? Then you wouldn't be Nia." Shayla took the money, then grinned. "Hey, if you decide you don't want this one," she said, referring to David, "give him my address and send him straight to my house. I'll gladly take him off your hands."

"I bet you would." Nia laughed and hugged Shayla, and they said good night.

Jay came out of the kitchen, his cheeks stuffed with hot dogs. Nia asked, "Are you ready for your history test next week?"

"Paganism, societal beliefs, world religions," Jay grumbled as he chewed and swallowed. "What does any of that stuff have to do with real life?"

"To be honest, I don't really know, Jay." She shrugged and wiped off a table.

"What do you believe in, Miss Nia?"

Jay's question caught her off guard. She stopped cleaning and tried to think. "I guess I was raised rather unconventionally. I don't really believe in anything until I see it. And I've seen things that are too bizarre to believe."

"Oh, yeah? Like what?" His face lit up with interest.

Nia wanted to avoid giving details. "Jay, why are you asking me all of this?"

"I don't know. Just trippin', I guess." He took out his iPod, plugged the earphones in his ears, and headed out the door. "Life is crazy."

"Yes, life is crazy," she chuckled to herself. She locked the side door, then turned off the light, but something in the darkness made her pause. Her nose caught a tiny whiff of sweet molasses, suggesting *he* was watching her from some secret, unseen place. The notion caused in her a paradox of emotion—both unnerving and strangely enticing.

David came out the guest bathroom, searching for her.

"Nia? Where are you?" He peeked into the game room. "Why are you standing in the dark?"

She came out and met him in the doorway. "What did you say my name meant in Welsh?"

"Radiance."

"Radiance," she repeated, with a hopeful glint in her eyes. "I like the sound of that."

David straightened his shirt. "Are you ready for our date?"

"I've been ready for a long time."

He took her hand, his grip confident and secure. "Then let's go make some magic."

CHAPTER 7

*D*avid walked Nia through her living room but paused at her front door. "I'll wait here while you get your sweater. It's chilly out tonight."

"I don't need a sweater. My body temperature naturally runs hot."

"Ooh, I like the way that sounds." He grinned. "But really, you could catch your death out there."

"I'll take my chances." She smiled and pulled him out the door.

David drove Nia to Spigolo's, a cozy, informal Italian restaurant in Santa Clarita that didn't require reservations. Built like a large brown brick cottage with red shutters, the restaurant featured a lovely wisteria-framed archway. Tuscan sunflowers, tulips, and calla lilies in large clay pots lined the porch.

Inside, the restaurant's dim chandelier lighting, colorful

oil paintings, and private tables separated by bright flower arrangements over wood partitions provided just the right ambience for an intimate first date. Nia marveled at the Tuscan Italian village décor.

"This feels like Little Italy. Do you come here for the food or the cozy ambience?"

"Personally, I come for the nude oil paintings." David nodded at a wall painting of a naked lady entangled in wild flowery vines.

"Stop it," Nia giggled as she elbowed him.

"No, I'm very serious." David kept his face straight, then grinned as their hostess seated them in a private booth beneath a wall tapestry of Venice's Canal Grande in muted colors. The low hum of guests' conversations drifted over the faint clack of dishes and silverware, while Dean Martin crooned "That's Amore" in the background.

Nia eyed the authentic cuisine on the menu with enthusiasm. "I'm starving."

"Good." David also read his menu eagerly. "I like a woman with a big appetite."

As Nia perused her dinner choices, she thought of the many dates she'd attempted in the past, during her breakups with Malcolm. The more she liked the guy, the weirder things would get, until finally events escalated into some sort of freak catastrophe and ended with her date bailing out. Nia hoped nothing would go wrong on her date with David, because she really liked him.

After deciding on the stuffed saltimbocca di pollo, David closed his menu and reached for his water glass but paused when he noticed the table's centerpiece. "Hmm, that's odd." David looked around, then back at the centerpiece. "A single purple rose?"

Nia's eyes locked on the purple rose, which hadn't been there when they'd first sat. She knew who'd placed it there, but she tried to play it cool.

"I could have sworn I saw white lilies a moment ago." David reached out to touch the rose, but she impulsively slapped his hand away.

"No! Don't touch that."

He jumped. "Why not?"

Realizing she'd overreacted, she tried to downplay it. "Um, because," she said, smiling nervously, "you don't know where it came from?"

"But it's just a rose."

"Maybe it is. Maybe it isn't."

Though baffled by her comment, he kept staring at it. "Intriguing. The color is so deep and textured, it almost looks unreal."

Irritated, Nia looked away from the exquisite rose. David had no idea that it had actually been placed there as a subtle threat to him, and she wanted to keep it that way.

She waved her hand dismissively. "It's probably a freak of nature, some hybrid trick that some scientist cooked up to fool people." She slyly scanned the restaurant crowd for *him.*

David remained confident and focused. "I can appreciate unique and exotic things. They're a real turn-on." He shifted his eyes from the rose and onto her.

The flirty grin on David's face pulled her attention away from her mysterious pursuer and back to him. Even in Jay's father's shirt, David looked appealing. His broad shoulders and firm biceps filled out the sleeves well, and the rest of the shirt hung nicely around his narrow waistline. Nia threw him a flirty look back, sipped her water, and tried to relax.

"You make borrowed clothes look good."

"I do my best," he said playfully, faking modesty.

David reached past the rose and took her hand. "You're great with those kids."

She smiled, comforted by the compliment. "Thanks. I love being around them. They're not bad kids. They just need a little direction and a place to belong. I open up my house to them, and they help me feel a little less lost."

"You feel lost?"

"Yeah, at times." Nia shifted in her seat, uncomfortable with the admission. She'd just met him and didn't want to come across as ditzy.

David gently squeezed her hand; his touch was warm and reassuring. "Well, tonight, you're not lost at all. You're with me."

Nia couldn't help but blush. David looked at her as if she was something special.

After a moment, he asked, "How'd you get a house like that so young?"

"My father made a fortune in real estate," she explained. "When I was seventeen, he had the house built for me and moved me out."

"He must have been heartbroken to see you leave."

"Not at all. He celebrated my departure over several bottles of Jack Daniel's."

David searched her face. "You're joking, right?"

"No." Nia smiled bravely. "But I'm okay with it. My father and I were never close. We lived more like roommates than father and daughter. After I was born, he retired from real estate, as well as from life, preferring to deal with his issues in the bottom of a bottle. Alcohol became his chosen form of therapy. 'Why do twelve steps,' he'd say, 'when I can make it to my kitchen bar in only five?'"

"You've been on your own since you were seventeen?" he asked, trying to understand her life story.

She nodded. "A big house, a huge trust fund, and a 'Good luck, kid.' That's what I got when he put me out."

"No wonder you feel sort of lost." David frowned empathetically. "What about your mother?"

Nia rolled her eyes. "Don't ask."

"Is she deceased?"

"More like MIA." Nia fiddled with the edge of her napkin. "She's been missing most of my life, and that's probably a good thing."

"Why?"

"When it comes to mothering skills, she belongs to a species of mammal that eats its young."

"That's harsh."

"That's putting it mildly." David had no idea of the magnitude of what she was talking about, and she thought it best to change the subject. "Enough about my weird life; tell me about you. Are you close to your mother and father?"

David's voice changed. "We talk occasionally."

"You seem so well adjusted. Were they good role models?"

"They did the best they could, I suppose." He shifted in his seat uncomfortably and looked around for their waiter.

The elusive waiter had passed their table several times but hadn't stopped to take their order. David lifted his menu to get the waiter's attention. Nia picked up his obvious hint that he didn't want to talk about his parents. A little offended, she fiddled with her napkin until the waiter finally came.

David diverted his attention back to their menus and asked Nia, "So, what are you having?"

CHAPTER 8

"I'll have the never-ending pasta bowl," Nia told the waiter. "When something's good, why should it ever end?"

Nia closed her menu, leaned forward, and smiled. David loved seeing the sparkle back in Nia's big brown eyes. He regretted being abrupt when she'd asked about his parents, but he avoided that discussion with everyone, even his best friend, who already knew about the family's tragedy. Outside of his family, Spivek was the only person who knew how his heart continually ached and how discord still existed between him and his parents. David steeled himself against the haunting memories.

After a moment, he gave Nia a look to let her know he was sorry for being discourteous. With a warm nod, she accepted his unspoken apology. Her eyes were so vivid and deep, he could get lost inside them.

The huffy waiter tapped his foot impatiently. David missed the usual waitress, a tall college student with a faint Tuscan accent and an extra-friendly demeanor. This waiter was new, and his incessant grimace meant he probably wouldn't be working there long.

David tried to make the best of it and placed his order, then added, "And please bring a bottle of Chianti and a plate of gnocchi. Thank you."

The waiter snatched the menus and left. Nia seemed undaunted by the waiter's rudeness. Her bright eyes sparkled with possibilities as she continued her train of thought. "Imagine if life was like a never-ending pasta bowl."

"How so?"

"Instead of ending, we could just ask for seconds."

"A nice thought," David said, chuckling, "but unfortunately, I don't think it works that way."

Nia frowned. "Too bad, though. Some of us could use a second shot at life."

David had no idea what she meant by that but could only guess she already had some regrets in her young life. The waiter returned and placed a basket of cold bread sticks on their table. David politely sent them back for warmer ones.

"Your eyes are amazing," he said. "They're so alive and full of light."

"Thanks." Her blush turned into a flirtatious glance. "But right now, they're so full of you."

David stifled a blush, trying to remain cool. "I'm enjoying your company, as well."

When the waiter brought their warm bread sticks and wine, Nia dug in.

He watched her enthusiasm, tickled. "I see you're not shy about eating on a first date."

"I *love* eating." She chewed with delight. "The key is to find fun ways to burn it off," she said, and caught his eye.

He asked, getting her innuendo, "Oh, yeah? Like what?"

Nia dipped her bread stick in her wine, then slipped it slowly between her lips while sucking the end of it.

David chuckled but squirmed a bit and sipped his water. "If you keep being mischievous, I may forget I'm a gentleman."

"Are you always a gentleman?" She paused, then continued sucking.

He watched her suck. "I try to be."

She rested the bread stick on her pouty, disappointed lips. "I was hoping it was only your day job. What time do you . . . get off?" She gave him a sexy wink.

David nearly spilled his water. "Whatever time you want me to."

They both laughed. This woman excited him. Unpredictable and daring, she kept him on his toes, and he liked that. She knew how to turn on the sex appeal yet maintain an innocent girlish quality.

He cleared his throat and leaned in, his voice low, serious, and sexy. "How much of this is teasing, and how much are you actually willing to deliver?"

Nia didn't answer him verbally but narrowed her eyes and pushed the bread stick all the way into her mouth. As the bread stick disappeared, she held his stare, slowly pulled it out, and started all over again, with a half smile on her face. David watched the way her mouth moved slowly and seductively around the crusty loaf, licking and sucking.

"Okay. Well." He raised an eyebrow and leaned back, then straightened his collar. "I guess that answers my question."

Her visual insinuation had warmed him up considerably and sparked activity in certain places of his body. He shifted in his seat several times, then gulped down his ice water to cool himself off. Finally, the waiter brought their main course. David had to take another minute to clear his mind of the sensual thoughts Nia had put there before he could bless their food.

After he said grace, Nia dove right into her endless pasta bowl. A few seconds later, she paused and patted her mouth with her napkin. "So, why hasn't some lucky woman snatched you up?"

David chuckled. "Don't beat around the bush. Get straight to the point."

"Okay, I will. I hate wasting time."

David cut into his chicken. "I'm not single by choice but by circumstance. It's going to take a special woman to figure me out."

"Are you that complex?"

"No, not really." David spoke honestly from his heart. "I like an independent woman who can take care of herself. But I *love* a woman who'll let me take care of her, not because she has to, but because she wants me to."

"So, you like taking care of people?"

"Old-fashioned, I guess. I was raised to believe that the man is the caretaker."

"Hmm, that's interesting." Nia twisted her fork in her pasta. "Are you still in love with your ex?"

Surprised, David paused with his fork in his hand. "What kind of question is that?"

"A valid one," she asserted archly.

He set down his fork. "I broke up with her months ago," he pointed out. "You broke up with Malcolm Smalls recently, I assume. Are you over him?"

"Absolutely."

"How can you be so sure?"

"Because I'm starting to fall for you."

Her response caught him off guard. He picked up his knife,

cut another piece of chicken, and chewed self-consciously, trying to play it cool.

Nia took another forkful of pasta. "You didn't answer my question."

"I forgot what it was."

"I asked if you're still in love with your ex."

He continued chewing, but the stuffing began to taste funny. He set down his fork. "What we had ended when she refused to get help for her obsessive behavior. I couldn't help her anymore."

Nia dug to the bottom of her bowl. "She had it bad for you. I can kind of understand that."

The stuffing left a bitter garlic taste in his mouth. "Cher-Ling was mixed up. She confused jealous obsession with true love."

Nia wrapped more pasta around her fork. "Men don't feel things as deeply as women."

"I disagree," David said. "We feel things, just in different ways."

"Maybe women need more reassurance than men."

He shook his head. "Love and insecurity are incompatible. A person shouldn't have to prove his love; it just is."

They ate in silence a few moments, then Nia reminded him, "You still didn't answer my question."

"I answered, you just weren't listening."

She set down her fork and gave him an appraising look. "I forgot I was having dinner with a lawyer. Way to dodge a direct question."

He gave it right back. "Ah . . . a woman as stubborn as she is beautiful."

"Are we having our first argument?"

"I believe so."

She smiled. "Does this mean it's over?"

"No." David removed his napkin from his lap and used it to

pat away a speck of sauce from her beautiful lip. "I'd say we're just beginning."

Nia's smile widened even more. "Good, because I was beginning to miss you already."

He caught her hand and squeezed her fingers. "I'm not going anywhere. How about you?"

Nia shook her head.

"Besides, I'm looking forward to dessert." He licked his lips in an unmistakably sexy way that made her blush. "I bet you have a sweet tooth, too."

"I do."

"Is it sensitive?" he asked, intimating other things.

"Yes. It's *very* sensitive." The look in her eye let him know she was thinking the same.

When he leaned forward, he could practically feel her body temperature rising. "It's going to take a very sensitive, very confident man to satisfy it."

She leaned forward, too. "I think you're right."

"I know I'm right." David held her gaze. "And I know who that guy is."

"Wow," she said dreamily.

"Define *wow*," he said, teasing her with her own words.

"You're really turning me on." Her voice fluttered with arousal.

Pleased that he'd evoked the same sensual heat she'd given him earlier, he watched her smooth complexion brighten and flush.

"You're radiant," he said, noticing her skin's new glow.

She squeezed his hands and pulled him even closer. He leaned over, trying to remain a gentleman, but he felt crucial body parts starting to betray him beneath the table.

"It's getting so hot in here," she said as she brought her lips close to his face.

He felt the heat in her short breaths. "I know."

She kicked off her shoe and slid her bare foot up his leg. Her toe crept past his knee and explored the swell between his thighs. His enthusiasm increased a few more inches. "I'm having a hard time containing things."

"I know," she said, working her toe. "I can feel it."

"We'd better stop before—"

"Before what?" she asked, panting in anticipation.

"I've got to get up, before this jackhammer lifts this table." David gently moved Nia's toe to the side and tried to get up, wondering how he'd conceal his *enthusiasm* as he walked to the men's restroom.

As soon David stood up, though, he bumped into someone.

A lady.

A diva like he'd never seen.

CHAPTER 9

"*E*xcuse me." David apologized and tried to back up, but the woman trapped him against the table.

"Don't apologize." She kept her body close up on him. "Please, bump into me all you like." The woman sucked up all of his vision, but he thought he heard Nia gasp.

She was as tall as she was scandalous looking. The woman's six-inch spiked heels put her dangerously at eye level with David. With vivid green eyes, a porcelain-like complexion over chiseled features, and bluntly cut hair that chipped at her chin, she was striking. Her hair reminded him of dark rum. Chilled.

David tried not to be obvious but he couldn't help scanning her body. It seemed to scream, *Look at me.* She was dressed in a form-fitting amethyst lambskin jumpsuit with a low-plunging V-neck. Prominent parts of her anatomy provided more than enough tension to hold the soft material in place.

At the uttermost depths of the V-neck, six silver studs pierced her navel and formed a tiny silver hook. When she saw David looking, she eased back a few inches to give him a privileged view. The material in her custom-designed attire was smooth, almost translucent, and the bottom half snaked around her voluptuous lower parts, flowing like an amethyst river going deep into the jungle.

David quickly pulled his eyes back up to her face, but not before stopping at her breasts, which were wrapped up tight in pure virgin lamb leather, a wardrobe malfunction waiting to happen. Struck guilty by the thought, David eased slightly to the side.

Deep-throated and raspy, her voice was like the slow lick of a tongue. "Do you like what you see?"

"I, uh—" David glanced back at Nia. A sharp scowl had crept into her pretty face, replacing her shock. David turned back politely. "You look, uh, impressive."

"I was going more for *dangerous*." She turned her gaze toward Nia. "What's up, Nia?"

"Hmph," Nia grunted curtly. The only thing more noticeable than the woman's devil-may-care attitude was Nia's reaction to her. David tried unsuccessfully to maneuver a safe gap between them, but if they were playing body checkers, she was winning. She obviously excelled in body maneuvering.

"You two know each other?" David asked.

"No," Nia lied.

"Yes, Nia and I go back. We've got history." Her loaded smile lacked affection, and her tone was deceptively casual. She said to Nia, "Long time no see."

"Yes . . . fortunately." Nia tilted her head slightly away as she talked. "What brings you out here tonight? An easterly wind? El Niño? Bad karma?"

Cold air seemed to whoosh over their table. But the woman

flashed an icy smile and sat down anyway, uninvited. With calculated smoothness, she slid her curvy bottom across the seat on David's side of the booth. Forever the gentleman, he politely remained standing.

"Sit," the woman insisted, and patted the small empty space next to her. She ignored the perturbed look on Nia's face.

Not wanting to offend, he sat on the edge of the seat. "So, uh, where do you two know each other from?"

"We were both in on a deal gone bad," the woman said, deliberately evasive.

Nia clarified. "But I was not a willing participant in the deal."

"Intent is irrelevant." Another whoosh of arctic air descended across the table.

David extended his hand. "I don't believe we've met. I'm David Wrightwood."

"I'm Mystical."

"Mystical?" David repeated, thinking her name fit her well.

"Folks call me Mysti." Her sly green eyes glistened at him.

"Folks call you a lot of things," Nia mumbled. "David, you should just call her a cab. She's trouble."

Mysti's eyes roved down David's shoulders. "David, feel free to call me . . . whenever you like."

"Pleasure meeting you, Mysti." He cleared his throat and tried to catch Nia's eyes for some sort of explanation, but Nia picked up her wineglass and drained it.

She waved the waiter over. "I need a refill."

David was glad for a break in the tension, but apparently, the waiter's courtesy had run out before his shift ended. "Wine refills are not free," he informed Nia.

David interrupted. "Please, refill her glass and let me be concerned about the bill. Thank you." The waiter left in a huff.

David felt Mysti scrutinizing him, and judging by her body language, she was obviously pleased with what she saw. "Nia, you've never mentioned David before."

Nia gritted her teeth as she replied. "That's because we don't talk."

"We should hang out more often," Mysti said.

Nia held her stare. "Your crowd is not exactly my crowd."

"Are you sure about that?"

Nia merely glared in response.

Mysti asked, "So, you broke up with Malcolm . . . again?"

"Not that it's any of your business, but Mal and I are finished. He's history."

Barely listening to Nia, Mysti turned her attention back to David. "I don't blame you. I'd drop a bicycle for a ride on a Harley any day."

As Mysti ran her white-tipped fingernails down her low V-neck, David resisted the urge to follow and kept his focus on her face. "Actually, this is our first date. We're getting to know each other."

"How cute," Mysti said, edging closer.

David, who was already perched half off the seat, almost lost his balance. He recovered it as the snooty waiter returned with a glass of red wine.

The waiter nodded his head toward Mysti. "Is she staying for dinner?"

"No," Nia said flatly.

"I'd love something to eat," Mysti said, looking straight at David.

Nia glowered at Mysti.

David turned to the waiter. "Bring her a menu, please."

Mysti stopped the waiter. "That won't be necessary. I already know what I want." Her jade-colored eyes pinned on David's body.

"I'll have whatever he has." Both David and the waiter stared at Mysti. Nia grunted. "And make sure the stuffing is very hot."

The waiter huffed and left.

David balanced himself on the edge of the booth and tried to make polite conversation. "Have you known each other very long?"

Nia fidgeted with her empty wineglass. "We met when I was six."

"Then you two must know each other very well," David commented.

"Mysti is not an easy person to get to know."

Mysti purred in David's ear. "I can be, under the right circumstances."

He cleared his throat as she ran her fingernails over the tip of David's water glass.

Mysti continued, "Nia was an only child. She missed her mother terribly and didn't have many friends, so I stepped in and tried to be like a big sister to her, but it never seemed to work out well."

Nia huffed in indignation, then added, "My father hated Mysti. He wouldn't allow her in our house."

"How is dear old Dad anyway? I'd go see him, but you know how jumpy he gets whenever I pop in."

"I'll give him your regards." Nia glared. "Or not."

After a few seconds of uncomfortable silence, Mysti asked, "Does David know about Rephaim?"

Shock lit up Nia's face.

David asked, "Who is *Ra-fi-eem*?"

"Rephaim is Nia's dark secret lover," she said in a low, raspy voice. "Very dark, very secret."

Alarmed, Nia yelled, "He's not!"

Unaffected, Mysti tapped the rim of David's water glass. "They are *very* intimate."

Nia adamantly protested. "She's lying."

"Rephaim keeps a close eye on Nia. He's very protective of her." Mysti added, with a wink at Nia, "She was practically made for him." She glanced toward the window as if someone was on the other side, and Nia's eyes followed.

David checked the window, too, but only mirrored darkness stared back at him. Befuddled, he asked again, "Who is *Ra-fi-eem*?"

"He's *nobody*," Nia insisted, but her eyes said otherwise.

David pinned his gaze on Nia. "Are you seeing someone?"

"No!" Emphatic and irate, she added, "I'm not *seeing* anyone but you."

Unmoved by Nia's vehement denial, Mysti looked straight at David. Her eyes were as convincing as they were green. "I'm giving you fair warning, David. You're messing with the wrong girl. Nia belongs to someone else."

"Shut up, Mysti."

Seeing Nia's ire, David challenged Mysti's assertion. "She denies being involved with someone else. Plus, she's sitting here with me tonight and not him. That says a lot."

Mysti matched his challenge. "Rephaim is one mean bastard."

"I don't scare easily."

"But can you last?"

"Excuse me?"

"Nia has dated her fair share of men, but none of them stuck around long enough to pose any real threat. Malcolm was with her under a special circumstance. He knew his place and, for the most part, agreed to stay in it. No one has ever been any match for Rephaim." Mysti iterated, "Rephaim is no ordinary man."

"The guy sounds like a bully to me." David remained steadfast. "I can't stand bullies."

Nia sat transfixed and speechless. "Rephaim is ruthless,"

Mysti warned David, as if Nia wasn't sitting right there. "He doesn't play by the rules. He makes up his own."

"Maybe he needs to be taught some manners."

Mysti leaned toward David. "If you mess with what belongs to Rephaim, he'll screw you in more ways than you can imagine."

"Mysti!"

"Rephaim is one *devil* of a man." Mysti smiled, picked up David's water glass, and took a slow sip. Before David had a chance to respond, the waiter returned with Mysti's order. He unapologetically interrupted their conversation and set the heavy plate down in front of Mysti with a clunk.

Mysti tasted the chicken. "This food is cold."

"Hot or cold, it tastes the same," the waiter replied.

David slammed his palm on the table. "That's it. I've had enough of your rudeness. Go get your manager. Now."

Mysti touched David's arm to calm him. "I'm a big girl, David. I can handle this."

"Mysti." Nia glared at Mysti with a strong warning in her eyes. "Don't."

Nia stiffened as if Mysti was about to do something, but David had no idea what. Mysti grazed her white fingertips along the bottom of her neck in a slow sweeping motion, then slyly grazed the waiter's apron. "It's already done," she told Nia, then turned to the waiter. "You eat it."

"Huh?" The waiter's eyes widened.

David was equally baffled. "Huh?"

Mysti pushed the plate to the table's edge, toward the waiter. Nia put her face in her hands. Mysti pointed to the plate. "You served this food cold. Now eat it."

David interrupted, "I'll go get his manager and let him handle—"

Before David could finish his sentence, the waiter dropped

down on both knees next to the table. Confusion, then help-lessness flashed across the waiter's face as he robotically kneeled over the plate of cold food and started lapping it up like a dog.

"Faster," Mysti said coolly as she admired her white finger-nail tips. The waiter involuntarily mashed his face deeper into the plate and ate ferociously, with stuffing flying everywhere.

"What the—?" David jumped out of the booth. "I'm get-ting the manager. This man has lost his mind."

David quickly found the manager and returned to the table amid avid stares from other guests. After cleaning his plate, the waiter remained on his knees, his eyes dazed, and food dripped down his shirt.

David pointed at the waiter. "Look! I told you. He's eating our food."

The manager quickly pulled the waiter to his feet. The baffled waiter mumbled, "Whaaa . . . what happened?" He fo-cused on Mysti, his eyes narrowing with accusation. "She made me do it."

The manager apologized to David's party, as well as the other guests that witnessed the strange behavior, and escorted the waiter into the back. David sat down, but this time next to Nia.

"Mysti is scandalous," Nia said, shaking her head. "Tell her to leave, David."

David looked across the table at Mysti, who appeared un-concerned about the events that had just transpired.

"I've dealt with many men, David." Mysti slid to the edge of her seat, preparing to leave.

"I don't doubt that."

"I know a real man when I see one." As Mysti stood up, she took in his physique. "Confident. Masculine. Stubborn. Firm." She smiled. "I'd love to see a lot more of you." Her voice changed from sultry to serious. "But for your own safety, cool it. Nia is already spoken for, and it's a done deal."

David bridled at the thought. "I'll let her be the judge of that. Until she tells me to leave, I'm not going anywhere."

With an angry huff at Mysti, Nia agreed with David.

Mysti ignored Nia and looked at David. "If you have a change of heart, give me a call."

"He won't. Have a nice life. Good-bye."

As Mysti left the restaurant, the entire roomful of people turned to watch her slink away. When David finally turned back around, Nia looked like she'd just been ambushed. "Are you okay?"

"No." Nia shook her head. "That woman is nerve wracking."

"Well," David conceded, "she's definitely eccentric but probably harmless."

"Mysti is *not* harmless," Nia said emphatically. "She's a witch."

"Calling names?" David handed her some water to try to calm her nerves. "Isn't that a bit unfair?"

"No!" Nia pushed the water away. "She really is a *witch*."

David raised his eyebrows. "You mean like, spells, hexes, the whole nine?"

Nia nodded. "Exactly."

"How do you know?"

"Because . . . Mysti is my *mother*."

David choked on his water.

$\mathcal{A}$fter Mysti left, Nia felt like someone had jabbed needles into her stomach. Mysti always had that kind of lasting effect on her. The fact that her wayward mother just happened to "pop up" during her date with David was no coincidence. Mysti was always scheming, and Nia knew that whatever she was plotting, it involved her terrific new love interest. Nia knew she needed to keep Mysti as far away from David as possible.

David cleared his throat after choking on his water. "Mysti is your *mother*?"

"Unfortunately, yes, but only in the loosest biological sense of the term."

David swallowed hard, trying to digest it all. Nia swallowed too, fearing Mysti had just ruined her chances with him. People in the restaurant continued staring, even after Mysti had left. David looked uncomfortable. "How about we skip dessert?"

Nia's hopes plummeted. "Okay."

David quickly paid the bill and left a large tip for the waiter, most likely out of pity for what Mysti had done to him. He escorted her out, and as he held open the lobby door, she asked, "I suppose you don't want to see me anymore?"

The night had grown cold, dark, and windy.

"First of all, I don't necessarily believe in witches, per se," David explained, taking his time to answer. "They could be misguided individuals trying to grapple with the mysteries of this universe." He touched her shoulder, and they paused under the black awning. "Second, if you'd told me your mother was Broom-Hilda and your dad was Count Dracula, I'd still be madly attracted to you. Nothing's going to change that."

His words struck her heart. She moved close and softly kissed his cheek. He smiled. "And did I mention I don't scare easily?"

"Now you're just trying to get another kiss."

"Exactly." He leaned over for another kiss. She gladly kissed him again, and they headed to the parking lot. A brisk icy wind blew over the Santa Monica Mountains and whipped at them fiercely. But Nia didn't mind the coldness. Her body had its own internal furnace that defied normal biophysics. Neither of them wore a jacket, only casual shirts and denim jeans. She could tell by the way his teeth chattered that he was cold.

"I'd offer you my coat but I don't have one." He wrapped his arm around her protectively. "Would you like my shirt?"

"That's very sweet, but I'm okay." She snuggled close, trying to block the breeze.

When they'd first arrived, no close parking spaces had been available, and David had to park far back. Now, since the dinner crowd had left, there were plenty of open spaces.

"Just for the record and my own personal curiosity," David asked, "does Mysti do the cape, floppy hat, and broom thing for Halloween?"

"Absolutely not." Nia left David's arm and walked slightly ahead of him, hoping he wouldn't ask too many questions. "Mysti has never touched a broom in her life. And as for a cape, she won't wear anything that's not imported and formfitting, preferring dead animals and reptile skins over cotton. She's too vain and proud of her youthful figure to hide it. Besides, Halloween costumes are child's play. Mysti is not playing around. She takes her craft seriously."

"Her craft?"

"Black magic, thaumaturgy, manipulation of the elements—whatever you want to call it."

Nia stepped off the curb. Only one lamppost lit the entire parking lot. David stepped off, too. "Where do you fit into all of this?"

"I don't. At least, not willingly. Being Mysti's daughter, biologically speaking, she's managed to get me mixed up in a thing or two." That was putting it mildly. David didn't need to know all the sordid details. Nia didn't even know the whole story herself. The wind slapped at their faces and backs. "You should have asked the boys to bring you a jacket, too."

"No, I'm fine," he lied.

The dim haze from the sole lamp turned the sky dirty black. When Nia heard a faint commotion near the back of the parking lot, she suspected something was going on. Small trees, landscaping, and bushes obstructed their view.

David didn't seem to notice. His mind was still on Mysti. "Is that why you two don't get along?"

"Tonight was a good night," she said wryly. "No one called 911."

"Wow." David tugged his collar closed. "What about your dad? Does he stay in touch with Mysti?"

"She's the reason why he drinks."

"I see."

"He hates it when Mysti *pops in.* She's considered a rebel, even in the occult community." Nia heard more noises and slowed, trying to stall. "Do you know anything about the dark arts?"

"No, can't say I do. Never been curious either. I grew up in a Christian home. I actually prefer to stay in the light." David chuckled uncomfortably.

Nia stopped completely. "You were lucky. I grew up in a house where anything goes, and often it did."

"Now that I'm grown, I still attend church most Sundays." David tried not to shiver. "Occasionally I make it to a Wednesday-night Bible study."

"So you understand how this whole spiritual thing works?"

"Oh, no, I didn't say that."

She turned and faced him. "I've never stepped foot inside a church."

"Never?"

She shook her head.

David looked around. "Why are we stopping here?"

"Because."

"Because why?"

"David, sometimes you ask too many questions." She heard a noise coming from the direction of David's car. A woman was arguing with someone, then yelled.

David heard it, too. "Sounds like somebody needs help."

He started forward, but Nia caught his arm. "I don't think she needs help." She'd recognized Mysti's voice and suspected that whoever had made her mother scream probably had a good reason.

The argument escalated, then they heard the loud crash of breaking glass. The sole lamppost burst open and shards of glass flew out from its globe. The parking lot went dark. David grabbed Nia and pulled her close, practically smothering her in his chest.

She clung to him too, but not because she was scared. "David, I can't breathe."

He loosened his grip but kept her close as they stood in almost total darkness. She felt his chest harden and his abdominal muscles tighten. He asked, "You okay?"

"I'm good." She kept her arms around his waist, squeezing him. His body felt alert, aroused, and ready for action.

"What was that?"

"Probably nothing." Nia tried to downplay it.

"I'll take you back inside, then go see what's going on." He tried to nudge her, but she wouldn't budge.

"No," she said, and kept her arms around him. "I'm staying right here with you."

❦ Chapter 11 ❧

*D*avid hated the dark. Not so much the dark itself, but what lurked inside the dark that he couldn't see. If he couldn't see it, he couldn't fight it. Rule number one in training as an athlete and a lawyer: confront your opponent head on.

After the lamp broke, they heard another sound. A low bass-like vibration emanated through the air, like from a stereo speaker, but it wasn't music. A man's voice rumbled but was indecipherable. Then they heard footsteps running away, the clacking of spiked heels on asphalt.

David nudged Nia back again. "You don't need to be out here. I'll handle this."

Nia remained resolute. "I'm not leaving you."

She was stubborn. Under normal circumstances, he'd put his foot down firmly and insist she go back inside, but this wasn't the time. "Okay, just get behind me."

"Okay," she said, but he still had to push her behind him.

David walked ahead, aided only by the weak rays of a distant streetlight. When his foot hit something, he stumbled and
looked down at a cement parking block. He stepped over it and
went forward.

As they walked through thinning rows of cars, Nia gripped
the back of his shirt, pulling him, but he kept moving forward.
They passed several small trees and bushes until they reached
the remotest section of the parking lot, a desolate area except
for his car.

And a purple Cadillac.

Parked perpendicular to David's limited-edition black
Jaguar XK, the darkly painted Caddy looked menacing. David's
eyes adjusted enough to take in certain details. A '65 Cadillac
Calais, two-door, hardtop. A classic.

Its body lay close to the ground. Polished wheels, thin
chrome lines accentuating its molded edges, hooded back
wheelbase, custom angled, winged taillights. The car was authentic, with all original parts. An amateur car buff himself,
David recognized the attention and detail put into it.

The two cars formed a T, with David's Jaguar as the top of
the letter at an unfair disadvantage. Though it had cost him the
price of a small house, his car suddenly looked like so much
fancy lightweight aluminum on wheels pitted against hard,
old-school, no-bullshit steel.

David stopped a careful distance away and kept his eyes
on the side view of the Caddy. Even at fifty feet away, the car
loomed threateningly, its body stretched long like desire.
Two hundred and twenty-four inches of impressive steel,
it boasted a custom paint job. Deep blood-rich purple with
embedded metallic flakes that stole spikes of light from the
darkness.

With no jacket and fighting off a shiver, David felt cold and
vulnerable to the wind. Nia tightened her grip on his shirttail

and stood next to him. The caddy appeared empty inside, but its darkly tinted windows made it impossible to tell for sure. Something moved—a shadow behind the wheel, slightly re-clined and sitting low.

David bent close to Nia's ear. "Do you know who that is?"

"No," she mumbled.

He didn't believe her. "It's him, isn't it?"

"Him who?"

He had no time to play the dumb game. He had a situation on his hands that he needed to deal with. "Let go of my shirt. I'm going to talk to him."

Reluctantly, she loosened her grip. The Caddy turned on its headlights. David shielded his eyes. Even from the side angle, the sudden light was blinding. Its rays lit up David's Jag like a glowing comet, forcing him to turn away for a second. He couldn't walk forward because the contrast of light and dark made it impossible to see a clear path.

A few seconds later, the Caddy dimmed its headlights. The intense light gradually descended to a low, ominous level. *A bully,* David thought, *someone who strong-arms others of lesser power through fear and intimidation.* David lowered his hands and thought about how much he hated bullies. He thought about his little sister and the horrible incident that had torn his family apart. All because of a bully.

David started toward the Caddy again.

"Wait . . ." Nia stopped him. He looked back a brief second. "Don't go over there."

"I'll just talk to the guy, try to reason with him." Not really believing his own words, he proceeded. He would indeed try to talk, preferring civilized conflict resolution to the alternative of violence. But most bullies weren't open to conflict resolution. If the guy would rather jump from his car and confront David man to man, then David was ready to do business that way, too.

He aimed his words at the purple Caddy. "If you came here for Nia, she's with me. And I don't play games."

Getting closer, he squinted, trying again to see the driver. He hated communicating with a shadow. Whoever was inside had a clear view of him, and that put David at another big disadvantage.

He walked slowly and cautiously. The shadow seemed to permeate the entire interior of the car. David second-guessed himself for not making Nia go back into the restaurant. If the driver had a gun, he'd rely on his natural quickness to duck fast and run low, but that would put Nia directly in the line of fire.

David closed in and veered slightly to the left, altering the angle of possible gunfire, figuring Nia would be clear.

The element of surprise boosted his adrenaline. Not knowing what to expect sharpened his senses and quickened his reactions. Like in his courtroom battles, he had to be prepared for the worst. Human subversiveness, disloyalty, deception, lies, and fury always surfaced in the heat of the battle. David thrived on this kind of adversity.

Mysti's words came back to him. *Rephaim doesn't play by the rules. He makes his own.*

More reason for David to proceed.

As he advanced, the Caddy sat deathly still, its hearse-black windows radiating a life force. The windows were rolled up, but David knew the driver could hear him.

"She doesn't want to be with you. Stop stalking her."

Slowly, the driver's window rolled down. A slow, fluid motion moved the glass halfway, leaving a gap, a hollow space near the driver's head.

David squinted but still couldn't see the man behind the wheel. It was as if the darkness clung to him, cloaking him in invisibility.

Nia stepped forward; apprehension weighed down her voice. "David, you don't want to do this."

"Stay back, Nia." He didn't take his eyes off the shadowy driver. "Get out of the car. Let's talk."

The window stayed cracked; the driver's door stayed closed. David interpreted the driver's noncompliance as cockiness.

"Nia doesn't want to be with you. If you still don't understand, get out of the car and I'll explain it to you."

He kept his voice low and even, careful not to show any signs of anger or frustration. First lesson in law school debate class: lose your cool, lose your credibility. David wanted the driver to show himself so he could see what he was up against.

A small, round red light appeared inside the dark space at the window. It seemed to originate from the dashboard, then travel in a zigzagging firefly motion toward the driver. The end of a laser pointer, or possibly some type of gun scope, but it stayed inside the car, then moved to the gap in the window. The driver flicked it. Tiny red ashes spilled toward the ground, disappearing into the blackness before hitting the asphalt.

A cigarette. The bastard was smoking!

After the flame made more circular motions, smoke wafted up from the window. David watched the small plume drift out the window and slowly evaporate in the night haze. The speck of flame expanded and increased in intensity as the driver pulled another drag. He'd only cracked the window to blow out smoke.

David stared at the lit butt, his frustration getting the better of him. He placed his hands in his pockets and turned slightly. He rocked back on the soles of his sneakers, appearing to back down or retreat, but he was actually testing the traction of his shoes on the asphalt. He'd rush the Caddy, but first he needed to make sure the sneakers he'd borrowed from Jay's father could handle his weight, the angle of his quick movement, and the friction it would cause. The last thing he needed was to slip and fall on his ass.

He'd wait for the driver to take another pull. The driver would have to drop the cigarette first before picking up a gun, if he had one, in order to shoot with his left hand. Since he'd already spotted the tiny raised silver knob and he knew the door was unlocked, all David needed were those extra seconds to snatch the door open, grab him by his neck, and yank him down to the asphalt.

Then they'd talk.

David saw the cigarette go back up. He broke out in a quick sprint and prayed the son of a bitch wasn't ambidextrous. Pro sports training had taught him how to angle his body and use his weight to increase his speed, then turn or stop on a dime.

David ran fast but before he could close the gap, the Caddy's engine started.

Loud, roaring thunder erupted. Powerful enough to stop David in his tracks. The engine's vibrations sent ripples through the asphalt that David felt through his sneakers' soles. He halted and spun slightly, like he'd hit a brick wall. The three-hundred-and-forty-horsepower engine's raw force poured from under the hood, bursting in fury, begging to break loose. The friction of its pistons reverberated, causing the Caddy's stretched-out body to bounce on its wheels.

Nia yelled something, but David couldn't hear over the engine's blast. Having been stilled in his tracks, he regained his balance. He waited, breathed, fists tightened.

After a series of loud revs, like a bully getting his point across, the Caddy's engine died down to a moderate, well-tuned hum. Still an effective nonverbal threat, it challenged David, strummed at his patience, clouded his better judgment.

He was already most of the way there, with only about twenty feet more to go, and the Caddy was still facing his Jag in a T formation. Even with its engine running, it couldn't back up or turn quick enough to hit him. If he ran fast enough, he could still get to the driver.

David took off. This time he heard Nia scream directly behind him. The Caddy's engine revved from zero to full throttle in one chilling second. Its cylinders fired; flame spit through its hood and out the exhaust pipe. Intake, compression, and combustion all exploded into a surreal skidding motion. With rims spinning, tread burning, and tires smoking, the car turned 90 degrees in an instant—way faster than any car that size and weight should be able to move. Thirty-five hundred pounds of steel bounced laterally on its tires. Menacing power roared at full throttle under the hood, held back only by a foot on the brake.

The driver pumped the engine. The motor thundered. White smoke shot from the wheelbase, like on race cars doing victory donuts, only the Caddy was no longer spinning; its aim stayed directly on David.

Flesh and bones were no match against steel. Unfortunately, that fact dawned on him a little too late.

The Caddy revved and bounced.

David took off.

The Caddy lurched full speed ahead.

David backpedaled, then turned completely and ran at Nia. He swept her up on his shoulder, carried her several yards, then tackled his body into hers, using his force to hurl them both into the narrow strip of landscaping dividing the parking lot. He knew he couldn't outrun the Caddy, especially not with Nia propped on his shoulder like a potato sack. If nothing else, the small tree trunks would absorb the majority of the blow from the Caddy's front fender.

Riotous sounds of heavy metal speeding through open space drowned out all thoughts. He didn't even hear Nia scream and he dropped and rolled his body over hers, breaking tree limbs and snapping twigs as he wedged their bodies between dwarf cypress tree trunks. Facedown in sagebrush, David looked up just in time to see the Caddy's headlights off the back of Nia's brown hair, coming at them full speed.

Brakes screeched. The Caddy skidded. David bore down as its tires' thick tread ground on the asphalt like a jet's landing gear.

The Caddy stopped inches away.

He turned around. Bright headlights obstructed his vision, but he made out the shiny chrome fender that had stopped two yards from where he and Nia lay. The engine idled, humming low.

Still bracing himself, David got up. Leaves, dirt, and branches fell from his clothes as he faltered back. He felt Nia get up behind him. A quick glance revealed a few superficial scratches on her cheek, nothing major. Her T-shirt was torn and her blue bra showed.

"You okay?"

"Yeah. You?"

He didn't answer but focused on the Caddy and its driver. The thick, suffocating smell of burning rubber filled his nostrils, threatening to gag him. He coughed it off.

The Caddy began backing away.

Instead of feeling relief, David felt denied. He wanted a man-to-man confrontation. He wanted to fight his way through his fear. He wanted to kick the driver's ass.

"Get out of the car!"

He stumbled back over twigs before he regained his footing and stepped to the side trying to get a visual through the windshield. Still, he could only see a faint outline of the driver. More leaves and foliage fell from his clothes. Heat from Nia's body brushed his arm. He tried to move her back, but she pushed forward.

The Caddy stopped a short way off and adjusted its head-lights, pointing its high beams at Nia, placing her in its spotlight.

All four windows rolled down.

David heard a click like from a speaker. Music played.

Rich, soulful-sweet music blasted from the Caddy's dark interior. Three loud, clear, high notes from an electric guitar, then percussion beats, followed by a smooth male voice that dove straight into sensuous lyrics: *"I've been really trying . . ."* The car's speakers pumped out Marvin Gaye's "Let's Get It On," with lyrics so suggestive and a melody so seductive, it'd make nuns think about having sex. David tried to ignore the enticing, pulsating music aimed at Nia, but it was impossible.

"Son of a—!"

The headlights surrounded her and made the blue lace in her bra glow. She backed up a few inches and tried to pull her torn T-shirt together but the wind kept it open.

With high treble and thumping bass, the car sounded like a concert stadium, like Marvin Gaye himself had awoken from the dead to perform live. Colorful lights projected from its equalizer flickered inside its dark interior like a light show from a disco ball, making the faint outline of the driver a little more defined. Broad-shouldered, resting a confident arm on the side of the door, body leaned back and slightly reclined, he used music now as intimidation.

The loudness of the bass made the car reverberate on its back tires, allowing the rays from its headlights to dance around Nia.

David felt punked. Dissed. Several times, all in the last ten minutes. An ultimate insult to a man trying to guard the integrity of his date. This bastard was making a play for Nia with David standing right there. "Get out of the car!"

David stood tall and kept his eye squarely on the shadow of the driver. He wanted to lunge for him but wasn't stupid enough to put himself in that kind of danger again.

He jumped in front of Nia, blocking the headlights, and yelled, "You and me! Let's you and me *get it on.*"

The driver increased the music's volume, drowning him out. David yelled louder. "Let's do this, man to man!"

The Caddy revved a few times, playing with its power, gunning to the rhythm of the music, toying with David, and flirting with Nia. David bit down on his lip.

With music still blasting, the Caddy turned slowly sideways—a phallic symbol showing off its girth before making a U-turn. It began to roll away, driving in a zigzag and bouncing on its suspension, as if slow-dancing or making love to Nia.

David yelled, "Hey! C'mon back, let's *talk!*" but the Caddy kept rolling, unhurried. A bully. David vowed he would take him down the next time he saw him, one way or the other.

*N*ia wanted to hug David, but he was still rattled by the driver of the purple Caddy. They got into his car and left the parking lot. Clearly, he didn't want to talk, and she didn't know what to say.

Instead of turning right onto the boulevard, David took a left and drove down a backstreet. She knew why. The purple Caddy had gone that way, and David was still mad. He wanted to confront the driver.

"I didn't want any of that to happen," she said with a sinking feeling that she was doomed. "I want to be with you. I wanted our date to go well. Do you believe me?"

David's grip stayed tight on the wheel, and he kept a lookout for the Caddy. "I believe you."

"Good." She exhaled.

David searched the residential neighborhood for a parked Cadillac, but he spotted something else. He hit the brakes.

"What?" Nia hoped it wasn't Rephaim again. She followed David's eyes over toward a devilwood tree. "Is that *Spivek*?"

David threw the car into park and jumped out. She got out, too. Several homeowners in the otherwise quiet neighborhood had gathered in their robes and pajamas around Spivek, who looked like he'd been ambushed but was unhurt. He'd been tied tightly to the tree with a long piece of amethyst-colored leather. His service revolver hung next to him, also tied up in an amethyst leather cord. Nia glanced around the dark trees and oleander bushes for Mysti, knowing she was somehow involved in all this.

David excused his way through the stunned residents and untied Spivek. "What happened?"

"Good timing. My arms were starting to go numb." Spivek rubbed his hands together, flexing his arms to get the circulation back into them. "The woman who crashed your dinner ambushed me."

"Were you spying on us?"

"Absolutely not," Spivek protested. "I stopped at Spigolo's to grab a quick bite and just happened to notice you on your date."

Already perturbed, David's patience was running short. "Please, just get in the car."

"But—"

"Or maybe I should just leave you out here?"

Spivek hurried and squeezed himself into the small backseat of David's Jaguar.

David drove off in silence, checking his rearview mirror every few seconds. First Mysti's intrusion, then the purple Cadillac, and now Spivek. He really had a lot on his mind. Crammed in the back, Spivek struggled to lean his wide body forward. He grunted, "I noticed something peculiar about the woman, so I put a tail on her when she left the restaurant."

Nia tried to hide her anxiety. "You followed Mysti?"

"Only as an informal precaution." Spivek turned back toward David. "After the woman argued with someone parked in a purple Cadillac, she ran off. Thinking she might be in some sort of trouble, I pursued her, only to have her turn around and ambush me. I think she pepper-sprayed me or something to cloud my vision. She disarmed me and tied me up." Spivek shook his head, befuddled. "I've been in law enforcement for over a decade. I still can't figure out how she did it."

"Where's your Jeep parked?" David asked, sounding tired and frustrated.

"Back at the restaurant." Spivek tried to move forward more but his body stayed wedged tight. "I'm telling you, Wood, there's something foul going on here."

David raised his hand, short on patience. "Save it, Spiv. I'm not in the mood right now." He made a sharp U-turn, drove back to the restaurant, and pulled up next to Spivek's red Grand Cherokee Jeep.

"We watch each other's back, right, Wood?" Spivek asked. David didn't reply, but Nia could tell they had a bond between them.

"Maybe you shouldn't have stuck your nose in my business." David remained irritable. He put the car in park but kept the engine running, got out, and lifted his seat forward.

Spivek pulled himself from the backseat but remained standing by David's door. He lowered his voice. "We've been watching out for each other since grade school. That's all I was doing tonight."

Nia perked up and listened. David softened a bit. "But I told you, I can handle myself."

"I know you can handle yourself," Spivek replied. "I taught you all your best moves," he joked, trying to lighten David's mood, then continued with concern in his voice. "But maybe subconsciously you're still trying to prove something."

"Am I being psychoanalyzed now?" David asked, his irritability returning.

"No, I'm just saying, after your relationship with Cher-Ling turned into a disaster, maybe you're a little too eager to get involved again and try to make things right this time. That, combined with the issue with your parents—"

"Don't go there." David cut him off sharply.

Spivek paused. "You're right." He backed off. "I shouldn't have interfered. I'll let you get on with your date."

As Spivek started walking to his Jeep, David shifted and hesitated, rethinking. He cleared his throat. "Hey," he called after Spivek with regret in his voice. "Thanks for being concerned."

Spivek nodded and got into his Jeep.

David got back into the car and they drove off, but he still wasn't talking much. As they headed south on Interstate 5 back to Northridge, Nia felt guilty. She knew David didn't need any additional trouble in his life, certainly not a woman who was being stalked by an obsessively jealous dark entity.

But now that she'd met him, there was no way she'd walk away from him, not of her own volition. If David Wrightwood was willing to stick around, then she'd do everything in her power to keep him by her side.

❧ CHAPTER 13 ❧

A half hour later, they arrived back at Nia's house. David had started to loosen up a bit. He sat on her red sofa beneath her impressionistic oil portrait of a sad-faced clown as she poured two Cokes and set the cans on the shelf, next to her glass menagerie of running stallions.

She went to the home theater system and turned on the MP3 player. She cranked up the volume, trying to clear her mind of the sexy Marvin Gaye song that kept echoing in her head, reminding her of *him.*

"Dance with me." She pulled David off her red sofa and started swaying her hips to Cheryl Lynn's upbeat song "Got to Be Real."

David joined in, but he let her do most of the dancing. "Where do you get all of this energy?"

"I was born with it."

"I believe it." Gradually, he began to relax and unwind too.

Nia let go and allowed the music to take control of her. Caught up in the rhythm, she lifted her arms above her head, bent her knees, curved her waist, and with self-assured, fluid motions, she swung her hips in quick, sexy swirls, showing off her innate sense of rhythm. She moved sensually and organically, better than a professionally choreographed dancer. Energetic and imaginative, her moves came straight from her soul. As she worked her body to the melody, she flashed a big, flirtatious grin at David.

David was obviously impressed, by the look in his eye. He watched her every move admiringly. He unbuttoned the top button on his shirt and laughed, sweated, and danced, trying to keep up with her. He threw in a few of his own rhythmic moves.

"Now you're showing off," Nia giggled, relieved that David had taken his mind off the other complications of the night.

"I'm just following your lead." David danced close, synchronizing his body movements with hers.

Nia marveled at his agile athletic moves and incredible stamina, and she couldn't help wondering about his other skills. "Is it true what they say about a man who can dance?"

He knew what she was hinting at. "Absolutely," he said, straight faced, then winked.

Nia laughed as they boogied, changed positions, and mixed up moves while improvising. They tried hard to outdo each other, with neither one wanting to back down first or show any sign of fatigue. They danced through three more songs until finally the music changed from fun and upbeat to slow and sensual.

When Boyz II Men started crooning "I'll Make Love to You," David backed up, catching his breath, but Nia kept going. Her moves changed from fun and playful to sultry, energy-stirred sensuality.

Invigorated by David's presence, Nia let the mood of the song sweep her up and take her to another place as she internalized the lyrics and interpreted their meaning using her body movements. Emotions deep inside surfaced and flowed through her. Unashamed, she expressed them with a slow, stirring, sultry dance.

Ablaze with passion, Nia closed her eyes. She tilted her head back and thought about David Wrightwood. Knowing he was standing right in front of her, watching her, she imagined him touching her and it thrilled her even more.

In slow, arousing, sexually charged movements, she glided her body through soft, intimate motions, using the sensuous beat as her only guide. Nia clenched the bottom of her T-shirt, lifting it slightly above her navel, exposing her bare midriff, and slowly tied a knot in it. Her tight-fitting, low-rise jeans clung to her curvy hips like a body glove just below her slender, curved waistline.

Nia sang along with the lyrics and imagined David touching her. She imagined him making love to her.

❧ CHAPTER 14 ❧

*D*avid's heart was pounding. Not because they'd danced through three songs. His pulse raced because of what Nia was doing in front of him.

Nia slowly slid her hand down her bare midriff, effortlessly flexing her abdominal muscles while grinding her hips in a slow, raw, feminine gyration. With no belt, her jeans clung to her body, held in place only by silver snaps. She rubbed her palm over her flat stomach, circled her diminutive navel, then slid the tips of her fingers beneath the first snap. She tugged gently at the blue lace on her panty, trapped between her jeans and her sweaty skin.

David hadn't sung to a woman in a long time, since back in his college days, and that was only after the singer had begged him to join her onstage. It had gone over well. His voice was above average, smooth, deep, and melodic, but he'd made no pretense of carrying his vocal gift any further. But now, as he began to sing "I'll Make Love to You" to Nia Youngblood, he wasn't showing off.

Every word he sang was for her ears only.

As he moved closer, his heart beat as loud as the music.

The small smile on her lips let him know she heard him, and she liked the sound of his voice. With her eyes closed and her expression hot and sensual, he could only imagine the racy thoughts that traveled through her mind at that moment. If they were even close to his, they shared a connection that was on fire.

He reached out and grabbed the empty loops that circled her tight jeans. Her jeans molded around her curvy body like a liquid glove. He loosened the knot in her T-shirt and ran his hands farther up her hot, sweat-dampened belly. He held her still and pressed her body tight to his, letting her feel what she was doing to him, letting her feel his hardness.

When she opened her eyes, she stared into his. The light emanating from her big brown eyes caught him off guard.

He stopped singing and whispered, "Radiance."

Her voice was breathy. "I love when you call me that."

He whispered again, "Radiance."

Her eyes narrowed as she moaned, "So . . . sensual."

"That's what you are."

As he brushed her neck with a kiss, she closed her eyes again. "I'm so sorry about the Cadi—"

He hushed her. "Shh. Don't apologize."

"I'm glad you're still here."

"I'm enjoying being here." He moved back up to her face. "Please, don't deprive me of those beautiful eyes." When she opened her eyes again, moisture filled them. His heart paused. "What's wrong?"

She stiffened. "I don't want this to end."

"Why would it end?"

"There are some things about me"—her voice wavered—
"that may scare you away."

"I told you, I don't scare easily." He reassured her with a
smile. "Tell me everything I should know. Don't hide anything
from me."

"David, I—"

"Are you in some kind of trouble?" He watched her lovely
brown eyes fill with apprehension. "I can help you. Let me
help you."

"I can't explain." She exhaled. "Just know that I really like
you. And no matter what happens, I would absolutely love for
things to work out between us."

He was just getting to know her and already he feared losing her.

"I'm not going anywhere." He drew her in tighter in his
arms. "I want to know everything about you. If you can't tell
me tonight, I'll keep coming back until you do. I promise." He
felt his body tighten, and his anatomy began to ache for her.
"Right now, though, I'd better go, or I'll end up staying the
whole night."

She wrapped her hands around his neck. "Stay, David."

He kissed her gently at first, tasting her sweetness and exploring the heat of her mouth, but when she pulled him closer
her passion ignited his. With confident and steady strokes of
his tongue, he claimed her mouth as his own, plunging deeper,
trying to taste the very essence of her. Like an uncut drug, her
effect on him was addictive. He couldn't get enough.

David wrapped his hands around her buttocks and lifted
her off her feet. Nia matched his passion, wrapping her legs
around his waist and her forearms around his neck. He backed
her up to the red sofa, lowered her onto it, and lay his body on
hers. He pressed his hardness into the crease of her jeans at the
juncture of her thighs.

She welcomed his body, met his tongue with hers, and sucked his mouth, hungry and desperate.

Steady and focused, he kissed her with deep plunges that lasted forever.

Connected by a strong yet invisible bond, they felt inseparable. Whatever he'd unleashed inside of her, he felt it, too, pulling him in. Something in him quaked. His heart rumbled.

The room shook.

He pulled away. "What was that?"

The steady rumble grew into a series of sudden jarring jolts. The jouncing rattled the glass menagerie of running stallions as they galloped off their shelves and fell to shattering deaths. The sad-faced clown portrait above the couch fell and came crashing down above their heads. He grabbed Nia and rolled her off the couch seconds before it hit them.

As they hit the floor, Nia's whole living room shook, and everything inside it trembled. Glass burst, pictures and décor crashed down, and furniture shifted.

"It's an earthquake!" David jumped up and rushed her into the hallway. He braced himself against the door frame and held her to his chest as the earth shook beneath their feet.

Nia screamed, "Stop it!"

After a few more jolts and aftershocks, the room settled down. All was quiet but David still held on to her. After several silent seconds, he exhaled. "Are you alright?"

She seemed steadier than he was. Quietly, she nodded and looked around.

Broken glass lay everywhere. The sofa had bounced away from the wall, her clown portrait had crashed to the floor, and the glass figurines had broken into pieces. The only thing remaining upright was the black-framed photo of a tyrannical yellow-eyed lion captured by her lens during her African safari.

David tried to ease her nerves, as well as his own. "Wow. That was some kiss," he joked, but his tone fell flat.

Finally, he released Nia. Her uneasy quietness added to the tension.

"I grew up in California and have experienced a lot of earthquakes, but none ever felt quite like this." David rubbed his chin. "This one felt . . . personal."

Nia walked to the middle of her living room. She looked more perturbed than frightened.

David headed for the door. "I'd better go check on your neighbors, see if they need any help. I'll be right back." He paused, "Are you sure you're okay?"

"I'm fine." Her voice was distant as she waved him on. "Go ahead. Just be careful."

David left, wondering if her outburst had been simply a nervous reaction, or if she'd yelled, "Stop it!" for some other reason.

CHAPTER 15

After David left, Nia's heart thudded inside her chest as she stood in the middle of her living room, alone. She closed her eyes and gritted her teeth. "Let me go!"

Silence ensued. When she opened her eyes again, David had stepped back inside. His face was more upset than when he'd left.

"Nia, nobody felt that earthquake but us," he said, then gazed around the living room. The red sofa was back in place against the wall. The figurines were sitting on the shelves unbroken, and the clown picture hung neatly on the wall. David shook his head. "What just happened here?"

Nia tried to think of an explanation that wouldn't cause more questions. "David, things aren't always how they appear."

"There's no way you could have cleaned things up so fast." He gazed at the unbroken menagerie pieces. "No way you could have pieced those back together."

"David, maybe it wasn't really an earthquake—"

"No," David insisted. "I'm not imagining things. I know what I felt."

Nia wrung her hands, not knowing what else to do. She confessed, "I wouldn't blame you if you left and never came back."

He turned to her. His face was tired and his eyes filled with concern. "Nia, I don't know what just happened, but the only thing that matters to me is that you're okay." He looked around again, then looked at her. Finally, he exhaled. "It's been a long night. Maybe things will make more sense tomorrow." He kissed her forehead and starting leaving. "Lock the door behind me. I'll call you in the morning."

Nia watched David get into his car through her window. She locked her front door, but she knew a locked door made no difference. Some things she couldn't hide from, no matter what she did.

Rephaim watched David Wrightwood back out of Nia's driveway. This time, he didn't wait in a Caddy but in a supernatural cocoon. Pure dark energy wrapped his slender muscular physique in an absence of light, and he moved with both beauty and lethal grace. In his present state, he was mostly invisible to the naked eye. His body converged with the other shadows and edges of the night and formed a tall sinewy outline, a fleeting apparition in the corner of one's eye.

REPHAIM WAS MORE than Nia's watcher. He was her protector and her guide, a conduit between this life and the one that awaited her in the afterlife.

Rephaim walked up Nia's driveway to her front porch. Not fully human, his hunger and lust for her companionship exceeded mortal boundaries, and his cravings for Nia drove him to inordinate, sometimes violent lengths.

Nia left the window and retreated into her house. She had no place to go where he couldn't find her. With a wave of his hand, Rephaim dimmed the streetlights surrounding her house, and a suitable layer of darkness settled over her neighborhood. Though equally effective in the light, he preferred to do his work in the darkness of night, a time when people let down their guard and slept in their beds under the illusion of safety.

Rephaim walked around to the back of Nia's house and scaled the exterior wall with the deftness of a panther. He slipped inside Nia's upstairs bedroom window, the one she always kept open, perhaps subconsciously, for him.

Like everything else he possessed, Nia had been custom-made specifically for him. The plotting of her conception and birth had been no accident. After watching the Youngbloods' sacred bloodline for several decades, Rephaim had finally found an opening to execute his preconceived entrance into the chaste and holy Youngblood genealogy through Nia's unsuspecting father. He'd needed a godly lineage to penetrate, to make his descent in the dark realm more powerful.

Rephaim had been present at Nia's birth and her unholy consecration when she was dedicated to him. An ambitious mother who dabbled in sorcery, an offer of power, and an opportunity—that's all it had taken for Rephaim, a mighty dark lord and ruthless prince, to gain an entrance into the sacred bloodline. Now, with Nia Youngblood as his lovely fleshly prize, he stood to gain unimaginable power.

But first he'd have to marry her.

When he entered her bedroom, Nia was already in the shower. Rephaim inhaled the perfume of her mango body wash. Disappointed, he scoffed at the artificial scent, preferring the sweet smell of her raw, naturally spicy carnal scent.

He walked around her bed, his large form intimidating and virile, as he prepared for his encounter with his future bride. He knew her well, her habits, her proclivities, her weaknesses, and her breaking point.

He moved closer to her bed and pulled back the covers.

When Nia exited the bathroom, he slipped back into the shadows and melded into the dark hollows of her dimly lit room. He'd never shown himself to her, not fully, not yet. All these years he'd only let her feel his overpowering presence.

Nia was nude except for a silk raspberry-colored thong. He took in the natural glow of her soft skin. Every glorious inch of her body glistened, still dampened by shower water. Her burnt-umber hair flowed loose and wild, gently grazing her shoulders. A few watery beads clung to its silken waves. The artificial scent began to fade, and her natural fragrance of wildflowers and cinnamon took over, bringing pleasure to Rephaim's nose.

Nia preferred to sleep in the nude, as her body temperature often rose during the darkest hours of the night, when he visited her and gave her erotic pleasures most women only imagined.

She didn't fully understand who he was yet or that she'd been dedicated to him as his wife. Rephaim would never leave her alone, and he'd never go away. Any attempt to replace him with an ordinary man would prove futile. For six years he'd allowed Malcolm Smalls a minor role in Nia's life, but for every transgression when he tried to become intimate with Nia, Malcolm had been chastised. No other man had ever made it beyond a first date with Nia. Rephaim had made sure of it.

Until David Wrightwood.

David had been the only exception. Rephaim hated resistance or rebellion in any form, especially from someone who was not his equal. David Wrightwood was merely a man. Men were weak and inferior in the broader scope of his dark region.

When Nia saw that the covers on her queen-size bed had been pulled back for her, she stripped them off completely and threw them on the floor, then looked around the room, searching for him. She knew he was there. She could *feel* him.

A silent breeze pushed back the window's curtain. Nia closed the window, turned off the light, and crawled onto her coverless bed.

Impulsive, impatient, and, at times, reckless, Nia constantly challenged him. Instead of waiting patiently until the day they would be together, she attempted to find love and companionship with a regular man. Fool's gold. No man could ever satisfy Nia the way Rephaim could. Deep down, she knew that, but she remained stubborn.

Nia lay on her bare bed with no sheets, clutched her pillow to her breasts, and closed her eyes. From the shadowy darkness, Rephaim emerged. Gifted in the art of soundless motion, he surrounded Nia's bed and circled her body with his ethereal presence. She clung to her pillow and squeezed her eyelids tight, trying to block his entry into her subconscious by holding on to thoughts of another man.

Rephaim endured her reverie and came closer, admiring every inch of her naked flesh like it was beautiful real estate that belonged to him. He yearned for the day coming soon when he'd finally claim his property.

"Nia," he whispered. His deep, ephemeral voice rained down on her like volcanic ash.

She'd fallen asleep. Under usual circumstances, he'd join her in that syrupy place between waking and sleeping, where fantasies merged with reality. There, he'd seduce her with erotic thoughts, apply soft touches to her secret places, and watch her body respond with writhes, quivers, and eventually orgasms. Some nights he brought her so many climaxes she'd clutch the sheets and cry sweetly, begging for him to stop.

But tonight was different. A NO VACANCY sign hung outside Nia's mind as David Wrightwood occupied her thoughts.

Rephaim held back a sneer of contempt and knelt even closer, bringing his face within inches of hers, as he silently cursed the man who'd dare try to take his place.

"Nia," he whispered again, allowing his hot breath to hit her cheek.

Sensitive and passionate, Nia had grown into a deeply sensual creature. He'd helped her become that way to prepare her for her role as his wife in the afterlife. Even her physical body had been beautifully predesigned using her mother's genes. Fate, planning, and foresight had endowed her womanly body with generous curves, along with a strong genetic predisposition for ambition and aggressiveness, all wrapped inside an attractive human package. The attributes of a strong will, bold aggression, and a fiery temperament would serve Nia well when she assumed her position as a dark queen.

Rephaim perused Nia's bare breasts. Firm and inviting, they held their shape even as she rolled onto her back, their fullness flowing against her ribs. The gentle blast of heat from his warm mouth hardened each nipple, darkening them like tiny ripened cherries, as her body began its lovely response to his presence.

He inhaled her essence as he moved his face slowly down the middle of her stomach to her tiny navel, then to the edge of her thong. Hovering so close, he licked his lips as he could almost taste her sweet sticky juices brewing just beneath the surface.

Nia tossed in her sleep and turned over. Rephaim admired the two firm mounds of smooth, tight skin separated by a silky strip of material in between. Her buttocks were like rolling hills, fertile and ready for harvest. Rephaim slowly opened his mouth and grazed his tongue softly along Nia's left hill, planting a soft kiss at its summit as he allowed his teeth to gently nick her skin.

He called her name a third time, a gentle utterance. "Nia . . . my wife."

She awoke.

WHEN NIA JERKED awake, she opened her eyes in the darkness. Her skin was sweaty, her body feverish, and her pulse raced. She'd been sleeping on her belly when she felt someone nibble on her buttocks. The room was dark but not empty. A tall shadow shifted by the window. Nia clicked on the light. An unusually sultry breeze blew through the open window despite the chilled night air and pushed the curtains back. She knew she'd closed that window before she'd fallen asleep.

Nia got up and closed it a second time, knowing that even if she locked it, he'd still come. She turned off the light and sat on the floor by her bed, wrapping the burgundy satin sheets that she'd thrown on the floor around her sweaty body. She covered her head, leaving only enough space to peek out at a world where she didn't fit in.

The familiar scent of warm molasses and damp earth swept across her nose, bringing with its sweetness a strong primal urge while conjuring images in her head of two bodies engaged in wild, frenzied sex.

He was still there.

Her secret regions began to quiver. She squeezed her legs tightly together and brought her knees to her chest. A bead of sweat rolled over her lip and seeped into her mouth. It spread across her tongue, assailing her taste buds with the sweet, salty savor of carnality and desire. She tried not to but consumed the fleshly flavor anyway.

"I can't do this. I want to be with David," she mumbled, trying to swallow away the taste.

A low-sounding bass reverberated from the expanding shadows. Nia stared at the dark edges of her room. The anticipation of hearing his voice caused her muscles to contract and her vaginal walls to rain down moisture. When he spoke, the deep, barely audible energy vibrated against her damp skin like an electrical current.

"You . . . are . . . *miinnne.*"

$\mathcal{D}$avid arrived at his office on Saturday morning a little late. He was tired, and his mind was preoccupied with Nia. Mrs. Wang greeted him with a hot cup of Starbucks coffee.

"Thanks," he said, and set it on his desk.

He frequently worked weekends, using the quieter time to do research on his cases. He opened a file and immediately dove in. David could have had his paralegals do the legwork, but he liked being well prepared before he went to court, and he preferred to know the details of his cases intimately. David knew that the devil was often in the details.

"I think I've got everything I need. Thanks," he told Mrs. Wang, who'd remained standing over him, but she still didn't leave.

She adjusted her pink wire glasses. "I heard you had a hot date last night."

Mrs. Wang was a great secretary. She had worked for him

since he'd joined the law firm three years ago. Great with cli-
ents, always professional and courteous, she even attended the
same church, but Mrs. Wang had a habit of mixing his personal
life with his professional one.

"Where did you hear that?" He closed the file and blew on
his hot coffee cautiously.

"A little bird told me."

"Was that bird stout with rust-colored hair and carrying an
LAPD badge?"

"Yes," she confessed enthusiastically. "Spivek called here
earlier looking for you. When I told him you were running late,
he mentioned your hot date. So I figured you'd gotten lucky,
scored big, and then overslept. Am I correct? Did you have a
happy birthday, Mr. David?" Mrs. Wang beamed and asked anxiously, "So . . . who is the lucky girl?"

David sipped his coffee, then set it down. "How about I
take you out to lunch one day next week and we can discuss
every iota of my private personal life then?" He reopened the
file. "But right now, I have research to do, and I'm guessing you
have some work at your desk."

After Mrs. Wang left, David buried himself in case files
for the next three hours, but he also kept one eye on the clock.
He'd wanted to call Nia earlier but remembered her mention-
ing she liked to sleep in on Saturdays. After last night, she was
probably as tired as he was. His cell phone's private line rang.
Without checking the caller ID, he snatched it up, hoping it
was Nia.

"Good afternoon, beautiful."

"I didn't know you felt that way about me," Spivek jested.

"Spiv? I thought you were Nia." David yawned.

"I called to tell you I just got two tickets to tonight's Lakers
game, close to the floor, and I knew you'd want one of them."

David grew eager. "They play the Spurs tonight. That's going to be a good game." But after he thought about it, he declined. "I'm going to have to pass."

"Wait a minute," Spivek asked in disbelief. "What could possibly make you pass on a Lakers game?"

"Her name is Nia Youngblood." David chuckled, remembering the way she'd danced for him last night. "Not even the Lakers can beat her moves. I'm hoping I get to see some more moves again tonight."

"Sounds like you're falling."

"I've never met a girl like her." David stared out his office window. "She's unique."

"Okay, well, you don't need me to tell you to be careful. But just one question," Spivek said, as his detective instincts began to surface again. "What's the story on her friend? I'm still debating whether to go after her and bring her in for assault on an officer. What's holding me back is that I still can't explain how she did it."

David was hesitant about telling his best friend but went ahead anyway. "Mysti is not Nia's friend, she's her mother."

"Her *mother*?" Spivek repeated, shocked. "She didn't exactly impress me as the motherly type, if you know what I mean."

"Yeah, I know what you mean," David concurred, recalling Mysti's audacious clothing style, racy aura, and flirtatious mannerisms. His next words slipped out. "She's a witch."

Spivek quipped jokingly, "Most potential mothers-in-law usually are."

David chuckled, too, then lowered his voice in case Mrs. Wang was eavesdropping. "No, seriously, Mysti is a witch," he said. "Nia's mother dabbles in the dark arts, but I think mostly she's just eccentric."

Spivek paused as he comprehended. "Doesn't that worry you?"

David thought about it. "No, because I'm dating Nia, not her mother."

"Okay, fine. Use your best judgment, but watch out for any boiling kettles."

David chuckled. "If I find myself in hot water, I'll call you."

"Yeah. I got your back, buddy."

Before hanging up, David added, "Oh, and tell Kobe I said don't be such a ball hog."

"Will do."

David hung up, but his phone rang again. Thinking it was Spivek, he answered, "And for the record, I *don't* think you're beautiful."

"You don't?" Nia asked, baffled.

"Nia?" David caught his blunder. "Sorry, I thought you were Spivek."

"Oh?" She sounded even more baffled.

"Let me start over." David cleared his throat and put on his sexy voice. "Hello, gorgeous. I've been sitting here thinking about you all morning."

"Now, that's what I like to hear," she purred. "We must have a connection, because I can't stop thinking about you, either."

"Yeah, we must." David tilted back in his chair, relaxing. "I enjoyed being with you last night. You gave me a birthday celebration I'll never forget, not even with therapy." They laughed. "I almost didn't want it to end."

Nia's voice grew reminiscent and a little sad. "When I was growing up, my dad never celebrated my birthday."

"Because of his alcohol problem?"

"No." Nia hesitated. "Because no one knows my exact birth date."

"Get out of here."

"It's true. When Mysti was pregnant with me, she never went to a doctor. I wasn't born in a hospital."

"Where were you born?"

"Don't know." Nia sighed. "Mysti and my father never married. They weren't even in a relationship. I'm the result of a one-night stand. My father didn't even know Mysti was pregnant until she rang his doorbell and handed me to him. Then she took off. I may have been a few months old. He didn't know, and she didn't tell."

David let her pause go uninterrupted.

She continued, "I never had a medical exam until I was about five or six, and that was only to get vaccinated so I could go to school. I had no birth certificate, so the courts ordered the hospital to make one up. My birthday is only an estimate."

David leaned forward. "You're serious?"

"Very," Nia said. "I don't go by the date they made up. I celebrate my birthday whenever I feel like it. If I wake up and decide today should be my birthday, then it is. Some years, I've had five or six birthdays. I just make sure I change my age once annually."

David listened, amazed. "I've never heard of anything like that."

"You should do the same."

"Huh?"

"David, would you like another birthday?"

"Ah, yeah," he laughed, amazed. "Why not?"

"Good," Nia announced. "Tonight, I'll come pick you up and take you out . . . for your birthday."

"That sounds strange, but exciting."

"Trust me, it will be."

David gave Nia the address to his condo, and they hung up.

Chapter 17

At seven o'clock, David looked through his upstairs loft window and watched Nia park her bright gold convertible Mustang Shelby in his condo's visitors' parking lot. She parked sideways illegally in the red zone, swung her door open, and got out without bothering to lock her car. Wearing no jacket, she had donned a white cashmere blouse and black low-rise pants. David was astonished at how she turned the simplest clothes into something special. When he saw her, he decided all of the questions he'd had from the night before could wait.

Nia walked fast, like she was in a hurry, looking over her shoulder three times while buzzing the security gate.

David quickly met her downstairs. "What's your hurry, young lady?"

She walked right up to him. "Seeing you."

"You parked in the red. You'll get another ticket."

She winked. "I'll give it to you."

"The way you look in those pants," he said, swallowing, "I'll pay all your fines."

Nia dropped the top on her gold convertible, opened his door for him, and even pinched his butt when he got in. This girl was irrepressible. She hopped on the freeway and immediately merged into the fast lane, letting the wind hit their faces and blow through her wavy hair. She roared up Interstate 5, heading north.

He watched her, amused. "You remind me of a roller coaster," he shouted over the wind. "You take off fast and never let up."

"Buckle up, boy. Here comes the loop!"

They laughed and proceeded north through Los Angeles. Even with the top down, he kept getting a whiff of something. "What's that smell?"

She grinned as if hiding something. "What does it smell like?"

He sniffed. "Smells like you're wearing perfume scented with . . . enchiladas."

Nia laughed. "You're right!"

"I didn't know they made Mexican-food-scented perfume," David teased.

"They don't. It *is* enchiladas." Nia pointed to the backseat, and David reached back and picked up a white CorningWare dish. The dish was still hot, and David nearly burned his fingers.

Nia smiled proudly. "It's our dinner, homemade enchiladas. I made them from scratch."

"I *love* enchiladas. You must have read my mind." David's stomach growled. "I guess we really do have a connection."

"They say the way to a man's heart is through his stomach," Nia shouted. "But if that doesn't work, I've got beer in the trunk. I'll just get you drunk."

"Sounds like a good plan."

Nia pulled off Interstate 5, exiting at the GRIFFITH PARK

AND OBSERVATORY sign. They drove past the park and headed up the hill toward the observatory, a light tan domed building in the hills overlooking Los Angeles. The area's thick trees, hills, and dense brush formed a small forest within the city, about two miles in radius and enclosed by five-lane freeways on most sides.

David checked his watch. "What time does the observatory close?"

"We're not going to the observatory. We've got private reservations a little farther up the hill."

Nia drove past the observatory's parking lot, where visitors parked to catch a shuttle the rest of the way up. She swung her car through a narrow gate marked WORK CREW ONLY and barreled up a dirt road, an alternative route to the observatory.

David's eyes widened with caution. "Does the word *trespass* mean anything to you?"

"No," Nia said, undaunted.

He did a double take. "Remind me to use insanity for your defense at your trial."

Nia parked near a small patch of land and hopped out. She opened her trunk and grabbed a white blanket. David carried the food and the ice chest as they walked up a slight incline. Nia stopped at the top of the slope and looked around at the city lights that lay before them, then at the night sky that hung low above their heads.

"Those stars look close enough to grab." She spread the white blanket on the grass. "This is perfect."

David looked around too, impressed with the landscape. "Is this where you take all of your men to feed them, get them intoxicated, then take advantage of them?"

"No, only you," she said, poking his chest playfully. "Actually, I've never been here before."

"Then how'd you know it was here?"

"Instinct." She plopped down on the blanket. "Just like the first second I saw you. I knew we should be together."

"But you played a little hard to get. You didn't believe it was my birthday." He sat down next to her with the food and drinks.

"Sometimes, I have a little trouble . . . believing."

"Faith is a beautiful thing." David helped Nia take out the enchiladas and serve them on paper plates. He removed beer from the ice chest and they drank it from the bottles. The enchiladas had stayed remarkably hot, and she'd made them so spicy they put tears in his eyes. He chewed, then coughed to clear his throat.

Nia handed him another cold beer. "Too hot and spicy for you, huh?" she teased.

"Not at all," he said, lying. He took a swig and bragged, acting macho, "This is like baby food compared to what I'm used to."

Nia grabbed his beer away. "In that case, you won't need this."

David laughed and got it back. He took another swig and coughed again, admitting, "These things are *hot*. What'd you put in them, rocket fuel?"

"You don't like my enchiladas?"

"They're killing me," he said, being honest. "But yes, I love 'em."

David kept eating. After four enchiladas and two cold beers, he was stuffed. Nia pointed at the dish, which was still half full. "There's more."

He waved his hand. "You cooked enough to feed a small tribe."

"I love to cook at night, when I can't sleep." Nia looked out over the city's lights, and her thoughts seemed far away.

"Why couldn't you sleep last night?" he asked, trying to bring her back.

She avoided his question and kept looking up at the sky.

"All the stars look perfect, almost surreal." She closed her eyes, as if dreaming. "Why do things that are so real and so beautiful sometimes seem so hard to believe?"

As David started to answer, something flashed in the sky. "Look, a shooting star." He pointed, then frowned. "No, wait. Is that a burning comet?"

The celestial object seemed to sear a black hole through the night sky directly above their heads, and it seemed to be shooting their way.

When Nia saw it her expression changed from contemplative to worried. David started to stand but she leaned over him, quickly and deliberately blocking his view. She kissed him. The second her warm, tender lips touched his, he forgot all about the comet.

Despite the chill in the air, Nia's skin felt warm and her mouth heated him up like an oven. He tasted leftover spices from the enchiladas that combined with her unique natural sweetness. The sensation caused his stomach to rumble again, hungry . . . for her.

He laid her back on the blanket and rolled his body between her legs. "Hmm, can I have seconds?"

"More enchiladas?" she teased.

"No. More Nia."

She kissed him again, and her warm scent reminded him of wild cloves and cinnamon.

He pushed his mouth into hers slowly and deeply, tasting all her spicy flavors and melding himself into her warmth. She felt vibrant, alive with passion, and he could practically feel blood surging through her veins. He pressed his chest into hers.

"I can feel your heart beating."

She exhaled. "It's beating for you."

He parted her lips again and sank his tongue into her mouth. When he finally let up, she whispered low and sexy in his ear. "Happy birthday, David. Again."

He brushed his lips over her neck. "Guess what?"

"What?" she moaned.

"Tomorrow's my birthday, too."

As they kissed, the heat between them grew in intensity so much that he forgot they were in a public place. He grabbed her knee and pulled her leg around him, then slid his hand beneath her white cashmere blouse, exploring the fullness inside her lace bra. She clenched her fingers around his butt and squeezed. David moved his body up so that his hardness pressed into the juncture of her thighs and positioned himself as if they were making love. He moved his hips in a slow grinding motion and caused her head to rock back while she moaned, as a prelude to what was to come.

"Ooh." Nia bit her lip. "You make me feel so good."

"I can make you feel even better," he whispered, "whenever you're ready."

Suddenly, a loud crack of thunder erupted above their heads. David looked up. In a matter of seconds, dark, heavy clouds had rolled in, blocking out the celestial lights. The night sky had grown dark and the air harsh and chilled as the temperature nosedived just below freezing. David rolled off Nia and shuddered, though Nia's skin remained warm.

"It's really gotten dark out here, and cold." His teeth chattered as he shifted against the icy jet stream that seemed to blow specifically at the heat beneath his zipper, killing his mood.

Nia must have sensed his change of intentions. She rose up. "Yeah, I think we'd better go."

David agreed.

CHAPTER 18

*D*avid loaded everything back into her trunk and they left the observatory. As Nia drove back down the winding path, blackness eclipsed the sky and dark clouds hovered just above their heads. She offered to put up her convertible's top but since she wasn't cold, he insisted she leave it down.

As they left the wooded area, she caught a glimpse of something tall standing at the edge of the trees. It was too erect to be a deer and was shaped like a man. She sped up, turned the corner sharply to get back on the main road, and hoped David hadn't seen it.

"What was that?" he asked, looking back.

"What?" Nia hated playing dumb, but what else could she do?

"That was him, wasn't it?"

"Who?"

David wasn't fooled by her act. "Please, Nia, playing dumb

doesn't fit you," he chastised. "You saw someone standing there watching us."

Nia didn't respond and kept driving, but David wouldn't take his eyes off her until she answered.

Finally, she admitted, "David, you don't understand—"

"Then explain it to me."

She merged onto Interstate 5 and headed south in light traffic. David folded his arms against the wind. His long-sleeved shirt wasn't enough to keep him warm, but he remained stubborn, determined to hide his coldness. She suspected it was some stupid macho thing.

"There's really no easy way to explain," she said.

"I thought we had an agreement," he said. "You tell me everything and I stay by your side and help you."

She turned on the radio, trying to divert his attention, but he kept staring at her. "David, it's not that simple."

"I'm not stupid, Nia. Don't you think I realize this guy is connected to all this weird stuff happening around you?"

"That's not what I meant. I know you're not stupid." Nia changed lanes and clicked on the cruise control.

"Then tell me what's going on."

He waited. When she still didn't answer, he clicked off the radio and faced her.

"Okay," she confessed. "Yes, I have strong feelings for you. Yes, I want things to work out between us, but . . ." She stopped and checked her rearview mirror.

"But what?"

"But there are some things that you don't need to know right now."

"Why not?"

"Because I don't fully understand them myself." She noticed something in the mirror, behind them.

"You're being intentionally evasive."

"Are you accusing me of lying?" She killed the cruise control and changed lanes.

"I'm accusing you of withholding information."

She checked her rearview mirror again. A dark object was tailing them, but it wasn't an automobile. She didn't know what it was.

David persisted. "Why don't you just admit that there's more going on with you and this guy than you want to admit and that you could use my help to get out of it?"

Feeling put on the spot, Nia turned the accusation around. "Why don't you just admit that you're cold and stop trying to prove something?"

"I'm *not* cold."

She watched the road but kept an eye on the rearview mirror. The dark shape blocked out headlights from distant cars.

David persisted. "Give me the guy's full name and address, not just some code name—*Ra-fi-eem.*"

"I don't know it." She kept driving, hoping David wouldn't look back.

"Then tell him to meet me somewhere."

"You *don't* want to meet him," she warned.

David clenched his fists. "You don't think I can protect you? Is that it?"

"I didn't say that." Nia changed lanes, but the shadow kept closing in on them.

David pressed his back hard against the seat. "If you don't think I'm man enough to protect you, then we've got a problem."

"David, stop it. This is not about whether you can protect me or not." She squinted at the figure in her mirror. With two arms, two legs, and a large frame, it ran effortlessly behind her car, like part of the night wind.

Nia sped up.

David frowned. "Slow down. You're driving too fast."

Nia pressed the pedal harder and watched her speedometer rise: seventy-five . . . eighty . . . eighty-five miles per hour.

"Nia, slow down."

The shadow hopped on the back of her car, but David didn't know it.

David gripped the safety bar. "Nia, slow down."

The shadow lay across the trunk of her convertible. It reached out its hand, grabbed hold of her black rubber-reinforced roll bar, and swung its feet forward.

The shadow, in the form of a man, sat on the back edge of her convertible with his feet planted firmly in her backseat and blocked out her entire rearview vision with his overwhelming body.

The sweet smell of hot molasses and wet desert sand accosted her nose. Sweat trickled down her throat beneath her cashmere blouse and drizzled over her lace bra, cooling her hot, hardening nipples.

With no discernable features, no eye color, no hair type, and no facial structure, the figure remained an outline of a man. Nia tried to stay calm.

David's voice rose. "Nia, slow down!"

Though the shadow sat on the backseat, his deep, low bass voice resounded close to her ear. "Go ahead, Nia. Tell him *who* I am."

Nia swerved. Her car entered the next lane, nearly side-swiping another car. Nia jerked the wheel, avoiding a collision. She overcorrected and veered dangerously close to the cement center divider.

David clutched the dashboard. "Nia!"

The shadow stayed on top of her backseat.

She gripped the wheel and regained control but didn't slow down. Her heart was racing faster than the car. "Leave me alone!"

"Fine!" David thought she was yelling at him. "Just slow the hell down!"

Nia screamed at the rearview mirror. "I don't want to be with you!" She whipped around. "I want to be with *you*, David!"

"*Who* are you talking to?" He followed her eyes to the rearview mirror and spun around.

As soon as David turned, the shadow leaned back and flipped off Nia's trunk. It grabbed hold of the tail end of a big rig truck as she passed it and ducked into its cargo section.

David jerked back around and looked at Nia. She tried to hide her shock and relief but failed.

CHAPTER 19

*N*ia was driving like a madwoman who'd just seen a ghost. Finally, she slowed and calmed a bit, but not before a California Highway Patrol officer flashed his blue and red lights at them. David's pulse had just begun to return to normal, but now he had another situation to deal with.

The officer approached them on the passenger side, his heavy black boots crunching the gravel. Being a defense lawyer, David wasn't exactly on the CHP's party guest list, but he'd been cordial with several officers who attended the same twenty-four-hour gym and knew Spivek. He hoped this was one of them so he could skate a ticket for Nia.

"Turn off your motor, please, miss."

Nia turned it off.

"License, registration, proof of insurance," the officer asked, following routine CHP procedure.

While Nia reached for her purse, David looked up at the

officer, hoping to recognize him. His helmet's flap shaded his face. "How are you tonight, sir?" A little kissing up never hurt.

The officer ignored David and spoke directly to Nia. "Do you know how fast you were going?"

David always hated that question. He thought it was the stupidest of all stupid traffic cop questions. Of course the driver didn't know. He was too busy speeding to look at the speedometer. If he'd cared enough to look at the speedometer, he probably would have slowed down.

David answered for Nia. "We were having a lively conversation, and she took her eye off the speedometer. It was my fault. You think perhaps you can let her go with a warning?"

"A *warning*?" The officer shifted his weight to his opposite boot. He straightened his heavy-duty jacket with his large, stiff black leather gloves, slightly curved at the fingers and winged at the cuff. "If her actions had caused injury or death to herself or others, wouldn't she deserve more than a *warning*?"

What was this officer's problem? "I understand your point," David said. "Fortunately, none of those things happened."

The officer's tone was formal and impersonal. "With all due respect, sir, you're just the passenger in this vehicle, not the driver."

Lose your cool, lose your credibility, David reminded himself, and bit back a curse word. He noticed the officer's helmet was not the usual CHP issue. It was missing the winged-wheel logo. On closer inspection, the metal badge on the outside of his jacket appeared smooth. No logo there either. The officer had on a belt, but no gun and no gun holster. He didn't need one; his large frame and body language were threatening enough.

The officer walked around the back of Nia's car and inspected her tags.

David whispered to Nia, "Don't worry about getting another

ticket. I've got connections. I'll call in a favor. Just cooperate with whatever he asks."

She whispered back. "I can't find my license."

"What?" He tried hard to keep his voice down. "Look again."

"I don't have it. I think I dropped it somewhere."

"Oh, shit."

When the officer returned to the passenger-side door, David noticed a small detail about his face he'd overlooked before because of the rotating red and blue bouncing through the night: the officer wore darkly tinted sunglasses.

It was nighttime.

"Who do you know, sir?" The CHP officer's voice was lower now. Darth Vader low.

David thought maybe the wind was distorting it, but the wind had died down. "Excuse me?"

The officer stepped back and cocked his head, as if to gain a better perspective on David. He stepped on a bottle. His heavy steel-tipped boot shattered the glass, breaking it with a hollow pop.

"You think you're connected, sir?"

"Excuse me again?" David felt the officer's severe scrutiny.

He raised a black glove and pointed a stiff, threatening finger at David. "You'd better make damn sure you're connected before you go making promises you can't keep."

David knew things were about to get ugly. He checked the officer's jacket for identification. There was none. "What's your name and badge number, Officer?"

The officer placed both gloved hands on his thick belt holster. "Step out of the car."

Nia stiffened. Panic cracked her voice. "Don't get out, David."

David had represented victims of police harassment, and he knew the best thing to do in a case like this was to comply. And pray for witnesses.

He went for the door's latch, keeping his hands in plain view, but Nia caught his arm. "Don't get out."

"It's okay." He slipped her his cell phone. "Anything happens, speed dial number one. It's Spiv's number."

"Sir, step out of the car. Now!"

David put his hands back in view and went to open the door, but before he could step out, Nia flipped her engine over and took off.

"Nia, don't!" David's door was flung wide open as the car swerved and barreled into traffic. He gripped the edge of the seat to stay inside. As soon as he gained his balance, he grabbed the door and yanked it closed.

Nia gunned the Shelby.

"Nia! You don't run from the police! It's a felony."

"That wasn't the police." Nia yelled what he'd begun to suspect.

David looked back expecting to see the motorcycle's flashing red and blue lights quickly catch up with them, backup patrol cars, and even helicopters for air support. But what he saw was no red and blue flashing lights following them, no helicopters. Nothing but the dark, quiet highway.

"Unbelievable," he uttered.

FARTHER BACK ON Interstate 5, the officer stood just to the dark side of the road, where the light didn't reach, and removed the helmet. He took off the black gloves and stripped off the uniform.

Nothing but darkness remained. A shadowy outline of a man stood near the motorcycle.

He wasn't alone. Another figure emerged from the brush. Not quite as fleshly or as dark, the second being was a shorter mixture of supernatural being and human. Rephaim greeted his younger brother, Zamzummims, with an impersonal nod, keeping his eye on the fading taillights of Nia's automobile.

"He's cocky."

"Who? The new man?" Zamzu asked.

Rephaim nodded. "He pretends to be unafraid, fearless."

"What are you going to do?"

"Put fear in him," Rephaim said in a steely growl.

At six foot six, Rephaim was an imposing figure against the night sky. He stood taller than most Nephilim, the offspring of human mothers and fallen angel fathers who'd given up their heavenly estate for sexual pleasures of the flesh.

Zamzu twitched slightly, a nervous habit, but covered it with a cough. He knew better than anyone how many different ways Rephaim could harm a mortal. He'd seen Rephaim's merciless terror executed upon his enemies over the past century, everything from drawn-out ancient torture to instant impalement.

Rephaim's confidence loomed even larger than his stature. "David Wrightwood needs to be eliminated, before I marry Nia."

Zamzu observed his brother's confidence. "When will you marry her?"

"On her birthday, a date I've kept secret." Rephaim's thick boot crunched the gravel. "I've waited so long for this. I'll let nothing get in my way."

"If you pull this off—"

"If?" Rephaim interrupted.

"*When* you pull this off," he said, correcting himself, "your power will be unmatched. Even I won't be able to approach you." Distress and envy seeped through his voice.

Rephaim had fought and killed to earn his way to the high position of dark demon lord. Nothing had been given to him; he'd had to take every power and position he held by force.

Zamzu was a hindrance, a vulnerability to Rephaim. Other, more conniving malevolent beings often used his weaker brother against him as a pawn to get to Rephaim. Zamzu was his Achilles' heel, and for that, Rephaim despised him.

Rephaim ignored his brother's obvious jealousy. "I will finally ascend to the highest great black throne. And Nia will take her rightful place by my side, as queen."

CHAPTER 20

When David and Nia arrived back at his condo over an hour later, David insisted on trailing Nia home. As he drove close behind her, he called her on his cell phone. "Come clean with me, Nia. What's going on?"

"But, David, you wouldn't understand. I don't even understand it all."

"For once have faith," David pleaded. "Put your trust in someone other than yourself."

Nia sighed into the phone. "Yes, someone is stalking me."

"Is his name Rephaim?"

"Not sure." She waffled. "Yeah, I think so."

"Let's go to the authorities—to the *real* police."

"I can't."

"Why not?"

"I can't really describe him. Besides, he's not . . . normal."

"Is he part of a gang? A crime lord?"

"A lord, probably, but not of ordinary crime. He's not . . . normal," she repeated.

David followed her as she exited the freeway and headed west on Devonshire Street. "You're not giving me much to work with."

As a lawyer, he'd represented many female victims, women who were bullied by men. He knew patience was key, but he had a hard time maintaining professional objectivity and not losing his cool. His tragic family background had made him intolerant of abusers.

"Are you scared of him? Has he threatened you?"

"Yeah, but not like that." Nia stopped at a red light on Reseda Boulevard and her taillights flashed. "David, just leave him alone. Don't mess with him."

Frustrated, David pulled in a deep breath and tried not to lose his temper like he'd done in her car when she'd insinuated he couldn't protect her. He didn't know anything about this Rephaim guy, and quite frankly, he didn't give a rat's ass what he was—a gangster, a criminal with mob ties, or a sociopath—he only wanted to kick his ass.

Nia pulled her Shelby into her driveway, and David followed close behind. When he got out, she practically jumped into his arms. Back to her usual energetic and passionate self, she kissed him as if nothing had happened. Keeping up with her emotional shifts was like running blind through a maze, but the prize was better than cheese.

He kissed her, then had to practically peel her off; he wanted to get her safely inside her home. But first, he needed to run a quick errand. He looked next door and saw the light on in Jay's bedroom. Jay was sitting on his bed, listening to his iPod. He reached for the dry-cleaning bag in his backseat.

"I'm going to tap on Jay's bedroom window and give him

his father's clothes back. Go inside and lock the door behind you till I get back."

Nia pursed her lips. "Now you're treating me like a child. I'm a big girl," she said sexily and cuddled closer. "How about I go inside and change into something skimpy, and wait for you on the rug in front of my fireplace?"

David raised an eyebrow. "Sounds good, but lock the door until I come."

He waited until she went inside, then he walked around to her back fence. Under normal circumstances, he would have knocked on the front door and introduced himself to Jay's parents, but it was late; they'd probably gone to bed and he didn't want to disturb them, but he needed to get the clothes back to Jay's father.

David laid the clothes across the fence, then hopped over. Before he could straighten back up, he heard the distinct *click-pull-clink* noise of a pump-action shotgun.

As he slowly turned, he saw a man wearing a pink bathrobe and a white shower cap aiming a shotgun barrel directly at his head.

David quickly raised his arms. "Whoa! What's going on?"

"I'll ask the questions." The man lowered the barrel just enough to inspect David's face. "Who are you?"

"David. David Wrightwood."

"Why are you jumping my fence?"

"I was trying to return some clothes." The man eyed the dry-cleaning bag on the fence. David hesitated. "Are you Jay's father?"

"I'll ask the questions." He studied David some more. "I've got a front door. Why didn't you knock on it?"

"I should have. I apologize. I didn't want to wake you."

"I'm awake."

"I noticed."

The man inspected David a final time, then hollered toward the window. "Jay!"

Jay opened the window and poked his head out. He saw David with his hands raised and his father aiming the shotgun at him. "Hey, Pops! Why are you out here jacking Mr. David?"

"I'm not jacking him. He hopped my fence."

David caught Jay's eye and nodded toward the clothes. "Aw, Dad, don't bust a cap. He's just bringing back your clothes."

Jay's father lowered the shotgun to his hip. David lowered his arms. As Jay left the window to come downstairs, David tried to ease the situation.

"Nice shotgun. You ever considered getting a nice guard dog instead?"

Jay's father straightened his shower cap; his hands remained a little shaky. "I don't go pulling shotguns on people every day. It's just that lately, especially at night, we've had a prowler."

"A prowler?"

"Yeah, a real sneaky joker. The other night I saw his shadow by my window. When I looked out, he'd moved by this fence. No sooner than I blinked, he was up on Nia's roof. A real fast mover. Part Spider-Man, part pervert."

David's suspicion rose. "What does this *joker* look like?"

"Tall."

"And?"

"That's it, just tall. Never saw much more than that." Jay's father finally released his grip on the shotgun and relaxed his trigger finger. "I mentioned the prowler to Nia, but she didn't seem too concerned. I told her I'd try to look out for her, too."

Jay came out the back door. He took the clothes off the fence, and handed them to his father. When he turned back to David, he gave a mocking smirk. "Ha! You looked real scared, dude!"

His father chastised him. "Is that how you address a grown-up?"

"It's okay. Jay and I are cool." David turned to Jay, faked a punch, and made Jay flinch. "Yeah, see. You'd look scared too if somebody pointed a Remi 870 at your head."

"Yeah, you right. You need these pants back, you know, and a fresh change of underwear or anything like that?"

David chuckled, but his heart was still beating fast. "Nah, I'm good."

"Alright, playa." Jay headed back inside the house, iPod dangling around his neck. He paused. "Oh yeah, I almost forgot. Dad, this is David, he's Nia's new man, a lawyer and stuff like that. Mr. David, this is my father. Y'all shake hands and stop all this neighbor-on-neighbor crime." Jay laughed and went back inside.

"Benton Wells," Jay's father said, extending his hand to David. "Folks call me Buddy."

David shook his hand. "I apologize, Buddy. Believe me, I won't ever do that again."

"Yeah, next time, ring the doorbell. Come in and have a drink, instead of getting a few pellets in your behind."

"Okay." David nodded but couldn't help eyeing the pink robe.

"Don't let this pink robe fool you, I *will* bust a cap," Buddy said in response to David's curious look, and began walking away.

David left and went back to Nia's house. She was waiting for him outside on the front porch, despite the fact he'd told her to go inside and lock the door. He shook his head, escorted her inside, and locked the door.

"Do you have a blood pressure monitor?" he asked.

"No. Why?"

"Because I think mine just went up." He glanced around, checking her place, then plopped down on her red sofa.

"What just happened to you?"

"I met Jay's father."

"Oh, Buddy? Nice man, huh?"

"Yep. Real nice." David left out the details and let out a long breath.

He spent the next half hour trying to relax his nerves. Nia had indeed slipped into something more comfortable—a very sexy red teddy. Like everything else she wore, she put the *umph!* in it. He bit his lip and tried not to stare but failed miserably. She saw the way he was looking.

"You like?" Nia asked, and struck a sexy pose on the rug in front of the fireplace.

"I like a lot." David felt his body responding to Nia's flirtatious look. "Maybe you should put on something else, like a raincoat."

Nia laughed. "Why? I've got nothing to hide."

"I see." He gave her a wide leer, and they both laughed.

"Besides, I feel so comfortable around you, like I'm free to be myself."

"Well, that's good, but—"

"But what?"

"What about me? Am I free to act on my impulses?"

Nia stretched out on the rug like a sexy feline. "By all means." She glided her leg slowly over the furry rug and rolled onto her side, showing off her curvy hips and slender waist. "But are you sure you can handle all of this?"

David slid down from the couch onto the rug. "I'm sure I can."

She rolled onto her belly. She flexed her back, stuck her butt in the air, and began crawling toward him like something wild and pretty, stalking him. She licked her full lips and let out a playful growl.

"Ooh, are you trying to scare me?" David crawled forward

bravely. "I told you, I don't scare easily, so bring it on." He made a movement like a lion tamer, cracking a whip.

"You wanna start a fire?"

"Is that what you call it?" He tugged at his belt.

"I mean in the fireplace, silly," she said teasingly.

"I knew that," David teased back.

Nia stretched out her leg and flipped on the wall switch with her toe. The gas-burning fireplace lit up with small blue-and-yellow-tinged flames beneath two pinewood logs. Nia rolled over on the rug again, this time on her back. She bent her knees and sank her toes into the white fur.

David watched, practically hypnotized. "You're making things hard."

"I hope so." She used her toe to loosen his belt buckle.

"I see you've got skills." He scooted closer.

"Wanna see what else I can do?" She brought her lovely face close to his and ran her tongue across his lips, sending thrills through his body. She pushed him back and climbed on top. Straddling him, she subtly moved her hips in a writhing, sexy motion while she massaged his pectorals through his shirt. He felt his body respond with a strong surge that pushed against the inside of his zipper.

She raised his shirttail and lifted his shirt, pulling it completely off his body. As she ran her hand across his smooth chest, she kissed the tiny scar that ran horizontally near his left nipple.

He stiffened.

Uncomfortable, he changed their positions by clasping his arms around her waist and rolling her over.

David pressed her back against the white fur rug and stared into her face. Nia's skin was warm, her breaths were short, and her body writhed with sexual vigor as her thick brown hair spread out behind her head like a dark, wavy halo against the furry white rug.

"I can feel your heartbeat," he whispered in her face as he slid down the thin straps of her red teddy. He rubbed her bare shoulders and attacked her neck with kisses, short, playful kisses that turned into long, deep, passionate sucking motions, tasting and licking her like she was covered in sweet melting honey and sugary spices.

David laid his body gently on top of her, grinding slowly as they kissed. When he tried to ease up, she pulled him harder.

A light whooshing sound came from the fireplace. He looked up and saw that the fire had increased, its flames expanding and growing larger and warmer, just like his member.

They kissed more, and he heard another *whoosh!* Flames shot up, igniting a larger inferno inside the fireplace. He eyed the fire extinguisher hanging next to the fireplace and tried to pull away. "Nia, the fire is—"

"I know . . . fire . . . burning . . . ," she mumbled as she pulled him back down and lunged into his mouth with more hungry, desperate kisses.

She was hot in every sense of the word, and he couldn't tell if all the heat he felt was coming from the fireplace or radiating from her body. Her skin felt like an oven door as he tried to hold on to her.

Nia unbuckled his pants. She grabbed the back of his neck, bucked her hips, and rolled him over. Her five foot five, one-hundred-twenty-pound body pinned him down with surprising strength. She ripped his belt from its loops and unzipped his pants. He felt his fullness burst loose and saw flames shoot out of the fireplace from the corner of his eye.

"Nia—"

She cut off his words, held his face, and smothered it with fervid kisses, driving him crazy. He lifted her up and flipped her over again. His muscles flexed and more blood surged to his manhood as he throbbed.

He hurried his mouth down her neck, clutched the lace, and ripped open her red teddy. A new wave of heat emanated off her body, causing him to start sweating. When she arched her back, her breasts jutted up at him. Two firm, voluptuous mounds of soft skin and flesh begged his mouth to make contact. When he did, her skin tasted hot and spicy, her nipples welcomed his tongue like hard ripe berries, and his mouth sucked at their sweetness, but he still couldn't get enough.

Another booming *whoosh!*

The fire surged with fury and emitted a loud sequence of pops like exploding fireworks. The flames grew higher, smothering and devouring the fireplace the same way David devoured Nia's breasts. Fiery embers exploded and shot from the fireplace onto the brick hearth. Several sparks leapt onto the furry rug, threatening to ignite it, but David quickly snuffed them out with his palm, without taking his lips from her skin.

Strong and weak at the same time, every muscle in his body flexed, tensed, and twitched as he wedged himself between Nia's thighs.

Nia clawed at his back. Her fingertips were as hot as the embers.

The fire raged like an inferno and the flames grew too large for the fireplace to contain. Blazes billowed out, scorching the decorative brick and attacking the back of David's naked body with hotness.

She pulled hard at his pants until they slid down and fell loose at his knees. She clutched his briefs and pushed them down, too.

Like the blaze, David's anatomy bounded out. He felt himself charging forward like a thoroughbred released from the gate. But before he could reach the finish line, a loud spraying sound erupted and something cut through the air and blasted his back.

"What the—?"

As he jerked around, a white burst of cloud rushed at him.

The blast hit him in the face and sprayed all over him and Nia. The fire extinguisher had gone off. Somehow, it had detached from the wall and activated itself, and was aiming its oxygen-depriving monoammonium phosphate chemicals directly at their bodies, covering them with a white layer.

Coughing and tearing up, they tried to shield their eyes from the blinding spray. David crouched low and kicked the extinguisher. Its red cylinder hit the fireplace bricks with a loud crash and rolled into the blazing fire. David quickly covered Nia with his body seconds before the pressurized contents exploded with an earsplitting boom.

David jumped up and flipped the wall switch off, killing the fireplace's gas burner. Nia got up and hurried into the bathroom, coughing. David quickly pulled on his pants and followed her, to check if she was okay.

Inside the bathroom, she'd stopped coughing. She stood at the sink and doused cold water onto her face and neck. She handed him a towel. He took it and dunked his whole face under the running water. He dried his face, then wrapped the towel around his neck.

He gazed at her, exasperated. "What's next?"

Hopelessness ran across her lovely face. She walked to the other side of the bathroom and slumped down on the clothes hamper with her back against the wall and despair clouding her bright eyes.

He'd upset her even more with his question, so he tried to make up for it.

"Maybe our feet kicked it off the wall," he offered as a

possible explanation. "Or maybe it was a sign from God, telling us we need to cool it."

He walked toward her, noticing her red teddy was torn but still clung to her body. "We were going at it so hot and heavy, we almost burned your house down. I guess getting blasted by a fire extinguisher worked better than a cold shower."

When he saw that his comment had brought a small smile to her face, he was glad. He sat beside her on the hamper. "I had no business going at you like that. After all, this is only our second date."

Nia banged her fist on the hamper. "But I was ready!"

Her outburst surprised him. "Yeah, I could tell."

"No, you don't understand." She got up. "I was ready to finally make love to a man."

He paused. "You mean, you've never—?"

She shook her head.

He stood up. "You're a virgin?"

She nodded, embarrassed.

"I had no idea. And I almost—" He backed up, loaded with guilt. "You should have told me."

"Would you have treated me differently?"

"Absolutely," he said.

"That's why I didn't tell you." Disappointed, she swung around, away from him.

"I would have treated you differently because your first time needs to be special." He turned her back to face him. "When we finally do make love, it'll be amazing." He touched her arm. "But we need to slow down, do things right. Do it for all the right reasons."

Nia frowned, frustrated. "But—"

"You deserve to be with a man who is deeply in love with you, not just someone who's hot and ready . . . because you're that special."

"But I thought . . ."

He saw the disappointment in her big brown eyes. "Love takes time. If it's real, you can't rush it. Not if you want it to last."

Nia gave a weak smile. She looked up at the ceiling and confessed, "Sometimes I feel like I'm running out of time."

"Nia, we've got all the time in the world." He wrapped his arms around her. "And I promise you, when I say those words—*I love you*—I'll really mean it."

She smiled again, this time stronger. He tugged her teddy closed. "In the meantime, stop throwing all this good stuff at me. A man can only take so much." She giggled and wrapped her arms around him. "I have to go now, and you understand why."

"Because if you stay, we'll burn my house down?"

"Exactly." They both laughed and he kissed her good night.

After throwing on his shirt, David left Nia's house, got in his Jag, and backed out of the driveway. When he turned around to go forward, a man appeared in front of his car. David slammed on his brakes.

"Get out of that car!" Buddy was standing in David's headlights with his shotgun pointed straight at David's front windshield.

David yelled through the windshield, "Didn't we already do this?"

"Get out of that car!"

David didn't want to get out. He didn't want to deal with Buddy again; he didn't want to do anything but go home and rest, because he was damn tired.

David threw his car into park, swung open the driver's door, and got out.

Buddy yelled at David, "Not you, *him*!"

He kept his gun aimed at David's windshield.

David was confused. "Who?"

"The prowler in your backseat!"

David jumped away from the car. "Oh, shit!"

He hurried next to Buddy, snatched the shotgun from him, and aimed it at his backseat.

Buddy said, "I was watching you when you came out. So was *he*. Only he didn't think I saw him. That's when he crawled into your car, the sneaky joker."

David's car door was wide open and the engine was running, idling in the middle of the street. He kept his eye peeled, staring through his windshield and into his backseat. Buddy stayed close behind his right shoulder. The light inside David's Jag would go off after sixty seconds to avoid draining the battery.

Slowly, David stepped sideways to get a better angle, before those sixty seconds were gone. The guy could have been squatting down low, ducking out of the line of fire, but he was cornered. There was no way he was going to escape.

"Get out of my car!" David yelled, just as Buddy had done a minute ago. He moved to a ninety-degree angle to the back window and held his position. "Let's *get it on* now. You still feel like dancing?"

Cautious but steady, David closed in on the backseat, trying to anticipate every possible scenario of the guy trying to run or fight. Buddy stepped back to give him a little space. Good. David didn't want any collateral damage.

Nia came running out the house. "David, what's going on?"

"Go back, Nia. I've got him cornered."

"But, David—"

"Go!"

He didn't know if Nia went back inside or not; he couldn't afford to take his eye off his car for one second. He'd already used up most of the sixty seconds on the indoor light's timer, but he still didn't see the guy.

The second the light went out, David rushed the car. He hit the latch and kicked his front seat forward. With no light, his backseat was like a black hole. Yet there was no way a large man could squat low enough to avoid being seen.

David stepped back. If the guy had escaped out the passenger side, he would have seen him.

David shoved the shotgun back into Buddy's hands and looked at Nia, who, being hardheaded, was still standing close behind him.

"Nia! I'm taking you to my place. If he wants you tonight, he'll have to go through me."

CHAPTER 21

*N*ia dropped her duffel bag in the middle of David's living room. It was late, about one A.M., and usually she was tossing and turning in her bed around this time of night, struggling with erotic thoughts, and contending with a strange bedfellow.

"I don't think this is a good idea," she said to David.

"What? You don't like my place?" David picked up her duffel bag and set it on his black leather couch.

"It's not that. I'm just not used to staying the night with other people."

"Didn't you do sleepovers as a kid?"

"Never."

"Why not?"

Nia walked to his mantel, snooped through his pictures. "My father wouldn't let me. He said he didn't want to put other little girls or their parents at risk."

"At risk of what?"

"Trouble always finds me."

David gave a little chuckle in agreement. Nia picked up a picture of him in his early teens. He was holding a little sweet-faced girl in his lap. "Who's this?"

"That's my little sister."

"Oh, how sweet! She's so pretty. She has your exact same eyes—dark and shiny."

David glanced at the picture, then turned away. "I'll take your bag up to my bedroom. I'm giving you my bed. I'll take the couch."

Nia followed David up the stairs but brought the picture with her. "What's her name? Where is she now? Does she live in L.A.? Can I meet her?"

"No."

"No what?"

David walked through the hall. "She doesn't live around here. She moved to Canada with my folks."

"She looks a lot younger than you."

"She is," he said as she followed him into his bedroom. "My folks had her late in life. She was unexpected."

"What's she like? Is she like you, smart but a little bull-headed?"

"She's nothing like me." David still didn't look at the photo. He tossed her duffel in the middle of his California king bed, then grabbed a few blankets from his closet.

"What's her name?"

"Her name is Melody, but we call her Beez." His body movements stiffened. He obviously didn't want to talk about his sister, but Nia was more than a little curious.

"How do you get Beez from Melody?"

He paused a moment, remembering. "She was always

buzzing around like a bumble bee, wouldn't keep still. I nick-named her Beez when she was two." David shifted and pulled back his bedspread. "I changed the sheets this morning so you're good to go."

He took the framed picture from her hand and held it at his side, facing away from him. "Anything else you need?"

"Yeah, you." Nia pushed David back on the bed and climbed on top of him, but something in his mood had changed, and she knew it had to do with Beez. "David, tell me . . . what's wrong?"

"Nothing," he said, but his eyes showed that he was lying. "Just tired."

Not wanting to push it, she let him up. She was just glad they were still together. "Okay. Just do me one favor before you leave me up here all alone."

"What?"

"Undress for me."

"Nia, it's late. We both need sleep." He got up off the bed.

"Please, David. No strings attached. I just want your body to be the last image I see before I go to sleep, so I can have sweet dreams."

Her plea brought a slight smile back to his face. Too tired to argue, he started undressing. As he pulled his shirt over his head, Nia watched how his body moved and his muscles flexed. She leaned back on the bed and tilted her head, taking him all in, as he stripped down to his black briefs.

David's physique was just right, not overly muscular but in darn good shape. At six-three, he was the perfect height, with a nice broad chest, strong biceps, a trim waist, and ath-letic legs, all of which he carried well with great posture and confidence. She drank in his whole body with her eyes. The only flaw on his smooth skin was the three-inch scar across his left chest.

"How did you get that scar, David?"

She wanted to go deeper, to understand and share his experiences, both good and bad. But David ignored her question, and that hurt her feelings.

"It's late." His voice was low and burdened. He picked up the picture and went to the door. He turned off the light. "Sleep tight."

After David left, Nia felt a tinge of betrayal. He'd wanted her to confess her life to him, but he didn't want to share something that had obviously affected him deeply. Perhaps he needed a little more faith, too.

Nia undressed down to her red lace panties and fell across his bed. His mattress was firm and supportive without being too hard. The covers smelled like him—a fresh, clean, breezy sandalwood. She closed her eyes, trying to remember every detail of his body, as she fantasized that he was making love to her on his king-size bed.

She hugged his pillow close to her breasts, remembering the way his tongue felt on her nipples. Nia shuddered as hotness ran through her. She slid his pillow down her belly and clamped her thighs around it, imagining it was him. She rolled over and dreamed hard. She wanted to be with David, even if only in her dreams.

As she drifted off into sleep, she didn't notice the faint clink of a lock being broken, or the window's glass as it slid open, or the dark hand that pushed its way through the miniblinds.

CHAPTER 22

At three A.M., David couldn't sleep. His fake leather couch felt hard and stiff, reminding him of the CHP officer's glove. All night he'd been hearing strange noises upstairs, like deep bass-like chords vibrating and muffled movements, but each time he'd gotten up to investigate, the noises stopped. He thought maybe Nia was playing tricks to get him to come up, but when he'd cracked open the door to check on her, she appeared to be sleeping.

David checked his security alarm system. High-tech electronic sensors monitored every door and window in his condo. Spivek had helped him install it, so he knew it worked. The digital LCD readout indicated no breach.

David lay back down and tried to relax. The last forty-eight hours had been an action-packed roller-coaster ride, some of it good, like meeting the girl of his dreams. Some of it hadn't been so good, but he didn't want to dwell on that right now.

He needed sleep. In a few hours, he'd get up and go to church. Since Nia had never been, he'd invite her.

Just as he began to doze off, he heard a loud noise from upstairs. He jumped off his couch, sprinted up the stairs, and burst into his bedroom. Nia was sitting upright in the middle of his bed, naked except for his pillow, which she hugged to her chest. Her hair looked tangled and wild, like she'd been pulling at it. Her legs were folded under her.

He turned on the light. "Nia, what . . . ?"

Her eyes were wide and dazed like she'd been dreaming and wasn't fully awake yet, and her pupils were dilated, as if she were in total darkness.

Slowly, her eyes shifted toward his window. He saw that the miniblinds were crooked, and one was broken. Suspicious, he checked the window but the lock was securely in place; however, the air near the window was colder, as if it'd been opened. A peculiar syrupy smell also filled the room.

"Nia, what's going on?"

She remained motionless, her forehead and neck damp from sweat. He noticed something in her hand, a crumpled letter. He removed it.

She'd been reading one of many love letters from his ex-girlfriend, but in the dark? The other letters were all open and scattered on the bed behind Nia. Cher-Ling's picture had fallen out of one of the strawberry-scented envelopes. He'd never removed the letters from the nightstand next to his bed. David winced at his omission.

He quickly gathered up the letters, wondering how she'd read them in the dark. He shoved them back into the nightstand, then sat on the bed in front of Nia.

Slowly, the daze evaporated from her eyes and she focused on him. She seemed surprised, like she hadn't seen him come into the room.

Worried, he gently shook her shoulder. "Nia, what's going on?"

A faint smile crept across her beautiful lips. "I'm going to die."

She kissed him gently at the corner of his mouth, then lay back down and immediately fell into a deep, hypnotic sleep.

Baffled, David spent the next few hours lying next to her, checking her breathing, her pulse, and her heartbeat. Other than having a fever, she seemed okay. Maybe she'd had a bad dream and it'd spooked her, put crazy ideas in her head, he thought. He slipped his hand around hers and stayed by her side the rest of the night.

❧ CHAPTER 23 ❧

Over the next few months, David and Nia were together like Batman and Robin. The New Year brought with it new possibilities and new hopes for companionship. When David wasn't practicing law and she wasn't mentoring her teens, they spent all their time together laughing, talking, playing, kissing, and arguing, but even the arguing was bearable because the making up was worth it.

David liked having Nia around, though sleeping on his couch was as hard as keeping his hands off her. She didn't make it easy for him either. Nia wore skimpy little seductive clothes around the condo. Even when David turned the heat all the way down and practically froze himself, Nia pranced around in teddies, camisoles, and short shorts, showing off that brick house body of hers and trying to get a reaction out of him. With the help of many cold showers and a few ice packs,

David kept his libido under control. But at times when she couldn't persuade him to give in, she'd pout.

One Thursday night before he went downstairs to his bed couch, she stopped him. "I don't have forever."

"Why do you keep saying that?" He knew her mood had something to do with the dreams she'd been having. Nia was a fitful sleeper. Sometimes he'd stand in the doorway and watch her toss, turn, and moan, struggling with her dreams. On more than one occasion, when he tried to wake her, she'd uttered nonsensical things about death, matrimony, purple roses, and other things he couldn't make sense out of.

"Don't be so impatient, Nia. We have all the time in the world," he said, but she looked like she didn't believe him. Of course, he'd left out the fact that every time they got hot and heavy, strange things happened, like earthquakes and exploding fire extinguishers. He wasn't sure if it was divine intervention keeping him a gentleman and Nia chaste or if she knew her mysterious stalker was somehow behind it all and she wasn't telling.

"We've already talked about this. I'd love to throw you on my bed and make mad love to you, but we decided we wouldn't rush it. That we'd take our time and do it right, so that what we have will last forever."

"Forever?" She repeated his word, trying to believe it. She ran her hand over his chest and whispered, "I hope you're right, David. I really, really hope you're right."

The next Sunday, David asked her to go to church with him. Uneasy, Nia declined saying, "I don't think I'd fit in."

Instead, she lay on his bed and watched him dress. He stepped into his suit pants and buttoned his shirt. "That's what you said last Sunday, and the Sunday before that."

"No. Last Sunday I said I wasn't ready." David swung the

tie around his neck. She jumped off the bed, lifted his chin, and grabbed his necktie. "Here, let me tie it."

"Well, when will you be ready?"

"I don't know," Nia said, jumbling his tie into a knot.

"You also don't know how to tie a necktie," David said playfully. He undid the knot and started over. "You'd like Pastor Kees."

"Pastor who?"

"Daryl Kees is the pastor of Grace and Mercy Cathedral, a young guy, very down-to-earth. We went to high school together. In fact, Spivek, Daryl, and I were all on the wrestling team. We've stayed friends all these years."

"Wrestlers can't become preachers."

"Why not?"

"I don't know. Just doesn't sound right."

"Wrestlers probably make the best men of God."

"Why?"

"Because they know how to contend with the opponent."

"Who's the opponent?"

"The enemy of our souls." David squared off the knot and put on his jacket.

Nia frowned, befuddled. "I'm confused."

"Come to church with me and maybe you'll get a better understanding. I already told Pastor Kees about you, told him I'd met the girl of my dreams. He's happy for me and wants to meet you."

Nia sat back down on the bed, nervous. "How about if you just tell me a few things I should know?"

Though he was disappointed she'd chickened out, David remained optimistic. He wouldn't pressure her. "No problem. Bible Study 101 begins tonight. We'll have our first lesson over pepperoni pizza."

"No, I'll cook. Succulent buttery lobster in red wine sauce with decadent devil's food fudge cake covered in hot caramel, as we listen to sensual music and cuddle in bed." Nia lay back on the sheets and cast him a seductive look.

David paused, gaping at her. For a moment, he forgot they were talking about Bible study.

"We'll read in the den," he said, catching his thoughts and straightening his tie. "Over milk and cookies."

They both laughed as he kissed her forehead and left quickly for church. He knew that having Nia staying in his condo with him was like playing with fire, but he just loved having her around.

Later that evening, they reached a compromise. Nia cooked salmon and lit candles, and they ate dinner at the table while David read Scripture by candlelight. Nia seemed genuinely interested and was surprised at certain basic Christian principles. David was amazed at how much she didn't know. They skipped dessert and cuddled on the living room couch as he shared his own personal experiences of faith and explained why he believed in God.

"I'm far from perfect, but I still believe," he said as Nia listened intently. When he finished, she fell asleep in his arms.

THE NEXT EVENING, Nia decided to give David cooking lessons. She donned a revealing azure negligee and kept "accidentally" spilling drops of creamy sauces and other lickable items on the front of it, making it even more transparent as it stuck to her deliciously attractive breasts. David could barely concentrate. He kept bending down close to her negligee and licking his lips. Every now and then, she'd stop and give him a little taste, to keep things interesting.

The lesson itself wasn't going too well. David couldn't master the necessary skills to crack open a raw egg with one hand

and empty its yolk into the batter without dropping in the shells.

When the phone rang, he eagerly answered it, glad for the interruption.

"Yes, I'll accept the charges," he told the operator.

Nia turned off the mixer. "Is that Cher-Ling, your ex-girlfriend, calling from jail again?"

He nodded. "Hello? Cher-Ling?"

Nia came closer. She'd mentioned that his ex-girlfriend had called several times over the past week when he wasn't home, and each time she'd hung up on her. David hadn't spoken to Cher-Ling in over three months. Though she'd brought the trouble upon herself by violating restraining orders and vandalizing his car, he still struggled with feelings of guilt, wondering if he'd done enough to help her.

Nia tried to tug the cordless phone from his ear, but he kept it. "Nia, stop. I need to see what she wants."

"She wants *you*! That's what she wants," Nia huffed.

David ignored the comment and asked Cher-Ling, over the phone, "Are you okay?"

"No." Cher-Ling had a real knack for being dramatic. "I don't belong here. I need to be with you, David."

Nia was practically crawling up his body to get to the phone. "Hang up on her," she hissed.

David left the kitchen and went into the living room to get away from Nia. She followed him, though, listening to Cher-Ling's voice as she shouted over the background jail noise. "David, you've got to come get me out of here."

At twenty-eight, Cher-Ling struggled to hold on to her modeling career. She'd maintained her tall, beautifully slender figure, but she'd never been easy to work with. Dealing with the added pressures of staying thin and flawless only added to her psychological issues.

"Cher-Ling, you know I can't do that."

"You have to. You have to help me sue the guard."

David stopped. "Did a guard assault you?"

"No, but every time I pass, she looks at me funny. I think she's jealous of my hair. Hers is always a mess."

David sighed. "Cher-Ling . . ."

"If you don't come, I'll do something—something terrible." She was more drama queen than suicidal, and he was reasonably sure she'd never do anything that would harm her complexion.

"No, you won't." He called her bluff.

"You're right," she conceded. "Why should I suffer for having beautiful hair?"

David was glad he'd pulled a favor and asked the DA to assign her to a jail section reserved for low-risk, nonviolent offenders. He worried that her "issues" would get her beat up.

"David, come see me. *Pleeease.*"

David turned his shoulder away from Nia, but she wiggled around him, listening in. "She wants you to come see her, huh?"

Cher-Ling heard Nia's voice in the background. "Who's that? Is that the home-wrecker who keeps hanging up on me?"

Nia heard her and fumed. "Who's she calling a home-wrecker?"

David left the living room and ducked into the hallway, trying to get privacy, but Nia followed determinedly. He told Cher-Ling, "Look, I can't really talk right now—"

"David, I *need* you." Cher-Ling started her dry-cry voice.

Nia finally managed to grab the phone away. "Hey, listen. David is seeing me now and I don't appreciate you calling here and—"

David took the phone back. He covered the receiver with his palm. "What do you think you're doing?"

Her eyes were filled with insecurity. "I'm protecting our relationship."

"Our relationship doesn't need protecting. It's fine. Now, go back into the kitchen and let me talk in privacy."

Nia looked up at him, stubborn as ever. "No! Hang up the phone."

David stepped into the bathroom, closed the door in Nia's face, and locked it. "Hello? Cher-Ling?"

Cher-Ling had hung up.

David walked out of the bathroom, pissed. Nia stood in the hallway, her arms crossed. He walked right past her like he didn't see her. She followed him back into the kitchen. As he put the phone on the cradle, she fired off. "Why did you even accept her call?"

He kept his voice flat and even. "Because she called me."

He went back to the island and looked at the raw eggs, chopped oysters, purple eggplant, sausage, mushrooms, bread cubes, and other ingredients for some elaborate dish he wasn't even sure he'd like. He sighed at the mess. "Let's finish this up."

Nia picked up a dish towel, but instead of cleaning something, she wrung it in her hands. "I heard her ask you to come see her."

Ignoring her, David tried to crack open another thin-shelled egg, but his fingers went straight through, puncturing the yolk. Disgusted, he threw the gooey glob in the trash.

Nia spoke as if she had the last word. "You're not going to see her."

"I'm a defense lawyer," he said patiently. "I go see people in jail. It's my job."

"Cher-Ling is not your client, she's your ex."

"Thanks. I didn't know that."

Even more enraged by his sarcasm, Nia rummaged through the cooking utensils she'd brought over and found a giant wire thing that looked more like an instrument of torture than something that belonged in a kitchen. She jabbed it into a glob of something in a bowl and started whipping vigorously. "So, are you going to see her?"

David ducked the question and picked up the last egg, but it broke before he could get it out of the carton. Infuriated, he asked, "Are these *trick* eggs?"

Nia ignored his question. Fine. He knew the eggs were rigged, anyway.

Why did he agree to a cooking lesson when he could have gone to the celebrity basketball fund-raiser with Spivek? He didn't need to learn how to cook. He had a phone, a credit card, and lived inside the delivery area of eight pizza joints.

"Are you going to see Cher-Ling?" Nia repeated.

Didn't she realize that if he'd ignored her question the first two times that he'd ignore it again? He sat on the stool and fiddled with the mushrooms. He was supposed to be doing something to them, but he'd forgotten what she'd said. "You've made a mess in my kitchen."

Before she'd come, his kitchen was easy to keep clean because he never used more than the fridge and microwave, and occasionally he'd toast something. Places existed in his kitchen cabinets and pantry that he'd never been. Elves could be living inside and he wouldn't know it. Nia loved to cook but not clean. He appreciated her elaborate meals but was sick of always having to clean up behind her. "Are you going to stick me with the dishes again?"

Nia dropped her whisk into the marmalade, purposely splattering the sticky stuff all over David's pants. "Are you going to see Cher-Ling?"

David went to the sink and wiped marmalade from his crotch. If he hurried, he could still make it to the basketball game before the fourth quarter.

He pointed to the diminutive poultry Nia had placed on an oven dish. "What's wrong with that chicken? Is it anorexic?"

Nia rolled dough and ignored his question. She probably figured out that he was trying to pick a fight as a distraction. He persisted. "Where did you buy it? Midget Farms?"

Nia chopped onions but was so mad, she didn't even cry. Biting her words, she hissed, "You're going to see her, aren't you?"

He kept looking at the small bird. "I think you need to return the chicken to the store and get your money back. Go ahead. I'll wait," he lied, checking his watch, and wondering what the score of the basketball game was.

"It's *not* a chicken. It's a Cornish hen!" Nia slammed down the onion. "Are you going to visit Cher-Ling?"

"It'll be *my* decision if I do or don't. I don't need your permission." David turned around, feeling like she'd transformed his kitchen into a torture chamber. "Now, stop grilling me and let's shred these damn mushrooms."

"You don't *shred* mushrooms!"

"Shred, chop, shake, peel, crush, stir, fry—I really don't give a flying fig what you do to them. Just do it so we can eat!" Nia emptied the bowl of mushrooms on his hand. "Oh. Now you're acting childish."

"Are you calling me childish?"

"Would you like a pacifier?"

They'd had squabbles before but this was their first major get-in-your-face argument they'd had since dating.

She glared at him. "Are you going to see her?"

"If I feel like it."

"Fine. I'm leaving." As she grabbed a handful of cooking utensils, he prepared to duck, not sure what she intended to do with them. She pointed a spatula at the uncooked hen. "I was going to stuff this for you, but now you can take it and *you* can stuff it yourself!"

She shoved the underweight poultry into his stomach. He grabbed it before it hit the floor. As she headed out of the kitchen, he yelled after her. "Call me when you *and* this chicken grow up!"

"That'll be never!" She left, slamming his front door.

CHAPTER 24

A whole week passed and Nia still hadn't called. David tried to call her several times, but she wouldn't take his calls. On Tuesday at six P.M., he drove to her house, knowing she'd be there mentoring the teens. Jay answered the door.

"What's up, Jay? Where's Nia?"

"Don't know," Jay replied, acting naïve. "Haven't seen her."

"You're standing in her house."

"Yeah, well, she said she's not home." Jay blocked the entry-way awkwardly. "She's not standing behind the door, either."

David tried to look past Jay, but Jay edged to the side. He waited a little longer, then said, "Okay, well, tell Nia whenever she gets back home from behind the door to call me."

"Alright." Jay paused before closing the door and gave David a hand signal indicating that Nia was, in fact, hiding behind the door. He whispered, "Don't give up, man. She still likes you."

As David turned to leave, he saw Nia's hand fly up over Jay's head and thump him. "Ouch!"

David walked anyway. He couldn't force Nia to see him, and he wouldn't beg. He'd give her enough space and when she was ready, she knew where to find him. He wasn't going anywhere.

By Thursday, Nia still hadn't called.

On Saturday, he went fishing with Spivek to try to take his mind off Nia. They rented a pontoon boat at Big Bear Lake. The water was clear and the trout were biting, but David found himself missing Nia so much that he absentmindedly baited his hook with a Lay's potato chip.

Spivek shook his head. "Never seen a girl affect you like this before."

"Me either." David chuckled but felt lousy.

Just then, David's cell phone rang. When he saw Nia's number on his caller ID, he grew elated. Before he could even say hello, Nia challenged him.

"Just answer one question," she said.

"What?" he asked.

"Were you thinking about me?"

"When?"

"Just now, before I called you."

David thought about it, then answered truthfully. "Yes."

"Don't lie to me, David."

"I'm not lying." He admitted, "I was thinking about you, wishing we were together."

Nia took a long, deep breath and let it out, sighing. "Good. Then it worked."

"What worked?"

"I'm still mad at you, but I miss you like crazy. So I sat here concentrating real hard, and I sent you thought waves."

"Thought who?"

"Thought waves." She paused. "Telling you that I miss you and that I want to be wherever you are." Nia sounded mellow and reflective, and a bit of melancholy tinged her voice. He'd never experienced this side of her.

"I guess I got your thought waves."

"Yes, you did." Nia sighed again, relieved. "Because we really do have a *connection*."

David held the phone. He didn't know what to say. It all sounded a bit esoteric but who was he to argue?

"Well?" Nia asked, waiting for a reply.

"I'm just happy to hear your voice, no matter how it happened."

CHAPTER 25

At six o'clock, Nia sat on a high stool in her upstairs den and let Shayla style her hair as she anxiously awaited David's arrival. Shayla had attended cosmetology school for six months before she dropped out. Despite her short attention span, she was an excellent hairstylist.

"Make-up sex is the best sex," Shayla said as she braided Nia's hair in long, silky rows and curled the ends.

"Shayla, please," Nia said, blushing. "That's private."

"Aw, c'mon, admit it. You and Malcolm used to break up all the time just to hit it again."

"Not true," Nia said, keeping her virginity a secret.

Shayla went on chitchatting about her own sexual experiences while Nia sat there trying to act like she already knew things. But in reality, she only knew as much about orgasms as her midnight visitor had shown her.

When the doorbell rang, it startled her. She hopped off the stool. "David's early!"

Shayla pointed at Nia's half-braided hair. "You can't go downstairs like that. You look crazy."

"I am. I'm crazy about him." Nia ran downstairs and swung open the door, but it wasn't David. She hurried to try to close the door, but Malcolm stuck his foot inside. She slammed it on his foot purposely.

"Ow!" He pushed his way in, hobbling on his injured foot.

Nia backed up. "Why are you here?"

He was all smiles. "I came to see you."

"Hello? News flash—I'm not your girlfriend anymore. We broke up."

"We always break up. Then we get back together."

"Not this time." She turned her back and walked into her living room. "And stop calling me, leaving messages, and sending me this stupid candy." She reached into her antique popcorn machine and pulled out a bag full of bow-tied candy. She poured it on his foot.

"Hey, that's imported chocolate!" Mal picked up some boxes and tried to stuff them in his pocket. "I paid good money for this."

"Give them to Judge *Vicky*. Had any more 'chamber meetings' lately?"

"Um, about that . . ." Mal cleared his throat. Nia knew he'd come ready with a smooth lie. "She forced me to have sex with her. I had no choice. She used her position to manipulate me."

Nia shuddered at the bad pun but chose not to comment. "Get out of here, Mal."

She turned and walked back toward the front door. He followed. "So, when do we get back together? Tonight?"

"You're crazy."

As she passed the stairs, she saw Shayla sitting there,

eavesdropping. Malcolm saw Shayla too but didn't acknowledge her and kept following Nia back into the atrium.

"I heard you're dating that lawyer—what's his name? Mr. Hotshot?"

"David Wrightwood. You know his name. He's the lawyer who beat you."

"That guy is not right for you."

"David is fantastic. Unlike you, he has morals."

"Okay, then *you're* not right for *him*."

Nia stopped at the coffee table. "How dare you!"

"Let's face it, Nia. You're a special case."

She crossed her arms over her chest. "How did I ever put up with you for six years since high school?"

"Because I'm the only guy who doesn't ask questions when all the strange shit hits the fan."

"Wow. How romantic." Nia rolled her eyes.

"Mr. Hotshot won't last. Nia, I'm telling you. He'll run."

"He's lasted this long."

"He's only sticking around for the nooky."

"The what?" Nia bristled.

"You know, he wants to get the cherry. It's a big thing for a man to be the first inside the cookie jar."

Nia huffed, irate. "David is not like that. He really cares about me. He may even be falling in love with me."

"Ha! Forget about it." Mal guffawed. "If he tells you he loves you, he's lying. Never trust a man who tells you he loves you *before* he even hits it. That's absurd. He's just trying to play with your head. Don't believe him."

Nia opened the front door and motioned for him to leave.

He frowned, surprised. "But, Nia, I thought we were getting back together. We've got to."

"Why?"

"Just trust me, it'll make things easier for *both* of us," he said, then glanced around, paranoid, as if someone else besides Shayla might be listening.

"Get out, Mal." Nia shoved him out the door and went back upstairs.

Malcolm walked back to his car and hopped in. He had to take a leak, so he found a Denny's restaurant and went inside. He walked into the restroom and checked it. Nobody was in there except him. Still, he was acting paranoid, so he bypassed the urinals, went inside a stall and closed the door.

As soon as he took aim, the lights went out.

Malcolm heard footsteps slowly cross the floor and stop in front of his stall. He glanced down at the bottom edge of a dark magenta suit that hung generously over burgundy leather shoes, and he knew.

It was *him*.

Mal tried to hurry and zip up, but the man's deep voice commanded, "Sit."

Mal looked down at the toilet. "But I don't have to—"

"Now." The voice was firm and threatening.

Malcolm didn't want any problems, so he sat. "Hey, I tried like you told me. She wants nothing to do with me."

"Quitting is not an option."

Mal squirmed. "Hey, we've been doing this for six years. Maybe it's time to move on and find another sucker to be with her. What's the point of all this anyway?"

"Do you like your job?"

"It's alright. You could help me win more cases, though."

"Your clothes?"

"Yeah, but—"

"Your money?"

"Yeah, but speaking of money—"

"Your *life*?"

Mal got quiet. Thanks to this intimidating dark figure who'd been bullying and bribing him since high school to date Nia, his life was pretty good. He wanted to keep it that way.

"Affirmative," Mal said, and waited nervously.

After a long silence, the ground started shaking and the stall's wall rattled. A jagged line cracked through the cement floor, like the San Andreas Fault, between Mal's expensive shoes.

"Holy crap!" Malcolm squirmed but stayed in place.

Moments later, he heard the footsteps walk away, but the restroom door never opened. The man whose face he'd never seen had vanished. Now Malcolm really did have to go.

ᑫ CHAPTER 26 ᑐ

At seven o'clock, David returned from Big Bear Lake, stiff from the long drive back to L.A. and dirty from fishing in the mountains. With his backpack in one hand and fishing rod in the other, he trampled through his condo's front door, ready for a hot shower and to go see his girl. As he reached behind the door to deactivate the alarm, he felt a pair of eyes on his back.

"Ooh. I like my men dirty," a woman's voice uttered, low and erotic.

David jerked around. Mysti was sitting on his couch. "How'd you get in here?"

"You left your door unlocked."

"No, I didn't."

"But you intended to." She stood up, grinning craftily. "You were hoping I'd pop in."

Dressed a bit more conservatively than when he first met

her, Mysti wore a figure-flattering mauve dress, knee length but still teasingly seductive on her long, shapely legs.

As she walked toward him, the dress clung to her curves. "I can tell you like a little danger and spice in your life, to keep things interesting."

"Actually, my life is already interesting enough."

Her jade eyes challenged him. "But you're dating my daughter."

"And?" His eyes dropped to her ankle-high buckskin boots and he wondered why something always had to die for this woman to get dressed.

"That means you're either a man with a death wish . . . or a fool." Mysti glanced toward the mantel, where he'd placed the framed picture of his little sister, Melody, whom he'd nicknamed Beez. "You don't strike me as a fool, David. So that means you're not afraid to die."

David's hand started to ache from the tight grip he kept on his backpack. He set it down by the door, wondering how she knew where he lived. "Does Nia know you're here?"

"What do you think?"

"I think you came for a reason. I think you should hurry and get to it."

"Nia is not normal." Mysti watched David carefully for a reaction. All he could think about was what the pot had called the kettle.

"I know. She's gorgeous," he said, subverting her point.

"Haven't you noticed peculiar things about her?"

"Her body temperature runs hot. That's a bit unusual, but—"

"It runs *very* hot," she said with a seditious grin.

"Why? Is it some sort of biological condition?"

"Part biological, part manipulation." She chuckled, adding, "Nia's also flame retardant, but I bet she's never told you that part."

"Did you do something to your daughter?"

"Not just me. Forces far greater have had a significant influence over Nia. Her birth was sanctified, but not in the way you think." Mysti cut her eyes toward the window. He could tell she was editing herself and withholding vital information.

"Nia's never been to a doctor, except once, and that was only to get vaccinated for school. When the doctor took her vitals—temperature, blood pressure, pulse—he thought his equipment had malfunctioned. They wanted to take a blood test, but I had to stop them."

David tried to focus on what she was saying, but Mysti was mentally distracting. His mind kept bending toward naughty thoughts. Pulling himself together, he stepped back, but Mysti narrowed the space between them, and her aura was so intoxicatingly strong, he felt heady and was having trouble thinking.

"Maybe Nia should go see a doctor and find out what's wrong."

"Nothing's *wrong* with Nia." She waved dismissively. "Nia doesn't even know herself all the powerful things she's capable of."

"And you're telling me all of this because . . . ?"

"Since you don't mind taking risks that could prove fatal, there are far better ways you could invest your resources." Mysti skimmed her lusty green eyes down his body and paused at the resources below his belt. "Perhaps in a more mature commodity, one that yields very high and pleasurable rewards."

Her ripe avocado eyes glanced at the stairs leading up to his bedroom. David felt the same forbidden sensation as when she'd brushed against him at the restaurant. He fought against a strange rage in his libido.

"To what new level of low would I have to stoop to date the mother of the girl I'm involved with?"

"Who said anything about dating?" she quipped nonchalantly. "We can get straight to the bed, or the floor, or the garage, or wherever you like."

"Stop with the games, Mysti. I'm not interested in you."

"Then why is your pole so erect?"

Alarmed, David looked down at his zipper. Mysti nodded toward the fishing pole in his hand that he'd been gripping tightly the whole time. He set it down.

Mysti gave a sly chuckle. "You and I should become friends, David. Maybe we could help each other."

"I don't need any help."

"If you keep seeing Nia, you will."

"Right now, all I need is a good shower to wash away this dirt." He threw her a chiding look.

With a nod, Mysti conceded. She moved toward the door. "Don't get too clean, though. You'll need some of that dirt to fight with very soon."

David reached out to open it. "Here, let me get that for you."

Before he could reach it, the door flew open by itself. David flinched but kept his cool.

Mysti smiled coyly. "Heed my warning, David. Don't get too attached to Nia. Hell has big plans for her." She blew him a kiss.

He watched the door close behind her on its own and thought to himself, *I need a new alarm system.* David headed upstairs for a quick shower before going to Nia's house.

CHAPTER 27

At eight o'clock, David rang Nia's doorbell. She greeted him at the door with a running leap, jumped into his arms, and hugged him like he'd just returned from the war. He dropped the bag he was carrying and held her inside his sturdy arms.

"I missed you so much, David." She kissed him deeply.

"Ooh, I like this. We should have squabbles more often," he joked.

She shook her head. "No, let's not split up again. Ever."

He saw the seriousness in her big brown eyes and agreed. "You're right. Let's not let foolish things break us apart."

David set her down and gave her the insulated bag containing two freshly caught rainbow trout. "Sorry I didn't catch more. It's not really the season."

"These are fine," she said, pleased. She took the fish into her kitchen and immediately started gutting them. He followed but didn't dare step foot inside her kitchen after their last blowup while cooking.

He watched her from the breakfast nook. "Aren't you even a little bit squeamish?"

"For what? Everything's got to die," she said, and chopped off the head. "It's the cycle of life. Just be glad we're at the top of the food chain."

Nia whipped up a delicious dinner of fried fish with macaroni and sweet yams while David prepared the table. They ate and chitchatted about how much they'd missed each other. Before they finished eating, Nia's phone rang. She answered, and her whole demeanor changed. She hung up abruptly.

"Is something wrong?"

"No. Yes. It's my father." Nia rose to her feet. "I've got to go over there."

"I'll go too." David got up also. "This would be a good time for me to meet him."

"No." Nia pushed him back down. "You stay here, finish your fish. I'll be right back." Nia hurried and grabbed her car keys. "This won't take long, hopefully."

David pretended to continue eating until she walked out the door. Then he grabbed his car keys and left to follow her.

He almost lost sight of Nia's gold Mustang on the 405 freeway because she drove too dang fast. He managed to spot her as she exited and tailed her down Palms Boulevard, through a series of quick turns, and onto a residential street. She parked in front of a modest bungalow with a single-car garage, hardly the kind of house where he'd expect a retired millionaire real estate investor like her father to live.

David waited until she went inside before he parked. He hoped she could tend to whatever family crisis had occurred before he got out and introduced himself. After a few minutes, he heard yelling and what sounded like a small-caliber gunshot.

David ran up the steps with one hand on his cell phone, ready to dial 911. He banged on the door. "Nia!"

Nia swung the door open. Her face was surprised, but she didn't look injured or scared. "David, what are you doing here?"

"I followed you," he confessed while trying to look inside the house.

"Why?"

David saw a man in his early fifties, his head full of thick black waves, graying slightly at the temples. He looked in good shape, a wrestler's body, not at all like the retired alcoholic David had pictured in his mind.

Her father barged to the door. "Who the hell are you?"

"I'm David—whoa!" He extended his hand but stopped when he saw the .22 caliber in her father's hand. Nia jumped in front of her father.

David frowned. "Nia, is everything okay?"

"Everything's fine . . . considering," she said tightly. "We were just having a family reunion of sorts. But now, thank God, it's over."

David caught a fleeting image of a woman in a mauve dress and buckskin boots darting past him, leaving abruptly.

Mysti.

David checked the pathway for blood, saw none, and surmised the shot had missed.

When Nia saw a few neighbors looking, she pulled David inside and quickly closed the door. "Dad, this is David. David, meet Jessie, my father."

Her father frowned. "What happened to Malcolm?"

"He's history."

"He's dead? Good. Never liked him anyway."

"I didn't kill him, just broke up with him."

"Too bad." Jessie Youngblood eyed David up and down. David kept his eye on the handgun. Nia saw and took the gun away from her father, and shoved it inside the curio cabinet.

"Are you dating my daughter?"

"Yes, sir."

Jessie took another look at David, then burst out laughing. He reached into his back pocket and pulled out a fifth of gin. "Here, you need this more than I do."

David politely declined. "Thanks, but no thanks."

Nia glared at Jessie and his bottle, then turned and threw David a flustered look for following her, but David was glad he did. He'd been more than a little curious to meet the man who'd impregnated a woman like Mysti.

As if reading his mind, Jessie asked David abruptly, "You met her mother yet?"

"Yes."

"And you still got both your balls?"

David winced, thinking of his encounter with Mysti earlier in his condo. "Actually, I find Mysti to be quite, uh, interesting."

"Yeah, like arsenic," Jessie said. "Did Nia tell you she's a bitch?"

"You mean a witch?"

"No, I mean bitch, but yeah, that too," Jessie added crassly, then turned to Nia. "Why is this boy up in my house? And where does he fit into this whole mess?"

Nia composed herself as best she could. "Dad, David wanted to meet you because you're my father, and he thinks I'm very special."

"Yeah, my daughter is special alright. You like scary movies, son?"

Nia frowned. "David doesn't scare easily."

"Ha! Yeah, right." Jessie added sourly, "Stick around. I thought I was brave, too. Now, I have all the courage I need, the Dutch kind." Jessie took a long, thirsty swig from the bottle.

"Mr. Youngblood—"

"Call me Jessie, no need for formalities. We're all in this shit together."

"Dad!" Nia scolded.

"Jessie, I wanted to meet you because I'm very serious about your daughter—"

"I'm serious too," Jessie interrupted irreverently. "This stuff is no joke. I wish it was." He waved the bottle all around. "I wish I could wake up from one of my drunken stupors and find out it was all one big prank. But that ain't gonna happen. It's real."

David frowned in consternation. "What exactly is real?"

"Nothing," Nia interrupted quickly. "He's drunk. Don't listen to him."

"Damn right I'm drunk. If it wasn't for the divine blessing of inebriation, I'd be cuckoo, sitting somewhere in a dark padded room playing with my spit." Jessie took another swig and eyed David with suspicion. "Why are you sticking around? What's in it for you?"

"I can't see myself living without Nia," David said. "My reward is simply having her in my life."

David smiled at Nia, who blushed, finally forgiving him for following her.

Jessie stared at David in amazement. "That's got to be the goofiest thing I ever heard in my life."

"If love is goofy, sir, then with all due respect, call me goofy."

"Okay, I will," Jessie concluded stubbornly.

But Nia also stared at David in amazement. Her face lit up with surprise, and her brown eyes radiated. "Did you just say *love*?"

David nodded. Nia blushed and rushed into his arms. He hugged her and looked deep into her eyes. "I love you, Nia Youngblood."

Nia gave a small squeal and searched his eyes, as if trying to believe him. He said softly, "I'm madly in love with you."

Finally, Jessie grunted impatiently. "Take all that stuff somewhere else. I have to live here."

"Nice meeting you, Mr. Youngblood." David took Nia's hand and opened the door.

Jessie grumbled. "Yeah, good luck with that. Now get out of my house. Go."

As David walked Nia back to her car, she could hardly keep her hands off him. She attacked him with more hugs and kisses. "I can't believe you said that, and in front of my father."

"I wanted him to know, too."

Nia stopped him on the walkway. "David, I've loved you from the first day we met."

He held her tight on her dad's front lawn, never wanting to let go, until she said, "We'd better go, before he turns the sprinklers on us."

ex Chapter 28 ey

*O*n Tuesday, three days later, while the other kids folded chairs and cleaned up for the day, Nia pulled Jay aside. She took him into the game room closet for a heart-to-heart talk.

"Jay, we've always been straightforward with each other. You're growing up now, getting hormones and crazy feelings. That's normal for a boy your age."

"What are you trying to get at, Miss Nia?"

"Your father told me that you've been spending a lot of time in your room listening to your iPod and staring out your window at my house."

"So?"

"He also said you've been acting kind of sad since I told you that David and I are in love."

Jay's eyelids flickered. "Still don't know what you're getting at."

"Jay, do you have a crush on me?"

He paused for a moment, then busted out laughing, holding his stomach.

Nia frowned. "What's so funny?"

Jay laughed even harder. "Miss Nia, you're cute, but you ain't all that."

Now Nia felt like the fool. "So, that's a no?"

"It's a no, but that was a good one." He smoothed his fingers down his chin, acting all cool and grown-up. "Miss Nia, I've got honeys lined up at school just waiting to get a piece of the Jay."

"The Jay?"

"Yeah, and besides, in case you haven't noticed, you're *waaay* too old for me."

"I'm not that much older." She added, growing a little annoyed, "Only eight years."

"That's a lot. You could practically be my grandma," Jay continued, oblivious to her grimace. "Plus, you knew me when I was just a kid, still wearing braces."

"That was just two months ago."

"Still, that's embarrassing. I'm a grown man now."

"You're only sixteen."

"Whatever." He turned toward the door. "Anyway, can I go now? It smells like feet in here."

"Go, Jay." Nia finished up with the teens, then checked the clock. It was after nine o'clock and David still hadn't called. Something was up. A little perturbed, she drove to David's condo.

When she arrived, a blue glow filled his living room and she could hear his TV. She used her key and opened the door. David was sitting on the couch. He looked up, saw her, and quickly clicked off the television. Guilt splattered his face.

"What are you watching?" Nia reached for the remote but he held it back. "Porn?"

"No."

"Then what was it?"

"Nothing." His expression told a different story.

Nia walked around him and clicked the television back on using the button. A DVD was playing interviews of several guys she'd dated during her breakups with Malcolm. They were confessing the weird stuff that happened to them when they'd attempted to date her.

Shocked, Nia bit her lip. "How did you get this?"

"Someone sent it anonymously." She followed his eyes to the coffee table. She picked up the opened envelope and recognized Malcolm's handwriting.

She listened a minute more as one guy attested to the fact that she was cursed and warned others to stay away from her, then clicked off the TV. Her hands trembled with anger and dread as she waited for David's reaction. Surely he wouldn't want anything else to do with her. Thanks to Mal.

"So, what now?" she asked.

He stood up. "What do you think?"

She searched his face. "I don't know."

"There's really only one thing left for me to do." He looked at the opened package, then took something from his pocket.

He got down on one knee. "Nia Youngblood, will you be my wife?"

"Oh, my God!" She gulped air, trying to breathe, as he slipped the ring on her finger. She shook with shock and disbelief. "Oh, my God!"

"Is that a yes?"

"Yes!" she exclaimed.

He stood up and wrapped her inside his arms. Shaking all over, she squeezed him back, laughing and muttering between joyful sobs, "I can't believe this. You're incredible."

CHAPTER 29

*L*ater that night, David was all over Nia, kissing, squeezing, and groping as they clamored through her front door. She couldn't keep her hands off him, either. They tumbled inside. He kicked the door closed, then pinned her against the wall, kissing, groping, grinding.

He heard a noise in her dark living room. "Aheem!"

Shayla, who'd been sleeping on the couch, lifted her head and grunted at them. Surprised, David asked Nia, "What's she doing here?"

She whispered, "I let Shayla move in."

"Why?"

"She and her aunt are bickering again. Her aunt wants her to start paying rent."

"That sounds reasonable," he said.

Nia pulled him into the hallway, shushing him. "Be nice,

David. Shayla can't keep a job for more than three days. She says people try to take advantage of her and underpay her."

"Then maybe she should have stayed in school and furthered her education. Sounds like Shayla needs a reality check." He shook his head. "Letting her move in was not a good idea."

"Why not? She's my friend."

"Are you sure about that?" He saw the confused look in Nia's eyes and wished he hadn't said anything. Now wasn't a good time to bring up the subtle advances Shayla had been making toward him, which he'd chosen to ignore. He checked his watch. "It's getting late, anyway. I'd better go."

He turned to leave but Nia grabbed his arm. "No, stay the night. Please."

"I can't." He scoffed, "Shayla's on the couch. Where would I sleep?"

"Upstairs with me, in my bed."

He backed away, reminding her, "Remember what happened when we crawled in bed together a few nights ago?"

"Yeah." Nia winced. "Another earth tremor."

"And the time before that when you pulled me into the shower with you?"

"Yeah." Nia grimaced. "Did your blister heal yet from the scalding water?"

"Yes, it did." David rubbed his butt and looked around suspiciously. "Besides, I mentioned those strange events to my friend, Pastor Kees, and he agreed with me. Whether they're signs from God or something else, it's best if I keep my passion under control until we're married. That would be the safest thing to do."

"Do you always do what's safe, David Wrightwood?" She rubbed her body into his.

"No, sometimes I get weak," he groaned. "Like right now."

"I didn't think so." She pulled him up the stairs, and he followed willingly, gazing at her butt in her tight jeans.

In her bedroom, Nia unzipped her jeans, bent over, and pushed them down to her ankles. David sat on her bed and stared at her thong, biting his lip.

"The things going through my head right now would get me kicked out of heaven. I'm going to sleep in one of the guest rooms."

"No!" He got up to leave but she blocked the door. "If something happens in the middle of the night, consider it an early honeymoon." She winked and helped him out of his clothes.

He turned out the light, lay down next to her, and tried to relax. Stiffly, he put his arm around her. With her back to him, she tried to spoon, snuggling close and pushing her behind into his groin, but he kept inching back, trying to keep a safe space between them. He wanted her bad but was determined to hold out until after the wedding.

After a few minutes, she whispered, "David?"

When he pretended to be fast asleep, she huffed and punched her pillow. He held still and steady but couldn't help being tickled by her angst.

A few seconds later, he whispered in her ear, "Love you, baby girl."

Nia heard David tell her he loved her and smiled. Though disappointed, she respected his honorable intentions. "Love you too, baby boy."

She tried not to toss and turn, but she kept fantasizing about how it'd feel to make love to David. He fidgeted also, probably thinking the same thing about her. She eased her butt back, determined at least to make contact with his body. Finally, he stopped inching back and relaxed, but she could feel his muscles tense as another part of his anatomy responded to her touch. Content with that for now, she finally drifted off to sleep.

She woke up a while later to his hard member jarring her back. She couldn't help smiling, happy to be awakened in such a way, but when she heard him groaning, struggling to contain himself, she felt a little sorry for him that he'd lost the fight and a little guilty that she'd contributed to his caving in under pressure.

"It's okay, David," she whispered.

She didn't want him to feel bad.

When she tried to turn around, he held her in place. He tightened his arm around her stomach and pulled her back, closer into him, slowly grinding as he grew even harder. His body felt sturdy, like a rock.

She closed her eyes and exhaled. She'd waited so long for this. She squeezed her thighs together tight, imagining him already inside. The sensation sent a slight tremble through her.

He clasped her thong and gently slid it down her thighs and off her body. She could feel that he was already naked.

He rolled her over onto her stomach and pinned her to the mattress, allowing his full weight to gently crush her. He moved her arms out, opened her hands, and spread out her fingers. He slipped his large fingers through hers, clasping her hands and pressing them on the mattress.

Her body heated up. Her internal juices percolated, bubbling up like a natural hot spring from the earth, making her feel helplessly wet. Her pulse beat inside her throat as blood flowed to crucial parts, energizing and preparing those places. She'd never felt so warm or so flushed. Hot moisture began to melt away her inhibitions.

God forgive us for what we're about to do, she uttered in her mind, more for David than for herself, as she felt his fullness throb against the roundness of her backside. Hard, firm, weighty, and fleshly, it pressed into her skin like a large hot prodding rod begging to get inside. She wondered if she could take on its girth.

She shuddered and moaned, "Mmm, David."

He slipped his hands under her stomach and clung to her body like a starving man to his last meal. His passion was palpable, his breaths hard behind her head.

Her body heat rose exponentially. She inhaled, bracing herself, as he began to lift her midsection slightly, positioning her for his entrance. With his other hand, he grasped her wrist, hooked her fingers on the headboard, and spread her thighs wide.

She held her breath as he unleashed his raw, hot desire and plunged into her deeply. The force rocked her whole body as he pounded mercilessly. She gripped the headboard and pressed her face hard into the mattress. She squealed, biting the sheets, in pain, agony, and sweetness. It felt surreal.

When he opened his mouth to speak, his hot breath singed the back of her neck. "Nia . . . my wife."

His deep voice shot fear through her body. In that instant, the sweet smell of burning molasses flooded her nose, and his dark, overpowering presence bore down heavily on her, like an anchor.

This was not David! She tried to lift her face to scream, but her voice got muffled in the sheets. Nia struggled under the weight to turn over. When she finally did, *he* was gone.

"David," she called out desperately, but David wasn't in the bed with her. The room was empty. She was alone.

Roiling with heat, terror, and confusion, her body shook. She knew she hadn't been dreaming because her thong lay next to her.

Where's David?

She heard groaning. It sounded like a woman in the throes of passion, and it was coming from downstairs.

Shayla.

The name caught in her throat as she tried to push back

the horrible thought that assaulted her mind. She grabbed her robe and raced down the stairs.

Unmistakable sexual moans emanated from her living room couch.

Where's David?

The pain that gripped her heart was too intense to allow her to think. She had to see it with her own eyes.

Nia ran into her living room. Shayla's moans escalated as Nia stood paralyzed in the dark and watched what looked like two bodies writhing beneath her white wool blanket. Shayla panted, "Ooh, David, oh yes."

Nia's heart threatened to pound through her chest as she flipped on the light.

Startled, Shayla jumped and rose up. A large vibrator fell from her hands and rolled toward Nia's feet.

Nia blinked as dampness clouded her vision. Shayla was alone on the couch.

Nia's chest rose and fell heavily, and her heart continued in an uneasy, pained beat as she realized her best friend was only masturbating while thinking of her man.

"Where's David?" Her voice came out flat and steely, like her gaze.

Shayla's mascara ran as thick as her embarrassment. "I don't know," she said. Guilt cracked her voice. "I thought he was upstairs with you."

Nia glared.

Shayla fell back on the couch, shamefaced and unfulfilled. She confessed, "Inspiration. That's all, Nia, just inspiration."

"What's going on?" The voice behind Nia startled her. She jerked around to see David entering from the hallway. With no shirt and his pants loosely fastened, he rubbed sleep from his eyes. "I thought I heard somebody call my name."

Gaining his focus, he saw Shayla indecently exposed. Then

he spotted the large vibrator on the floor. Shayla flung the cover around her and buried her face.

"Oh." David backed up, embarrassed. "I didn't mean to—I'll leave."

Nia caught him in the hallway and grabbed his arm. "David!"

When he saw the panicked look in her eye, he froze. "What's wrong?"

"Please tell me you were upstairs just now, making love to me," she pleaded desperately.

He looked at her, bewildered. "Nia, I didn't touch you."

CHAPTER 30

Nia ran into the bathroom and locked the door. She turned on the water and blasted the shower. David banged on the door. "Nia, tell me what's wrong. Please, so I can help you."

She stood outside the shower stall and squeezed a small, round mirror inside her trembling hands. Slowly, she slipped the mirror between her thighs. Barely able to hold the mirror steady, she checked herself for blood, semen, or torn skin as her private areas still throbbed.

There was nothing there, other than her body's own moisture.

Still a virgin physically, but emotionally, it had all seemed so real.

Distressed, Nia dropped the mirror and it shattered loudly on the tile floor. Hearing it, David knocked again.

"Nia, please! Are you okay?" His voice sounded panicked.

"Yeah," she mumbled faintly.

But she lied.

David jiggled the knob, wanting to come in. He explained from the other side of the door, "I'm sorry I left, but you kept tossing and turning, and I got weak. I had to leave."

She stepped into the shower. The hard, cold streaming water pounded her sensitive skin. She started scrubbing, trying to cleanse her body, her mind, her spirit, but even the hardness of the soap between her thighs reminded her again of *him*.

Nia flung the soap away from her. She slid down with her back pressed against the wall and squatted in the shower. The water pelted her from above, making a wet mess of her hair, and she didn't care.

David knocked again. "Nia, open the door. At least tell me what is wrong."

"David?" she called from the shower.

"Yeah, Nia. I'm here."

"Please"—she held back a sob—"take me to church with you on Sunday."

A pause.

"Sure," he said. "Just open the door. Let's work this out together."

MORNING FINALLY CAME and David kissed Nia good-bye, leaving her curled up on the den's sofa, where he'd spent the rest of the night hugging her.

As David headed back to his condo to get ready for work, she dragged herself into the kitchen to make orange juice. She felt dehydrated and, more importantly, dispirited as her body and mind struggled to reconcile what had happened.

Shayla must have heard David leave. She came to the

doorway. She still had Nia's favorite white blanket wrapped around her, and her voice was hoarse. "You probably don't want to talk to me."

Nia didn't respond. She removed the oranges from the bowl.

Shayla began trying to justify her actions. "Hey, I know that whole thing looked bad, but you've got to understand, David is fine and—"

"And he's *my* boyfriend," Nia said, whipping around.

Nia was still angry at her, but her emotions splintered in different directions. She turned back around, tossed the oranges onto the cutting board, and began chopping them in half with a butcher's knife. "What you did was inconsiderate," she said, scolding Shayla.

"What about you, Nia?" Shayla said. "You're greedy."

Nia turned around again, gripping two oranges. Her friend had a lot of nerve.

Shayla moved forward and narrowed her eyes at Nia. "You've got David." She nodded at Nia's engagement ring. In all the commotion, Nia hadn't had a chance to tell her David had proposed. She was surprised Shayla noticed it.

"You've got Malcolm who still wants to be with you," Shayla continued. "And you've got *him.*"

Nia dropped one of the oranges. "Who are you talking about?"

"You know who I'm talking about." Shayla circled around Nia and dragged her white blanket on the floor. Accusation filled her smudged eyes. "That tall, sneaky buff guy who lurks outside at night. I've spotted him a few times on the ledge by your window."

Nia swallowed hard.

"Don't think I don't know that he sneaks in sometimes."

Shayla smirked. "I've heard how you toss, turn, and moan around midnight. He must really be good."

Nia clutched the knife in her hand. She was supposed to be chopping oranges but right now she couldn't move.

Shayla admitted, "I haven't gotten a real good look at him yet. He moves like a shadow, but the guy must really be packing."

Shayla moved closer and lowered her voice, though nobody was there but them. "I heard your bed squeaking last night, Nia. And I heard what you asked David in the hallway. So much sex flying around, you forgot which one you were with?" Shayla chuckled. "It takes a guy with huge balls to sneak in and do you while David is right downstairs."

Nia grabbed Shayla. "Shut up!" Enraged, she pushed her back against a cabinet. "You don't know what you're talking about."

Shayla stared at the knife in Nia's hand. Her eyes widened, then she glowered. "You'd actually cut me, Nia, over some dick?"

Nia caught herself. After a tense moment, she released Shayla.

Shayla jerked away. "I thought I knew you, but I guess I don't know you as well as I thought." She pulled the blanket back up on her shoulders. "You're full of surprises." She backed away from the knife that Nia still gripped in her hand. "Is that some street shit that tall guy taught you? I can tell he's rough, got some gangster in him."

"I'm sorry, Shayla, I didn't mean to—" Nia dropped the knife. "It's not what you think."

"What else could it be?" Shayla shrugged. "You've got your *cakes* and you're eating them too. I want to be just like you when I grow up."

Nia stiffened at her sarcasm. She exhaled and tried to collect her emotions. "Please, don't say anything to David."

"Friends don't snitch." She looked down at the sink full of oranges, her eyes tainted with jealousy. "They share."

Shayla stole one of the oranges from the sink. "Just don't slip up and blow it. Or things could get pretty ugly."

Shayla bounced the orange in her hand and walked out.

CHAPTER 31

Church services at Mercy and Grace Cathedral started at eight o'clock sharp on Sunday, but David and Nia were running late. David hated getting to church late, but Nia kept coming out of her bedroom dressed in clothes suited more for a nightclub than a church.

"What's wrong with this one?" Nia asked him for the fifth time.

"That dress is cut so low, it gives a whole new meaning to the hymn 'Swing Low, Sweet Chariot.'"

Nia huffed and tried on two more dresses that were equally as hoochie. Finally, David went next door and asked Jay to borrow one of his mother's shawls.

"For who, you?" Jay teased.

"Yeah, Jay, it'll go good with my suit." David added, "Blue, preferably."

He returned to Nia with a conservative oversized shawl

that matched her slinky blue party dress. He threw the shawl across her bare shoulders and said, "Perfect. Let's go," and they headed for church.

When the white-gloved usher led them to a seat, Nia whispered to the lady, "We'd like something in the back, please, close to the exit."

The usher ignored Nia's request and took them all the way up front, five rows from the altar. Nia, who was already very nervous about her first time attending church, took it personally. "I told her I wanted to sit in the back!"

David felt everyone looking at them. "Shh, it's okay. This is fine."

The usher extended her arm, opening her white-gloved hand to guide them into the pew. David tried to sit quietly, but Nia remained standing, opened her purse, and took out a five-dollar bill. She wadded it up and crammed it inside the usher's white glove, in front of everybody.

The usher frowned. "What's this?"

"A tip," Nia said. "Isn't that why you have your hand out?"

The usher gave Nia an agitated look and walked way. David tried to explain, lowering his voice, "You don't tip ushers at church."

"How was I supposed to know?" Nia turned around. "Hey, bring me my money back!"

David quieted her. "Shh! Let her keep it."

"But she had an attitude."

People turned in their seats to see what was going on. David tried to relax and calm Nia. He knew she was nervous. In fact, she'd been on edge ever since the night he'd proposed—the same night she ran and locked herself in the bathroom, thinking he'd made love to her. She refused to tell him exactly what had happened.

Regardless, David was happy she finally came to church with him, especially since he'd asked her to be his wife. If he was going to spend the rest of his life with this woman, he wanted to be able to share his faith with her.

News about their engagement had already spread fast to the church, courtesy of his secretary. People in the church lobby had congratulated them on the way in. David spotted Mrs. Wang sitting in a middle row. She waved, and he waved back. Mrs. Wang had taken a tremendous liking to Nia and had already appointed herself as their wedding planner.

David pointed to the nicely decorated altar. "Would you like to have our wedding ceremony here?"

"In a church?"

"Of course. Where else would we get married?"

"What's wrong with Disneyland?"

"Disneyland?" he asked, amazed. "For a wedding?"

"Yes, it's the happiest place on earth. Don't you want our wedding to be happy?"

David left that conversation for another time. After the church made announcements and the choir sang, the preacher took the podium. David asked the man seated in front of him, "Where's Pastor Kees? He was supposed to preach today."

"The pastor got called away on an emergency. This guy is filling in for him."

"Oh." David leaned back, chagrined. He'd called Pastor Kees the night before and told him he was bringing Nia. Since she'd never been to a church before, Pastor Kees promised David that he'd prepare a special easy-to-understand sermon about the basics of salvation, Christianity, God, and the devil. David had been looking forward to it, but now he was disappointed. This fill-in preacher was long-winded and his points were complicated at best.

David looked over at Nia. She kept shifting uncomfortably in the pew. He whispered, "What's wrong?"

"I feel like eyes are on the back of my head."

David turned slightly. A few people were staring at Nia, mostly men who were distracted from the sermon by Nia's unconventional beauty. David gave them a polite but firm nod, letting them know that she was with him and they should probably look elsewhere, like at the preacher.

He pulled the shawl a little farther up her shoulders. "No one's watching you. Relax."

After the sermon, the preacher gave the altar call. Nia leaned toward David. "Why is he making people come up there?"

"For special prayer requests."

Nia frowned. "But isn't God everywhere? Can't he hear them if they stay in their seats and pray?"

"Well, yeah, but—I'll try to explain it better later." He touched her hand. "Do you want to go up there?"

"Heck no!" Nia jerked her hand back. "I don't want all these folks listening to what I have to say to God. That's *personal*."

David hoped that after a few more church visits, she'd start to catch on. Given the circumstances, Nia's first visit to church was going reasonably well—until he spotted a tall, model-thin woman with long, black, silky hair doing a pony-like strut up to the altar.

As the woman passed their pew, she paused slightly and eyed the engagement ring on Nia's finger. She blew an air kiss at David. David was so stunned his mouth fell open.

❧ CHAPTER 32 ❧

"Is that—Ch-Ch—" Nia stuttered from shock as David's ex-girlfriend blew him a kiss and continued to the altar. "Is that *Cher-Ling*?"

Nia recognized her from a picture she'd found in the love letters David still kept in his nightstand. David's astounded expression confirmed it was her.

Cher-Ling strutted up to the altar like she was on a runway in a New York fashion show. She stopped, turned, and flung her long, silky hair across her shoulder, completing her turn on the catwalk. She wore an outfit straight off the pages of *Vogue*, a gold glittery number usually reserved for celebrities on red carpets—something Nia would never wear in a million years, not even for Halloween. Nia felt plain and dumpy, smothered by the big ugly shawl that David had made her wear.

Cher-Ling whispered something to the fill-in preacher. He stopped the organ music and spoke into the mike. "We have a special prayer request by this lovely young lady who's been away for a while. She says she's had a lot of time to think and reflect back over her life, and she has something she'd like to share with the church."

Nia raised her eyebrow. David stiffened in his seat. Cher-Ling swung her long hair behind her narrow shoulders with a dramatic flair and took the mike.

"Yes, um, greetings, everyone," she purred in a super-sugary, fake voice. "As some of you may remember from last year when I visited here, I'm David Wrightwood's girlfriend."

"Ha!" The exclamation escaped Nia's mouth without warning. Several people turned and looked in her direction. David touched her arm to quiet her.

His ex-girlfriend continued, "Things didn't turn out the way we'd hoped, and I had to go away on my, uh, sabbatical. But now I'm back, and I'd like to tell him publicly that I missed him and I know how much he's missed me, too."

Cher-Ling batted her lashes at David. Nia bit her lip and glared at Cher-Ling as she continued. "No matter what happened between us, David, that caused us to split up, I forgive you, and I'm looking forward to us getting back together."

Nia blurted out, "Back together, my ass!"

The church people gasped.

David said, "Nia, calm down."

Cher-Ling pretended to ignore Nia. "I'd like to ask the entire church to pray for us to get back together."

"Stop! Nobody pray!" Nia stood up, her eyes glaring. "That floozy wasn't away on *sabbatical,* she's a jailbird! David didn't miss her and they're not getting back together. She's lying. Where's the lightning?" Nia looked up at the vaulted ceiling.

"This is a private matter between David and me," Cher-Ling sneered at Nia. "You shut up! You home-wrecker!"

Nia snatched the shawl from her shoulders and gripped

it like a noose. She left the pew and headed toward Cher-Ling. David tried to grab her, but she slipped away from him. The white-gloved usher tried to block Nia, but Nia put a move on her and faked her out.

Once Nia was in the aisle, two more ushers came at her. Like she was playing backyard football, she outmaneuvered them. David was on her heels, but Nia zeroed in on the goal line: Cher-Ling.

She came nose-to-nose with David's psycho panty-model ex-girlfriend, in all of her pompous glory. "What did you just say to me?"

Cher-Ling put her skinny little hand on her skinny little hip and gave Nia attitude. "I said, shut up, you raggedy little ragamuffin." She pushed Nia's forehead.

Infuriated, Nia picked up one of the lovely white orchid floral arrangements and banged it over Cher-Ling's head. David tried to grab the flowers, but Nia wouldn't stop swinging until all the petals flew off the orchids.

Cher-Ling grabbed for Nia's dress but got a mouth full of flowers instead. She squealed, spitting out white petals, "David is mine, you little thief!" She lunged at Nia, grabbing her at her waist.

"You want prayer? Here, I'll give you some prayer!" Nia pushed Cher-Ling headfirst into the altar.

Chaos erupted and a nasty scuffle ensued as David and several deacons pulled the two women apart.

❧ CHAPTER 33 ❧

*A*fter the melee, Pastor Kees called David and Nia into his office. He'd returned from what had turned out to be a fake emergency call, only to find his church in an uproar, and David's new fiancée was at the center of it. David pulled his vinyl chair next to Nia's chair and sat.

Pastor Kees smiled pleasantly at David. "So . . . this is your fiancée?"

David hung his head, too embarrassed to look his friend in the eye. "Pastor Kees, meet Nia. Nia, Pastor Kees."

They shook hands.

Nia quipped to the pastor, "She started it."

"Who started what?"

"David's ex-girlfriend picked a fight with me by saying she and David were getting back together."

"Is it true?"

Nia frowned. "Of course not."

"Then why do you let a lie upset you so much?"

Nia had to stop and think about it. She straightened the blue shawl on her shoulders. "Guess I never looked at it that way. I apologize for behaving badly in your church."

Pastor Kees turned to David, but before he could say anything, David tried to defend himself. "I had no idea Cher-Ling had been released from jail or that she'd show up this morning. Had I known, I would not have brought Nia here today."

Pastor Kees poured ice water from a pitcher into two glasses. "That's not what concerns me."

"It's not?"

"No. I'd like to know why your fiancée feels so insecure about her relationship with you that she felt she needed to beat your ex-girlfriend with flowers."

David took the water, frowning. "You say that almost like it's my fault Nia jumped on Cher-Ling."

Accusation filled Pastor Kees's eyes. Nia looked accusingly at David, too.

"Hey, hold on. Nia knows I love her. She knows I'm faithful to her. Go ahead, Nia, tell him." David nudged Nia's knee, but she didn't affirm it.

After a second, she confided in Pastor Kees. "I think David went to visit her in jail, but he won't admit it."

"I don't bring it up because it's a sore point with her," he said wearily.

"Why would he go visit her when he knows I didn't want him to?"

David cleared his throat. "Translation: Nia has insecurity issues. Her last boyfriend cheated on her."

"Men don't feel things as deeply as women, and sometimes they lie about what they really feel."

Pastor Kees frowned at Nia's last comment. David used the

opportunity to reiterate his point. "Nia has a hard time trusting and believing in love. She struggles with the concept of faith."

"David is stubborn."

Pastor Kees opened his appointment book. "What day should I schedule you two lovebirds for premarital counseling?" He looked up at Nia. "And possibly anger-management classes?"

"Tuesday." David sipped his water.

"Friday." Nia gulped hers.

"In the meantime, until we can settle on a day, would you mind if I say a prayer for you two?"

"Definitely not," David said, getting in the last word. "We need it."

He looked at Nia. She sneered at him, then shifted again in her chair, looking extremely unsettled.

She tugged at the shawl uncomfortably, wiped her damp neck, and gulped down more water nervously.

David locked hands with his fiancée as they bowed their heads and closed their eyes. "Okay, we're ready."

Pastor Kees started praying. "Dear Heavenly Father, we ask that you bless this couple and unite them in Your heavenly love as You help them find their way . . ."

Nia's grip on David's hand tightened, almost cutting off circulation to his fingers. He lifted his head and peeked at her. The blue shawl had fallen off her shoulders, and she was gripping the side of her chair with her other hand.

Pastor Kees continued, "We ask that You set them on the right path to happiness and holiness . . ."

Nia's chair started to rumble and vibrate. David tried to catch her eye without interrupting the prayer. He mouthed, "What's going on?"

Nia shrugged innocently and kept a tight grip on his hand and the chair.

Pastor Kees continued, his head still bowed, "We ask that You allow no one and nothing to separate them . . ."

Nia's chair lifted two inches off the floor.

Seeing it, David exclaimed, "Holy—!"

Pastor Kees continued praying. "Yes, Lord. *Holy* is Your Name . . ."

David heard a low, vicious growl come from Nia's direction. Pastor Kees heard it, too. He ended the prayer with a quick, "Amen!"

David frowned at Nia. "What the heck was that?"

"I don't know. I didn't do it," Nia said defensively as both men stared at her.

David sniffed. "Something's burning."

Nia's eyes widened.

Pastor Kees inhaled. "I smell it, too. It smells like burning plastic."

Noticing a waft of smoke, David leaned over and looked at the back of Nia's chair. The vinyl was smoldering.

"Nia, you're melting the chair!"

Nia's hot exposed skin was melting the vinyl, turning it into a gooey mess.

Pastor Kees jumped up. "Good mercy! Should I call a doctor or the fire department?"

David grabbed a church fan and started fanning her frantically. His eyes widened with concern. "Nia, are you okay?"

Nia picked up the entire pitcher of ice water and gulped it down, spilling water all over the low cleavage of her dress. Steam rose off her dress.

"I'm leaving." She handed the blue shawl to David. "I told you I wouldn't fit in."

David got up and started after her. "Wait. You're riding with me."

"I'll catch a cab home. I wouldn't want to spook you any-more today," she said sadly, then left the office.

Pastor Kees raised his hands, confounded. "Hey, would someone please tell me what's going on here?"

David shot him an exasperated look. "It's a long story. For now, just send me the bill for the chair and the orchids." He hurried out the door.

CHAPTER 34

*R*ephaim had a cab waiting curbside for Nia as she rushed out of the church. In his invisible form, he came to her side but remained deathly quiet, allowing her to think she was all alone. They left the holy place together.

Rephaim stretched his arms and straightened his tie, glad to be away from the claustrophobic quarters. Thanks to the fill-in pastor's negligence, Rephaim had gained a temporary foothold inside the church. Instead of praying for sanctification before he began the service, the prideful substitute preacher had spent idle time in Pastor Kees's office, entertaining thoughts of envy and lust, allowing a dark entity like himself to ride in and settle in the corners of the church and lay in wait to wreak havoc.

Rephaim had crouched low and hidden his shadowy, diaphanous body behind Nia's chair. Like a guard dog protecting his property, he tried to fend off the holy man's prayers with a low, vicious growl. When that didn't work, he used supernatural trickery to raise Nia's body temperature to an inordinate degree, until her skin melted the chair. Such a cunning ploy created an effective distraction and gave Nia a reason to leave.

Nia paused, thinking it odd that a cab should to be waiting at that precise moment. Yet, in her haste, she hopped in. Rephaim, as invisible and shifting as the wind, slipped into the backseat next to Nia.

"To Northridge, please," Nia said, and closed the cab's door just as David rushed out of the church, but he was too late to catch her.

The taxi driver knew nothing of Rephaim or why his cab had stalled directly in front of the church. He was content that his engine started again and he had a passenger's fare.

Nothing had been a coincidence. Not the taxi. Not Cher-Ling's arrival or antics. Not even Pastor Kee's false emergency call away or the fill-in preacher.

Rephaim took great pride in the careful planning and manipulation of events that surrounded Nia.

But he hadn't foreseen David Wrightwood's entrance into her life.

Nia mumbled to herself, "I told him I wouldn't fit in."

Rephaim moved closer and watched Nia's beautiful brown eyes begin to fill with tears. He whispered, in subsonic waves, *No, Nia, you don't fit in,* confirming her negative thoughts and doubts.

She didn't fit in, not in this world.

And certainly not in David Wrightwood's world. David was a man of faith. Rephaim had groomed Nia not to believe in anything, certainly not in love.

In David's world, she could never be happy. And he could never satisfy her, not the way Rephaim could.

Nia knew he was near. He could tell by the way the muscles in her shapely legs contracted and the heat bumps on her neck arose.

Rephaim leaned forward and let his warm breath caress her cheek. Nia touched her face.

She pretended to look out the window and watch the other cars while she tried to ignore the tingle in her innermost parts and the heat that was growing there.

The ring David had placed on her finger drew his eye.

The clear diamond glittered. Its crystalline rays cast sharp daggers of light into his displeased gaze.

Rephaim despised the sharp twinge of jealousy he felt pierce his chest at that moment. Such a feeble emotion was unfitting for a demon lord of his high standing. Ruthlessness was his guiding force and evil his catalyst. All other emotions were frivolity.

Rephaim moved closer to Nia, slightly depressing the cushioned seat next to her. She felt his presence.

He focused his thoughts on her.

You belong to me, Nia.

His palpable desire served as his only form of communication.

She heard him.

He smiled.

As for David Wrightwood, he'd deal with the man who dared engage himself to Nia Youngblood. Rephaim would take him out, in a way that only he could. After all, the art of possession was only one of his many dark hobbies.

❧ CHAPTER 35 ❧

*D*avid couldn't get ahold of Nia all afternoon. He knew she was stewing about Cher-Ling's appearance at church, even though he'd had nothing to do with it. Finally, he decided to go to her house and talk to her. The longer she dwelled on the incident, the worse it would get.

When he pulled into the driveway, her house was dark, but her car was parked outside.

When he saw the front door was half open, he pushed it and walked in. "Nia?"

There was no sound, movement, or any sign of life inside her house. He flicked on the light switch in the atrium, but it didn't work.

"Nia?"

He looked up the dark staircase toward her bedroom and slowly stepped into Nia's living room. None of the light switches worked. He noticed a strange syrupy smell and wrinkled his nose, wondering if she'd cooked pancakes.

"Nia, are you here?"

Just when he thought the house was empty, he heard a noise at the wet bar and went to investigate. An eerie, faint purple light pervaded the entire house, and its shifting magenta rays had no apparent source as they cut through the darkness.

David stood by the bar and tried to find his bearings, but things seemed out of whack. He thought he saw a shadow slowly rising behind the bar, but when he blinked, it left.

A bottle toppled off the shelf and smashed. Broken glass and red wine spurted out at him, staining his white shirt with crimson.

"Damn!" David jumped back and looked around but didn't see anyone in the room.

The purplish strobe made his white shirt glow, and the dark red wine stain looked like blood. A drop had splashed onto his lip. He tasted it; it was acrid and sweet.

David heard another noise in the next room. When he walked into the dining room, at first glance, it appeared empty. Then a shadow arose at the opposite end of the long table.

A sepulchral voice was emitted by the shadow. "Have a seat."

David squinted, wondering if Nia was playing one of her pranks.

"No thanks. I already ate." His thin voice bounced off the dark walls, echoing back at him.

Like a gracious host, the shadow extended its arm, and the chair closest to David slowly slid back by itself.

Hairs arose on David's forearms.

What the hell is going on? he wondered. He pushed the chair back into place, feeling for invisible wires. He looked again at the host.

"Nice trick," he said, unsure who he was talking to.

A centerpiece sat in the middle of the long table. It was about three feet high and made from some type of shiny brass, narrow at the top, flared at the bottom, but he couldn't make out what it was. He'd never seen it there before, and the table seemed much longer than he remembered.

"Where's Nia?"

"She's with me," the deep voice responded.

The crease in David's forehead deepened, and the acidic aftertaste from the drop of wine burned his tongue and pricked his nerves as realization settled over him.

"You hurt her, your ass is mine," David warned him.

"Why would I hurt something that already belongs to me?" His voice was disguised with some kind of vibrating bass effect, and the trick with the lights made it impossible for David to identify him.

"You coward."

"Are you scared?"

A tougher edge entered David's voice. "Bullies don't scare me, they just make me mad."

"Fear is the first sign of respect."

"Who are you?"

"Someone to be both feared and respected."

The shadow rushed at David suddenly, moving so fast that David almost didn't see him coming. David dove to his right, feeling a hot rush of air as the man swooped over him.

The force of his momentum knocked over the centerpiece and it rolled down the table in his direction. David grabbed the statue by its narrow top and swung its flared brass base at the man's head but missed. The man was too fast. David had barely swung it a second time before the man knocked him against the wall.

The statue dropped from his hand.

The dark form rushed at him again, this time knocking him backward onto the table. David tried to rise quickly, but something like a heavy pressing force kept him pinned down on the table.

David put all of his strength into trying to get up, but he couldn't punch or grab what was pinning him down. Blood rushed to his head. His fists tightened. He tried to calm himself so he'd know where to swing in the maroon light.

The man's face blocked out the ceiling as his shadowy body hovered over David like a heavy thundercloud, eclipsing all light. The man's face appeared as dark as iniquity.

His deep, angry voice rumbled loud in David's eardrums, threatening to flood his mind with debilitating fear.

"Call me *lord.*"

David exploded in defiance. "Get off me!"

With a mighty heave, he pushed the dark figure off, then jumped to his feet and reached for the brass statue. He swung it hard enough to break the man's skull, but the man moved with the quickness of lightning, ducking the blow.

He knocked David backward.

Quick on his feet, David recovered and stayed upright in fighting position.

The man threw a blunt, forceful punch that carried the strength of several heavyweights and rattled David's body. David took the blow to his stomach, but he felt it all the way down to his toes. It hurt like hell and he rocked back, trying to offset the impact.

David's back hit the wall. He threw up his guard and tried to block, like Ali against the ropes, but another blow straightened him up. Yet another strike carried a lasting force that pinned his arms back against the wall.

The man struck him again, this time with a swipe of

something razor sharp that sliced open the front of David's wine-stained shirt. With his chest bared and breathing hard, David tried to free himself but invisible nails fastened him to the wall.

A sound like thunder pierced the darkness as the phantom rushed at him, throwing himself into David's chest with the thrust of a freight train.

"Uhn!" The impact knocked the wind out of him.

His vision failed, the room seemed to spin, and dark magenta rays crisscrossed. The table bounced in and out of focus as dizziness rocked David's head. He tried to shake it off and stay focused.

The man appeared again in the center of David's foggy vision. David sneered. "You bastard."

The man moved like a lion in a stalking motion. Powerful, quick, and agile with predatory instinct, he circled David like prey that was still standing while planning his next strike.

"You *will* bow."

David followed the deep vibrating voice with his eyes. Before he could refocus, the man leapt at him again, attacking David with a savagery reserved for beasts. He delivered another hard blow to David's midsection.

David's chest tightened and his rib cage contracted, squeezing around his heart like a protective cage.

In that second, David couldn't think straight. His mind became a jumbled maze with no clear path out. David squeezed his eyes closed. Wetness dampened his lids. He silently and desperately scolded himself. *Stay focused!*

He snapped open his eyes.

"You dirty bastard."

"Let me in!" The shadow rammed into David again, the force powerful enough to penetrate David's very soul. He felt the wall behind his back crack amid the thunder, and every cell in his body compressed and resisted. Darkness threatened to close up his throat.

To survive, he had to retreat into an inner sacred place where his thoughts scrambled as he struggled to hold on to everything dear to him: his faith; his love; his little sister, Beez; his future wife, Nia.

His thoughts then turned to whatever threatened to strip those precious things away from him.

A bully.

The enemy of his soul.

David gritted his teeth. With every measure of faith he had, he prayed.

This time when the thing barreled at him, David hunkered down. Coming back around mentally, he grunted and heaved. "Uhhnnn!"

He hurled himself from the wall, and with renewed strength, he charged at the shadow.

Like they were two gladiators, their collision shook the atmosphere.

The air grew charged, like in an electrical storm. Two mighty forces clashed and collided, ramming into each other with a sound like a clap of thunder.

Their jarring forces rebounded and bounced off each other.

David again flew back into the wall, but this time, the deafening noise ceased, the magenta rays slackened and dissipated, and the room stopped spinning.

David breathed.

His white shirt hung off his broad shoulders like a tattered, bloodstained rag. Fog continued to huddle around his mind, but he knew he was safe now.

But Nia wasn't.

Haze clouded his vision as he focused on the statue lying on the floor. It was a mini brass replica of Nia in a wedding dress and veil. He knew she was in trouble because her voice seemed to emanate from the statue. Fear gripped his heart as the statue called to him, *"David..."*

ᥬ CHAPTER 36 ᥫ

*T*he moment Nia clicked on the light switch and saw David crouched in the dark, staring at something on the floor, she knew.

"David?"

She rushed to him. Exertion, exhaustion, and fleeting fear covered his face. For a second, he wouldn't look at her. He kept his eyes pinned on the floor.

"David!" she yelled, scared that he wasn't alright.

"Where did it go?"

"What?"

"The statue." Dazed, his eyes slowly rose to her face. "You."

"David, I don't understand. Are you okay? Please tell me you're okay." She saw his shirt slit open, and for a horrible second, she thought the red stains were his blood. But his chest was smooth and dry, except for small beads of perspiration, and the strong, sweet smell of fermented grape indicated the stains were from wine.

He clutched her arms. "Did he hurt you?"

She wanted to ask, "Who?" but she knew.

Slowly, she shook her head.

David forced himself to his feet, despite his obvious pain. She tried to help brace him but he winced and pushed her back.

"Why didn't you come?" he asked her, squinting at the fluffy white towel she had wrapped around her body and her skin, which was still slightly damp with milky water from her bath. She immediately felt guilty, looking at his slightly swollen face and the bruises just beginning to develop on his chest and arms, knowing they were only small indications of the internal trauma he must have suffered as she bathed upstairs by candlelight.

"I'm sorry, David. I didn't hear anything."

She cursed herself for wearing headphones while soaking in the tub.

Unsteady, David moved toward the man-sized crack in the wall, cringing slightly. His body was rigid, his face taut. "You didn't *hear* anything?"

Nia came forward, trying to explain. "David, I—"

She reached out for his arm but he recoiled from her touch.

That small reaction from him sent shock waves of hurt through her.

David backed up. He found his car keys deep inside his pocket, pulled them out, and clutched them in his hand.

"I need some space right now."

He turned and headed out her front door. Night had fallen.

REPHAIM SPIT VENOM as he watched David Wrightwood leave. Once the man was out of his sight, he stalked across Nia's roof and slammed his fist into the chimney. Several bricks broke loose and crashed to the ground, exploding on Nia's walkway. One angry stomp and he could have caved in half of her house, yet he'd failed to possess David Wrightwood.

Rephaim tried to compose himself. He had to wield his power in a way befitting a dark lord, because he knew someone was on the roof with him, watching him.

"Woman, why are you here?" He'd seen Mysti spying through a window earlier, trying to see how he'd handle the man who challenged him for Nia.

Mysti sauntered nearer to him, but he kept his back toward her. "I have a vested interest in all of this," she said silkily.

"Your interests have ceased." He turned around. "You have no more business here."

Mysti was a unique specimen of a woman, the human embodiment of ambition and fearless thirst for power. Rephaim stood on the edge of the roof and remained in his darkest form, a faint black outline to the regular human eye. But Mysti's eyes had been trained in darkness. She had immersed herself into his world in her early youth, embracing the ominous pleasures and pains it had to offer.

Mysti's natural innocence had been stolen from her. Dangerous curiosity replaced purity, and ambition overruled her inhibitions. She had worked her way up the ranks of human deviltry and made a deal with the demon lord himself, Rephaim.

"You've been adequately compensated," he said, noticing her wanton stare.

"I want more."

At one time in their past, her blind ambition was beauty to his eyes. A young female hellion was a lovely sight for a male demon lord.

She saw the scrutiny in his eyes. "That's how you looked at me once, not long ago."

"Not all history is worth repeating," he said, and broke his stare.

She walked closer to him, purposely filling his vision. "You never touched me again, at least not the way I wanted you to."

"And you never stopped hating me for it."

"And I never will." Mysti gazed out over Nia's dark backyard, longing in her eyes. "But my hate has never bothered you."

"Why should it?"

She opened her fingers and let the wind flow between them. "You only wanted to use my womb and take the fruit from it. You figured my unholy blood mixed with the Young-bloods' holy seed would give you an edge, a better chance of winning Nia over."

His expression remained stark. "You knew my plans before you agreed."

"But I didn't know all of your plans."

"You still don't. You never will."

"I know that your attempt to take over David Wrightwood failed," she said, smiling sardonically. "I know that whatever was inside of him was stronger than you. You can't control David the way you take over and control Malcolm."

Mysti took pleasure in throwing failure in his face, but Rephaim remained confident, undaunted. He muttered, "There are other ways."

Mysti persisted, probing. "I know that you're planning to take Nia as your bride very soon, but David Wrightwood has blocked you. I also know that you're running out of time." Her smile turned shrewd. "Nia's true birthday is coming. You're not the only one who knows the date. I was there, remember?"

He studied Mysti. Her ambition had driven her to research his dark plans, and in her conniving, she sought his secrets, flaunting what she'd already discovered.

"Twenty-five years. That's how long you had to persuade

her to be your wife. You were so sure of yourself, you waited all this time to take her as your human prize. Making Nia your bride now will bring you even more power. You'll both take up thrones and rule an even larger kingdom."

"You've been studious. Casting powerful spells over weak mortal men hasn't been enough to keep you entertained."

"Dedicating my child to you has brought you high standing in the underworld, but now, if you marry her, you'll go from being a prince to being a king. Nia would be a young queen. That's a lot of power for one ordinary woman to possess— much more than what you gave me." She ran the white tips of her short fingernails along her forearm. "Without my contribution, none of this would be possible."

"You've been adequately compensated. You accepted the dark gifts I granted to you."

"That was before I realized how much both you and Nia stood to gain."

He cut his eyes away from her to end the conversation. "That part doesn't concern you."

"It does now." Mysti refused to be swayed. "Your brilliant plot seemed foolproof, but now things have gone awry."

"I *will* have her."

"Not without my help."

"You fool yourself if you think I need your help," he thundered. "Have you forgotten how much more powerful I am than you? You are privileged even to stand in my presence right now."

"I have influence over Nia. After all, I am her mother." Mysti smiled devilishly.

"Stay out of this, Mystical. Your biological ties hold no merit. Nia detests the very ground you strut on." Rephaim smiled back at her, his smile just as sexy and malicious.

He sat down on the apex of the roof and placed his large feet on the steep incline.

"Nia Youngblood is stubborn, passionate, independent, and very much her own woman. Her rebellious nature, inherited from you, is the very thing I've counted on all these years to win her over. Her strong will is my inroad and her downfall."

"But Nia has begun to put her faith in David Wrightwood and the god he serves, a force you can't control," she pointed out.

"No. Nia's faith is still up for grabs, and this story is still far from over. The ending will not be without its own surprises."

"You're as cocky as you are evil. I've always *lusted* that in you." Mysti smiled with fervent disdain in her eyes. She dug her spiked heels into the sharply sloping tile roof and stood with her back to the sky.

Rephaim remained seated, looking up at Mysti's beautifully endowed body and her lovely, icy face. He wondered if screwing her for one long blood-curdling hour would help ease a bit of his tension.

Her greedy green eyes reflected back a portion of his lust. "You've deprived me once. As mother of the bride, I won't be deprived twice."

Mysti's eyes flashed dark jade as she hooked her fingers around the wind, grabbed its energy, and quickly converted it into a series of sharp jade-colored daggers aimed directly at Rephaim. The jagged daggers sliced through the wind and pierced his head and body. He threw his arm up, diverting several, but many more hit him and sent supernatural shock waves through his body. Each one was sharp enough to weaken a normal man, render him helpless and send him to his knees begging for mercy in the face of a powerful Wiccan pythoness like Mysti.

Rephaim doubled over. The force and suddenness of Mysti's attack caught even him, a dark demon lord, by surprise.

She came closer, her chest heaving, her heels piercing the tile, and her fingers still clenched and glowing with energy borrowed from Mother Nature. Rephaim could almost hear the edges of her lips curl into a slight grin as she attacked him, the one who had initiated her into true power. Such ruthlessness was intoxicating, even for an accomplished witch.

Rephaim allowed Mysti a few seconds of her bout of treachery before he rose up, even taller than before, and unleashed his anger like a tornado. He lunged at her. His powerful left hand gripped her neck, clutching her carotid artery.

The force threw them off the roof.

Rephaim slammed Nia's mother down on the ground. Her back flattened a patch of grass on Nia's front lawn, instantly killing it. He lay on top of her, his unmitigated force pressing into her, making it impossible for her to breathe.

"Did you think that because I didn't get into David Wrightwood tonight that I was weak?" He kept his hand pressed into her upper neck. His strong fingers were like blunt claws against her skin. He could feel Mysti's blood struggling to pulsate through her vein, throbbing beneath his hand.

He whispered into her lovely, cold face, "Did you forget who gave you your powers?"

Naked fear filled her eyes.

At last, he eased his grip, allowed her blood to resume flowing.

Mysti let out a wispy groan. Her whole body shivered and twitched, like tiny spasms in the aftermath of powerful sex. Rephaim kept his body on top of hers, cast-iron hard and potent, allowing her to feel a small portion of what sex with a powerful dark entity like him had been like.

Dangerous.

Soul splitting.

He warned her, "You don't want to become my enemy, Mystical. You don't really want to fuck with me."

Mysti bit down on her lip, biting back fear, rejection, and dashed hopes. Her voice was strained but charged with fury. "Kill me or get off."

Rephaim let out a dry chuckle but didn't release all of the pressure from her neck, not yet. "When I chose the mother of my future bride, I chose correctly."

Mysti matched his stare in silent defiance.

"Your ruthlessly wicked qualities will serve Nia well in the next world as my queen," he said, rubbing Nia's future power in Mysti's face.

Mysti didn't bat an eyelash.

He added, "But Nia has something you'll never have." He kneeled down, bringing his face close to hers. He licked her lips with his hot tongue. "My attention."

When he finally released Mysti from his clutches, she jerked away.

Rephaim stood up slowly, his towering form, his physique, and his powerful countenance absent of all light. Mysti knew exactly how he looked when he assumed the form of a regular man, and that vision contributed to her lust for him.

"Leave my sight." His deep voice reverberated in the night.

Rephaim watched Mysti back away from him. With gall, she turned and walked away on one broken heel, the determined sway never leaving her seductive hips, while she murmured obscenities.

He thought about something else Nia had that Mysti did not. Purity.

Nia needed to remain a virgin until he took her as his wife, or else the black ceremony he'd planned would be ineffective. But Rephaim wanted Nia to remain a virgin for selfish reasons, also. For another man to touch his future bride would be unspeakable. To erase that possibility, he needed to eliminate David Wrightwood from Nia's life, one way or the other.

CHAPTER 37

*W*hen David woke up Monday morning in his condo, he immediately ran upstairs to check on Nia, forgetting that he'd left her at her house. He regretted his decision, but in that moment, after battling the malevolent shadow in her dining room, he was angry. Letting his temper get the best of him, he'd taken out his frustration on Nia. How could she *not* have heard?

The fight was loud as a freight train. He'd been brutally rammed and practically crushed through a wall while battling for his life, all while Nia soaked in a milk bath upstairs.

Ah, man! David thought as he punched the couch where he'd fallen last night, nearly passed out, too exhausted to climb the stairs to his bedroom. His body still ached, but he'd be okay. Professional sports training camp had taught him to work through his pain and force his body to function even when it wanted to quit.

He worried about Nia. He grabbed his phone and called her. When she answered on the first ring, his panic eased. "Baby? Are you okay? I'm sorry—"

"It's okay. I understand." Her voice was sleepy and a bit sad, but she sounded like she was alright.

They talked for a bit. Both avoided the obvious issue, like the elephant in the room, only theirs was a svelte, stealthy, mean son-of-a-bitch shadow. After he promised he'd take off early from work and come see her, they hung up. He showered, dressed, skipped breakfast, and left for work.

Two hours after arriving at the office, Mrs. Wang buzzed him with a call. He'd spent the first hour bent over his desk just trying to get his head right, not taking any calls. Now he felt better; he just had a whole lot of unanswered questions.

"Who is it?" he asked.

Mrs. Wang whispered, "It's your crazy ex-girlfriend. I disconnected her three times and told her she deserved every whack Nia gave her with the orchids, but she keeps calling back."

After the church incident, he hadn't heard from Cher-Ling, and he was glad.

"Go ahead and put her through. I'll handle it." Mrs. Wang reluctantly put the call through. He took a moment before he answered. "Why are you calling me?"

Cher-Ling huffed. "Why are you being so cruel to me, David?"

"After that stunt you pulled at church, I'm considering rein-stating the restraining order. Bye." He started hanging up.

"Wait." Cher-Ling did her usual dramatic pause for effect. "I'm sorry."

He exhaled, still annoyed. "You need to apologize to Nia."

"Who?"

"Don't play dumb with me. Nia Youngblood, my *fiancée*. You know, the woman I told you about. I even showed you her picture when I visited you in jail."

Cher-Ling let out a disbelieving grunt.

He continued, "I explained to you that I've moved on, that I'm in love with Nia, and that I'm going to marry her. I also told you that you have an addiction—"

"A disorder."

"—and that you need to get help."

"I don't need help. I need you."

"What you need is a doctor's updated diagnosis and a new prescription. You've gotten worse."

"You said you'd help me." Tearful, Cher-Ling whined. "David, please. You promised."

He switched the phone to his other ear, wanting to hang up, but she'd hit his weak spot. Helping people in distress, especially women, had become his compulsion, a way to try to ease his own inner turmoil. She knew that and used it against him.

"First, admit that you have a problem and that you need to get help," he said.

"I have. I do."

He hesitated, then brought up his list of contacts on his computer. "Here's the number of my friend's office. She's a psychiatrist. I'm looking at her online schedule now. She has an opening in about an hour. Call and get that appointment."

"I can't."

"Why not?"

"I don't have a car."

"Catch the bus."

"I can't."

"Why not?"

"It's public transportation. My designer shoes will get dirty. I need you to take me."

"No. Get there on your own."

"If you won't take me, I won't go."

"Don't play games with me, Cher-Ling. I'm really not in the mood."

"I'm not playing games. You said you'd help me, David. You promised."

David sighed. He knew he'd put himself in a bad situation, but the sooner Cher-Ling got help with her bipolar disorder, the sooner she'd get on with her life and leave him and Nia alone.

"I'll take you to your first appointment only. After that, you take the bus. Be ready in twenty minutes." He jotted down the address where she'd been staying since her release and hung up.

He rushed to take Cher-Ling to her appointment, drove east on Wilshire Boulevard past the office buildings, then turned south on Figueroa Street, past the Staples Center, and drove into a residential area. He double-checked the address and pulled up in front of the town house. He got out of the car and pushed the doorbell.

Cher-Ling opened the door dressed in a revealing outfit, a cross between a nightgown and a stripper's work clothes.

"Oh, David. What a surprise!" Cher-Ling played coy. "I'm not quite ready but come in and get comfortable while I find something to wear."

David looked at her gown, then at his watch. "I'll be in my car. If you're not out in two minutes, I'm leaving."

"But, David—"

"One minute, fifty-five seconds." David walked back to his car.

A few minutes later, Cher-Ling came out, overdressed. She wore a dramatic saffron miniskirt and matching blazer with a hat and scarf, all with designer embroidered logos. She strutted to his car as if it were her chariot waiting.

David rolled his eyes and ignored her theatrics. He held

the door open for her, wondering how he'd ever gotten involved with her in the first place. He watched her slip her attractive model figure and smooth, long legs inside his car. He closed the door and blamed his mistake on normal male libido.

DAVID WAS LATE getting to Nia's house. He'd told her he'd see her at noon, but it was after two o'clock. Fooling with Cher-Ling and her problems had made him late.

As he pulled into her driveway, Nia was on her front porch, ripping up a piece of red paper and complaining loudly. Several teens gathered around her, and they too looked upset. He hopped out quickly.

"What's going on?" he asked, walking up to the porch.

"This!" Nia stuffed the paper shards into his hands.

"I can't read this."

"It's a notice from the city," Jay explained. "They're going to close us down."

David looked at Nia for clarification. She ran her hand through her waves, trying to collect herself.

"The city of Los Angeles says I'm in violation of several city ordinances and fire codes and that I'm 'contributing to the illegal congregation of minors.'"

Her voice cracked as she bit back her anger.

"They've given me fourteen days to cease and desist. If I don't, they'll send out the sheriff to arrest me."

David felt his own anger surfacing. He calmly told the kids to go into the backyard so he could speak to Nia privately. All the teens left, except Jay.

"I know who snitched on Nia," Jay confessed.

Nia's face lit with curiosity. "Who?"

"My mother." Jay gazed down at the porch, overcome with guilt and embarrassment.

"But why?" Nia asked, baffled.

"Don't know." Jay kicked his sneaker into a potted plant. "She just don't like you, Miss Nia."

"What did I ever do to her?" Nia's ire rose again.

David stepped in. "Okay, Jay. Thanks for telling us. We'll handle things from here." Not wanting to put Jay in the middle of it, he sent Jay into the backyard with the other kids.

Unlike Jay and his father, Claudia Wells was an unfriendly woman who never bothered to speak first. It was obvious from her body language that she didn't like the way Buddy watched out for Nia, sometimes standing guard over her house at night. The fact that her young son had an enormous crush on Nia didn't help. David knew jealousy was the reason Claudia had complained to the city about Nia's home-based youth center.

After Jay left, he turned to Nia. "Let's go over there and calmly talk to Jay's parents to try to work something out. Maybe if we can persuade her to retract her complaint, the city will leave you alone. Most problems can be solved by simply talking," he said, feeling like a hypocrite. He didn't want to talk to the Shadow Man. He wanted to kick his ass.

Nia didn't want to go. He had to nudge her.

In his haste to get out of the car, he realized he'd left his keys in the ignition. "Hold on, I left my keys," he told her.

"No, I'll get them. You go on ahead of me."

"You're stalling."

She headed toward his car.

David rang the doorbell and talked to Buddy about the situation. Buddy agreed with David and asked Claudia, who was in the kitchen baking something stinky, to come out and meet with Nia. Claudia entered and spoke curtly to David, carrying a pan of whatever she'd been cooking. With a fake smile, she offered one to David. Small, round, and lumpy, they were too dark to be oatmeal cookies.

"Thanks." He held it and sat on the plastic-covered couch, trying to make small talk while waiting for Nia. "Nia is looking forward to talking with you and reaching a resolution," he lied.

When Nia finally walked in, she wasn't smiling and wasn't even trying to fake politeness. She spoke curtly to Buddy and Claudia, then sat on the stiff reupholstered couch next to David. David took one look at her perturbed expression and he knew things were about to go downhill.

When Claudia saw Nia, she grew stone-faced and didn't offer Nia anything. Instead, she pulled the tray just out of Nia's reach. Nia saw Claudia's obvious shun, reached over, snatched one of the lumps, and bit into it. She chewed roughly, glowering.

Even Buddy looked pessimistic. He murmured, "This should be interesting."

David cleared his throat and turned toward Claudia. "Now, about your complaint to the city—"

"This is bull crap!" Nia exclaimed.

"What?" Claudia pulled her tray back, insulted.

David looked at Nia, shocked. "Nia, what are you talking about?"

"I'm talking about everything. This nasty cookie, her complaint to the city, and what you did, David." Nia glared at David.

"What *I* did?"

"Don't try to act innocent." She pointed the burnt cookie at him. "You said you love me, but you're still seeing Cher-Ling."

"I'm not seeing Cher-Ling."

"Oh yeah?" Nia pulled Cher-Ling's saffron scarf from her jeans' back pocket. "Then why was this under your car seat?"

Realizing Cher-Ling had left her scarf in his car intentionally so Nia could find it, he took the scarf from Nia. "I took her to a doctor's appointment."

"So you're her personal chauffeur now? Is that why you were late?"

Conscious of Buddy and Claudia watching them like a Blockbuster movie, David lowered his voice. "Stop it, Nia. You're making a scene."

Nia grew more livid. "I won't let you make a fool of me. Malcolm already did that. Just be honest, David. I refuse to be in love with a man who is still in love with someone else." She got up to leave. "I'm done here."

By the time David got to the porch, Nia was at his car. "Where do you think you're going?"

"To return this scarf." She held up his car keys. "And I'm taking your car so you can't follow me."

Nia burned rubber as she peeled away in his Jaguar and left David standing in the empty driveway.

Buddy came out. "Hey. Need a lift?"

CHAPTER 38

*A*s Nia drove, she unfolded the piece of paper on which David had scribbled Cher-Ling's name and address. She drove past the Staples Center and hung a left on Chick Hearn Court, then another left. She parked in front of a town house, got out, and rang the doorbell. Nobody answered. Someone peeped through the curtain. Nia banged on the window.

When Cher-Ling finally opened the door, she was dressed in an elaborate lounging outfit complete with silk robe and Victoria's Secret lingerie underneath with feathers. Her makeup was camera ready.

"Oh, it's you," she said, overly dramatic and disappointed. "I was expecting David."

Nia gritted her teeth and handed her the scarf. "Not my color."

Cher-Ling tossed her long jet-black hair behind her shoulder and took back her designer scarf. She eyed Nia's hair and scrunched her nose. "You're right. Not much goes with that wild dead-tree color."

"It's raw sienna with chestnut highlights."

"Raw and nutty. Oh, how special."

"Let's cut the bull and get straight to it." Nia walked inside without an invitation. "I know you left that scarf in David's car on purpose, hoping I'd find it. Well, I did. And I came here to tell you to stop begging my fiancé for a ride."

"I didn't have to beg David. He insisted on picking me up." Cher-Ling sat on her couch and crossed her mile-long legs. "David still cares a great deal about me. He's always been so protective of me."

Nia was not impressed. "David is like that with most people. He likes helping, so don't take it personally."

"I know David Wrightwood a lot better than you do." Cher-Ling's tone was biting. "When he cares about a woman, he really cares. And he doesn't stop caring just because circumstances change."

"What are you trying to say?"

"I'm saying"—she annunciated as if Nia was stupid— "David still *loves* me."

Her words cut straight to Nia's heart. Nia tried to cover her hurt. "No, he doesn't."

"Then why did he come visit me in jail?"

"So, he *did* visit you?"

"Oh, didn't he tell you?" Cher-Ling giggled. "Silly boy."

Nia tried to stay calm and focused. "That doesn't mean anything."

"Oh yeah? Well, like they say, a picture speaks a thousand words." Cher-Ling pulled photos from a decorative box next to the couch and handed them to Nia.

Nia flipped through them. They were of David and Cher-Ling, during his visit. Cher-Ling was dressed in jailhouse gray pants and a white shirt and had her arm around David's waist as they both cheesed for the camera. In the next picture, David handed Cher-Ling a small gift-wrapped present. Nia's mouth fell open. "He brought you a gift?"

"Of course." Cher-Ling grinned. "That's what people do when they still love someone. Look at the next picture when I opened his gift."

Nia looked. The next picture showed Cher-Ling pulling an edible thong from the gift box. "Ah!"

Nia flipped to another picture. David was pulling off his shirt, getting undressed, and Cher-Ling was helping him. Nia could even see the tiny scar near his left nipple. "What's this?"

Cher-Ling smirked. "It's called a *conjugal* visit."

Nia gasped. She wanted to cry, but first she wanted to wring Cher-Ling's skinny little neck. She threw down the pictures. "You hussy!"

She tried to grab her but only got a handful of feathers. Cher-Ling jumped off the couch.

"David is not going to marry you. He still loves me!" She ran out the front door.

Nia was on her heels. "Let's see if he still loves you after I pull all your hair out."

Cher-Ling fled out into the yard. "Not my hair!"

Nia caught the edge of Cher-Ling's robe and tried to rein her in, but David caught her. She was so mad, she hadn't seen him jump from Buddy's pickup truck and run up the yard.

He grabbed her. "Nia, stop it!"

"David, you lied to me!"

"I didn't lie to you."

She kept kicking at both him and Cher-Ling. "You said you didn't love her anymore."

"I *don't*!" He swung her around and sat her down in the

grass. He squatted behind her and held her arms. "Calm down, Nia. Stop it!"

She yelled, "I saw the pictures, David!"

"What pictures?"

"The ones you took during your *conjugal* visit!" She tried to sock him. "You even bought her a gift."

"A gift?" He kept his clutch tight as he figured out what she was talking about. "She'd bought that herself over a year ago and left it at my condo. It had been in the back of my closet collecting dust. I wanted to get rid of it, along with her love letters and a bottle of her perfume that she'd also left. So when she asked me to bring them to her in jail, I did."

"But what about the picture where you're getting naked? How do you explain that?"

He knew that question was coming. "She spilled the perfume all over me. I took off my shirt because I didn't want to walk around a jail smelling like women's perfume. She'd paid the guard with the money on her books to take those pictures, just before he got me another shirt."

He gave Cher-Ling a scathing look and continued. "As for *conjugal* visits, they don't even have those in the county jail."

"They don't?" Nia glared at Cher-Ling as well.

David stood up and brushed grass from his pants. "I'm not going to keep explaining my actions to you, Nia. You're going to have to trust me, or this is not going to work."

He left Nia on the grass to think about it while he gave Cher-Ling some harsh words.

Out of breath and feeling silly, Nia plucked the grass for a second. When she stood up, her voice was apologetic. "David, I'm sorry. Can you forgive me?"

David grumbled, "Nia, I swear, you've got to stop doubting me."

"I'll try."

He saw the sincerity in her eyes and finally gave in. "Okay. Let's go."

As Nia followed David to his car, Cher-Ling stood nearby in a come-hither pose, trying to lure David back. Angered by her audacity, Nia started at her again, but David caught her arm.

"Nia?" he said in a warning tone.

"Sorry," she said, and got into the car with him.

⌘ CHAPTER 39 ⌘

A week later, Nia remained on her best behavior, trying to make up for her last blowup with Cher-Ling and to prepare David for the surprise news.

"You did *what*?" David nearly spit out his red wine.

"I moved up our wedding date," she repeated, and set a plate of spicy orange cashew chicken in front of him.

"Why?"

"Because . . . why wait?"

"You didn't discuss this with me first."

Nia sat next to him and dug into her sweet-and-sour hand-rolled egg rolls as if nothing was wrong. David pushed her plate away from her.

"In case you didn't know, marriage is a two-way street. You don't decide to hang a left all by yourself and expect me to come along for the ride."

"You make it sound like the Indy 500. We're just getting

married." She pulled her plate back to her. "It's all been taken care of. Eat your food."

David was growing more upset. "Getting *married* is a big decision. It's not something you rush into."

"I'm not rushing; I'm just speeding things up."

"But we'd already agreed on a date. Everything was set."

"Mrs. Wang and I put our heads together yesterday and knocked out all the preordering and arrangements. The florist, the cake, the band—we even found a dress for me already made. The invitations went out last night, overnight priority mail." She went on, as though adding a minor detail. "David, honey, we're getting married next weekend. Have some more wine?" She tried to fill his glass.

He blocked his glass. "I can't believe this! You're incredible."

"Um, thank you?"

"No, don't thank me. I'm having a hard time trying to figure you out." He got up angrily, bumping the table. Her wineglass tilted and spilled. "Does this have something to do with Cher-Ling? Are you still brewing about her?"

She didn't answer.

"I thought we went over this." David paced, irritated. "I thought we were done with this already."

"You don't understand." She grabbed a cloth napkin and tried to blot the wine.

"I'm trying. I'm really trying, but you're making it difficult."

"You were in love with Cher-Ling."

"I *was.* Past tense."

"You say you love me now."

"I do."

"But you also said love was *forever.* If you fell out of love with her, how do I know you won't fall out of love with me?"

David stopped pacing, but he had no answer.

"If you want me to believe you, then prove it." She threw down the napkin and stood up. "Marry me. Now."

"Nia, it doesn't work like that!" David yelled. "People get married every day, and it doesn't prove a damn thing."

She turned away. She wasn't buying it.

"You've got to start believing *first.*"

She yelled back. "It's not easy for me to *believe.*"

"Why not?"

Nia threw up her hands, confused and frustrated.

David calmed down and reached for her hands. "Baby, you've got to already know that I love you. The ceremony is just a public expression of what we already have."

She stared at him, trying to understand.

He met her stare. "The only part that really matters is the vow we take before God. But before we even take those vows, Nia, you've got to already have faith that this love between us will last. You don't have to fight with Cher-Ling or move up our wedding date to prove anything." She turned away guiltily.

"Look at me." He raised her chin back up to his face. "I'm madly in love with you. I'm not going anywhere. When you need me, I'll be right here."

Nia felt ashamed. "I'm scared, David. I just don't want to lose you."

He took her in his arms and held her. "Baby, we've got all the time in the world."

She asked glumly, "So, you want me to move the wedding back?"

David exhaled. "No, leave it as it is. I'll go along with it but—"

Nia gasped, excited.

He pointed his finger at her nose and warned her. "If you *ever* do anything this impulsive again—"

"I won't. I promise."

As they settled back down, he took her hand in his and patted it. "In light of your news, now I've got a surprise for you."

"You do? What?" Nia perked up.

"Now that we're getting married in only a few days, you can't stay here anymore."

"Huh?" Her happy expression fell flat.

"That's right." He picked up her keys and nudged her toward the door. "No teasing me with your sexiness. No more cold showers. With only five more days to go, I can hold it; let it build up for our wedding night."

She swallowed hard. "Are you serious?"

He opened the door to let her know he was serious.

"You're doing this to get back at me, aren't you?"

He smiled with a playful glint of revenge in his eye.

"But David, what about the food?"

"I guess I'll have to eat it all by myself, to teach you a lesson." He nudged her out the door. "C'mon. I'll see you home."

❧ CHAPTER 40 ❧

$\mathscr{F}$or the next few days, Nia nearly went crazy not being able to see David. He was serious about staying away until the night of their wedding rehearsal. She lit a single gold candle and placed it by her bed, then cradled the phone between her ear and pillow.

"You can't hang up," she whispered to David over the phone. "Since you won't let me see you, you've got to stay up all night on the phone with me talking dirty."

"It's not dirty."

"What do you call it?"

"Two people in love describing what they're going to do to each other after they're married."

"Okay, then let's do that." Nia loosened the straps on her teddy and imagined David lying in bed next to her. "I'm going to rip off all your clothes and throw you on the bed."

David chuckled. "Then I'll flip you over and straddle you."

"Tie me up?"

"No, I'm not into bondage. I'll hold you down with something else."

"What?"

"Guess."

"Um, is it big?"

"Big enough to do the job."

"Is it sturdy?"

"Yes, very," David said, self-assured. "You can even hold on to it, if you like."

Nia let out a lazy chuckle. "What does it look like?"

"It's indescribable."

"Will I like it?"

"Yes, very much." David chuckled sexily. "I guarantee you will."

Nia squirmed a bit and moaned as she stared up at the ceiling. The candle flame flickered.

David got quiet, his voice low and serious. "Now let me ask you something."

"What?"

"How much can you take?"

"Ooh." Hotness rushed over Nia, and her insides pulsated. He was already driving her crazy and only using words. She clasped her knees together and tried to contain her passion, but she felt ready to explode. How much better would the real thing be?

She took a moment to fantasize while listening to him breathe. "What's that playing in the background?"

" 'Sexual Healing' by Marvin Gaye."

"Turn it up."

"I will, but first I want you to do something for me."

"What?"

"Set the phone down and lay back. Let your hands roam all over your body. Do whatever you feel . . . but don't, not even for a second, take your mind off me."

"Okay." Nia placed the phone on her pillow. David turned
up the music so she could hear. Her hands drifted to places
on her body where she wanted David to go, rubbing, squeezing, massaging . . . Seven seconds. That's all it took for her
chin to go up, the back of her head to hit the mattress, and her
body to respond with feverish passion to David's imagined
touch. She moaned his name, knowing he could hear her.
"Oooh . . . David."

She could hear him moan also, his voice sweet and masculine, filtered through the phone. "Ahh . . . *Radiance*."

When he called her that, her thighs closed together
tightly and her insides contracted in one long, deep, wet
squeeze. She called his name again but it caught in the back
of her throat. For a few wonderful seconds, her vision faded,
the ceiling seemed to disappear, and hot tears filled her eyes
as she imagined his face over hers and his juicy lips smothering hers.

After a moment, she picked up the phone, regaining her
voice. Low and breathy, she pleaded, "David, please come, just
for tonight, just for a couple of hours. I can't wait any longer."

David caught his breath but remained slightly winded.
"Baby, I can't even drive like this. Three more days, that's all,
and then we'll be doing this for real."

She heard the sound of his mattress as his body pressed
into it. She moaned, wishing she were beneath him, taking the
weight of his anatomy. She kept listening as he started the song
over again. He groaned, "This is crazy. You've got me so hot,
baby, I can't think straight."

"Just don't hang up."

"I won't, Nia."

"Don't ever hang up on me."

A chuckle slipped from his mouth and turned into a sexy
moan. "I won't ever hang up on you, baby."

✿   ✿   ✿

Nia awoke a few hours later and thought she heard David calling her name on the other end of the line. "Nia . . ."

She snatched up the phone. "I'm sorry, baby, I fell—"

"Turn over." David's voice sounded different.

Groggy, she thought she'd misheard him. "Huh?"

"Look behind you." Now she knew it wasn't David.

She turned over.

Her dark lover lay beside her in the bed.

Nia froze. The phone slipped from her hand.

The gold candle had burned down to its last half inch of wax, and the room had grown dim. Dark shadows shifted, and faint rays of light swayed as the candle's serpentine flame flickered.

She had never seen *him* so close, or so real.

She stared at his dark outline, a very real man, fleshly, tangible, but his features remained hidden. His body was immense, with a smooth, expansive chest.

He whispered at her in the dark. "Don't believe his love, Nia." His words filtered through the air like a low, slow-beating drum. "It's fool's gold. There is no forever with him. Your eternity is with me . . ."

She shook her head. "No."

He grabbed her wrist. His skin burned hotter than hers did. The heat he emitted was electrifying, igniting her senses and adding fuel to her already burning flame.

She wanted to get up, wanted to run, but all the strength left her body. The air thickened with the smoke pouring from the dying flame as its vapors mixed with the thick, sweet smell of burning molasses.

She stared at his dark form through the expiring light.

"Forever, Nia, that's how long you'll be with me."

Spurred by his touch, images flickered through her eyes

and visions of matrimony, death, purple roses on a casket, and a royal black throne flooded her mind.

He let her go.

She fell off the edge of her bed and crawled away. With her back pressed against the wall, she was afraid to look up, afraid he would still be there.

She finally lifted her eyes. He had gone but had left something on her bed. Nia cautiously scooted closer to see.

A purple rose on a long black stem, its thorns smoothed down to a pearl-like finish and its thick, velvet folds enclosed around a beautifully swollen bud. However, when she came near and touched it, the flower's folds opened and bloomed widely in her hand. For all the fear she felt, something else inside of her begged to be opened . . . opened to other dark possibilities.

❧ CHAPTER 41 ❧

*D*avid woke up early the next morning, slightly before dawn. He quickly picked up the phone, checking to see if Nia was still on the line.

"Good morning, sunlight," he whispered. When she didn't answer, he figured she'd fallen asleep, too, in the wee hours of the morning. He would let her sleep peacefully while he made another call.

He reached for his cell phone, leaving the other line open so she wouldn't think he'd hung up on her. He dialed his parents' phone number in Canada, double-checked the time, and allowed for the three-hour time difference: 7:45 A.M. in Ontario. His parents were early risers.

David listened to the rings, counting them. He didn't call much anymore, since they'd forbidden him to speak to Beez. By the third ring, his heart was beating too fast, and he didn't know if he'd be able to talk. He knew they were checking the caller ID, deciding whether to take his call. Finally, someone picked up.

"Hello?"

"Hey, Ma." She already knew it was him. Why couldn't she just say his name?

"Who's calling?" she asked. The question stuck in his chest.

"It's David." He swallowed. "How are you?"

She paused. "Satisfactory."

"How's Dad?" His question came out too fast. His nerves played tricks on him.

She paused again. "He's the same as he's been."

David pulled in a deep breath and released it slowly. "I'm doing okay."

He thought about how happy times fly by in the blink of an eye, but tragedies are embedded and frozen in time, their vivid memories lingering on for years.

"Hey, I've got some news. I'm getting married." He waited.

After a moment, she responded, "That's nice. Very fortunate for you. Not everyone has things turn out so well for them."

He straightened the pillow on his bed. "Is Dad there? Maybe he'd want to know, too."

He heard his mother move the phone away from her mouth. He heard muffled voices as she talked to someone in the background. When she got back on the phone, she didn't say anything. He only knew she was there by her breathing.

He asked, "You think I could tell Beez myself? I mean, she always talked about being in my wedding when we were kids and—" David regretted his words the moment they spilled from his mouth, and he wished he could take them back, but like so many other things, he couldn't. "I mean, if you could just hold the phone up to her ear and—"

"No, David."

The silence after that was almost unbearable.

As she resumed speaking, her voice became devoid of any small attempt at warmth. "Obviously, Melody *can't* be in your wedding."

"I know, I just meant—"

Click. The line went dead.

She had hung up on him.

A sad image of Beez burned in his brain. Twelve years later, and they still blamed David for what happened. Moreover, so did he.

CHAPTER 42

*R*ephaim was ruthless. However, like all ruthless leaders, he wasn't untouchable. He had his Achilles' heel. Mysti knew that well. She'd spent her spare time studying him, longing for a way to touch him.

The only one who could get as close to Rephaim as she needed was Zamzummims, his younger brother. Envious, resentful, and disloyal, Zamzu had agreed to meet with her at the Northridge Mall, and he knew beforehand it wasn't to pick out a Hallmark card for Rephaim.

They walked in a crowded section near the food court, blending in with other hungry shoppers in search of the golden sale. Zamzu ogled a girl passing by in a tight black T-shirt with a devil's skull imprinted on the front in silver foil. He smiled and flashed her a glimpse of his sharpened incisors. She smiled back and kept walking.

In his human form, Zamzu was unremarkable. Short,

unassuming, and approachable, he was the exact opposite of his older brother, Rephaim. Zamzu didn't turn any heads when he entered a room. Rephaim not only turned heads, he stole breaths and stopped pulses. Most people were smart enough not to try approaching him.

Mysti led Zamzu to a table and they sat down. "Nia's real birthday is fast approaching."

"So?" Zamzu smacked his lips indifferently.

"That's when Rephaim plans to make his move on Nia."

"I don't know when the girl was born. You and my brother have kept that date a secret."

"We've had to." Mysti didn't elaborate on the reasons why.

Mysti had many secrets. At sixteen, she'd been too ambitious for her own good. When she stole a rare manuscript tucked away in the bowels of a small run-down bookstore and followed its instructions on contacting the dark realm to a T, she'd had no idea how effective it would prove to be. However, she didn't get to the dark lord Rephaim right away. She'd had to make the rounds up the hierarchical ladder.

Zamzu brought Mysti's attention back to the matter at hand. "What'd you call me here for?"

Mysti leaned forward. Her crafty jade eyes zeroed in on Zamzu's weatherworn face. "Aren't you tired of bowing to Rephaim?"

He leaned forward too, and his perpetual scowl grew even deeper. "Lady, I've been bowing my whole life. I can't even see the sun rise for living in the shadow of the Mighty Dark One's ass."

When he referred to Rephaim, his left ear twitched, an uncontainable nervous habit he tried to cover with a black bandana. He pulled the cloth lower on his head. "What exactly do you want from me?"

"A little guts."

Zamzu was many things but not stupid. He knew she was asking him to betray his brother. "What's in it for me?"

"There's a lot of power up for grabs."

His coal-black eyes drank in Mysti's cold beauty and her hot ambition. "This is about more than just power." He tilted his head. "You still want him, don't you?"

Mysti didn't answer. She met his stare with equally dark indifference. "Are you in?"

"Suicide? That's not my thing." He got up to leave.

Mysti flicked her fingers wildly and shot a sharp, crackling green bolt of cold energy up at the ceiling, shattering the roof. The mall's lights went out, and in a moment the food court had cleared, with only the slowest people still scrambling to get away.

With the speed of a hawk, she snatched off Zamzu's black bandana, and tied it around his throat like a noose in one smooth motion. His demonic reflexes kicked in instantaneously and he shifted form, sliced through his own bandana with his claws, and went for her throat, but she quickly blocked him with her own set of sharp steel blades, which she'd whipped from her cleavage.

"Go for it." Her green eyes flashed even more coldly in the darkness as she stood ready.

Zamzu held his position, studying her. They stood in the dark facing each other, both breathing hard, both pissed with the hand fate had dealt them. After a second, he backed off.

"You just may be insane enough to pull it off."

A small calculating grin curled her full lips. "So," she repeated, "are you in?"

Zamzu nodded slowly, then gave a warning. "But if you dare challenge Rephaim, you'd better bring your A game. Anything less and that sadistic mafioso will bury us both alive."

ᕲ CHAPTER 43 ᕲ

$\mathcal{F}$riday night finally came, the night before their wedding, when Nia would get to see David at their wedding rehearsal. Tension and worry stole her usual peppy mood as she drove to the church during an unexpected storm. With all the mysterious things going on in her life, she tried to relax and focus on becoming David's wife.

When she saw him waiting for her on the church steps, she parked, hopped out, and rushed into his waiting arms, kissing him fiercely. They'd only been apart five incredibly long days, but it had seemed like a decade.

Other people hurried inside the church as the rain pounded and the strong winds blew in the late-season freak storm that raged, threatening to ruin their wedding. But Nia and David stayed on the church steps, kissing and hugging, oblivious to the raging tempest.

Nia tried to rid her mind of her dark lover lying in her bed next to her. "Things will be so much better once we're married. I'll have you in my bed to keep away the bogeyman."

David pulled her close to his chest like he always did when he wanted to feel her heartbeat. He whispered in her ear. "I missed your light, Radiance."

As she kissed him again, a thunderous roar rolled off the dark clouds, erupting above their heads with deafening noise. The lights inside the church flickered. David held her tight. "Half the city of Pasadena is experiencing a power outage. Hopefully, it won't affect us."

"We'd better go inside."

As they walked into the main sanctuary, Shayla stood idly near a back pew. Nia didn't have many close friends, because of Rephaim, so when she needed to choose a maid of honor, she chose Shayla, despite their falling out. She had to. The last thing she needed was to offend Shayla and have her blab to David about Rephaim's nighttime visits.

When they saw each other, they exchanged looks. Nia kept walking.

David noticed. "What was that about?"

"Just girl stuff." Nia shrugged and played it off. Changing the subject, she asked, "So, is Beez coming?"

David's reply was short. "No."

Disappointed, Nia asked, "Why not? I've really been looking forward to having Beez as my bridesmaid. I'll pay to fly her in from Canada and we can make all the necessary arrangements. She can stay at my house—"

"I said she's not coming. Leave it at that," he snapped.

Irked, Nia bit her lip and pulled David to the side. "How come every time I ask you about Beez or your parents, you get in a mood? Why can't you just open up?"

"Rehearsal's about to start." David checked his watch evasively.

Nia's nerves were already on edge. She had the usual bridal jitters piled on top of far more serious issues involving dark stalkers, lust, and betrayal, not to mention lack of sleep, her best friend's secrets and subtle blackmail, and early PMS. This was all way more than any new bride should have to go through. Now David was adding to her inner turmoil by constantly eluding her questions about his family. They were getting married tomorrow, and he still wouldn't open up to her.

Fed up, she was about to let him have it when Pastor Kees touched her shoulder. He brushed close by them as he headed up the aisle. "I'll meet you two lovebirds at the altar."

David knew he'd ticked her off, and he was glad for the interruption. "Pastor Kees is waiting for us. We don't want to make another scene, now, do we?"

Out of respect for Pastor Kees, Mrs. Wang, the teens, and everyone else who'd attended their rehearsal, Nia took a deep breath and tried to pull it together, putting her emotions on hold for the time being.

The wind and rain escalated outside, and the church windows rattled. Pastor Kees yelled over the chatter and noise, "C'mon, folks, let's get this rehearsal under way. Everyone take your places."

Nia and David walked to the altar and faced each other. Suddenly, a blaring clap of thunder exploded directly above the church, bursting through the atmosphere so forcefully it broke out a large stained glass window. As the glass shattered, the lights inside the church went out with a loud *thwack!*

Frightened shrieks erupted in the darkness. Nia's heart missed a beat as faint light poured in through the broken window.

After a moment, Pastor Kees gathered his voice. "I think we've just been struck by lightning."

One of the teens started crying. "It's spooky in here."

David asked, "What about the backup generators?"

The janitor yelled from the back. "Those went out, too."

With no lights, the church loomed larger and darker than normal. The dim rays that filtered through the broken window fell near the back doors of the church. As Nia's eyes gradually adjusted, she realized that the moment the lightning struck, everybody had run to the front of the church . . . except for one man.

She didn't remember him being there before the lights went out. Nia squinted, and something inside of her squirmed. She reached for David's hand, but he'd gone to the back to help the janitor inspect the generators.

Pastor Kees stayed out front to keep everyone calm. "No need to panic. The storm, the rain, the lightning, it's all just part of nature." He reminded them, "God says, 'Fear not.' So don't let fear overtake you."

Despite the pastor's comforting demeanor, two of the younger teen girls continued to cry. Nia knew how they felt. She touched Pastor Kees's arm. "Do you see someone sitting in the last pew?"

He bent slightly and peered at the back. "Yes. There's a gentleman sitting there."

Nia had hoped she was seeing things. "Do you know who he is?"

Pastor Kees looked again. "No. I can't see him clearly."

Nia slowly walked to the side, taking the two crying teens by the hand and escorting them back to Pastor Kees, all while keeping her eye on the man. His larger-than-life size made the pews around him look miniature. He remained motionless, like a shadow, but Nia saw the slightest movement of his head as he followed her with his eyes.

Silent and unmoving, he wore a dark magenta suit. His jet-black hair caught stolen light from the broken window. Long, thick strands with slight waves were pulled back and tied into a masculine ponytail. The way he wore his hair reminded her of an ancient warrior or a tribal leader. Even from where she stood, strength emanated from his chiseled facial bone structure and his strong jawline. Shadows hovered about the rest of his face.

Nia's nerves were already frayed, and his effect on her was unsettling. She felt trembly and very warm. The muggy air inside the church thickened with a sweet smell of dirty rain. The wilted petals of a nearly dead orchid resting on the pew closest to her began to push out and rise up, and their unnatural scent infiltrated the atmosphere.

The man in the back pew stood up.

"Perhaps I can help." His voice was smooth and deep, like organ music. Everyone quieted, and all eyes turned toward this man with the tall, muscular physique and commanding presence.

As he moved forward, pheromones wafted like thousands of tiny darts of attraction, pelting her and setting her aflame. With each step closer he took, Nia's body temperature rose, her heart palpitated, and her hormones betrayed her.

"If the bride will allow me . . ." He'd left the broken window's light rays and walked up the aisle as the large shadowy outline of a man, but with a few more steps, he'd be close enough to look at her face to face. After all these years, Nia still hadn't seen his face clearly. Her heart pounded. *Not here. Not now. I'm trying to get married.*

Averting her eyes, Nia looked down at her hands. Her lips quivered, but there was no escaping his deep voice as he approached.

"I can make things better . . ."

Fear and apprehension overtook her. "Oh, God. No."

She panicked and ran out.

Nia rushed out the side door behind the pulpit and into the dark hallway. The electricity outage had turned the church into a dark maze, but she didn't stop. She ran past Pastor Kees's office, the prayer room, and the utility room, until she reached the staff restroom. She slammed the door behind her and locked it, knowing that locked doors only kept out normal people.

Nothing was normal about the man in the dark magenta suit. She hadn't stuck around long enough to see his face. She didn't need to. She knew it was him.

Nia paced the dark restroom and pounded her fist against the mirror, confused, scared, excited.

Yes, despite the fact that she was in love with David and was about to marry a *real* man who offered her happiness, goodness, and even holiness, her dark pursuer excited her in a sensual way that drove her crazy.

But she'd be damned if she'd give in to him.

Nia tried to talk sense into her head, knowing that all the good things she wanted in life she could never experience with *him*.

Nia straightened herself in front of the mirror and thought, *I love you, David. We're getting married tomorrow. Nothing can stop us.*

Her nerves would not get the best of her. Everything would be just fine. She was strong, self-determined, and in love with David Wrightwood. She'd find David and let him protect her.

She just needed to *believe* in his love.

Nia thought she heard David's voice outside. She collected herself and opened the door, but the hallway was empty. She smoothed down her hair and started walking back toward the sanctuary. As she turned the corner, she saw David standing in the hallway with his back toward her. He bent forward slightly. A woman's hand draped the back of his neck.

The lights came back on.

David was kissing Cher-Ling.

❧ CHAPTER 44 ☙

*D*avid had been struggling in the dark utility room, trying to help the janitor fix the generator, when he saw Nia run past. He went out into the dark hallway to look for her, calling her name. When he didn't find her, he headed back toward the main sanctuary, but he heard a noise. Before he could turn around, he felt her arms around his waist.

Feeling guilty, he quickly apologized. "I'm sorry for snapping at you earlier about Beez."

As he turned, she pulled him to her lips, eagerly accepting his apology. He bent forward and kissed her deeply and passionately but noticed something odd about her—she was too tall and too thin. When he tried to pull away, she grabbed his neck and kept him bent forward.

The generator finally kicked in, and the lights came back on.

He heard footsteps running away. When he finally broke free, Cher-Ling looked up at him.

"I'll be da—!" Shocked, he backed up. "What the hell are you doing?"

"Kissing you and enjoying it tremendously," she said, grinning. Raindrops rolled off her fur collar, and the back door where she'd snuck inside the church remained slightly ajar behind her.

"I thought you were—" He paused, remembering the footsteps that had just run away. "Nia!"

He turned and rushed in that direction, but when he got to the sanctuary, Nia wasn't there.

Mrs. Wang sadly informed him, "Nia just ran out, crying."

David stood there a moment, his heart beating irregularly as he realized what had happened. He ran after her.

He rushed through the double doors of the church, wiping his mouth to get rid of the taste of Cher-Ling and cursing himself for letting this happen. The rehearsal wasn't even half over and already so many things had gone wrong.

He caught Nia at the bottom of the steps.

"Nia!"

She whipped around. Raindrops mixed with tears as they streamed down her face.

"I wasn't kissing *her*. I thought she was—"

"Liar!"

He tried desperately to explain, but Nia wouldn't listen.

"Baby, I love you. Have faith—"

"Faith?" Disbelief dimmed her eyes. "Screw *faith*! I just saw *proof*."

They stared at each other on the church steps. Her lips trembled. She wiped tears and rain from her face. "You still love her."

David tried to come closer but she backed away, all hope drained from her face.

"Why did you ask me to marry you, David? How could you be that cruel?" Bitterness and anger underscored each word.

She turned and stumbled through the mud to her car.

He followed her, pleading, "Nia, baby, but you know I love you—"

Malcolm was leaning against her car, holding an umbrella, as if he'd been waiting for her. He watched her coming and collapsed the umbrella. "Nia, what happened?"

"David just kissed his ex-girlfriend!" Nia jerked her car keys from her pocket, but they slipped from her trembling hands.

"I told you not to believe him." Malcolm bent over to pick them up, but David quickly blocked him. He snatched them up. Nia reached for her keys but David held them.

"Nia, no matter how things look, you've got to believe that I love you—"

"Don't believe him, Nia." Malcolm interrupted and shoved David out of the way. "His love is worth about as much as fool's gold."

David punched Malcolm in his jaw. A strong right jab delivered on point threw Mal back against the Mustang. David was about to counter with a left hook, but before he could connect a second time, Nia jumped in the way.

"David!" Nia shrieked. They stared at each other.

Malcolm's expensive shoes slipped in the mud and he collapsed to his knees, bleeding from his mouth. Alarmed, Nia kneeled, checking him.

David rubbed his bruised knuckle. "Nothing's wrong with him," he grumbled. "He just got his ass kicked."

As Nia helped Malcolm up, she turned, glaring at David. "I believed you and you made a fool of me."

"No, Nia—"

She held up her hand. "Nothing you say matters to me anymore."

Stunned by her words, he stood still.

Despair filled her eyes. "I *saw* you."

She took her car keys from his hand and gave them to Malcolm. Malcolm opened her door for her, and she got in. Holding his bleeding mouth, Malcolm walked around Nia's car and opened the other door. Just before he got in, he gave David a *fuck you* look.

David banged on Nia's window. "Nia, don't leave. Please."

She rolled it down and for a brief second, he regained hope. "I should have stayed with Malcolm." She pulled off her engagement ring and threw it at him. It fell in the mud. "At least he didn't lie to me about loving me."

❧ CHAPTER 45 ❧

$\mathcal{D}$avid yelled over the thunder and rain, "Nia, I didn't lie to you!" But she kept going.

He picked up the ring and jumped in his car to follow her, but as soon as he threw his car into reverse, a florist van pulled up behind him, blocking him in.

"Move out of the way!" he hollered, but the van turned off its headlights and stayed put. David caught a fleeting glimpse of a dark magenta suit behind the wheel. He jumped out and yanked open the van's door, but it was empty.

A few people had exited the church and witnessed the unfortunate scene. Both Pastor Kees and Spivek, who'd arrived late due to an overload of police calls because of the storm, came over and offered their empathy and help.

"Just help me move this damn van!" David threw the van into neutral, and the three men struggled in the mud to push it out of the way, but by the time they'd cleared a path, Nia was long gone.

David kicked the side of his car and slumped against the door. Pastor Kees tried to console him. "She's emotional right now. Hopefully, she'll calm down and reconsider."

Spivek placed his hand on David's shoulder. "I'll put in a call and have my patrol cars keep a look out for Nia's gold Mustang. If they see it, they'll pull her over, detain her for a few minutes, give her a chance to cool off."

"I can't lose her, man." David gritted his teeth.

Spivek squeezed his shoulder, then headed for his car's radio. "If we find her, I'll call you."

Pastor Kees stood by silently and watched as David got back into his car.

As he drove away, a sinking feeling attacked his stomach. Thinking he was going to be sick, he pulled off the road and opened the door. As he hung his head out, only hot, angry tears flowed from his face. The roads were flooding, and the storm was making the streets hard to see at night.

David closed his door and drove through several cities looking for her before returning to her house. When he got there, her house was dark and her driveway empty.

Hours had passed and it was nearing midnight, but there was still no sign of her. David sat in his car, waiting, watching his front windshield wipers, and hoping for another chance to prove his love.

∽ CHAPTER 46 ∾

*T*he moment Nia walked into the hotel room with Malcolm, she knew she'd made a mistake. She believed David had betrayed her, but sleeping with Malcolm would only make things worse.

"Mal, I'm sorry. I can't do this." She turned around to leave, but he caught her hand.

"David played you for a fool. I told you he didn't love you, but you didn't listen." Malcolm tried to soothe her with kisses to her neck but it didn't feel right.

"Yeah, but you don't either," she said, pushing him away.

Malcolm fingered his busted lip, growing impatient and angry. "You said in the car that you might as well be with me. So what's the problem?"

"I was upset and confused. I still am, but don't try to take advantage of that." She walked around him, and headed for the door.

He blocked her. "You can't just leave."

"Malcolm, I have to go. I'll pay for the room, just move out of my way."

"It's too late," Malcolm said, and reached for her arm.

"I said, no!" Nia jerked loose and ran to the other side of the room.

Malcolm kept coming at her, but something about him had changed. The way he walked, the look in his eye, even his voice had changed, deepening to an eerie, low bass.

"Nia." When he said her name, the incendiary vibration in his voice gave her goose bumps.

"Malcolm, what's wrong with you?" she yelled at him, but he was no longer the Malcolm she knew.

As she moved away from him, her back hit the wall. With no place to escape, scared, tears began to fill her eyes. Mal's face blurred. With effortless strength, he grabbed her and tossed her on the bed.

Nia screamed, "Mal, stop!"

She kicked, swung her arm and pounded his already busted lip, and even jabbed him with her keys, but he acted as if he didn't feel it.

"Finally, we will be together," he said, his voice exotic and deep. Dizziness and heat swept over her. "Nia . . . my bride."

He straddled her and covered her mouth with his. When he exhaled, his breath was like a hot lethal injection of poison. The blast knocked her head back, and she felt like she was choking. Her lungs burned. She squinted and tried again to hit his face, but his features seemed to change as she slipped from consciousness, and that would be the last thing she remembered.

REPHAIM WAITED UNTIL Nia stopped struggling, then he laid her down gently on the pillow. He kept his mouth covering hers and continued to exhale in one long, deep, hot breath. For six full minutes, he breathed into her, filling her constricted lungs with a sweet, poisonous aphrodisiac from his half demonic body.

With her eyes still open, she choked. Strong lethal toxins attacked her nervous system, muscles, and arteries. Her body convulsed.

Rephaim held her gently in his arms. He watched the life drain from her lovely face and the light leave her bright brown eyes.

Her heart slowed, and finally, it ceased beating.

When it was all over, he closed her eyes for her.

He rose from the bed and gazed down at her. "My lovely . . . Nia."

CHAPTER 47

*D*avid awoke inside his car to the sound of his phone buzzing. He'd dozed off while parked in Nia's driveway. His private line lit up with a 911 page from Spivek. He speed-dialed him right back. Spivek got straight to the point.

"A patrol car spotted Nia's Mustang in front of the Radisson Hotel."

"I'm on my way."

"No, Wood." Spivek stopped him, his voice heavy with concern. "Meet me at Northridge General Hospital."

"Why?"

"Just do it." Spivek hung up.

David froze. Panic rushed through his body. He gripped the steering wheel and started his car. He skidded off, heading for the hospital.

David pulled into the emergency parking area at the same time as the ambulance carrying Nia. Spivek was following close behind in his detective car, his strobe light flashing. David got out and ran to the ambulance. Paramedics rolled Nia out on a stretcher and started rushing her inside the ER.

She wasn't moving.

"Nia! Oh my God!" David grabbed Nia's hand as two EMTs tried to hold him back.

He pushed past them, trying to get inside the restricted entrance, and Spivek rushed over and grabbed his arm. "Let them go. They've got to resuscitate her!"

"Resuscitate?" David frowned as dread and urgency filled his body. "What happened? Why isn't she breathing?"

Spivek said something about finding her inside a hotel room unconscious, but David stopped listening when he saw Malcolm sitting in the backseat of Spivek's police car. He ran over, reached inside, and hurled Malcolm out.

David clutched Mal's shirt in a deathlike vise grip and jammed him against the squad car. "What did you do to Nia?"

Shaken up, Malcom tried to push back. "I didn't do anything to her."

Spivek and another officer tried to separate David from Malcolm, but David kept pressing. "What did you do to her!"

"One minute she was okay," Malcolm grunted. "The next minute she was passed out with no pulse. I called an ambulance. That's all I know. I swear!"

Frantic, David ran back into the ER, but this time they couldn't stop him. He shoved past the guard, ran through the hall, and found Nia lying on a table. When he saw her, motionless and lifeless, he shrank to his knees.

Nurses rushed past him. They placed a mask on her face and hooked her to machines while a doctor pumped her chest with both his hands. When that didn't work, they quickly hooked her up to a defibrillator and delivered several quick electrical jolts to her chest. Each time her body bounced, David's insides rocked with pain and emotion.

"Oh, God! Oh, God! Please!"

After several long attempts, one nurse said, "We can't resuscitate."

The doctor looked at the machines, baffled, then mumbled, "Expired." He picked up a clipboard and wrote down the time of death.

"No! Nooo!" David hollered so loud that two other doctors came with the security guard to help escort him out.

David was inconsolable.

❧ CHAPTER 48 ❧

At two A.M., David sat outside the ER with his face in his hands, bent over in a chair. Spivek paced near the coffee machines. When the attending physician came out, David was so spent that he couldn't stand up. Spivek came and stood by David's side.

The doctor said, "I'm afraid all attempts to revive Miss Youngblood failed. Her official time of expiration was six minutes to midnight, though phantom readings continued on the monitors, for some unknown reason."

David kept his face buried in his hands. "What did he do to her?"

"Preliminary cause of death appears to be natural causes," the doctor said.

David looked up. "*Natural* causes?"

"Yes. Until an official autopsy can be performed, it seems her heart simply gave out."

"There was nothing wrong with Nia's heart." David stood up. "Nia's heart was fine!" He clutched Spivek's arm. "Malcolm did something to her. Arrest him."

Spivek tried to calm him, frowning sympathetically. "Without evidence of foul play, we can't hold Malcolm. I'm sorry, buddy."

Spivek left David alone with the doctor for privacy. David pounded the wall. "She didn't just die!"

The doctor backed away slightly, being cautious. "When was the last time she'd been to a doctor? Had diagnostic tests run? Had an EKG?"

David couldn't answer those questions.

The doctor ran his pen down his clipboard, circling specific number values on Nia's chart. "Miss Youngblood's premortem estimated vitals would have been erratic, to put it mildly. Even after death, her body temperature remained nearly a hundred and twenty-five degrees. That's way too high, even for a living person." He showed David the numbers, but they didn't mean anything to him.

The doctor continued. "The patient's readings were highly abnormal. Her heart ceased pumping, yet electrical impulses and atypical vibrations remained on the monitors and even on the readouts. There's no way to explain it, other than to say it's highly unusual and even medically impossible. Even postmortem, her body remains an anomaly."

David ran his hand down his face, confused, trying to process everything, but mostly his heart just ached.

Finally, the doctor lowered his clipboard. "Have you notified her next of kin?"

The question rattled David. He shook his head. "No, I haven't notified anybody."

Already hours had passed, but for David, it seemed like time had stood still from the moment Nia slipped away.

The doctor put his pen back into his coat pocket. "Orderlies will move Miss Youngblood's body and she'll be processed. If you'll leave your number with the nurse, she'll advise you when the final report has been made, and someone related to the deceased can return and claim the body." The doctor left.

Standing alone in the middle of the room, David shook his head. "This can't be happening."

He walked unsteadily to the nurses' station. "Where do they take the people who—?" He stopped.

The nurse, who'd been listening, knew what he was trying to ask. "They take the bodies to the basement, but only staff is allowed down there. Nia Youngblood was just taken down."

David's lip trembled.

The nurse continued sympathetically, "If you're not ready to leave yet, have a seat and try to relax. Just be sure to give me your contact information before you leave."

"Where's the bathroom?" He needed to wash up. The nurse pointed him down the hallway.

David headed in that direction but bypassed the bathroom and caught the staff's service elevator down to the basement. He turned several corners and went down several long, empty hallways until he found a windowless room labeled with a small, engraved silver plate: MORGUE.

David pushed the door open slightly. He saw a monitor by the door listing the names of the deceased patients. Nia Youngblood was number eight.

David tried to go in but couldn't. His legs failed him, his knees gave out, and he slid his back down the wall. He sat on the floor just outside the morgue.

"Oh, God, Nia. How did I let you slip away from me?" He placed his hands in his lap and cried. "How did I lose you?"

His words bounced off the sterile walls as his shoulders shook. "I was supposed to protect you. I'm so sorry."

Images of Nia's face, along with Beez's, flashed through his mind. He felt his parents' scorn rip through his chest all over again. He doubled over. "Not again."

He lifted his chin and pleaded to God. "Please, it can't end like this. Give me another chance. I can't go through this again."

David lowered his face into his hands, knowing that what he was begging for was impossible.

After an interminable, heartrending while, David got up. His eyes were sore from crying, and his whole body ached from pain and grief.

He heard someone walking down the hallway toward the morgue, perhaps a staff orderly. He'd become disoriented and needed to ask for directions to find his way out, but the footsteps stopped before reaching the end of the hall.

David stepped forward and looked around the corner, but no one was there.

Rubbing his eyes clear, he looked back toward the morgue's door.

A man was standing there.

Instead of an orderly's white uniform, he wore a high-end, tailor-made imported suit in the deep, rich, dark color of fresh blood, like something a very successful, very fashionable, highly proficient crime lord would wear. The man had that kind of air about him.

David's grief-stricken mind took an extra moment to comprehend.

It was him.

The driver of the purple Caddy.

The shadow that had attacked him in Nia's dining room.

The man who'd stalked Nia when she was alive and now had the nerve to show up here at the morgue after she was dead.

David's throat tightened. He swallowed hard and clenched his fists. "What in the hell are you doing here?"

Rephaim didn't respond. He stood partway in the door's shadow. The tract lighting exposed his lower face but not his eyes.

Rage, resentment, and turmoil brewed just beneath David's restrained surface, threatening to burst forth. "If you're still looking for Nia, you're too late. She died."

The edges of Rephaim's lips curled up into a salacious smile. "I know."

Fury overtook David, and he rushed at him. Rephaim shifted abruptly like a shadow. Instead of hitting flesh and muscle, David hit the gray wall behind him. His left shoulder absorbed the brunt of the blow, and the force pushed him back and spun him around.

Rephaim disappeared into the morgue and slammed the door shut behind him. David tried to pull it open, but it stuck. He backed up and jump-kicked the door. When it flew open, the man had Nia's body cradled in his arms. David lunged at him, but again, Rephaim eluded him, and he crashed against the steel horizontal body cabinets. He jumped back up, breathing hard and grimacing with pain. He jerked around looking in all four directions, but Rephaim was gone, along with Nia's body. David stood alone and shaking inside the morgue.

Rephaim knew Zamzu had entered his parlor, but he didn't know why he'd come. He remained standing over Nia's dark polished casket, with his back to the door. "You're not allowed in here unless summoned, and I didn't summon you."

Zamzu uttered some excuse but Rephaim ignored his brother and continued gazing at Nia, whose body he'd stolen from the morgue.

She lay perfectly still, as if floating on a beautiful white cloud of death. He'd lined her casket with the finest imported white silk and lace, adorned with precious pearls and other jewels as rare as she. He'd removed Nia's clothes and redressed her in a plain white slip made of finely spun spider silk that would lie beneath her wedding gown.

Zamzu approached Nia's casket and looked at her too, but not with nearly the same amount of adoration. "In light of the recent events, I thought I could be of service."

"You?" Rephaim scoffed. "What could you possibly do for me?" Overwhelming pride filled his regal eyes as he looked again at Nia. "I told you I'd take her, and I've done just that."

"But she's dead. What good is she to you now?" Zamzu stepped back, unsure of his brother's reaction.

Rephaim smelled his fear. He ran his hand along Nia's glistening casket and answered his brother's question indirectly. "I've constructed Nia's casket from heartwood, a rare type of wood that has become resistant to decay."

He touched Nia's arm. "The world needed to see Nia's death so no one would come looking for her."

"But David Wrightwood saw you steal her body."

Rephaim turned quickly. "Were you spying on me?"

Zamzu saw the fierce scrutiny in his brother's eyes. He backed away. "No."

Zamzu's left ear twitched. Rephaim noted it.

"I purposely allowed him to see it," Rephaim lied. He hadn't anticipated David standing at the morgue, but so be it. "Let David's grief debilitate him and his fears consume his faith," he sneered, and circled Nia's casket. "His interruptions won't interfere with my plans for her."

Rephaim glanced at the faceless clock on the wall. "Very soon, I'll awaken her and, in a black ritual ceremony, take her as my wife."

Without disclosing the intricate details of his plans for Nia, Rephaim adjusted the lace surrounding Nia's face. He was not willing to share his knowledge or his power with his younger brother, who'd been of no assistance to him through the century as he'd fought and maneuvered his way up the dark hierarchy.

Rephaim removed a piece of cloth from his suit pocket and polished the smooth, shiny heartwood as Zamzu stood by silently observing him.

"My dear brother, do you remember the last time you attempted to betray me? And how I handled the situation in such a way as to ensure you'd never attempt to double-cross me again?"

Zamzu's expression fell flat as he remembered the violent incident. He nodded. "I'm not that stupid."

"Good. Because I desperately hope you're not planning to interfere in my plans as I take my new bride. You are my only remaining blood relation in our Nephilim tribe, and I'd hate to have to sacrifice you." Rephaim returned the cloth to his pocket. "Who else is better suited to wipe the excrement from my shoe at the end of a busy day?"

Rephaim's slight evil grin quickly turned into a ferocious display as he shifted into his demonic form and flashed razor-sharp fangs. Zamzu flinched but held his expression steady. In the next second, Rephaim had shifted back to his normal handsome state.

Again, he noted how his brother's left ear twitched.

"Leave me now," he commanded.

Zamzu exited.

He'd deal with his brother later. Right now, he had more work to do. Final preparations for Nia's rebirth and their union had to be made. Rephaim took one more look at Nia, then closed her casket. His hand lingered on the shiny brass latch.

Her casket stood on an altar-like brass frame in the center of his parlor. Six purple candles lit the dark room, and the soft flames from the candles emitted a gentle purplish glow over her temporary resting place. Rephaim placed the large brass candelabra in the center behind her casket to be lit during the black ceremony as a symbol of their eternal union.

He laid a single long-stemmed purple rose on top of her casket and left Nia Youngblood to lie dead inside his parlor.

Over the next few hours, Nia's body would undergo a transition. Heat from the poisonous toxins and other occult forces that he'd breathed into her would begin to permeate her body. Her cells would begin to agitate and accelerate, like tiny microwaves, regenerating unholy cells from holy ones. Her five mortal senses would amplify, her carnality would intensify, and the most sensual parts of her body would ignite and catch fire, creating in her an unquenchable sexual desire that only he would be able to satisfy. All of this was part of a skillfully crafted diabolic plan he'd set in motion twenty-five years ago at her conception, between Mystical and Jessie Youngblood.

Under his watchful eye, Nia's virginal body would be reborn into darkness.

At the appointed time, after the process was complete, he would awaken her.

She would become a new erotic dark being, still fully human and with the same mind, but possessing a unique spiritual attribute usually reserved for angels . . . and demonic princesses.

Very soon, Nia's afterlife would finally begin.

Chapter 50

At seven A.M. on Saturday morning, David left the hospital. Cruel light from the newly arisen sun attacked his eyes. Today would have been his wedding day. Instead, he'd plan Nia's obituary.

He'd spent all night pacing the floor of the morgue, demanding that the hospital administration search the entire building for Nia's missing body. Even in his frustration and grief, he didn't disclose information about this so-called *Ra-fi-eem* or his seemingly supernatural powers, other than to tell them there had been an intruder. When no one could find Nia's body, David knew he'd have to deal with Rephaim on his own terms.

In the meantime, he could only hope and pray Nia's soul was somewhere safe and protected by God.

David needed to notify Nia's parents. Telling Jessie would be simple enough, but contacting Mysti would present its own difficulties. He drove to Jessie Youngblood's residence in Mar Vista and knocked on the front door. If Jessie had gotten drunk the night before and had a hangover, this news would surely sober him up.

David heard Jessie moving around inside. He knocked again.

"Go away!" Jessie's voice was hoarse.

"Open the door, Mr. Youngblood. I've got bad news."

"Bad news?" Jessie swung open the door. The fermented alcohol on his breath hit David's nose. "You can't possibly tell me anything worse than what I already know."

David kept his place at the doorway. "Nia died last night."

Jessie stared back at David through bloodshot eyes. His jaw was tight and he looked like he was bracing himself. "Of course she died. What did you expect?"

Jessie's blasé response shocked David. He stared at him in disbelief. Jessie said, "Nia was doomed from the beginning."

"Nia was *not* doomed."

Jessie waved his hand dismissively. "You have no damn idea what was going on."

Jessie tried to close the door, but David blocked it. Long-brewing resentment and ire surfaced in that moment as David thought about his own father's recalcitrance. He turned his anger on Jessie. "You were her *father*!" Fuming, he pointed his finger in Jessie's face. "Fathers are supposed to support their children, even when they make a mistake!"

Jessie fumed back. "Nia didn't make the mistake. *I* did!"

David held Jessie's angry stare for several seconds. Finally, Jessie eased his jaw, unclenched his fist, and backed away but left the door open for David to step in.

David didn't want to go inside. He didn't want to be around the man who'd put Nia out at seventeen years old to fend for herself, or to be reminded of his own father, who'd turned his back on him when David was nineteen. But he went inside anyway, out of respect. Jessie was still Nia's father.

Jessie picked up a cognac bottle and slumped into his recliner. "From the time she was born and her mother handed her to me," he said irritably, "Nia had death written all over her."

David remained standing, listening.

Jessie took a long pull from the bottle and continued. "Nia was already a few months old the first time I saw her. I never knew exactly when she was born. Her eyes were already big and bright, the color of two brand-new pennies." He chuckled, then his laugh fell flat. "I wouldn't let myself look into them too long, didn't want to see the mistake I'd made, didn't want to get too attached."

David sat on the edge of the sofa. Jessie turned the bottle to his lips, took another drink.

"I figured if Nia turned out to be anything like her mother, she wouldn't want to get attached to me, either, but I was wrong. That little bright-eyed baby grew into an affectionate and caring girl with a heart so big it scared me. And that only made it harder, knowing what fate had in store for her," Jessie explained painfully.

David listened but didn't understand. Jessie was drinking, and David was reluctant to believe the words that spilled from the lips of a drunk.

Jessie lifted the bottle slightly and eyed the copper-colored brandy. "I used to be a preacher."

"A preacher?" David didn't try to hide his incredulity.

Jessie opened his end table and dug to the bottom. He slowly pulled out a worn, leather-bound black Bible and handed it to David. David read the gold letters inscribed on the cover: REVEREND JESSIE YOUNGBLOOD.

Jessie idly swirled the liquid around in the bottle. "My father was a preacher, too. In fact, I come from a long line of strong men of God."

He looked at Jessie, then at his bottle. "What happened?"

His eyes darkened with regret. "Mystical."

David watched as Jessie shifted uncomfortably and the weight of bad decisions burdened his face. "I never touched a drop of liquor until the night I met her," he recalled. "With one look, she got me. A woman who could make a man forget everything he believed in with one simple stroke of her fingernail across his arm. I should have known something wasn't right about her."

Jessie's hand tilted. David watched, waiting for liquid to spill. He continued, "Mystical didn't want me, she only wanted my seed. So she took it. Nia was conceived that same night."

"Why did Mysti target you?" David asked. "Why did she want to have your child?"

"Don't ask me to explain how evil works. It just does. Mystical wasn't working alone. Someone had sent her to me."

David thought about Rephaim.

Jessie took another swallow. "Nia was never intended to be a part of this world. They had otherworldly plans for her. By the time I realized my mistake, it was already too late and there was nothing I could do. So I tried to find my peace in the bottom of a bottle, to keep from going crazy."

After hearing Jessie's story, David was convinced that foul play continued, even though Nia had died. He needed to find her body and give her a proper burial. That was the least he could do.

David tried to hand the Bible back but Jessie wouldn't take it. He placed the Bible on the stand between them.

"I learned by studying the Bible never to give the devil a foothold," David said. "If he tries to take it, you fight. You hold on to what God has given you, and you don't give up." David stood up. "God gave me Nia."

Jessie didn't respond.

David walked to the door and opened it. "God gave me something to fight for. Whatever hope, courage, or love Nia put inside of me, I'm not letting go of it. Not today, not tomorrow, not ever."

⌘ CHAPTER 51 ⌘

When David left Jessie's house, he knew Jessie wouldn't contact Mysti to tell her about Nia's death. The responsibility fell on his shoulders, but he didn't know how much more weight he could bear. She had no phone number, no address, no place of known employment; David had no idea how to get in touch with Mysti.

Physically and emotionally depleted, David drove back to his condo. He stood in the middle of his bedroom next to his bed, where Nia used to sleep, and his body trembled. He needed to get himself together, if that was possible.

He stripped off his clothes, got into the shower, and let the hot water beat down on his head. His muscles were tense with stress, his left shoulder ached, and the back of his neck was tight with nerves. Steam rose and the air inside his bathroom grew thick, almost smothering. He was tired of crying. The water's hard stream helped drown out his sobs as he closed his eyes and pictured Nia standing in front of him at an altar, dressed in all white as his bride. That was the way she was supposed to look today when they got married, instead of motionless on a table.

"Nia, I'm sorry—" He turned up the water pressure. "I swear, I'd marry you a thousand times, if only I had another chance."

SEVENTEEN MINUTES AFTER Rephaim laid Nia to rest in her casket, she opened her eyes. She choked and coughed, trying to catch her breath. Her lungs burned like someone had poured dry fuel into them. As she coughed more, puffs of fine powdery dust were expelled from her mouth.

After finally catching her breath, she wondered where she was. The dark, confined space startled her. She pushed up on the compartment's door, which loomed above her head, and sat up. She felt dizzy and her head felt heavy as the room seemed to spin crazily. Flickering candlelight distorted shapes and sizes, and the colors inside the dark room seemed to glow with a purplish haze. A faint sweet smell, like boiling sugar in a refinery, greeted her nose, and she looked down at the delicate white lace adorned with pearls and precious jewels that touched her skin, and at the shiny box that surrounded her body. *A casket?*

Alarmed, Nia quickly felt her cheeks. She ran her hands down her arms and legs, feeling her body. She was warm, and her skin felt soft. Her breathing was shallow, due to nerves, but was otherwise sufficient.

Nia was baffled. If she was dead, then someone had forgotten to turn off her mind, her thoughts, her senses, and her emotions.

How could that be?

A sound in the next room interrupted her thoughts. Someone stirred, moving about, setting things in place. Whoever it was had probably put her in the casket. She needed to leave, quickly and quietly.

As she climbed out, her arms were shaky and her legs unsteady, but she kept moving, too afraid to keep still. She snuck through the dark purplish haze, her white slip brushed against the wall, and she bumped into a tall brass candelabra, tilting it. She steadied it on its base but knocked over a purple candle. The burning wax spilled on her hand and she panicked, and desperately whispered the only name that came to her mind: *"David . . . help me."*

DAVID HEARD A noise and turned off the shower but kept his hand gripping the knob. Water continued to drip from the faucet and from his cold, wet body.

He thought he'd heard someone call his name. He stilled himself and listened.

The voice sounded like . . .

No, she was gone.

David got out of the shower and dried off quickly. He threw on a pair of pants and a shirt, yet he couldn't resist. He sat on his bed, breathing hard, but quieted his heart and listened again, though he knew what he was thinking was impossible.

Grief had led to insanity.

He got up and tried to shake it off. He left his bedroom and paced his condo, spotting items that belonged to her—stuff she'd left in his condo, knowing she'd be back. The pink T-shirt she'd thrown on the floor of his closet. A battery-operated Superman toothbrush. Her hair comb with one tooth broken.

When he picked up the comb, an overwhelming surge of grief shot through him, but he felt something else also. Something dangerous, like hope.

He grabbed his car keys and left. He needed fresh air right away, as his condo's walls were starting to cave in on him.

David drove aimlessly, in no particular direction . . . until he heard her call his name again.

It was a low, desperate whisper. *"David."*

He swerved, nearly clipping a tractor-trailer heading in the opposite direction as his Jaguar ran off the road. He skidded to a stop, parked on the shoulder, and waited.

NIA'S BODY MOVED faster than her mind. She ran through several murky hallways before spotting a narrow door. She blew through the exit, barreled outside, and came upon an iron gate. She kicked the gate open and tumbled down an embankment, a sharp, rocky incline full of rocks and dead weeds, before rolling to a stop. She wasn't hurt.

Crouching, she looked back up at the house from which she'd escaped. Sleek and modern, with no windows, it was perched precariously at the top of a rocky hill. Nia blinked. The structure seemed to vanish inside the bright rays of the late morning sun.

She looked farther down the canyon. A city stood in the distance, with tall buildings and streets that she recognized. Nia started running toward the familiar landscape. Her bare feet were unshielded against the dirt, rocks, and ditches, but she set a steady pace and just kept running.

DAVID TRIED TO keep his mind clear and tried not to let grief distort his thoughts. He spotted a dirt path near where he'd run off the road and turned down it to get away from other traffic. Guided only by shaky hands and a thumping heart, he followed the trail until he reached a wider, rocky road, a road seldom traveled.

From the corner of his eye, he saw something white running in the desert, parallel to his car, darting past Joshua trees and over tumbleweeds. Perhaps it was a deer or a large coyote.

He couldn't tell because the sun was glaring around the object and blurred his eyes.

He slowed as he came upon a fork in the road.

Without warning, the figure cut across his path, passing directly in front of him. He slammed on his brakes and skidded on the rocks, but he was too late. He'd hit it.

Whiteness tumbled over his windshield, rolled across the roof of his car, and spilled off his trunk. Panicked, David threw his car into park and jumped out.

A white object lay sprawled in the road.

He ran closer.

A woman in a white slip with waves of sepia hair flung across the back of her head rolled over in the dirt. When he saw her face, he jumped back. David's reflexes turned him around in a circle—shocked, confused, and in disbelief, he spun three hundred and sixty degrees—before he faced her again. He felt his soul leap inside his body.

Afraid to touch her, afraid to say a word, he stood still. She moaned as she rolled over, her body uninjured, just shaken. Her face was every bit as lovely as when she'd stood in front of him at the altar during their wedding rehearsal the night before.

CHAPTER 52

*D*avid crouched in the middle of the dirt road next to Nia. The same intense sunlight that had crucified him earlier that morning now glowed sofly around the edges of Nia's brown hair. As he stared at her, a wavy lock fell across her penny-colored eyes. He reached out to move it but hesitated. "How do you explain this?" he asked.

She took his hand and brought it to her face, staring back at him. "I can't."

In awe, he moved his hand across her cheek. Warm, soft, and smooth, her complexion was even more beautiful than he'd remembered. "But I saw you lying on the table. The doctor wrote down your time of death. Six minutes to midnight."

Emotions began to arise inside of him. Where he'd felt loss, despair, and anger moments before, he now felt a surging rush of hope, love, and passion. He stuttered, "I—I thought I'd lost you."

He pulled her to him and clutched her warm body,

holding her like he never wanted to let go again. Still unsure if this was real, he whispered, "Nia, I need to feel you."

He held her face to him and plunged his tongue deep inside her mouth. As she sighed, her mouth's moist heat was even more intense than when he'd last kissed her. He moved uncontrollably, smelling her sweet spice, caressing her warm curves, and feeling the passion of her kiss, a sensation he never wanted to lose again.

Nia clutched his neck and pulled him farther into her. Her body responded fervently to his touch, writhing against his hardness, as they lay on the dirt road.

His mind had trouble comprehending. "Nia . . . you're alive."

He moved his hand under her white slip and clutched her thigh. Soft, vibrant flesh responded to his grip with erotic twitches. He pushed up the white slip and rushed his hands up her body. He grasped her breasts and squeezed their wonderful fullness as her nipples hardened with sexual desire. He pushed himself into her, kissing, tasting, grinding, exploding with physical affection, while trying to get his mind around the fact that she was really there—her face, her body, her soul.

He wanted to feel all of her. He slid himself down and buried his face between her breasts, kissing her warm flesh, trying to feel every part of her body, until a realization stilled him, and he froze.

"Nia." David sat up slowly, stiffening as dread filled his face. "I can't feel your—"

"Heartbeat."

NIA INHALED AND braced herself as she watched David's expression change and horror fleet through his dark, lovely eyes. He pulled away, troubled and confused. Though she understood, still his reaction hurt her.

Somewhere in the desert as she was running, she realized that her heart should have been racing and her pulse pounding. But she'd felt only an eerie stillness in her chest. She was scared and confused, but had kept running.

Nia quickly lowered the white slip around her shaking body and tugged nervously at her hair, having no explanation or words of consolation to offer David, or even herself.

As David stared at her, his lips quivered. "What's happening, Nia?"

His eyes scampered to her chest

"David, I—" She paused, searching for words. "I think I'm still dead."

❦ CHAPTER 53 ❧

*W*hen Rephaim returned to his parlor and saw Nia was missing from her casket, he went ballistic.

"Nooo!" he hollered in a demonic rage. His deep voice boomed through the dimly lit air, rocking the black altar. The walls shook, the candelabra vibrated, and the flames on the purple candles blew out.

In complete darkness, Rephaim bowed his head, clenched his fists, and cursed everything holy.

"Her transformation is not complete," he snarled, his temper at its brink. "She is not yet ready!"

Rephaim himself had underestimated the power of Nia Youngblood's life force. Impatient, impulsive, and incessantly strong-willed, Nia had gotten up of her own free will, before the poisons and incantations had time to take full effect.

"Zamzummims!" Rephaim hollered, summoning his brother

in a loud rage. His brother appeared before him immediately. "What do you know about this?"

Rephaim pointed his finger at Nia's empty casket.

Zamzu acted surprised. "Nothing."

But Rephaim held to his strong suspicion that his brother was in some way connected to Nia's disappearance.

Perhaps fearing for his safety, Zamzu remained steadfast in his reaction. "What happened? Where'd she go?"

Rephaim lowered his gaze to Nia's casket. "Nia's life force was stronger than even I'd imagined." He touched the edge of her casket. "She arose early, before it was time."

Even in total darkness, his demon eyes canvassed the lace pillow where her head had lain just moments ago. A cringe of regret knotted his countenance, and anger pierced his abdomen as thoughts of failure tried to steal away his confidence.

"She's in limbo," he uttered, trying to squelch the human emotions of sadness and fear. "Nia's body is in a suspended state of animation. Until the transition is complete, a war wages inside of her, as two sides battle for her soul, one holy, the other unholy. She has not yet chosen sides. Whichever side she chooses, her spirit will follow." His jaw tightened. "She's vulnerable to external influences, both godly and ungodly."

The nerves in his neck and face jutted out as he touched the lace. "Things will happen to her body that she won't understand. She'll be capable of unordinary things." He swore silently. Even he was no longer sure exactly what Nia was capable of.

Rephaim closed her casket and covered it with a black cloth taken from an ancient Egyptian tomb. He turned and regarded Zamzu harshly. As his brother bowed his head, his left ear twitched.

"If you are somehow connected, reconsider your actions," he warned Zamzu. "Choose life instead."

Rephaim dismissed his brother.

He'd go search for Nia. He knew her sensuality would be piqued, and her spiritual and sexual appetites would be raging at full force. Yet she'd be emotionally fragile. His worst fear was that somehow she'd reunited with David Wrightwood.

He'd have to find her, then handle her with care and gently guide her to the dark side. He was prepared to move heaven and earth to make her his bride.

"I'm so close," Rephaim whispered as he left his parlor. "I won't let her slip through my hands."

CHAPTER 54

As David drove Nia back to his condo, the ride seemed long and the air thick with uncertainty and tension. She guessed neither of them knew what to say or how to articulate what they were thinking and feeling.

David opened the door and she walked inside. She felt like she'd been gone forever.

They stood in the middle of his living room, staring at each other.

Finally, David asked, "How did we find each other out there in the desert, in the middle of nowhere?"

She spoke cautiously, her mind still trying to process events. "Because we have a connection."

He hesitated, then slowly reached out and touched her warm arm and rubbed it softly. His touch felt good, and for a moment, her body fooled her, feeling as if everything was okay. But when she pressed her hand to her chest, she felt only stillness and an empty pang. She looked at David and realized another reason for her emptiness.

"Why didn't our *connection* stop you from breaking my heart?"

Hot tears filled her eyes as she remembered seeing him kissing Cher-Ling the night before, at their wedding rehearsal.

"Nia, I—" Words seemed to fail seeing him as his hand slipped from her arm. "I thought she was you."

"You thought she was me?" Disbelief and anguish spilled through her voice.

"I know it sounds like a lie, but it's the truth."

"David, I can't—" She paused. "I can't believe that."

"But, Nia, I swear," David said, coming toward her, but she raised her hands and backed up. Heavy tears brimmed at the bottom of her eyes, threatening to topple down her cheeks.

"I can't believe anything anymore. It's too hard," she said, shaking her head.

As the tears began to fall, she stared back at him, but her vision clouded. "I miss you, David. I miss what we had."

"Don't say that, Nia," he pleaded. "We still have each other."

She turned away, feeling lost, but he persisted.

"It's not over. It can't be over." He tried to turn her back around, tried to talk to her as if there was still hope. "Nia, I'm going to help you. Whatever went wrong, I'll make it right."

She tried to listen but his words sounded empty. She covered her wet face with her hands.

"Look at me." He held her arms and tried to blot her tears. "What happened between your parents when you were born? What did Mysti do to you? Who is this guy, Rephaim? What does he want from you?"

The image of her dark lover assailed her, flooding her mind with erotic thoughts. She shook her head. Sadness over losing David and anger at his betrayal attacked her emotions. She tried to back away.

David gripped her arms and shook her. "Think!"

"I can't!" she yelled back. She jerked out of his embrace. Overwhelmed, she shouted, "Leave me alone!"

Her body, her senses, her emotions, and her conflicting desires all seemed amplified. Frustrated, she threw up her hands. "I don't *know*."

David calmed a bit, apologizing. "I'm sorry."

She muttered, confused, "I don't know how this happened or who did this to me."

David gritted his teeth. "I'm positive Rephaim's hand is in all of this."

Somehow, she knew it, too. The probability that Rephaim had interfered in her life both horrified and thrilled her. If she'd truly lost David, could he be the one to ease some of her pain?

"Please," David uttered. "Don't give up on us, Nia."

Her emotions jerked back and forth like a boomerang.

"You want to save me, but how?" Nia challenged him. "The worst has already happened. Our relationship is ruined, and as for my life . . ." She held up her arms pitifully. "You told me we had *all the time in the world.* Now look at me."

His gaze reflected all the sadness she felt.

Nia's tears poured. "After all of this, how can you make me believe again?"

"But, Nia—"

She refused to listen. "Can you make my heart beat again?"

He continued pleading, trying to make things better with empty words, but she shook her head. "You're not a miracle worker, David. You can't make me believe again."

Feeling lost but angry, she walked toward the door.

"I don't even know if I *want* to believe again." She sniffed. "It hurts too much when things fall apart."

She walked out, leaving him alone in his condo to figure it all out and to see if his faith would be of any use to him now. As for her, she was no longer sure of anything.

○○ CHAPTER 55 ○○

*D*avid couldn't believe he'd allowed Nia to walk out the door. He took off after her, but she moved fast and disappeared across the lawn. He didn't understand how he could lose sight of her that quickly.

David darted across the lawn and circled the hedges. With no sign of Nia, he ran toward some kids playing near the pool and questioned them. He also asked a woman walking her poodle if she'd seen a woman in a white slip run past, but they all said no.

David spent the next hour searching for Nia. Finally, he drove to her house in Northridge, thinking maybe she'd hitched a ride. When he got there, her driveway was empty but he knew her gold Mustang remained parked at the Radisson Hotel from the night before. He banged on the door, thinking she could be inside. Her house was quiet, and there was no answer. He went around back and crawled through a window she always left open.

"Nia," he called as he searched her house.

Realizing she wasn't there, he went out the front door and closed and locked it. As he left her house and jumped back in his car, his mind was in turmoil, determined to find her. He moved so quickly that he hadn't noticed the pair of long legs seated next to him.

David flinched and dropped his keys.

Mysti reached over and picked them up. She held his keys in her fingers, toying with them, and in her other hand she balanced a cigarette, watching him, amused.

Obviously, she didn't know about Nia's death. He had to tell her, but he didn't know how to say it or where to begin. "There's something I have to tell—"

"I already know," she said, and took a pull on her cigarette.

"You know?" he asked, surprised by her casualness.

She nodded and added inscrutably, "Way more than you do."

Mysti's attitude only added to his growing frustration. Nia's father was drunk and David couldn't trust his words, but maybe her mother would drop her Elvira routine long enough to shed some valuable light on the whole terrible situation.

"What exactly do you know, Mysti?" He ran his hand over his tired face, trying to maintain his composure. "And please don't play with me. I'm not in the mood."

"Nia is not really dead," she said, getting straight to the point.

Though David already knew this, hearing Mysti say it out loud still jarred him. He listened.

"Medically speaking, yes, she is deceased, but not according to spiritual laws." Mysti flicked her ashes out the window. "Nia is in a suspended, demonically induced state."

"What does that mean?"

"Exactly what I just said." She pulled another long drag and let it out slowly, as if giving David time to comprehend. But no matter how much time she gave him, he wasn't going to get it. He stared at her impatiently.

Mysti shifted slightly in her seat and crossed her long legs. "Rephaim will bring Nia back to life—or at least give her a heartbeat—in the same instant that he takes her as his bride."

"His *bride*?" David frowned angrily.

"He's going to marry her in a black ritual ceremony. Once he does that, she'll be his forever."

"No." David shook his head. "He can't do that."

"Yes, he can, and he will," Mysti assured him.

"But how? Who is Rephaim really? *What* is he?"

"A demon. A dark lord. A very powerful creature."

"Nobody has that kind of power but God. Who gave Rephaim the right to toy with Nia's life?"

"I did, as her birth mother. Before Nia was even conceived in my womb, I made some deals."

David narrowed his eyes at Mysti. "What kind of wicked motives could a mother have to allow a curse like this upon her child?"

Mysti didn't answer.

David clenched his jaw and tightened his fists, trying hard to restrain the fury he felt toward her at that moment. She must have sensed it because she edged away from him slightly, defensively. A thousand more questions filled his head about Rephaim and the extent of his power and evilness, but he was too upset to ask. David exhaled hard and loud, and tried to focus. "Tell me about Nia. What's going to happen to her?"

Mysti continued. "Nia's heartbeat will start again at the moment they consummate the marriage, when Rephaim has sex with her." Mysti's green eyes intensified.

David struck the steering wheel with his clenched fist. In a low, strained voice, he vowed, "I won't let that happen."

"Nia's *rebirth* will take place at the exact time she was born on her real birthday."

"When is her real birthday?"

"Today."

David flinched. Mysti seemed amused by his shock.

"Six minutes before midnight—exactly twenty-four hours after her death last night. After that, it'll be too late to save her."

David looked at his watch.

Mysti informed him, without looking, "Eleven hours, thirty-six minutes, eight seconds . . . and counting."

"Does Nia know all of this?"

"Nia knows next to nothing. Rephaim figured it was best to keep her in the dark all of these years and I agreed."

"Why?"

"If Nia knew she was damned, don't you think she would have done something, like prayed or tried to find Jesus, to keep from dwelling in hell for the rest of eternity?"

David looked at Mysti questioningly. "If you are that spiritually aware, what's your excuse for not seeking Jesus?"

"I thought about joining the heavenly choir once, but I didn't like the way the robes fit." She winked sarcastically.

David frowned and ignored Mysti's antics. "How do I save Nia?"

"What makes you think Nia wants to be saved?"

"Why wouldn't she?"

"Have you ever gotten a real good look at Rephaim?" she asked slyly. "Rephaim is one hell of a man."

She wrapped her lips around the tip of the cigarette and pulled hard, sucking the glowing flame toward her. She blew out a long swirling snake of smoke as she recalled with passion, "He has a body to die for." She chuckled ironically. "But his appeal goes beyond just the physical. Intellectually, emotionally, and even spiritually, that man has a way of breaking a woman down, making her want to sell her soul just to spend one long, hard, throbbing night with him."

Mysti rubbed her legs together, twisting slightly in her seat, and gazed up at the bright midday sun. Her jade eyes grew deep with lust. "Sex with a powerful dark demon lord like Rephaim is out of this world. He gives orgasms that erupt like volcanoes."

Irritated, David asked, "And you know this because . . . ?"

"I've experienced it. Believe me, once is *not* enough." Her eyes flashed with jealousy and envy; she was obviously thinking about being in Nia's shoes.

David exhaled. Anger tightened his muscles, and his patience wore thin. "You still haven't told me how I'm supposed to save Nia."

"You don't even realize the power you have, David. You've got to figure out how to convince Nia that what you can offer her is just as good, if not better." Mysti's eyes dropped to his zipper.

He raised his hand. "Don't go there, Mysti. This is not about sex."

"It's not *only* about sex," she corrected him. "But never underestimate the power of a good climax." She put out her cigarette on his dashboard. "This is about two alpha males battling for dominance over little Nia's soul. Remember I told you that part of Rephaim's appeal is spiritual, too. Nia is looking for something to believe in."

Her last comment cut straight to David's heart; he remembered the despair in Nia's eyes when she told him she no longer believed in love.

He asserted somberly, "I do love Nia."

"But she doesn't believe it."

David couldn't argue. It was true.

"The only thing that matters is what Nia believes," she continued. "Whatever Nia believes, Nia becomes."

"She's confused. She feels betrayed."

"Her faith is up for grabs." Mysti saw the uncertainty in his eyes. "Now is not the time to doubt your faith, or your virility." Her eyes fell back over his lap as she handed him his keys. "Besides, there's nothing more sexy than watching two alpha males battling for sexual and spiritual dominance."

She got out and leaned back through the window. As he put the key in the ignition, she watched him.

"Why are you helping me? What's in all of this for you?" he asked, knowing she was up to something.

"Can't a mother simply care about her baby girl?" Mysti grinned, full of bullshit.

He watched her slink away, wondering what her true motives were. But right now he had no time to waste on Mysti. He had to find Nia and make her believe again. He also had to do whatever it would take to stop a dark, malevolent being from making Nia his wife.

CHAPTER 56

*A*t three P.M., Nia's hormones were raging and her emotions surging as she wandered through the busy streets of Los Angeles alone. She didn't understand the strange longings she felt or the strange erotic compulsions that gripped her psyche, but she knew something odd was happening to her body.

Like when she'd slipped away from David. She saw him give chase and figured she couldn't outrun him, so she stood still and held her breath, planning to talk him out of following her. But he ran right past her, calling her name. Somehow, she'd blended in with the atmosphere. When she looked down at her body, only a transparent haze, like heat rising from asphalt, existed where her torso should have been.

Her body felt different, too, ironically more alive and vibrant than before. She could move much faster than normal, and when she didn't want to be seen, she held her breath and her body became transparent.

Like now.

Nia didn't want anyone to see the sad look on her face or the desperation in her eyes. Loneliness, alienation, and confusion dominated her soul as she walked invisibly past people and landmarks that seemed foreign to her now. She felt like she'd always felt, like she didn't belong.

With no direction in mind, she walked fast and thought about David and Rephaim. One man she'd thought she knew but who had apparently lied to her; the other she'd never dared to meet, except in her dreams.

In less time than normal, she'd somehow traveled from David's condo in Culver City to her house in Northridge and found herself standing on her front lawn, staring at her gold Shelby Mustang parked in her driveway. She walked to her own front door, feeling like a stranger.

Her door had been left unlocked. When she went inside, the house was quiet. She saw her keys on the table, and memories of the night before began to come back to her in wisps.

She'd been in such a hurry to go see David at their wedding rehearsal that she'd tilted over the lamp by the door. Nia set it back upright and continued up the winding stairs. She thought about how happy she was to finally see David after a long week, about the freak storm that knocked out the church's electricity, and about the dark stranger who appeared at the back of the church.

Nia paused at the top of the staircase and thought about *him*. A wave of heat and anticipation washed over her as she remembered his tall, masculine body walking up the aisle toward her, his face covered in shadows. She gripped the banister to steady herself.

Aroused yet confused, she entered the hallway. As she walked toward her bedroom, the disturbing vision of David kissing Cher-Ling assailed her mind. Anger overtook her, and she stopped and closed her eyes, trying to clear her head, but the image wouldn't fade, and neither would the pain. She remembered how Malcolm had shown up and tried to console her. In her heartbreak, she'd thought making love to Malcolm would help ease the pain, but she came to her senses when they walked into the hotel room. Though David had broken her heart, she was still in love with him. She tried to dissuade Malcolm, but he became violent.

That's when he killed her.

A new surge of rage overtook her. Incensed, she headed for her bedroom phone. She'd call the police, tell them what Malcolm did, and have him arrested. But when Nia opened her bedroom door, she found Malcolm in bed with Shayla, having sex on her favorite satin sheets. She froze.

CHAPTER 57

*N*ia couldn't believe her eyes. In one long, angry breath, she exhaled. As the vapor-like cells of her body began to materialize, she screamed, "Mal!"

Mal jumped off Shayla. He swung around and looked at her, squinting skeptically. "Nia?"

"I live here, remember?"

His eyes grew large. "Nia!"

Both Mal and Shayla scrambled frantically, with their naked bodies tangling in the satin covers as they clambered to get off the bed.

Furious, Nia lunged at them both, but Mal moved quickly and pushed Shayla into Nia. He grabbed his pants and ran out of the bedroom. Shayla tried to run too but tripped over Nia's foot and landed sprawled on the floor by the bed, blocking Nia's path.

Nia tried quickly to step over Shayla and go after Mal, but

she stopped. She whipped around. "How could you do this? You were supposed to be my best friend!"

Shayla tried to squirm away but Nia cornered her.

Shocked and too afraid to speak, Shayla blubbered incoherently and tears began to stream down her cheeks in black mascara trails as she lay there naked. Nia yanked the sheet off her bed and threw it at her. Shayla twisted it around, clutching it to her chest. Her face wrinkled with fear and confusion at seeing Nia . . . alive. Finally she calmed enough to speak. "Nia, you had all the guys. I had nobody."

"That's no excuse. You were screwing my ex-boyfriend in *my* bed!" Nia cringed, then shouted, "You knew Malcolm and I had history. I confided in you. You knew how he constantly hurt and betrayed me. He was no good."

Shayla sniveled pitifully. "I couldn't do any better."

Nia suddenly felt dizzy as her anger at Shayla melted into pity. She looked down at Shayla, realizing that low self-esteem had plagued her all her life, and now Nia felt sorry for her. "Oh, Shayla. Damn it. You can do better. Didn't you hear what happened to me last night?"

Shayla stiffened and nodded slowly. "Mal said it was an accident."

"Mal *killed* me." Nia bit her bottom lip to keep it from trembling. Now wrath wracked her body as she paced around the bed, trying to get a handle on her vacillating emotions. "He couldn't even wait until they put me in the ground before he started banging my best friend."

"I'm sorry, Nia." Shayla sniffed as she apologized. She wiped her smudged eyes on the sheet and looked at Nia skeptically. "But how did you—"

"Come back?" Nia finished her sentence for her. "I don't know yet."

Shayla backed away slightly, perplexed and troubled. "Are you still—"

"Dead?" Nia placed her hand on her chest and felt for a heartbeat. "Don't mean to scare you, Shayla, but yeah, I think so."

Nervously, Shayla scrambled to her feet. "Okay. I think I'd better go now."

"Yeah. I don't blame you." Nia watched as Shayla clutched the sheet and ran from the bedroom.

After a minute, Nia left too, to look for Malcolm.

Forget about calling the police; she wanted revenge. She wanted to put the fear of God in Malcolm by giving him a supernatural butt-kicking.

Nia hurried out the front door and ran into her front yard. She stood by the acacia tree, looking up and down the block for Mal. Someone tapped her on the shoulder and scared the living daylights out of her.

$\mathcal{L}$eaning against the tree trunk, bouncing a cigarette between her fingers, Mysti asked coolly, "Hey, Nia. What's up?"

Flabbergasted, Nia yelled, "What do you mean 'What's up?' Look at me." She held up both her hands. Mysti glanced causally down her body. Irate, Nia huffed, "And don't act like you don't know."

Mysti didn't deny knowing Nia had expired. Nia waited for her mother to have some kind of reaction to her death, and when she didn't, Nia asked, "Is that all you're going to say? *'What's up?'*"

Mysti remained her usual iceberg-cool self. "What would you like me to say, Nia?"

"How about explaining to me how I got in this predicament? What did you do to me? How do I get out of this dead situation?"

"If you think I have all the answers, I'm flattered." Mysti flicked her cigarette.

"You're always scheming, Mysti. I know somehow you're involved in this."

"You're right," Mysti admitted. Her honesty shocked Nia. Mysti looked around the yard as if someone might be watching. "But let's not talk about it here. Follow me."

As Mysti walked to her white SUV and got in, Nia remained by the tree protesting, but her complaints went ignored. She needed answers, and Mysti was hiding some. Reluctantly, Nia got into the SUV with Mysti and they drove off.

Despite Nia's questions, Mysti didn't say much as she drove. She pulled up in front of a popular hangout in the Valley, Club XO, an upscale daytime club for people who couldn't wait until the evening to party. Nia cast a wary look at the partygo-ers, then threw Mysti a questioning look. "It's the middle of the day. Plus, I'm dead," she added indignantly. "I'm not exactly in the mood to get my party on."

"Let's hang out, grab a few drinks." Mysti parked her SUV in the red zone and started getting out. "I can't think of a better reason to tie one on."

Nia didn't for one second trust her scheming mother's nonchalant air. She rubbed her forehead and followed Mysti inside the club. Mysti slipped the bouncer a twenty, and he let them in through a side door. She led Nia to the bathroom and handed her a satchel she'd taken from her SUV. Nia opened it and pulled out an exotic red and black designer dress, one of Mysti's signature snakeskin outfits.

Mysti pointed to Nia's clothes. "That white slip just isn't working."

Nia slipped the dress over her head. Since she and Mysti were about the same size with the same curvaceous figure, the soft snakeskin dress made from the original reptilian scales fit Nia perfectly, hugging all her voluptuous places. Mysti also gave Nia a pair of six-inch spiked shoes.

Nia smoothed down the dress, ran her fingers through her hair, and stumbled to the mirror, inspecting herself. She murmured, "This is so not me."

Mysti regarded the dress. "You could use a little bang in your wardrobe."

They left the bathroom. Nia followed Mysti deeper into the club, and they sat at one of the bars. Mysti nodded to the bartender, who promptly brought them two banana daiquiris.

Nia sipped hers thirstily, complaining, "This is all your fault."

Mysti didn't touch her drink but lit another cigarette. "I didn't kill you, if that's what you mean."

"I know Mal killed me, but I'm betting you had a hand in all this. I'm thinking you put some kind of spell on me at my birth, dooming me to a weird and unusual death, all, of course, for your ultimate gain."

"Relax. It'll be fun," Mysti said, then turned to watch the dancers. Nia didn't know if Mysti was talking about the club or her predicament.

Inside, the place looked like the usual upscale nighttime club, with strobe lights, three huge bars, smoky air, mirrors, and the pervasive scent of alcohol and lack of inhibition. It also boasted a large, shiny dance floor where people danced like they never wanted to go back to their normal daily-grind lives.

Despite the devil-may-care ambience, Nia couldn't take her mind off her tragic predicament. "So, Mysti, tell me," she asked, "what kind of hex did you put on me?"

At forty-plus, Mysti looked better than most women half her age. With a tight body, fluid motions, and drop-dead gorgeous looks, she turned men's heads. Mysti fiddled with her unlit cigarette while tapping her foot in rhythm to the loud music.

"Everything I did was motivated by two things."

"What?" Nia asked.

"Power. And more power."

"Power for who, you?"

"Of course," Mysti said, like the answer should have been obvious.

Nia sighed. "You're amazing. Remind me to nominate you for mother of the year," she said, rolling her eyes.

Mysti smirked at the comment. "By the way, I ran into David earlier."

"I find that hard to believe. You don't run into people, you haunt them."

"He's really broken up over your death."

"Yeah." Nia pretended to be unmoved. "That makes two of us."

She didn't want to talk about David, although she hadn't stopped thinking about him since he'd run into her in the desert, literally. She finished off the last of her daiquiri. "What am I doing here?"

"Drinking."

"No, I mean, what am I *doing here*?" Nia discreetly ran her hand over her cleavage and added somberly, "With no heartbeat."

Mysti glanced at Nia momentarily, then continued tapping her foot to the music, as if she hadn't heard the question. Nia rearranged herself on the bar stool, knowing Mysti was simply being her usual obstinate self. She tried a different question.

"How long did you know my father before you screwed him?"

"Never bothered getting to know him, just screwed him. It's so much better that way," Mysti answered without missing a beat.

Nia recoiled and continued their very first mother-daughter talk. "So, what happens to me now?"

"For the next seven hours, you'll go through hell," Mysti said casually. "Then things will get really bad."

Nia cringed. "What can I do to improve my situation?"

She scratched her white fingernail tip on her cigarette, lighting it without a match. "Have another drink."

Mysti nodded and the bartender rushed two more banana daiquiris in front of them. Nia immediately sipped hers, but Mysti got up. "I need to make a call," she told Nia, then winked. "Sit tight."

Mysti took a few steps away and removed her tiny cell phone from her belt. As she pushed speed dial, Nia listened to the tone of the buttons. The sequence sounded familiar. Mysti was calling David.

Nia continued sipping her daiquiri while debating whether to get up and leave. After their blowup at his condo, she didn't want to see David, yet she missed him tremendously. Her mixed emotions swayed back and forth like a pendulum. Her body also responded to her high-flying emotions with strong, unmistakable tingles in her private places, letting her know that her pheromone levels raged at an all-time high.

As Nia continued to flip-flop over whether to stay or leave, she self-consciously glanced around the club. Several men gawked at her, all with the flirty-slash-lustful gaze that she'd seen so many times. She chuckled and murmured to herself, "I am so off the market."

She rolled her eyes, dismissing their gawking stares. Besides, none of the men at the club caught her attention anyway.

Except for one.

CHAPTER 59

$\mathcal{L}$eaning against a beam, with his head cocked slightly to the side, the man stared at Nia from across the room. His eyes were light golden, almost translucent. An abnormal eye color for humans, the catlike hue was especially striking against his darkly vibrant complexion.

Floored by just one glance, Nia paused with her drink at her lips. If she'd had a heartbeat, it would have skipped. Having never seen his face before, she had no idea who the man was. She averted her eyes quickly and sipped her daiquiri. *This is silly,* she thought, referring to his mesmerizing eyes, *probably just a reflection off a strobe light.*

When Nia looked again, he was still peering at her, and his gaze reminded her of something, but she couldn't think of what it was. Alone and off to the side, he stood out from the crowd like he was in a world of his own and he owned it.

Strong sexual vibes emanated from him like sound

waves, and Nia felt the sensual tension right off the bat. Her palms began to sweat and the tingling in forbidden places rose to a higher intensity. She glanced around at Mysti, who was still talking to David on the phone. Her hearing had amplified, and she could hear the desperation and urgency in David's voice from where she stood. It was making her crazy with confusion.

When she looked over again, the man had leaned off the beam and started coming toward her. Mysti must have sensed the man approaching too, because she paused her conversation and looked in his direction. By the time the man reached the bar, Mysti had hung up and was watching him, but she stayed a distance away.

The man was dressed casually in a loose-fitting, light tan herringbone sports jacket with two buttons and light-colored slacks. His walk was every bit as relaxed as his appearance. A white V-neck shirt lay smoothly beneath his sports jacket, and a light brown fedora covered his head. He turned every woman's head as he walked across the room, and a few men's, too. One woman placed her hand to her chest to catch her breath.

When he finally drew near, he stood dangerously close to Nia, penetrating her private space with his strong masculine aura and shattering that invisible bubble that strangers use to guard themselves.

Or maybe Nia was extra sensitive right now. Maybe she'd only imagined that his huge physique and his strong presence were overpowering her senses and pulling her to him. Discreetly, she tried to cool herself and regain her composure. She carefully set her drink down and glanced his way.

He didn't say anything.

Up close, his eyes burned even more intensely, smoldering with unknown intent. If he hadn't smiled, she would have thought he was angry about something.

Since he didn't start the conversation, she tried to think of something to say. "I noticed you were staring at me. Is there a reason why?"

He cleared his throat before he spoke. His voice flowed deep and smooth, with great confidence and a subtle, assertive sensuality. "Why would any man stare at a stunning woman?"

He turned slightly, and the broadness of his shoulders stirred her. She picked up her drink and noticed her hand shaking. She struggled to stay composed under her sudden attack of nerves.

"A lion," Nia remembered as she set her drink down.

He tilted his head slightly, his eyes warming with interest, as he waited to hear more.

She continued, "That's where I've seen your eyes before—on a lion, stalking me during my African safari."

He listened but offered her no response.

"I got out of the jeep and found myself face-to-face with a king of the jungle, nothing between us but my camera and his wildness." The same heat that had swept over her then rushed over her now. "Five hundred pounds of raw muscle, massive claws, and ferocious biting power. I should have feared his ruthless savagery, yet all I could focus on was his eyes."

She looked again at the man's face and gripped her cold drink. Sweat from her hand mixed with condensation on the glass and seeped down, forming a puddle on the bar. Feelings of exuberance and fear took over her. Erotic thoughts attacked her mind.

"It's you, isn't it?"

It wasn't a question. She knew.

Rephaim smiled, but his eyes never left hers, their cat-like hue almost ablaze. "Happy birthday, Nia."

Startled, Nia knocked over her drink. The glass rolled off the bar and shattered on the floor. She backed away as her emotions betrayed her. Fear mixed with excitement. She pushed through the crowd of people and searched for an exit sign. When she couldn't find one, she ducked through a storage area, then out a back door.

Immediately, the sun's bright light hurt her eyes, like when walking out of a movie theater back into the daylight. Her pupils constricted painfully as she took a few more steps down the sidewalk, away from the club, wobbling on her mother's spiked heels.

The back door opened again. Nia jumped, expecting Rephaim, but it wasn't him. Mysti had followed her outside.

Nia faced her mother, her palms still wet with perspiration. "You set me up."

"I had no idea Rephaim would come here," Mysti said starkly. "If I'd known, I wouldn't have brought you."

"I don't trust you. Never have." Nia took off a spiked heel and gripped it.

Suddenly, a black Jaguar pulled up. David got out. When he spotted them, he hurried over.

Mysti murmured to him, "You're a little too late."

Seeing David again, Nia's emotions somersaulted. Lust and love collided, and the sexual feelings Rephaim had given her moments ago alternated with deep tugs of love lost and betrayal in her gut.

Nia looked back and forth from David to Mysti.

"You called him here." She glared at Mysti.

Mysti didn't deny it.

She turned to David. "Since when did you earn a spot on my mother's speed dial?"

David reached out for her arm. "Nia, I've been looking everywhere for you."

She pulled back. Her body was still hot from the lion's gaze. "I told you, you can't help me. I'm in this alone."

"You're not alone. I'm here for you." He held out his hand, but she ignored it.

Accusation filled her eyes. "Are you in cahoots with Mysti now, the mother of all schemers?"

"I'll do anything to save you."

"Save me?" She raised her arms slightly, hopelessly. "Haven't you noticed?"

David looked around as if he was looking for someone else and not really listening to her.

"David, you're so busy trying to save me, you keep forgetting about my feelings," Nia said in a mass jumble of confusion. She waved her hand to get his attention back. "It's my birthday. Did you know that?"

David's face immediately registered knowledge, as well as guilt, as he glanced at Mysti.

"You knew," Nia said. She felt betrayed yet again. "And you didn't even bother to tell me. I expected that from my mother, but not you, David."

She removed her other high-heeled shoe and tossed both of them carelessly against the building. She started walking away.

"Wait—" David came after her.

She walked faster and ducked into a dead-end alley. Instead of running, she pressed her back against the bricks and held her breath.

David turned in to the alley but hurried past her. When he saw the dead end, he looked up at the empty ladders and fire escapes, then walked back to the end of the alley. He looked in her direction, but she could tell his eyes saw nothing but the dirty bricks behind her. After a moment, he left the alley.

What's happening to our connection? she wondered, almost wishing he could have seen her.

She couldn't believe David had formed an alliance with Mysti, of all people. He knew how much Nia abhorred her.

And why had he kept her birthday a secret from her? How long had he known? For twenty-five years, she'd wondered when it was, and now she'd found out from a stranger, someone who shouldn't even have been a part of her life.

Nia kept her back pressed against the wall, trying to sort through her anger, disappointment, and strange joy of self-discovery. A hefty black crow meandered down the alley after feasting on putrid delicacies from the large overflowing trash bins. The bird stopped near her feet but it couldn't tell she was standing there or it would have flown away. She was out of place, just like she'd felt her whole life.

She heard David say something to Mysti, then he got back in his car and took off. She heard Mysti's spiked heels as she walked back toward her SUV. Nia stayed in the foul-smelling alley a few minutes longer, until the stench of trash became unbearable.

When she stepped out of the alley, Rephaim stood in front of her.

His large frame blocked her pathway and consumed her vision. Though she'd been transparent to David and the crow, he peered directly into her eyes.

Stunned, she asked, "You can see me?"

He smiled. "Follow me."

"Where?"

"Does it matter?" He angled his broad shoulder, and she saw a long purple Cadillac parked at the curb, perpendicular to the alley. The classic car took up the entire curbside, but she hadn't seen it parked there moments ago. Rephaim motioned toward the passenger door, which was already open. "Let's go for a ride."

Thrilled by the invitation, Nia stood still. Apprehension glued her in place. "I can't go with you."

He removed the fedora from his head, and his jet-black

hair fell in regal waves around his shoulders. In one smooth motion, he tied it back with a torn piece of raw leather.

"Do you have anywhere else to go?" he asked, perhaps already knowing the answer.

Anger, fear, curiosity, and longing guided her thoughts as Nia looked up at the man who'd made her life a living hell, inhabiting her dreams, haunting her fantasies, and sweetly torturing her body during long, steamy nights of erotic thoughts, teasing touches, and explosive orgasms.

"No, I don't have any place else to go," she admitted as Rephaim smiled and ushered her into his car.

CHAPTER 60

*T*he grooves in the leather felt snug, as if the Cadillac's seat had been cut, designed, and custom-made for her body. Nia hesitated, then leaned back. The leather conformed easily to her shape.

Rephaim brought his engine to life and slowly pulled away from the curb. Unlike David, he seemed unrushed and very confident about what he was doing. He drove through the congested city streets unobstructed, hardly having to use his brakes. Red lights seemed to yield as they proceeded at a steady pace.

In addition to its spotless beige interior, his Cadillac boasted authentic 1965 parts and genuine chrome controls. Shiny chrome-plated molding lined the dashboard and steering wheel, and the automobile sparkled with arresting flare, with great attention given to every minute detail. The smoothness of the engine camouflaged the power lying beneath the hood. Nia knew a thing or two about horsepower, being an avid race-car fan herself. A light aroma scented the air, reminding her of warmed brown sugarcane.

"Where are you taking me?" she asked.

"Somewhere you belong." Rephaim kept his luminous eyes on the road, but his body language let her know his focus remained on her.

She kept talking, trying to quell the tension and heat building in specific parts of her body. "I'm not going back to your house, in case you're in the mood to fit me into any more caskets."

"Yours was a casket never meant to be buried." He changed the dial on his XM satellite radio, but she wasn't paying attention to the music.

"All caskets are meant to be buried. That's what they are—burial boxes."

"Not yours."

She thought about it. "Actually, it was kind of pretty. Sort of like *Pimp My Ride,* only it was *Pimp My Casket.*" She chuckled uneasily.

He smiled, amused.

"You don't look like the type who sits around watching MTV," she added, rattling on nervously. She couldn't believe she was riding in a car with *him.*

A momentary glance from him sent her hormones reeling.

She shook her head, trying to conceal her erotic twinges. "If the casket wasn't for my burial, then what was it for?"

"It was only a temporary resting place, a box designed to hold a very precious gift."

"A gift? Since when do people give away dead girls as presents?"

"You're not so much dead as you are in transition."

" 'In transition,' " she repeated dubiously. "Great euphemism."

She gazed out the darkly tinted window at the clouds that hovered over Los Angeles. Smog had mixed with the fog and rolled in heavily from the coast but was uncommon that far inland. She could barely see out the window as her body's elevated temperature created condensation hazing the insides of the glass.

She wiped a clear circle on the damp glass. Commercial businesses, office buildings, and city streets had given way to vacant fields, dense brush, and looming trees on a flat terrain. She marveled at the change in landscape.

"I've lived in Los Angeles my whole life, but I've never seen this part of the city," she said.

"Not many have," he said.

"As long as there are no hidden cemeteries, I'm cool." She tried to relax, telling herself that the worst had already happened. What else could happen? But Mysti's words echoed in her mind. *You'll go through hell . . . Then things will get really bad.*

"You're not the bogeyman, are you?"

"Do you believe that I am?" he asked casually.

"I don't know what I believe." She sighed and pressed her head against the headrest. Her mind drifted to David again. *Just believe. Have faith,* he'd told her. Now look at where she was.

The smooth hum of the engine and vibration of the road helped lull her thoughts back to *him.* Her body felt licentious and intoxicated by his strong presence, and her senses felt vibrant and active.

She continued trying to allay her fears by talking. "Besides, even if you were the bogeyman, what could you possibly do to me now?" she asked with a nervous chuckle.

As if in reply, Rephaim stopped the car.

He walked around and opened her door. She got out and gazed over the landscape, a beautiful area of dense foliage blooming with exotic plants and dotted with hot springs that shot up warm bubbling water from beneath the earth. In a small clearing, fruits, vegetables, and other bulbous plants flowered.

"Wow. This is amazing. Guess we're not in Kansas anymore." She turned to him. "What is this place?"

"It's sacred ground."

She could believe that. She started to walk toward it, but he stopped her.

"Wait."

"What? I'm already barefoot."

He gazed at her bare feet, then eased his way up her shapely curves to the hem of her dress. "Take off your dress."

Nia arched her eyebrows. "Pardon me?"

"Your dress, it's borrowed, is it not?"

Nia looked down at the snakeskin dress that Mysti had given her, hating it because it made her feel like a reptilian hooker. "Yes, as a matter of fact, it is."

"Do you want its owner's aura to follow you into the garden?"

She shook her head vigorously. "No. I don't want her aura following me anywhere."

"Then you must remove the dress."

Nia looked down at the dress again, warming to the idea of casting off the scaly reminder of her mother's transgressions. "Okay, but turn around."

Rephaim obeyed.

Nia slowly lifted the dress over her head, removing it. Her white slip underneath was made from an unusually strong but softly spun, sticky material. Sleeveless and strapless, it clung to her body just above her breasts, flared slightly at her hips, and ended just above her knees. Nia flushed at the thought that he'd already seen her naked when he'd placed the slip on her

and remembered the many times he'd visited during the midnight hour as she slept nude.

Nia tossed the dress near his feet to let him know it was
off. When Rephaim turned back around, she'd expected his
eyes to roam down her body lustfully, but he kept his eyes
pinned on her face. Somehow, his possessive stare made her
feel more naked than if she'd stripped bare.

"What about you?" she asked, filled with sensual curiosity.
"Are you going to get undressed?"

He smiled at her anticipation but said, "I live here."

"So?"

"Every part of my body has already been consecrated."

Nia raised an eyebrow, wondering what that meant as she
glanced down his body. From the nice way his body filled out
his clothes, she could tell he was well endowed.

When he saw her looking, mischief peppered his sexy
grin. He took Nia's hand and led her forward. The moment she
stepped into the garden, her senses burst into a vibrant alert-
ness. She walked toward the clearing, her curiosity piqued.

"Wow."

Myriad smells accosted her nose. Sweet honey, lilac, rose,
wood sap, minty geranium, rosemary, basil, and more formed
a potpourri of aromas as sweet and spicy scents intermingled
with intoxicating fragrances. Even the sounds in the garden
were alive and organic, bristling in her ear. The low strumming
flap of a hummingbird's wing; the gentle crackle of a narrow
stream trickling into a small lake; the chirp of a cricket as it
rubbed its wings; a gentle breeze fluttering the leaves of a papaya plant; the scuttling of something small and spiny into the
brilliantly green low-lying moss.

Nia walked into the middle of the garden and stood
beneath a colorfully blooming tree with thin branches that
arched and drooped, heavy with blossoms, their tips nearly

touching the ground. The tree looked like an exploding fire-work, shooting its branches forty feet into the sky, then showering down its blossoming limbs over Nia's head.

Nia felt tiny beneath it. "Amazing."

"It's a Chinese weeping cherry tree."

She touched a blossom. Its delicately soft, milky pink petals had not yet opened.

"These buds look like teardrops," she said, careful not to separate it from the tree, as it remained dependant on its main source for life.

Rephaim looked not at the bud but at her. "Beauty in sadness, joy in pain, death in life; nature has an intricate way of mixing two opposites."

He touched her hand, stroking his thumb between her fingers. His touch was electrifying, evoking erotic images in her mind of their two bodies entwined in a gyrating carnal love dance.

Nia recoiled, her back brushing the tree's bark. Rephaim plucked the bud from the tree, and it fell loose in his hand.

"You killed it," she protested. "Now it'll never produce fruit."

He lifted both her hands and placed the tiny bud inside, then closed her hands together and folded his hands over hers. The soft velvety petals felt cool against her palm.

Rephaim clasped his hands around hers, crushing the tiny bud and generating preternatural warmth between them. The combined temperatures of their bodies produced a brand-new surge of heat. Nia tried to pull back, but he kept her hands inside his.

"Never underestimate your own power, Nia."

She felt something stir inside her hand. A vibrant, new fertile hotness erupted as he released her hands. When she opened them, the bud was gone, and a single ripened cherry lay on her palm.

Deep purple-crimson skin stretched over its plump body, struggling to contain the fruit's ripe, sweet juices surging inside.

"Whoa!" Nia gaped. "Where did the bud go?"

"It's right here," Rephaim said, indicating the cherry. "Same bud. Just a new manifestation."

Nia gently rolled the swollen fruit on her palm. Its skin looked ready to burst and give way to the blood-colored juices inside. A dull ache attacked Nia's stomach as hunger pangs surfaced and a deep, throbbing yearning erupted.

"Nice trick," she commended as her mouth watered and her hunger grew.

"This was no trick." Rephaim's eyes stayed intensely focused on her. "This is the miracle of union."

Nia gazed at the fruit as its aroma assailed her nose, and she imagined its sweetness inside her mouth. Rephaim was watching her carefully.

"This is the power of two souls that come together emotionally, spiritually, and sexually. It's strong enough to tilt the universe."

He raised the fruit close to her mouth. "Go ahead, taste."

Nia's hunger escalated as she stared at the cherry. "I didn't realize how hungry I was." She licked her lips, then looked past the cherry and into Rephaim's translucent eyes. "But I think you're mistaking me for that other girl. What was her name, Eve?" Nia remembered how David had explained to her the original sin in the Garden of Eden.

"I haven't mistaken you for anyone. I know exactly who you are."

His intimate gaze aroused her, but she took his hand, placed the cherry inside, and closed his strong fingers around it. As she squeezed, the cherry's bloodred juices seeped through his fingers and dripped down his knuckles. Her deep craving made her want to lick the juices from his fingers, but she fought off the wanton urge and walked out of the garden, away from Rephaim's sweet, tempting words, away from his tempestuous touch, and away from his eyes' tantalizing gaze.

Her highly volatile urges and vacillating emotions had left her light-headed but still yearning. She was both relieved and disappointed that he didn't follow her. As she walked past his Cadillac, its long body jutted like a phallic symbol, reminding her again of Rephaim's powerful appeal. She passed the looming trees and fertile foliage and kept walking through the unfamiliar landscape until she reached a fork in the road. Unlike the one she'd been at in the desert, this time she was alone.

Not knowing east from west, Nia looked around. With no compass and no clear direction to follow, she sat on the foggy road. Damp black soil smudged her white slip. Thick clouds drifted low above her head, brushing over the treetops and looming over the landscape. Nia strummed her fingers impatiently on her knees while waiting at the crossroads. She felt lost. She closed her eyes and waited for a sign or something to help her find her way.

❧ CHAPTER 61 ❧

Rephaim had stood by passively and watched Nia leave the garden of her own free will. He could have easily stopped her, but he didn't want to use force, at least not yet.

Nia possessed certain supernatural privileges but was unaware of most of them. Though endowed with certain physical and spiritual advantages, she remained fully human and therefore was subject to the normal human weaknesses, among them impatience, impulsivity, and oversight.

He couldn't push her too hard or else she might break.

Rephaim had to be patient and calculating in his handling of her. He would use her heightened sensitivity to his advantage to aid in seducing her toward the dark side, but she had to come of her own free will.

Rephaim left the garden and returned to his mansion to finish preparing for their black wedding ceremony. Only a few more hours, and he'd find her, bring her back, and marry her.

CHAPTER 62

When David left Club XO in the Válley, he drove around the block, then circled back. He didn't trust Mysti. He only tried to use what she knew to help Nia, but he didn't feel comfortable doing it, and he hated that Nia had accused him of being in cahoots with her. Mysti was the type of person who promoted her own self-gain in any situation, even one involving her daughter's tragic demise and unfathomable return.

That's why he'd returned to the club, parked discreetly in front, and was watching Mysti as she climbed into her SUV. She could make the simplest event, like bringing her legs up and placing them into an automobile, look like a sexual act. David realized that Nia had inherited a great deal of her sexuality from her biological mother, and he'd enjoyed it when that sexual energy was directed at him. But now, with Nia out there somewhere doubting his love, he didn't know what danger might befall her.

He hoped that following Mysti would lead him back to Nia.

Mysti took off in her SUV in an unfamiliar direction, and after the first turn, he lost her. Her white SUV vanished in traffic. David returned to Nia's house to check one more time before heading back to the desert where he'd found Nia that morning, praying that their connection would somehow bring them back together.

WHEN NIA OPENED her eyes again, she was no longer sitting in the damp black soil, at a crossroads, but she was sprawled on her front lawn in Northridge. A few hours had passed, and judging by the sun's position in the sky, it was late afternoon. She rose just in time to see David's black Jag pull away. He'd been looking for her and had apparently missed her by seconds. Lately, their connection seemed to have a faulty wire.

Other people had gathered at her house. Over two dozen teens that she'd mentored over the past years stood at her front door. Dressed mostly in black and other somber colors, the girls wore hoods covering their hair, and the boys pulled up their sagging pants out of respect.

Their sad faces told the story. They'd heard the news of her untimely death and were holding an impromptu memorial, bringing cards, teddy bears, and small candles to place on her front porch.

Jay stood at the top of the porch, his face the saddest of them all. Nia knew Jay and the other teens couldn't see her. She wanted to go comfort him and tell him she was still around, but she stayed near the tree without interrupting her own memorial service, not wanting to traumatize the kids.

"She cared about us," Jay said over the group, and they listened like he was their leader. He'd come a long way since he was the mischievous little fellow she'd first met, and he was growing into a sensitive young man. All he needed was a little more time and attention, and she hated that she couldn't give him that anymore.

"Miss Nia put up with our crap and she didn't judge us. She was cool like that."

Jay's bottom lip quivered. He bit it, fighting hard to keep from crying. She'd told him that a man could cry and still be a man, but under peer pressure, he struggled with showing his emotions. She stood by the acacia tree in her front yard and listened.

"We're going to miss her. We can never replace her. Ain't even gonna try." Jay set his candle down on the porch steps.

The other teens did the same and began to leave. One by one, they wandered off in different directions like lost souls. She'd always told them to stick together because traveling alone was so much harder. She'd believed in togetherness, once upon a time.

After the others left, Jay remained on the porch and spoke aloud from his heart, as if she were there. "I lied, Miss Nia, I did have a crush on you," he said sadly. "But I knew you were out of my league."

Jay pulled the red legal notice off her door, crumbled it up, and threw it behind the bushes. He left her porch and walked across her yard back to his house, where his father had been waiting by the fence. Buddy placed a comforting hand on Jay's back and walked with him into their house.

Nia wiped her eyes and retrieved the red piece of paper. She smoothed it out and read: NOTICE TO CEASE AND DESIST THE IL-LEGAL CONGREGATION OF MINORS, FROM THE CITY OF LOS ANGELES DEPART-MENT OF LAW ENFORCEMENT.

Her home-based youth center had officially been shut down. She chuckled at the irony and silently cursed Mal for killing her. Not only had he ruined her life, but he had helped deprive these teens of a place to go.

Sad and frustrated, she started to leave when she noticed

somebody hiding near the bushes. Dressed in all black with a hood pulled low over her face and wearing dark shades, Shayla had waited until everyone else left before approaching Nia's porch. Nia ducked back and watched her guarded movements as she cautiously walked up the steps and placed a candle. After a moment, she hurried off the porch and rushed down the block.

Nia followed Shayla, figuring a mouse would lead her to the cheese.

CHAPTER 63

*M*alcolm had parked around the corner in Nia's gold Mustang since his flashy, expensive car had gotten repossessed. He was good at spending lots of money, but not good at paying his bills. He waited for Shayla. As Shayla hurried inside the car, Nia quickly crawled in through an open back window. Although they couldn't see her, she squatted low in the backseat.

As Mal took off, he fidgeted in his seat and kept checking his rearview mirror, obviously distressed. He asked Shayla, "Did you tell anybody we saw her?"

"Of course not," Shayla huffed, her own nerves showing. "I'm not stupid."

"Nobody would believe you anyway," Mal said, and drove hurriedly, like he had someplace else to go. Tension and guilt filled the silence as they rode.

Finally, Shayla asked, "Did you really kill her?"

"I told you, no!" Mal snapped, and tugged at his collar, adding, "It was some sort of freak accident."

Nia stayed quiet, but her body tightened with feelings of betrayal and outrage. Mal pulled up in front of Shayla's aunt's apartment just a few miles from David's church but kept the motor running.

He cleared his throat. "You're an okay girl, Shayla, but you're not really my type."

Shayla turned in her seat, appalled. "What are you trying to say?"

Nia sat up and listened, bracing herself for Shayla's sake, because she knew what was coming next.

"I'm trying to say," Mal explained as he reached over and opened her door from the inside, "lose my number."

Embarrassed and angry, Shayla let out a squeal, then bit her lip. Empathizing, Nia felt her pain. After a moment, Shayla said, "You're not my type either, Malcolm." She got out and slammed the car door. "Nia was right. I can do better."

As Mal drove off, Nia fumed.

When he stopped at a red stoplight at a busy intersection near the freeway, she couldn't take it anymore. She exhaled, materialized, and lunged forward, clasping her arm around Mal's neck. She pulled hard, pinning him to the headrest.

Mal hollered and fought back. His foot slipped off the brake and hit the gas, and her Mustang barreled into the intersection, colliding with oncoming traffic. A minivan clipped their front end and spun them around before they skidded into another car, causing Nia to lose her grip.

Shaken up but not seriously hurt, Mal got out and ran.

Nia jumped out and ran after him. She followed him along the freeway, up the steps, and onto an overpass enclosed in a fence. She caught up to him halfway across the pedestrian walkway and tackled him, yelling, "You killed me! Just because you were horny?"

"I didn't do it!" he protested. He kicked her away and jumped back to his feet.

Nia stood up also, her chest heaving from ire and exertion. "Yes, you did. I was there, remember?"

Severely winded and freaked out, Mal puffed hard, his eyes shifty, looking ready to take off running again.

"Yeah, I was mad and horny," he admitted, bending over, trying to catch his breath. "And yeah, I lost my temper, but then something happened. I don't know what."

He straightened up and frowned at Nia. In that moment, his cocky self-confidence vanished and Nia thought she saw sincerity in his troubled countenance.

"It's not my fault, I swear, Nia. There's way more going on than you think."

Something in her wanted to believe him, but, cautious, she remained skeptical. "I suppose next you're going to tell me the devil made you do it."

"Yeah, he did!"

When Mal tried to lie foolishly and shift the blame to someone else, Nia became enraged. She slammed his back against the wire fence and scowled, shouting, "You liar!

At first, shock lit up Mal's expression.

But a few seconds later, he closed his eyes, and when he opened them, a sardonic smile slid across his face. Cocky irreverence replaced his fear as his voice deepened and he sneered at her.

"Nia, I'm glad you're dead. When you were alive, you caused me more trouble than you were worth."

Reflexively Nia slapped Mal.

In the same instant, his back ripped through the wire

fence and he fell off the overpass into the freeway traffic below. His body hit the top of a passing U-Haul. Nia watched in horror as he landed on his back, arms sprawled, motionless. The U-Haul continued north on the I-5 freeway for several more miles before it pulled over.

A few drivers that had witnessed the incident stopped their cars and pulled to the side of the road. Stunned, they got out and looked up at the overpass.

A little boy spotted Nia standing near the torn wire. Pointing at her, he yelled, "Look! That lady in the white slip pushed him. She killed him!"

Shocked, Nia backed up. She turned and ran down the steps heading in the opposite direction. Dread and fear overtook her, along with a strange rush of power, excitement, and revenge.

Suddenly overflowing with peculiar, shameful sensations, Nia stopped and clutched her stomach. She knelt near bushes at the freeway's off-ramp. Horrified by the sordid thrills that charged through her body, her soul seemed to ache as she crouched, trying to curtail the eerie energy that rushed through her. Duplicitous thoughts of evil clashed with her desire to do right and frightened her.

A few seconds later, a purple Caddy pulled up and Rephaim got out. When he touched her shoulder, her body shuddered as if the internal war had suddenly intensified.

"What's wrong?" he asked, his voice strangely soothing.

"I just killed someone." Nia trembled.

"Did they deserve it?"

Nia didn't answer for fear she would say yes.

As if sensing her silent affirmation, he comforted her. "You did nothing wrong, Nia."

Along with his slight squeeze of her shoulder, Nia felt a new surge of devious impulses, but this time, she wasn't as afraid.

❊   ❊   ❊

As REPHAIM PUT Nia in his car, he looked up at the overpass where moments ago he'd possessed Mal's body, then pushed himself through the wire fence. The fall from the overpass onto the U-Haul had been exhilarating. Possession, treachery, and death had always had that kind of reviving effect on him.

Rephaim had to do it. Nia needed help moving to the dark side. What better way to lure her over than to let her feel the sweetly deceptive adrenaline surge of killing someone.

He smiled wistfully as he got into the Cadillac and started his powerful engine. He leaned close to her ear as he pulled away and whispered, "Tell me, Nia, did you feel a sexual rush when you killed him?"

CHAPTER 64

$\mathcal{D}$avid had left Nia's house and gone back to the desert to search for her. When that proved futile, he felt hopeless, but quitting was not an option. He thought of every place she might possibly go and decided to drive by Mercy and Grace Cathedral.

He winced when he saw the large green church, knowing that he and Nia were supposed to be getting married there right now. Pastor Kees was in the parking lot, unloading canned goods for the homeless from his van, when he saw David's Jag enter. He dropped the cans and flagged him down.

"I heard about Nia," the pastor said as he hurried to David's rolled-down window and began offering his condolences.

David cut him off. "She's come back."

Pastor Kees paused. His face registered shock and disbelief. David gave him a second, acknowledging the pastor's amazement with a nod, but he had no time to go into details.

"You've known me a long time, Daryl. You know I

wouldn't lie about something like this. Right now, I need you to believe me."

Pastor Kees nodded, but David could see he remained slightly skeptical. He asserted, "I saw her. I touched her. I felt her." He pounded a clenched hand on his steering wheel, remembering. "She slipped away from me twice, but I'm trying to find her right now."

Seeing David's distress, Pastor Kees sighed, believing something certainly was going on. "What can I do to help?"

"There's a man after her. He may not be fully human. Nia's mother says he's a demon." David chose his words carefully. "He wants Nia's body and her soul. I could use your insight on this."

The minister shook his head. "I'm a pastor, not a demon hunter." He stood at David's car door, silent, thinking. After a moment he asked, "Even if you do find Nia and this man, what are you going to do?"

"Fight him," David said firmly.

"How?"

"With my fists, a big stick, whatever I can get my hands on." David clenched his jaw. "I swore to God that if I got a second chance, I wouldn't lose this time around."

The minister's expression filled with concern. "But you're missing an important fact."

"What?"

"You don't bring a knife to a gunfight," his friend advised him, using a familiar cliché to make his grave point. "And you definitely don't fight demonic powers with physical strength."

David looked around the church's parking lot impatiently for any sign of Nia. "Right now, I don't know what else to do."

"You're making a big mistake."

"This is something I have to do." David let up off the brake and edged forward. "Nia is out there somewhere in trouble and she needs my help. I've got less than six hours to find her. If I don't stop him, I'll lose her forever."

"But, David, my friend, I think you're going about this the wrong way."

He shifted his car into drive. "I can't be wrong. Nia's life depends on it."

David drove away from the church and hopped back on the freeway.

CHAPTER 65

*R*ephaim watched the internal struggle transpire in Nia's pretty eyes as she tried to come to terms with the "murder" she'd just committed.

He had her in his possession again. Now all he had to do was take her back to his parlor and, at six minutes to midnight, claim her as his eternal bride.

As he began to drive away, someone yanked open the passenger-side door.

"Nia!" David Wrightwood had found them. He yelled and grabbed Nia. "Get out of the car!"

As David yanked Nia from the car, Rephaim threw the Caddy into park and jumped out, wondering how David had found her and if they had some kind of connection that was beyond his interference.

David tried to run with Nia, but Rephaim quickly blocked him. He threw a blow to David's chest, knocking him back, but he quickly recovered his footing and stood his ground, face-to-face with Rephaim.

David reached again for Nia. "Nia is mine."

After being yanked from the car by surprise, Nia recovered her footing as well. She pulled away from David's grip, incensed. "I don't belong to anyone."

Her words jarred David and injured his confidence. Rephaim could see the uncertainty in David's eyes and thought, *Good. Doubt is always better than faith.*

Rephaim grinned. "You heard the lady. She's her own woman."

Rephaim reached out his hand for Nia, and when she took it, an upsurge of pride stimulated his male libido. Having Nia dead and so close with her hormones brewing so fervently also ignited his own sex drive. Their impending consummation was sure to be earth shattering, and he'd give her sexual delights she'd never dreamed of.

He gently nudged Nia back inside the car and watched the faith dwindle in David Wrightwood's eyes. Rephaim closed Nia's door and locked it.

As he walked around the Caddy to the driver's side, he sneered at David, knowing Nia could not hear him. "In less than four hours, her body and soul will be mine eternally. Since you're not invited to our wedding, I'll e-mail you a picture."

Rephaim got in and took off, but David pursued them in his own car. Rephaim could have easily turned his car, along with Nia as she rode inside, into metaphysical vapors. He could have changed himself into his supernatural form, fully equipped with powerful claws, sharp fangs, a winged back, and ferocious fire in his eyes. But he didn't want to scare Nia. She remained fragile and he needed to win her confidence gently, not push her over the edge. He needed her to be off guard and to go willingly where he planned to take her.

Rephaim sped away down the nearly empty city street. Traffic was light, and he gunned his purple Caddy. David kept up with him in his black Jaguar, both cars pushed to their powerful limits. But Rephaim's Caddy didn't burn regular gas. It ran on determination, fueled by evil. He rounded a sharp curve, then entered a one-way street going the wrong way. Rephaim played chicken with other cars while luring David along. Both speeding cars missed head-on traffic by inches as Rephaim tested David's fortitude, and David stayed right on his bumper.

Rephaim turned off the one-way street sharply, and his Caddy reeled dangerously to the left. Nia wasn't wearing a seat belt, and she slid into Rephaim. No safety grips were installed inside the Caddy, and he'd planned it that way so she'd only have one thing to hold on to.

"Just cling to me," Rephaim said to Nia while the car skidded wildly. His Caddy barreled up a slope, then swooped down on the other side, bouncing on its wheels. With nothing else to clutch, Nia grabbed hold of his arm and hung on.

Rephaim took another corner at top sped, accelerated, then skidded onto the freeway. David kept up. His driving skills were almost as impressive as his foolishness. He'd already gone far beyond the boundaries of an ordinary man who should fear for his life. David Wrightwood acted as if he had a death wish.

But it'd take more than guts to defeat a powerful dark warlord like Rephaim. David was about to learn that the hard way.

Rephaim hit his brakes and whipped his Cadillac to the side of the freeway, skidding a few feet on the asphalt shoulder before jerking to a complete stop. David skidded to a dust-filled stop behind him.

Rephaim jumped out of the Caddy. He wanted Nia to see him whip her lover's human ass.

Rephaim walked swiftly toward David. "Do you *really* want to fight me?"

David got out of his black Jaguar and walked just as swiftly toward Rephaim.

Rephaim said, "I've given you every opportunity to back down, but you won't take it. You have no idea who you're messing with."

He lunged forward with a paralyzing blow.

"Neither do you." David surprised him with a quick and powerful left jab, using Rephaim's own momentum to help power punch.

Rephaim backed up and fingered his nearly broken jaw. He spit and smiled. Demon hybrids didn't bleed, but they did feel pain. But nowhere near the kind of pain he was about to inflict on David Wrightwood.

CHAPTER 66

*D*avid kept his fists positioned in front of his face, protecting himself while looking for an opening, ready to strike first. This bastard Rephaim was tough. David had hit him with his best left jab, a jab that would knock a man unconscious, or at least break open a bleeding mouth. But the guy had shrugged it off and smiled back at him.

In his peripheral vision David saw Nia get out of the car. The wind caught the edge of her dirty white slip, fluttering it.

"David!" she called, but he couldn't take his eye off Rephaim, or else he'd lose.

A few cars passed on the freeway. One honked, but no one had apparently called the police. This was Los Angeles. Fights on the side of the freeway were not unusual, especially for commuters. Sometimes drivers exchanged insurance information, other times they exchanged blows.

But there'd never been a fight like this before, an all-out battle over a woman who was already dead.

Nia yelled again, "David, stop it!"

David kept his focus on Rephaim's strange-colored eyes as he crouched in front of him like a wild animal ready to strike. "He's responsible for your death, Nia."

"No, Mal killed me."

"This guy was behind it."

"I don't believe you" Nia yelled, unwilling to listen. "You're just trying to prove something—prove that you can save somebody. Go back to saving Cher-Ling, you seem to enjoy saving her."

Rephaim used the distraction to strike. He swung a sharp right; David was fast and blocked it, but he wasn't ready for Rephaim's lightning-fast left uppercut.

The force of Rephaim's punch rocked him back. He tried to break his fall with quick footwork but it wasn't enough and he fell. As he hit the asphalt, he rolled before Rephaim could get over him good, and he knocked the tall bastard's feet from under him.

Rephaim didn't go down all the way, but his stumble gave David enough time to jump back to his feet and run at Nia. He grabbed her arm. "Quick, Nia. Get in my car."

She pulled back. "David, stop trying to be a hero."

David didn't even see Rephaim coming, the son of a bitch was so fast. Rephaim reached over Nia's shoulder and grabbed David like he was a rag doll, practically lifting him off his feet. David had never been grabbed like that before. He threw a flurry of punches into Rephaim's abdomen, hard enough to knock breath from the lungs of a normal man. He knew Rephaim felt them by the anger in his banana-colored eyes.

Rephaim hauled David over and slammed him on the

hood of the Caddy. The metal banged against David's back with jackhammer force. His adversary pressed his left forearm against David's chest to pin him down and delivered a series of exploding blows with his right fist to David's face. The back of David's head hit the hood, and he felt blood spurt from his right jaw, then drizzle warmly down his chin.

The blows blurred David's vision, but he refused to lose consciousness. Through the seething pain, he focused and maneuvered his knee inside Rephaim's clutches and delivered a sharp kick to Rephaim's midsection.

Grunting, Rephaim backed up a few feet.

David rolled off the hood down to the asphalt. He gripped the side mirror and quickly pulled himself back up.

Nia ran around the perimeter of the fight, yelling mostly at David, even though the other bastard was doing most of the fighting.

"Stop! Please, just stop!" She was irrational, not thinking straight, yelling at the one who'd come to save her.

David threw his hands in the air and backed up. "All right. All right."

Rephaim paused.

Breathing hard, David stepped slightly toward Nia, and he asked her, "You really want me to leave?"

"Yes, I want you to leave. Fighting like this is stupid."

David kept his palms up as a sign of truce, backing down. "Okay, I just want to tell you one thing before you leave with him."

He moved a little closer to Nia; so did Rephaim. Her voice shook. "What, David?"

"This." David threw everything he had at Rephaim, knocking him back off his feet. He followed the surprise blow with a quick succession of debilitating kicks to Rephaim's body that he'd learned in his Krav Maga class last summer. He delivered another set of powerful blows to the back of Rephaim's head, then pushed him down with the heel of his shoe to make him stay down, kicking him one more time for good measure. *He doesn't play by the rules . . . he makes up his own,* he remembered Mysti saying. Well, so could he.

"David!" Nia yanked his arm.

With no time to be a gentleman, he grabbed her. "Nia, this is serious. Shut up and get in my car!"

But Nia twisted out of his grip with a strength that surprised him, and she slapped his face so hard it caused him to spin around halfway. "What the—?"

He grabbed his face and looked at her hand, expecting to see a skillet or a waffle iron, something that would explain what he'd just felt. Nia's hands were empty.

Faster than he could blink, she was back inside the purple Caddy, and so was Rephaim.

Rephaim sped away with Nia inside his car. As he passed, he looked at David. His expression was cool and calm, like David hadn't just beaten the holy crap out of him. Rephaim leaned close to Nia, grinned at David, and kept going.

David caught a glimpse of Nia's face. Sadness, guilt, and resignaion. She looked like she truly believed she was not worth saving.

But David refused to believe that. He kicked up asphalt trying to get back to his car, but by the time he started his engine, the Caddy was nowhere in sight.

❧ CHAPTER 67 ❧

*N*ight fell and so did David's hopes, but the thought of surrendering his girl to a dark entity made bile rise in his gut.

He wouldn't do it.

Tired of driving all over the city looking for her, David swung his car to the side of the dark road. He tried to pray to god but frustration hampered his thoughts. He got out, and hollered up at the black clouds. "Mysti! Get your ass down here. Please!"

He needed to fight dirty. Who knew more about getting dirty than Mysti?

The woman suddenly appeared, leaning on his car's trunk, a lit cigarette glowing near the tips of her white fingernails. "Since you said *please*."

David got straight to the point. "Rephaim has got Nia."

"I know."

"It's three hours till midnight. I don't have much time. What do I have to do to get you to help me?"

Mysti smiled as she slipped up on his trunk and crossed her long legs. "I want you to talk to Nia."

"Don't you think I've already tried that? She won't listen to me!"

"You've got to *make* her listen."

"And tell her what?"

"That you love her."

"She already knows that."

"She no longer *believes* it."

David paced, thinking. He kicked a tire and paused near the door. He looked at Mysti. Her bone-straight hair and shapely body carved a black outline against the nighttime sky. Her gleaming green eyes were all he could see of her danger-ously attractive face.

He moved closer, scrutinizing what he could see of her. "There's more to it than that, isn't there?"

She used her cool body language to camouflage her true motives, but he wasn't fooled. He asked, "What do you stand to gain from all this?"

"A blood transfer."

"A what?"

"Rephaim plans to marry Nia and make her his queen. Once that happens, Nia will be one of hell's most prominent queens for the rest of her eternal life . . . unless she transfers her rights."

"To you?"

"Exactly." Her honesty was as blunt as her heart. She ex-plained, "Such a transfer of power is permitted only once dur-ing an entity's lifespan and can only be done between blood relatives." Mysti smiled. "I am her *blood* relative."

"Mystical, the ultimate schemer." David shook his head,

understanding her motives now. "Assuming all of this is true, why would Nia want to grant you such a favor? She doesn't even like you."

"Because she'll want to come back to you—*if* she believes you love her."

David frowned. "How could she come back?"

"In a blood transfer, the two parties switch lives," Mysti said, flicking her cigarette. "I would become queen and sit at Rephaim's side. Nia would come back to this world and resume life as a regular woman. We'd exchange places."

"Sort of like *Trading Spaces,* only *Trading Lives.*" David chuckled dryly. "Does Rephaim know about this?"

"Yes, but he doesn't think I know. That's why he'll be powerless to stop it."

David cocked his head, amazed and disgusted. "So, your whole reason for helping me is that you can gain more power?"

She nodded.

"I don't blame Nia for hating you."

Mysti smiled as if David had complimented her.

She gracefully lowered herself from the trunk of his car and put out her cigarette on his taillight. "So, do we have a deal?"

David withheld his answer, remaining skeptical. "Assuming I go along with this, how would I find Nia?"

"She's at Rephaim's house. Zamzu knows how to get us through the gate."

"Zam-*who*?"

"No time for more questions," Mysti said as she turned and started walking down the road to an unknown destination. "Follow me."

David hesitated. Everything in him knew he should never follow a witch down a dark road, but he needed to find Nia. "God help me," he muttered, and followed Mysti.

CHAPTER 68

*W*hen Nia walked into Rephaim's house, the bright and festive décor surprised her, a stark contrast to the room's appearance when she'd escaped earlier. Showers of sheer, deeply-colored gossamer streamers decorated the high-vaulted reception area. A unique, subtle Mardi Gras theme pervaded, with shining beads and metallic masks giving the feel of an unusual masquerade. Green, gold, and royal purple foil was draped around large antique stone pillars. Muted light bounced off various-sized candles placed inside dark-colored glass jars.

Nia picked up a white flower petal from the mantel. "Who's having a party?"

"We are." Rephaim's warm, sensual smile sent a tingle up her spine. "This is our celebration."

She blushed, despite the sick, empty feeling in her stomach from seeing David slammed across Rephaim's hood and beaten. Even though she remained upset at David for betraying her, breaking her heart, keeping secrets, and conniving with Mysti, she still had feelings for him. She'd tried to stop the fight, but both men were so angry, they'd pushed her aside. Seeing David like that ripped at her emotions and rattled her core. Leaving with Rephaim was the only way she could put an end to the violent combat.

At the same time, another feeling was kindling inside Nia, one she'd pushed back for twenty-five years.

The incendiary feeling of freedom.

Killing Malcolm had sparked it. The horrific event had jarred any hopes she ever had of being righteous.

Righteous was what David wanted her to be. He'd taken her to his church, given her mini Bible studies, and had tried to explain Christian principles and blessings, but it all had seemed so foreign to her. She'd attended his church and tried to fit in, but her efforts ended in disaster, and her failure to fit in had made her spirit plummet.

Now she could stop trying.

"Yeah, it *is* my birthday. How 'bout that?" she said, trying to perk herself up.

Rephaim took her hand. "Happy birthday, Nia."

Hearing someone say it for real, after so many years of pretending, stimulated a feeling of liberty deep inside that she'd never felt before.

Rephaim's mesmeric eyes evoked an even deeper soul stirring, one as spiritual as it was erotic. With her senses piqued and her mind open, for the first time Nia allowed herself the freedom to feel whatever sensation came her way.

Rephaim led her to an elaborate banquet table. An elegant thronelike black chair sat at each end, and a covered brass statue rested in the middle. With no heat lamps or burners needed to keep the food warm, the hot food simmered in its own juices beneath silver-plated dome covers. Nia lifted a cover and sniffed the seasoned meats, brewing spices, and warm sweets. The strong, seductive aromas stirred her hunger and sparked a ravenous appetite inside of her, as if she'd been starving for twenty-five years.

Rephaim stood on the other side of the banquet table with his arousing physique looking every bit as delectable as the food. Each time he came close, he elicited a tumultuous high inside of her and a deep desire to attain some type of satisfaction.

Nia reached for a food dish, but he caught her hand. Knowing she was famished, he was teasing her.

She protested softly. "But it's my birthday, and I'm hungry."

"There'll be plenty of time to eat later," he said as he led her away from the table. "But first, we need to tend to the ceremonies."

Not sure what he was referring to, she walked with him across the spacious celebration hall and noticed two large antique sterling silver bells tied to an arching post. As he walked her under the archway, she slid her hand along the smooth surface of one of the bells.

"These decorations are for weddings, not birthdays."

"Both are celebrations," he said persuasively as he adjusted one of the purple roses on the archway. "In some ancient cultures, reaching the age of twenty-five is a sacred rite of passage from bondage to freedom."

"Freedom?"

"Yes. Freedom to choose one's own destiny."

She marveled at how he seemed to know what she'd been thinking only moments ago. "It may be my twenty-fifth birthday, but I feel just as lost as ever."

"You're not lost, Nia." His light-colored eyes flashed, warm and seductive, and caused her thoughts to wander. "There's a place waiting for you."

"Where?"

"Come, I'll show you." He guided her outside onto a sweeping terrace that winded along the side of his palatial home. The generous upper balcony overlooked his humongous estate. "Look over there. What do you see?"

She looked out over the breathtaking view. "I see the desert valley where I live, but the dark clouds are obstructing the city lights."

As Rephaim came closer, she could feel the heat emanating from his body. His huge chest gently brushed against her bare shoulders. "On the other side of those clouds is a world that hates you," he said quietly. "A world that doesn't understand what you are and has no place for such a rare creation as you." He turned to her. "Nia, you don't fit it."

His words stilled her. She was starting to believe they were true. Thoughts of David flooded her head, along with all the hopes they'd shared and promises he'd made to her. "But David—"

Rephaim interrupted. "No ordinary man can satisfy you the way you need to be satisfied."

Her empty stomach churned with deep cravings that remained unquenched. She protested, "But he said he loved me."

"Shh . . ." Rephaim gently placed his finger to her lips. His voice was like a seductive whisper. "Love *never* existed."

He gently clasped her shoulder, turning her all the way around toward another sky looming on the opposite side of the terrace. In the absence of stars, this sky's intensity was forebodingly thick and heavy and seemed so impenetrable she couldn't make out anything beyond the tip of Rephaim's finger as he pointed into the pitch-blackness.

"Another world awaits you, one that will embrace you."

He pulled her back against his chest and slipped his strong, warm hand around her stomach. Nia's pulse raced. Even though she had no heartbeat, heat surged through her body as

his words tranquilized her fears and tantalized her thoughts.
She wanted to believe there was a place where she'd fit in, yet
she didn't trust this coming from the lips of the one who'd dis-
rupted her life.

She turned and faced him. "You've made my life a living
hell."

"I brought you pleasure," he asserted without flinching.
As she stared into his dangerously handsome face, he replied
with self-assured confidence, "Even when you tried to push me
away, your body begged me to stay."

"I was confused."

"You knew what you wanted. You understood the pleasures
I offered you, but you were afraid." He pulled her close. "Now
you can stop fighting and give in to your wanton desires."

When her body touched his, her womanly muscles contracted. His large, strong hands seemed to master her body—
touching, rubbing, squeezing in just the right places with skilled
accuracy, causing heated moisture in pleasurable places.

Overwhelmed, Nia closed her eyes.

"Ooh, this feels so seductive," she sighed, then added, "but
so wrong."

After a few more breaths, she opened her eyes and peered
at him through slanted lids, nudging him away.

He let her go, but not far.

"Everything that's holding you back has died. Tonight, all
of your taboo fantasies can become real."

He closed the small space between them. "And I know
every one of your erotic dreams, Nia. I gave them to you."

A raw heat crept into her womanly regions. She pressed
her thighs together and her internal walls tightened, oozing
sweetness. He walked around her slowly and slipped his hands
around her abdomen, capturing her from behind. He pulled
her backward into him until her butt melded into his bulging

thigh muscles and his hard, swollen groin ironed her back.

He whispered, "Tonight is your birthday, a chance to be reborn."

As he lowered his hands to her hips, her sensual secrets betrayed her and her forbidden fantasies began to surface in the form of slight fervent jolts as her body grew more alive, seeking pleasurable gratification.

He turned her around. "I'm the only one who can satisfy you."

She stared into his eyes, starting to believe him. A clock chimed in an adjacent room, breaking the tension. Startled, she jumped. "What was that?"

A ruthless glimmer appeared in his eyes. "A reminder of the lateness of the hour."

Grateful for the interruption, Nia broke free of his hot embrace. The unrelenting heat of his body combined with his persuasive touch made it hard for her to think. She left the terrace, heading in the direction of the chime. She walked through the expansive banquet room and into a dimly lit parlor. Purple candles lined the walls, and tall brass candelabra stood near the front. The room resembled a small church sanctuary. A six-foot oblong box rested in the center, covered by finely woven jet-black material that reminded her of Rephaim's hair. The covered box formed a makeshift altar.

Nia stared at it. "That's my casket, isn't it?"

He didn't deny it.

The magisterial clock chimed again, and its brass hands pointed to eleven o'clock.

She asked, "What time was I born?"

He came close. "Six to midnight."

Rephaim surprised her with a sudden kiss. He pressed his lips against hers and parted her mouth with his tongue. Once inside, his firm tongue probed her like a hot viper, sending shock waves through her body and weakening her knees. When she started to fall, he caught her. His mouth never left hers.

He lifted Nia, cradling her sensitive, fragile body in his strong arms, and kissed her deeper. Sexual fires raged inside her as he carried her into another room.

When he released her mouth and set her down, tears filled her eyes, but she didn't know if they were tears of joy or fear. Uncertainty gripped her heart but her deep craving for stimulation overruled her inhibitions. Her legs grew weaker as flames burned in her erogenous zones. Woozy and feeling intoxicated, she leaned into him, looking at her surroundings.

"Where am I?"

He held her unfalteringly. "In our dressing room."

Smaller than the other rooms, dark shadowy mirrors covered the walls, and two large antique armoires sat erect beneath the low vaulted ceiling. Five massive beams crisscrossed in the ceiling and were held in place by one supporting beam propped perpendicular to the floor.

The armoires' doors were highly polished, with a shiny silver latch adorning each one. Rephaim opened one of the armoires, and a beautiful wedding dress glowed in the darkness. Bright, vibrant, and virginal white with layers of lace and fine silk interwoven with pearlescent jewels that seemed to swirl, the entire dress flowed like a white river, possessing a life force of its own. Its train spilled out of the bottom of the armoire. Nia knelt and touched the fabric that lay near her bare feet.

"Wow, it's beautiful."

Rephaim ran his hand across the back of her neck and moved it slowly down her spine, unzipping the dirty white slip she still wore. The slip loosened around her breasts and fell forward, but she curled her arms, catching it and holding it to her chest. Slowly, she stood up and turned toward him, clinging to the front of the slip.

He touched her arms; his smooth, low voice resonated deep inside her body. "*Qi* and *jing,* pain and pleasure."

She didn't fully understand. He whispered to her in the dark.

"The moment I enter you, our life forces will unite. Our sexual energy will explode into a force so powerful it will cause your heart to beat again."

Hot wetness burned inside her walls, causing her insides to expand and contract at its opening, as he attacked her neck with prolonged erotic kisses. His fervid mouth preyed on the hollow of her neck, and he ran his strong, sweltering tongue down her collarbone. The heat rushed down her body like volcanic lava, and images barraged her mind of their bodies entwined in erotic postures, pulsating to the rhythmic beat of an unseen drum.

Nia exhaled heavily. Her glowing brown eyes stared up at the crisscrossing beams, where she seemed to lose herself and the disquiet in her soul seemed to float away.

He bent his face deep into the curve of her neck and uttered her real name. "*Abomi'Nia,* that's who you really are." His insidious breath bashed her sweltering skin. "You were born here in this room and consecrated at my altar as Abomi'Nia."

"What does it mean?"

"Abomination," he whispered.

Nia closed her eyes, trying to digest what he was saying.

"Your whole life has been leading to this moment," he said. "To answer to that name would be to accept your destiny."

Nia shuddered at the possibility that her true home was with this mysterious erotic creature who knew her so intimately.

Nia uncurled her arms and allowed her white slip to fall.

Rephaim stood back. The stolen light inside his eyes fell across her naked body, drinking in her beauty. His brilliant hazel eyes glowed with lust like two small solar storms as he ran his hand down his private regions, slid down his zipper, and began to undress.

❧ CHAPTER 69 ❧

*R*ephaim slowly ripped the clothing from his upper body. He lowered his pants, allowing his extraordinary manhood to fill Nia's vision. A hot, sweet deluge erupted inside her body as she stood naked in front of him.

He opened the second armoire. A long-tailed black tuxedo hung inside. Regal and princely, its girth filled the width of the armoire, and its fabric was spun from the same shiny black material that covered Nia's casket and mirrored Rephaim's jet-black hair. The groom's attire, like her dress, seemed to possess a life force of its own.

Rephaim removed the tuxedo from the armoire and slowly leaned forward, inserting his arresting male anatomy into the black fabric. Nia watched as he tucked his formidable male flesh, swollen and aroused, inside the slacks and raised the zipper over the huge bulge.

"When I climax, my potent energy rushing inside your

body will jolt your heart and give you a new, powerful life." He covered his expansive chest with a fine silk shirt and began to button. "Our sexual union will bind us together eternally, and you'll reign by my side as queen in a world that embraces you."

Just then, the dressing room's door burst open and David charged in.

"Everything he's telling you is bullshit!"

Rephaim jerked around. His powerful hand gripped his tuxedo jacket and fire flared in his eyes as he glared at David. "Who led you here?"

"Your brother." David ran and drop-kicked the supporting beam from beneath the five crisscrossing sectors in the ceiling, caving in the roof. As the massive wood structures came crashing down, David rolled quickly on the floor out of the way, pushing Nia to the opposite wall. The beams split the dressing room into two separate sections—her and David on one side, and Rephaim on the other.

Rephaim spotted Zamzu standing at the door next to Mysti, watching as David Wrightwood crashed through his dressing room. His eyes blazed with fury at his brother's treachery.

Zamzu turned and tried to run, but Rephaim was much faster. His claws protracted and he hooked his brother behind his neck, inflicting four vertical bloodcurdling gouges into Zamzu's skin. Demon hybrids didn't bleed, but they did feel pain.

Zamzu hollered. "Awww!"

Angered yet astounded by this brother's stupidity, Rephaim whipped him around and pinned him to the wall with one powerful thrust. Zamzu's feet barely scraped the ground as Rephaim yelled.

"Why did you lead David Wrightwood here?"

The fire in his breath burned Zamzu's face. His brother squinted and tried to turn away, but Rephaim wouldn't let him.

Zamzu sputtered, "Mysti said David was the only man who could challenge you."

"Mysti was wrong," Rephaim snarled. "Guess who'll die first, you or the man?"

Zamzu grunted, "I'm guessing . . . the man?"

"Wrong." Rephaim sank his powerful claws into Zamzu's belly. With one lethal stroke, he separated vital organs from his brother's body, body parts necessary for even a half demon to live.

Zamzu gasped, hurling out pathetic final words. "You selfish bastard . . . you could've shared your power."

Rephaim laughed deeply and evilly, then jeered in a low, even voice. "I don't share."

Zamzu tried to spit in Rephaim's eyes, but Rephaim turned his head slightly, avoiding any saliva. Zamzu closed his eyes and his world darkened permanently.

Seeing Rephaim take off after Zamzu, Mysti ran down a back hallway, away from the dressing room and wedding parlor. She knew Rephaim's mansion well, having spent many sleepless nights inside his guest rooms, hoping one of her powerful incantations would bring him back to her bed in the midnight hours. But they never did. Instead, he'd only used her womb as an incubator for the seed of a preacher man whom she'd raped and dedicated their offspring to himself.

Young, ambitious, and foolishly fearless, Mysti would have done anything for the powerfully seductive dark warlord.

After Nia was born, Rephaim became obsessed with her. Nia eventually grew into a woman and Mysti aged, but Rephaim, ageless and semi-immortal, remained in his glorious prime, decade after decade.

Mysti ran through the hallways, her spiked heels clacking

madly on the tile, but she didn't regret the actions that had
brought her to her present predicament. David Wrightwood
was Mysti's one last chance to try to even the score. Rephaim
never thought a mortal man could ever challenge him or steal
the heart of his future bride, but the first time Mysti laid
eyes on David, she knew that if any man could, he would be
the one.

She followed a corridor that stretched the length of the
mansion, then circled back in a parallel hallway and returned
via a different route to the wedding parlor and dressing room.

Mysti ran out to the adjoining balcony. A valley several
hundred feet deep separated her from the room where David
had barricaded Nia.

Though she couldn't see his face, Mysti yelled to David,
"You've got less than five minutes to convince her or it's all
over. *Make* her listen." Mysti leaned over the balcony. "Nia is
what Nia believes!"

Before Mysti turned around, she could feel him behind
her. Rephaim's presence was so overwhelming it was unmistakable. A born ruler, he wielded his power well, like a huge
and powerful rod, a beautifully potent phallic symbol. He and
Mysti had so much in common and would make a fantastically
evil couple, but why couldn't he see that?

Mysti turned around slowly.

Yellow rage swirled inside his eyes. "You betrayed me."

"Rejection is a bitch. How does it feel?"

Even in the face of her own possible death, she still
wanted him. She'd watched his glorious bare body plunge
into the wet warmth of the hot springs that bubbled in his
garden as she stood in the bushes wishing she was that water.
Rephaim's sexual energy was so potent that the earth itself
boiled around him.

He ignored her overt signs of lust. "Rejection by you I can

live with. But nothing and no one will ever come between me and Nia."

His round and slightly curved claws protracted as an extension of his body. So many nights she'd fantasized about how any part of his body would feel inside her again.

Anger tightened his jawbone as he slowly wrapped his fingers around her throat and clutched her neck tightly. He brought her face close and uttered, "You and I have unfinished business."

The tips of his claws pressed into her skin, threatening to puncture a main artery. She was scared to move. He whispered in her face. "I will lay you down one more time."

With lightning speed, he whipped her up, whisked her into the next room, and flung her back against a pillow. As he lay her down, a mad rush of desire and anticipation filled her. "Finally, I get to feel your fury inside of me again."

He breathed hot and heavy against her ear. "Guess again." He rose and placed his hand on the hinge connected to a casket's door. When Mysti realized he was throwing her into Nia's casket, she flung her hands up over her head.

"No!"

Rephaim slammed the casket shut and secured the latch. "My wedding gift to Nia," she heard his deep, ruthless voice say on the other side of the door, "will be her mother buried alive."

Horrified, Mysti listened to his heavy footsteps as he walked away.

IN THE FRAY, Nia pulled the dirty white slip back up on her naked body and ran toward the wall near the balcony, away from the beams that crashed down. She pressed her back against the wall and screamed at David, "Why did you come here? You shouldn't have."

"I love you, Nia. Can't you see that?"

"All I saw was you kissing another woman," Nia yelled back. "You never proved you loved me."

"I can't prove it!" He slammed his fist into the wall. "Nobody should have to *prove* love, it just is. If you weren't so damn insecure, you'd realize that."

"If you weren't so damn blind, you'd realize that you destroyed any belief I had in love. Just let me go, David. You can't save me."

David tried to grab her, but she pushed him back. With a snap of her wrist she tore open his shirt and pointed at the scar on his chest. "Who are you trying to fool, David? You can't even save yourself."

Her words stilled him. She wanted him gone from Rephaim's house as quickly as possible, for his own good. If he didn't go, she was sure he'd die there. She spoke fast and nervously. "You refused to open up to me about that scar, so one day I pushed redial and called your parents."

David stepped back but his shirt remained open, a stunned expression on his face.

Nia continued, "They told me what you wouldn't tell me. They told me what happened to Beez and how they blamed you for it. You were so busy playing the hero, you never dealt with your own hurt and guilt. Save yourself, David, before you go trying to save me."

As realization sank in, he paused. She'd discovered what he'd been hiding all these years: the issues he couldn't deal with and the guilt and shame he'd been silently trying to compensate for through his actions and his profession.

David grew silent.

Then, in a burst of rage, he knocked over one of the giant antique armoires. "It was a night intruder and I was scared!"

He kicked a hole in the armoire's thick wood. Afraid, Nia jumped back, thinking that in his anguish, he also might lash out and hurt her. In his turmoil, David wrung his hands.

"It was dark, and I couldn't see what was happening. Our parents weren't home." He punched the wall. "She was my little sister! I should have protected her."

Nia kept a safe distance. "You were just a kid yourself, David. You did what any scared kid would do."

"I did *nothing*!"

The pain in his voice echoed against the mirrored walls, and Nia felt it, too.

"I ran and hid in the closet. I fell on a wire hanger and cut my chest," he confessed, without looking down at the scar. "When the intruder left, I ran out, called for help. Beez's throat had been slashed. The knife clipped a nerve in her spine."

David slid down to the floor. "My little sister is a paraplegic, in a bed like a vegetable, for the rest of her life."

His voice shook. He took a moment to recover. "The way my father looked at me in the emergency room, I knew he didn't care that I'd survived. He yelled at me, 'Why didn't you protect your little sister? Why didn't you *do* something?'"

As David leaned against the wall his forehead pressed into the dark mirror and his own sad reflection bounced back at him, haunting him.

She kneeled and whispered softly. "It wasn't your fault. The intruder hurt Beez, not you."

He shook his head. "My parents blame me, even to this day. And so do I."

Nia's voice thickened with sympathy. "But who told you you had to be a hero?"

Wracked with guilt, he asked, "How can I enjoy my life when my little sister's life is ruined? I turned down a contract to play professional sports to become a lawyer, to find justice, but after all these years, I still can't find it."

David broke down, and his body shook with sobs. Nia reached out, wanting to ease his pain. "Sometimes there is no justice, and you just have to accept it."

David looked up at her. "I can't let him have you, too. I can't lose again."

"It was never about you winning or you having to *save* anybody. It was about *us*. I just wanted you to love me." She looked at the wedding dress spilling out of the armoire. "Now it's too late."

"No, don't say it." He held out his hand, pleading.

"Whatever faith was trying to grow inside me has died completely."

As she turned away from him, he reached out, touching her ankles. "No. Nia, please—"

A loud crash erupted in the room. Nia shrieked as Rephaim burst through the fallen beams. Rage distorted his handsome face, his tuxedo shirt hung limply off his huge body, and claws protruded from his fingertips.

CHAPTER 70

*R*ephaim looked like a monster. Terror-stricken, Nia ran out to the terrace and looked over the railing for a way to escape, but the balcony loomed over a deep cliff with no way to climb down. She whirled back around.

David was still on his knees near the balcony's doorway. His eyes were red and clouded from crying, and his expression was dazed, like he had no more fight in him.

Rephaim saw David weak and bowed, and like a lion closing in on its prey he stalked toward him. Predatory, feral, and ferocious, Rephaim whipped his hands, jutting his claws out an inch longer. With a sinister grin, he licked his sharp teeth, preparing to slaughter David.

Nia ran back inside and pulled the back of David's shirt. "David, get up. Go! Run!"

David struggled to his knees unsteadily and gathered himself enough to push Nia back. "No."

"David, please! He's going to kill you."

"No," he repeated, and clambered to his feet.

David turned his back to Nia and faced Rephaim. Extending both his arms, he braced himself inside the terrace door's threshold, grasping hold of each side of the door frame and positioning his body between Rephaim and Nia.

"I won't bow. I won't move." David slurred his words, but she understood what he was saying, and so did Rephaim. "I won't try to fight to prove myself anymore. I'll just love her with everything I've got."

"David!" Nia gasped. .

"You *can't* kill me." David looked Rephaim in the eye. "If I can't live and protect her, then I'll *give* my life to save her."

"David, no—!"

Before Nia could finish her scream, Rephaim struck David with one swift and powerful mortal blow. The slicing pounce struck David's chest at a vertical angle, rocking his entire body and thrusting him out on the balcony.

Though she fell behind him, Nia saw the blood spurt from David's chest.

Rephaim reached over David's slumping body and grabbed her.

As the massive clock began its booming chimes, counting down six minutes to midnight, Rephaim rushed Nia into the wedding parlor. Even without her wedding dress on, he pulled her to the black altar, snatched up the ancient unholy scroll, and began their wedding ceremony, frenetically reading strange words in an archaic language.

Nia didn't understand them, but she knew what they meant. She stared at the single purple rose lying on the black altar. Its thick, sweet smell was sickening in her nose. The candles burned all around them, their flames gyrating up toward heaven, a serpentine fire.

Realization hit Nia, and she murmured, "He loved me."

Rephaim kept chanting.

"I should have believed it without seeing."

Hearing Nia, Rephaim paused. He snarled, "Love doesn't exist, it's all fool's gold." He clasped her limp hand tightly with his left hand. "You made your choice. You chose darkness. You chose me."

With her eyes in a daze, she murmured again. "I was the fool."

Rephaim spat angry words, chiding her, then resumed his chants, but all Nia could hear was one loud unintelligible roar that overshadowed all else, like disbelief had overshadowed her life. Now all she wanted to do was silence the roar.

Erupting in fury, Nia knocked the black unholy scroll from his right hand.

Rephaim turned to her, his face evil and glowering. "How dare you defy me!"

Unflinching, Nia knocked over the candles. Spurts of fire sprang up in a dozen places. Smoke and flames began to fill the chamber.

Enraged, Rephaim grabbed her arms and tried to force her to bow before the black altar, but Nia fought back. Something deep inside her had ignited like a mighty force of wind and filled her with a new reviving heat that empowered, not consumed.

Lashing out with her foot, she kicked over the altar. A sound like a woman's scream came out when it hit the ground.

Rephaim raised his clawed hand to strike her, but Nia immediately rammed her body into his lower half. With all she had, she knocked Rephaim down and they tumbled over the dark wood casket, knocking off the latch. Mysti scrambled out and looked around, stunned. When she saw Nia attacking Rephaim and the room catching fire, she fled.

Nia and Rephaim writhed violently on the ground, not as the erotic entwined images that had once filled her mind, but as two opposing forces battling for her soul. She clawed at him with her fingernails, kicking, biting, punching, and fighting Rephaim for her life.

A trained and ruthless warlord, Rephaim found an opening and slammed Nia's back against the burning floor. "You are my wife, Abomi'Nia!"

"I am not your wife," Nia grunted against his strength. "And my name isn't *Abomi'Nia!*"

He pinned her arms and slapped her across her face, but she broke free and slapped him back five times harder. As they fought, flames consumed the wedding parlor and the edge of Rephaim's white shirt caught fire.

"Surrender to me, or we'll both burn," he yelled.

Nia whispered her words slowly, with a defiant smile on her face. "I don't burn."

Gathering all her strength, she coiled back her legs and kicked him hard. Rephaim stumbled back. The flames all around them licked his tall, strong body as he tried to fling them off, jerking away from their stinging burns. Surprise and dismay overpowered his rage. His veins smoothed, his jaw twitched, and his claws retracted as he staved off Nia's unrelenting assaults.

Like a wounded lion, Rephaim arose. His hair splayed wild and loose in a thick black mane around his handsome face.

Nia scooted back, her chest rising and falling sharply. Her eyes remained focused on Rephaim and she was alert to the flames surrounding them.

"Twenty-five years . . ." He bit back any sign of defeat. "I've watched over you. Now you've come into your own power, and you challenge and fight me with a new type of strength. You've become what you believe."

Nia rose to her feet. Rephaim's light gold eyes reflected

the fire. He pointed his finger at her. "Don't think this is over, Abomi'Nia Youngblood."

Rephaim disappeared through the flames.

As soon as Rephaim vanished, Nia screamed, "David!"

She darted through the flames out to the terrace, where David lay sprawled. The fire hadn't yet reached the terrace, but black smoke billowed out the door, filling the night sky with thick gray plumes.

Nia grabbed David's shoulders and clutched his head to her breast. She placed her hand over his torn, bloody chest and applied pressure to his fresh, deep wound, trying to staunch the blood flow, but David's blood kept gushing. Nia cried and prayed, and her body's heat rose so high that her hand seared David's skin. The strange heat from her body melded together subcutaneous tissues and coagulated his blood, providing a temporary closure. After several nerve-wracking moments, David opened his eyes. He murmured, *"Radiance."*

At that moment, Nia's heart started beating again.

As she kissed David's temple, a new surge of life sprung up inside her, a life that had never completely left.

Nia wrapped his arm around her neck and hoisted him to his feet. She walked him to the railing, where an unfriendly black smoky sky greeted them. As Rephaim's castle began to collapse in the flames, Nia peered down into the abyss that loomed beneath them, believing they could survive. She kicked the railing loose and together, they jumped into the void, trusting their fall to someone greater than themselves, a god of second chances.

CHAPTER 71

*T*wo weeks later on Saturday morning, Nia and David stood before a justice of the peace. The words *justice* and *peace* held new meaning for them after what they'd gone through. Together, they'd jumped off Rephaim's terrace and landed in a small lake with dried-up springs near a withered garden. The same garden Rephaim had deluded her into thinking was so beautiful. They hadn't known it was there before they jumped because dark clouds had obstructed their view. That same night, Nia showed up with David at the emergency room, and doctors treated him for a deep chest wound that had punctured a main artery. Nia's touch had saved his life.

As for Nia, the ER doctor immediately recognized her as the woman who had been DOA the night before and whose body had gone missing. After examining her, the doctors could not come up with a scientific explanation for what had happened to her. Her body temperature and vital statistics remained abnormal, in addition to other physical anomalies. The doctors settled on a preliminary diagnosis of poison-induced coma, minus vital signs, with atypical, nonexternal resuscitation phenomenon. They traced the uncommonly potent toxin residue in Nia's lungs back to a rare and exotic form of opium that affects the body's nervous system with its naturally occurring sedative compounds.

Nia had remembered how strangely Malcolm had behaved just prior to attacking her in the motel room. She had told David, and together they'd surmised that Malcolm had probably been possessed by Rephaim, who then breathed some type of supernatural opium into her, thrusting her into a suspended state that mimicked death. During this time Rephaim had planned to really kill her and take her soul as prisoner.

"The heart is a strong muscle," one doctor advised. "It has an intrinsic ability to beat, if you can stimulate it and get it going."

David and Nia took that to mean that their love was stronger than death.

Malcolm survived the fall from the freeway overpass but suffered four fractured ribs, a broken leg, and a cracked pelvis as his punishment for being Rephaim's puppet. Whether or not he learned from his sins they didn't know, because he'd skipped town.

Nia forgave Shayla, blaming her low self-esteem as the determining factor behind her actions, but she also kicked Shayla out of her house. "I forgive you, but I don't necessarily trust you," Nia told Shayla, and handed her a check made out to a cosmetology school so she could go back and get her license.

David called in a few favors with the city's redevelopment lawyer and located a nearby abandoned warehouse where Nia could continue her teen tutoring and recreation center. Nia paid cash for the building and hired contractors to renovate it.

David stood at the podium before the justice of the peace, a little stiff from the chest wound, but he wore his navy suit and white shirt well. Nia wore a simple white dress with no veil or train, and her hair was brushed high inside a small tiara, with thick wavy tendrils falling softly and framing her face. She held a bouquet of white lilies, no roses.

As they stood at the podium, Nia whispered, "I have a surprise."

"Please, no more surprises," David sighed, but smiled.

"You'll love this one." She pointed to the door as Mrs. Wang pushed his little sister, Beez, in a wheelchair.

Surprised, David rocked back, grabbing his heart. As he stared at his little sister, he was speechless.

"I flew her in from Canada," Nia explained. "Your parents objected, but since Beez had recently turned eighteen and she wanted to come, they couldn't legally stop her." Mrs. Wang brought Beez forward, and Nia kneeled down and placed her bouquet inside Beez's hands. "She's our maid of honor, David."

David kneeled at Beez's wheelchair. He brushed his little sister's hand against his cheek and closed his eyes. With no words, he told her he loved her. After a moment, he collected himself and rejoined Nia at the podium.

Jay, Buddy, and Mrs. Wang stood as witnesses, and Spivek took David's side as his best man. "Congratulations, buddy," he said, and handed David the ring.

As the magistrate began the ceremony, the door opened and Pastor Kees hurried in. Surprised to see him, David asked him, "Didn't you have a prior commitment?"

"I slipped away," Pastor Kees said. "I couldn't bear to let someone else marry my longtime friend to the woman he loves."

Nia slipped her hand inside David's shirt, gently touching his healing scar, which intersected the old one. Together,

368   ᏔᏭ Lᴇxɪ Dᴀᴠɪs ᏔᏭ

the two wounds formed a cross, a symbol of resurrection. "A true hero fights with his heart," she said, and they began their vows.

David and Nia were married in a very brief ceremony that only lasted a few minutes, but they took vows before God to love each other forever.

As the sun spread its golden rays across the Pacific Ocean, Nia and David's plane touched down in Lanai, Hawaii. They rented a car and drove deep into the tropical rain forest. Carrying a bottle of champagne in one hand and a seashell in the other, David led Nia down a dirt trail through lush foliage. They ducked into a cavern during a surprise torrential downpour and drank champagne from the seashell as they waited out the rain. Nia laughed, spilling bubbly over David's unbuttoned tan shirt and baggy flowered shorts. She donned a red floral sarong that wrapped snugly around her breasts and her curvy hips.

Moments after the refreshing downpour ceased, the earth warmed back up and the green forest came alive with sounds and movements in the swaying leaves of fertile tropical plants.

David led Nia farther down the winding dirt trail to a hidden cascading waterfall where splashing waters rolled off small hanging cliffs and over rock beds. Surrounded by looming palm trees, the secluded waterfall was a honeymooners' dream, a romantic tropical paradise and peaceful respite from the rest of world.

A tropical breeze blew the mist over the water and into the papaya plants. Birds and butterflies skittered over the trees and across a small grassy area, near a patch of sugarcane.

David brushed his lips softly against hers as he guided her into the misty pool. Warm turquoise freshwater surrounded their bodies, and the thick mist emanating off the waterfall moistened their skin. The sounds of the water splashing over the falls lulled Nia, and the subtle current massaged her erogenous zones as her bare feet stepped over black volcanic rocks formed by a hot spot in the earth's mantle beneath the water.

David took her hand as they floated and bathed in warm turquoise water, laughing and dreaming of their romantic future together. After a few moments of leisure, they found their footing and came together in the warm, shallow water.

Nia's bright brown eyes glistened. "Finally."

He came closer. "Yes, finally."

"Remember all those nights we spent on the phone talking about how we'd make love after we were married?"

David smiled knowingly. "Yes."

Nia held up her arms, and in a slow reveal, she untied the front of her red floral sarong and let it fall open, exposing the curvy insides of her breasts and her bare lower region. As David pulled her closer, the muscles in his lower abdomen tightened. She removed his shirt, then pushed down his loose, drenched shorts. Beneath the water's clear surface, his striking manhood drew her eyes, full, throbbing, and awaiting her touch.

Slowly, she bent her knees, held her breath, and sank her face beneath the water's surface. His throbbing muscle hardened even more as she took him, tasting him like the sweet juices of ripe mangoes. David's whole body flexed and contracted from pleasure and desire, and he pulled her up and brought her close. The island's warmth mixed with their bodies' natural heat and increased the flames already being fanned in Nia's secret realms.

David lifted her from the water and laid her down on the small mound of soft pili grass beside the waterfall. He whispered in her ear. "Do you still have sexual fantasies?"

"Yes."

"Who's in them?"

"You are, David." She clung to his neck and pulled him closer. "Only you."

He unwrapped the bottom of her sarong and made love to her beneath the waterfall. Thick, warm mist sprayed across their bare bodies as sweet moans and unintelligible murmurs escaped both their lips.

Nia bent her head back, and her words caught in her throat. "My first time," she groaned, gripping his shoulders. "It's like . . . heaven."

"Hold on to me," he murmured as he clutched her body, rocking. "Don't ever let go."

As David plunged deeper, she closed her eyes. A sweet succession of soft orgasms quaked through her. Both powerful and weakening, they jolted through her body like so many lovely electrical currents. David stroked over and over endlessly, unable to get enough of her. Exhausted, but still wanting more, they collapsed inside each other's arms. David relaxed his biceps and fell across her chest, his body still firm and trembling inside of her.

When she opened her eyes, the moisture from her tears fogged her vision, and she squinted through the swirling mist at the dark, stately outline of a tall man in a black tuxedo. Regal and princely, he stood just to the left of their panting naked bodies, eyes blazing like the rising sun, while holding a white overflowing garment. His deep voice floated on misty vapors, vibrating close to her, letting her know only she could hear him.

"I saved your dress, Abomi'Nia." Rephaim smiled and held the dress out to her.

Nia closed her eyes tightly, hugged David harder, and prayed silently, "Please, God . . . make him go away."